CURSED! BLOOD OF THE DONNELLYS

KEITH ROSS LECKIE

A Novel Based on a True Story

CURSED!

BLOOD

OF THE

DONNELLYS

Douglas & McIntyre

Douglas and McIntyre (2013) Ltd.
P.O. Box 219, Madeira Park, BC, VON 2H0
www.douglas-mcintyre.com

Poem on page 216 ("So the spirit bows before thee"): Excerpt from "Stanzas for Music" by Lord Byron
Poem on page 216 ("But the sword outwears its sheath"): Excerpt from "So We'll Go No More a Roving" by Lord Byron
Poem on pages 297–98: Excerpt from "Gentlemen-Rankers" by Rudyard Kipling
Poem on pages 311 and 319: Excerpts from "Oil in My Lamp," traditional
Edited by Pam Robertson
Cover design by Anna Comfort O'Keeffe
Text design by Carleton Wilson
Printed and bound in Canada
Printed on 100% recycled paper

Douglas and McIntyre (2013) Ltd. acknowledges the support of the Canada Council for the Arts, which last year invested $153 million to bring the arts to Canadians throughout the country.

Nous remercions le Conseil des arts du Canada de son soutien. L'an dernier, le Conseil a investi 153 millions de dollars pour mettre de l'art dans la vie des Canadiennes et des Canadiens de tout le pays.

We also gratefully acknowledge financial support from the Government of Canada and from the Province of British Columbia through the BC Arts Council and the Book Publishing Tax Credit.

LIBRARY AND ARCHIVES CANADA CATALOGUING IN PUBLICATION

Title: Cursed! Blood of the Donnellys : a novel based on a true story / Keith Ross Leckie.
Other titles: Blood of the Donnellys
Names: Leckie, Keith Ross, 1952- author.
Identifiers: Canadiana (print) 20190125020 | Canadiana (ebook) 20190125039 | ISBN 9781771622394 (softcover) | ISBN 9781771622400 (HTML)
Subjects: LCSH: Donnelly family—Fiction. | LCSH: Lucan (Ont.)—History—19th century—Fiction.
Classification: LCC PS8573.E337 B56 2019 | DDC C813/.54—dc23

For Mary, my soulmate, my lover, my rock.
Thank you for your great ideas and for your patience.

Author's Note

THIS NOVEL IS a fictional account inspired by the lives of the Donnelly family that once lived in Biddulph Township, Ontario. Occasionally details including names, dates, events and locations have been changed or invented for the sake of the narrative.

Since the massacre of the Donnelly family on February 4, 1880, the story has been told and retold in newspapers, magazines and books. There were the Kelley novels of the 1960s and the Reaney plays of the 1970s and the deeply researched non-fiction books by Ray Fazakas. There have been at least two musical albums, many poems, documentary films and recently a full-cast live Donnelly musical. I admire and thank those writers who have gone before me to try and sort out whether the Donnellys were cruel, vindictive monsters or innocent lambs to the slaughter. This novel explores that complex and compelling ground in between and brings the epic Donnelly story to new generations who will find chilling comparisons to events in the world today, where more than at any other time in history, huge numbers of refugees are fleeing violence, persecution and starvation to find hope, prosperity and a new life in a new land. Like the Donnellys, they may find themselves burdened by racism, ignorance and religious tensions of the old country.

Acknowledgements

AGAIN I WOULD like to thank the writers that went before me finding their truth in the Donnelly story in books and plays and poetry and song. I would like to thank my agents, Bruce Westwood and Meg Tobin-O'Drowsky, for their encouragement and trust. Special thanks for excellent early editing work by the highly skilled Barbara Berson, who is both tough and passionate. Later editing by Douglas & McIntyre editor Pam Robertson was insightful and supportive. My thanks to Nicola Goshulak and managing editor Anna Comfort O'Keeffe at Douglas & McIntyre for pushing authenticity and truth and guiding the book to print.

Contents

PART TWO

PART ONE

Prologue

Spring assizes—Old Court House, London, Ontario. June 2, 1880.

"Take the book in your hands, son. That's right. Now, do you promise to tell the truth, the whole truth and nothing but the truth, so help you God?"

I knowed this was a powerful question when he asked it 'cause what I said could mean the lives of six men, but I were ready to tell my story.

"I'll do my best, Mr. Irving."

"Just answer yes or no, Johnny."

"Yes, sir. Yes."

"Please tell the court your full name and age."

"I am Johnny O'Connor, sir. I am twelve years old as of last November fifth."

"Good. Now tell us about yourself. Where do you live?"

"I lives with my ma and da. We got two acres on the edge of Lucan town out by the Roman Line near the church. My da does odd jobs and keeps chickens and my ma takes in laundry."

"Good, good. Now what was your association with the Donnelly family?"

"Well they lived up the Line from us and long as I remember they'd often be talked about in stories of the various doings and goings on around town."

"Goings on?"

"Well, you know, like the fist fights and wooing the girls and barn burnings and various mischief and whatnot going on. The good stories was most often about them Donnelly boys, whether they did all those things or not. I liked that 'cause they was just down the road, they was real and you could see them, like trees in the woods or stones in the cemetery."

"Right. Now Johnny, you worked for them on their farm. Is that so?"

"Yes, sir. I did. Miss Johannah come to my ma summer before last and asked if I'd be free to do chores some days."

"Did that worry you? Were you scared to work for the Donnellys? With their reputation and all?"

"I were a little excited sir, no question, but not scared. I was some pleased. After school I'd walk the three miles to their place to do chores and make a few pennies and sometimes stay overnight for early morning doings. They treated me good, almost like family. And I must say working for the Donnellys give me some standing with the lads at school."

"So how did you get along with Johannah Donnelly? How did she treat you?"

"Oh, she were a fine woman, sir. Fed me well and gave me clothes too small for her boys. It were a good farmhouse, big and finished inside and Miss Johannah kept it clean. There was a nice Jesus and the Virgin Mary hanging on the wall. They was good Catholics."

While I was answering Mr. Irving's questions I got to thinking about Miss Johannah and it were like I could almost hear her voice in my head, so often had I heard it. Now there was one for telling stories. She'd tell me about times going way back to when she were a little one across the sea in old Tipperary. She said she growed up quite a lady, the daughter of the manager on a big estate with servants and all and horses to ride. And not a year after that, she said, she was across the ocean here on her knees in the dirt, her nails broken and her hair in tatters, working a farm with the man she loved. She would laugh about it, say to me, "Imagine that!" and call herself a fool. She'd show me the smooth round stone from the Ballyfinboy River that she kept in her apron pocket and tell me it were the only thing she had left from Ireland. It had flecks of green and red in it and she'd say the green was for Ireland and the red for the blood of her family. The stone was her good luck charm and kept her safe. It would slow down my chores considerable listening to Miss Johannah's tales but she loved to tell them and I loved to listen. Near the end she would make me sit with her and talk my ears off. It was like she knowed what was coming and wanted to get it all out for memory's sake.

"Johnny? Did you hear me?"

"Sorry, sir. What?"

"How long had you been working for the family before Jim Donnelly came home from prison?"

"I would say more than a year, sir."

"All right. Now was Jim Donnelly ever abusive to you, Johnny? Did he ever hit you or kick you?"

"No, sir. He could be gruff but he were always fair and even with me."

Now I knew these was the easy questions and soon they'd be asking me about the night of February 3 and it's not easy going back to that bloody night and remembering and thinking and dreaming and then telling about it. You knows how a dream can sometimes get mixed up with real life and then for a moment you're not exactly sure what were one and what were t'other? I was sleeping out at the Donnelly place, and this wild dream come furious to me. It started with the sound of distant thunder like I've never heard. A hundred hooves come, hitting the frozen ground, and I saw two dozen horsemen riding close and hard on that frosty winter night along the flat Roman Line north of Lucan town. And in my dream the steel on the horses' hooves were kicking up ice and dirt and I remember the horses' eyes was wild, mouths frothing, coats all lathered, frosty breath. There was torches in the hands of some riders and the broken, moving light showed them to be strange creatures for sure. They were men, but none like I'd ever seen. Some wore women's dresses, hiked up to ride. Others was sporting feathered hats tied on with rope, and carnival masks like I seen at the Idyll in Guelph. Others was wearing clown paint or had their faces blacked up. They all rode with one hand to the reins because in the other was the tools for their purpose, clubs and pitchforks. A few held rifles. There was bottles of whisky passed between them as they rode and long drinks managed without slowing down.

My eyes had opened from that dream on that night and I was a little trembly from it. The thunder had stopped but I could feel them out there, those men from my dream, horses left behind now, creeping toward us in the house with their tools quick and quiet. I was lying in the big bed beside Old Jim with moonlight coming in the little window above my head and the fire in the kitchen stove had burned low so I could see my breath. In the other big downstairs bedroom, I could hear Johannah and Bridget sound asleep, breathing soft. Big Tom was asleep as well, snoring on the cot in a small room off the kitchen.

I raised myself up to the window, pulled the curtain aside and peeked out. It was all true, the dream. I seen them, their eerie bodies in the torchlight, armed men in wild costumes, spread out across the yard, coming for us. I called out once to Old Jim that there was men outside, but it only came out a whisper. I was frozen, looking out the frosted window, then suddenly a ghoul's painted face was right there, his nose two inches from mine own, looking in at me, and we locked eyes like, and he was one of the Ryder boys and I prayed to Jesus and all his angels to forgive my past sins and, in the name of everything that was holy, to please deliver us all from these demons…

"Johnny? Did you hear me? I asked you, how was it that you came to be at the house that night?"

I heard the question Mr. Irving was asking me, but Johannah's voice had come into my head and the courtroom was suddenly far away. I were there again, in that house on that night, and saw her in the kitchen. I was hiding from them under the bed in the first bedroom and I could see her through the open kitchen door, on her knees on the bloody floor with three bodies down and the men standing around her. She was saying her prayers.

"Johnny? Are you all right?"

It was Mr. Irving again from far away, but I was back in the house and I seen Miss Johannah turn from her prayers and look right at me.

"Johnny?"

And we stared at each other and I felt her strength flow into me to help me survive that night and I closed my eyes and hid behind the laundry basket before they started to put the clubs to her again.

Of the Earth

IN ONE OF her earliest childhood memories, Johannah Magee sat on the bank of the Ballyfinboy River on a hot summer day with her toes in the cool black water as an old man rowed past in a small boat painted green. The boatman smiled pleasantly at her and paused to tip his cap, and she remembered the drops from his one lifted oar blade created pretty concentric rings in the smooth surface of the river. She waved at him and he blew her a kiss, then he slipped his oars into the water again and continued on his way, disappearing around the bend. Johannah was overcome with a deep sadness to the point of tears, because she believed the nice man and his rowboat no longer existed. She had no way to explain her sorrow to her nanny, but at that point in her young life she believed that everything she could see or taste or touch in the world had been put there for her benefit and when she looked away, those things simply ceased to exist. People would have conversations in her presence, plowmen would plow fields, ships would sail out on the sea, and they were all there for her momentary amusement and pleasure and when she turned her alert green eyes elsewhere, those things would disappear. She was not perceptive enough for this to come from arrogance or entitlement, but rather she simply assumed the universe was a performance staged by God for her alone. When she was much older and remembered this strange little fantasy of hers, Johannah Donnelly wondered if perhaps, for at least a short while, every child saw the world that way to help them ease into the disappointment of a reality in which they were not literally the centre of the universe.

Another fantasy the young Johannah had was that her mother and father weren't really her parents but had kidnapped her as a baby. Her real parents, her beautiful, compassionate, idyllic mother and father, were out there somewhere searching for her. Such had been the lonely yearning of her little heart.

Sadly for her, Johannah's parents, Mary and George Magee, were not kidnappers, but her real mother and father. They lived in the manager's house, called Ballymore, where her father ran the Cavendish estate for an absentee landlord outside the town of Borrisokane in County Tipperary. She was their only child. Theirs was a formal household—her father, usually gruff and distracted by his work, hardly realized she existed in the early days, and her mother kept a distance from her for reasons she never understood. Her mother was a pale woman who wore an expression of concern and seldom smiled. Johannah did sense that deep within her mother's shell she loved her but any hugs or kisses were always cool and perfunctory. Perhaps, Johannah often thought, it was a son they had wanted.

On the outside, Ballymore House was a grey stone block of a building, largely devoid of imagination, sacrificing gentility for size, without a porch or pillar, gable or gazebo to soften the stark, stern simplicity of its design. The narrow windows were small in number as if to keep the darkness in. The interior fared better under her mother's influence, with several fine framed landscapes and watercolours gracing the walls in an attempt to bring some warmth to the place. Her mother arranged flowers in the spring and brought in novels by Shelley and Owenson and Austen, which were left lying around. Johannah would discreetly borrow them, for she learned to read early and loved the new worlds these writers provided.

Miss Jane Rafferty was their housekeeper and Johannah's nanny and also her advisor, co-conspirator and friend. She provided the warmth and affection Johannah so needed in her life, and her favourite place was buried in Raffy's ample bosom, her strong arms around her in a good night embrace that signalled no doubt about her love. Raffy could read her palm and tell her fortune. They would examine maps of the world together, compare drawings of exotic dress from other countries and make up wild stories about their adventures together in other lands, saving a princess from monsters or discovering a cave of pirate treasure guarded by huge eels. Raffy was the source of joy in Johannah's early life but Johannah became aware early that like her mother, Raffy feared Johannah's father, a heavyset, powerful man with a red face and eyes that were rarely still.

One night when Johannah was ten, she was in the library reading Scott's *The Heart of Midlothian* when she was surprised to hear her mother's voice raised in anger. Her father had returned that day from one of his business trips to London. Johannah entered the foyer just in time to see her father slap her mother's face with the back of his hand. When Johannah gave a little gasp, both parents turned to her and it was her mother who spoke.

"Go to your room!" she said angrily, as if it was Johannah who had inspired the slap, and the command sent her bolting up the stairs.

Later, as Johannah brooded on her bed, Raffy brought her tea to see that she was all right.

"It will pass, Johannah."

"I hate him."

"Don't hate your father."

"Why does she let him do it?"

"It's not easy to understand the bond between a man and a woman. Sure each one's a mystery, as you'll find out."

"She's a fool to put up with it."

"Now don't you be talking like that about your mother. She's a fine woman that loves you and she does have a lot to be dealing with. Drink that tea before it gets cold and I'll tell your fortune."

In following days Johannah would often catch her mother sadly day-dreaming.

"Mother? Are you all right?"

"Of course," she would say. Then something unrelated, like, "Have you tried on the new petticoat? I want to know if it has to go back. Go and try it on now or you'll forget."

Johannah thought that they did share something, perhaps. Maybe her mother also felt as if she had been abducted by kidnappers and her real family, beautiful and idyllic, was still out there somewhere, searching for her.

On Johannah's eleventh birthday, her father surprised her by giving her a remarkable gift. He was a three-year-old gelding of a milky white colour including tail and mane, just shy of fourteen hands, making up in agility and speed what he lacked in size. He had been named Cuchulain after the great warrior of Irish myths. Her father had bought him for her at Smithfield Square on one of his many trips to Dublin.

She insisted, against the strong wishes of the stable boys, on bridling and saddling him herself. On that day and almost every day thereafter, Johannah and Cuchulain rode across the rough pastureland of the broad estate, Johannah straddling him barefoot with her dress tucked under her knees and his sure hooves beneath her, his legs pumping, as if she were mounted on a warm little whirlwind.

Though Johannah and Cuchulain became close comrades-in-arms, she also had many playmates among the two score of tenant children whose parents worked for her father. Their whitewashed stone cottages with thick thatch roofs dotted the verdant pastureland west of St. Patrick's Parish Church on the edge of the estate. Each had a yard and animal pens for a pig or chickens, sheds for tools and a garden patch for peas and beans and potatoes, and children were always playing outside among the animals. There were the Ryan twins, Devon and Michael, and the Donnelly children, Jim and Theresa, and little Donald Murphy, known for his angelic singing voice, and his blind sister Maive, as well as Martin and Brid O'Day, who won the Waterford junior dance championship, and several more.

Her favourite and best friend was Lucy O'Toole, her same age and as Viking fair as Johannah was dark, a blonde-haired, blue-eyed waif with skin so translucent you could see the purple lines of her veins pulsing in her arms and temples. Lucy had a firm belief in the existence of fairies and the little people as passionate as her belief in God and his angels and she would tell such good stories about them and their meetings with humans. Johannah found the lives of the tenant children substantially more interesting than her own. She did of course know that she had privilege—she resided in the manager's house, her clothes were expensive and her father had power—but with these friends she felt, for the most part, as accepted in their warm homes as anyone else, given neither fault nor favour.

Almost every day after tea, in good weather, Cuch and Johannah left Ballymore and took the long way to Lucy's, across the glen and up onto the ridge, behind which you could see beyond the estate to the brown Ballyfinboy River meandering through the fields and small woodlots on its untroubled way through Lough Derg, past Limerick and on down the Shannon to the sea. It was the route by which she and Lucy vowed they would one day set off to find the house of the Black Dwarf from Walter Scott's book, or journey to London like Jeanie Deans did in *The Heart of Midlothian*.

On one particularly fine afternoon, Johannah and Cuchulain rode up along the ridge and then through the woods, then down again, skirting well wide of the leg-breaking bog. Johannah slowed Cuch briefly for a walk along the long, cool, willow-shaded path by the fishing stream, a tributary of the Ballyfinboy, then brought him back up to speed across the hard pasture, where they cleared two of the sheep walls her father had forbidden her to jump. Johannah was a skilled rider for her age, instinctive and without fear, following Cuchulain's moves through whatever jumble of rocky paths they would careen. Lucy once told her she must have led great cavalries in one of her previous lives. It was only on Cuchulain she felt such freedom, practically free of gravity itself as Cuch barely touched the earth. It seemed entirely possible they could simply ride on like this forever.

Approaching Lucy's cottage, Johannah steered clear of the vegetable patch and the great blind pig named Rosie, which the O'Tooles kept on a tether west of the house, and pulled up outside the door.

The O'Toole cottage was as tiny as the other tenant houses, with a dirt floor and tattered curtains, braced-up broken furniture and a small pen inside holding three younger pigs without names and a goat named Willy in one corner. Blue peat smoke hung in a cloud just above their heads and completed the host of rich and pungent aromas assaulting Johannah as she stepped inside the crowded little hut. But it was the place where children from the other families gathered before supper to tease and be scolded, play cards and checkers beside the fire and listen again and again to Granda O'Toole's tales of monsters and little people and The Great Disaster. Irish history was all divided between the time before and after The Great Disaster, which was the invasion of Ireland by the English armies in 1649 under the commander they called Cromwell. Johannah's father would never have allowed such talk against the English, who were his bread and butter, though he was as Irish born as anyone can be, and Johannah was thrilled by the forbidden stories. On this day she and Lucy, leaning against each other, braiding each other's hair, listened closely to the old man's dramatic retelling.

"The armies from hell under the devil himself Cromwell set forth across the sea in huge black barges. Sure we prayed for God to send bad weather but it did not come. The barbarians landed on the beach and our lads come down to beat them back from whence they came. We fought with spirit and courage under several of our great lords. Chieftain Peter Donnelly, the great-great-great-granda of the Donnelly family, led the charge. In those times we had only clubs and spears and short bows, not the broad steel and armour of the English, nor their crossbows, and only a tenth of their cavalry. And so the miracle did not happen and our men were defeated, falling before Cromwell, wave after wave after wave."

Though all were familiar with the story, no one spoke for fear of interrupting the rest.

"Then came the day the English soldiers surrounded our town of Borrisokane. The old men and older boys that were left fought them with sticks and stones but in moments they were overwhelmed, captured and taken away. The next morning, the women, the great-great-grandmothers of the women here, they went to the Englishman's camp to bargain for the release of their men and boys. As they approached, they found the path was lined either side with what looked like long piles of turnip or cabbages. Ah, but they weren't cabbages, my loves. These were the heads of their husbands, sons and fathers, every one. They had refused Cromwell's demands and met their fate." He was coming to Lucy and Johannah's favourite part. "Cromwell's demands were simple. The Irish would give up ownership of their lands, curse the Pope and swear fealty to the English king or die. As their men had done before them, the women of Borrisokane refused and offered their heads instead of submitting to the Englishman's conditions. They do say that in the face of such courage, Devil Cromwell's frozen heart melted and for one day he grew weary of slaughter and let the women live, and their children too. So Borrisokane survived and the women kept their heads. Cromwell seized their lands, mind you, writing up legal deeds for his lords in England. And that is why the O'Tooles, the Ryans and the Donnellys are tenants on their own land to this day."

Lucy's father was usually a quiet man, listening to his father-in-law's stories, but on this one day his eyes grew intense as the story ended. He spoke out as if the events had happened last Thursday.

"What gave them the right? What gives them the right now to raise our rent and restrict the common land? Them, old Cavendish and that thief Magee…"

"Quiet now, Tom," Mrs. O'Toole chided under her breath. "The child…"

His eyes glanced over at Johannah. "She should hear it. If she comes to us, eats our bread, she should know. I won't seal my lips in my own house!"

"Shhhhhh."

"I won't be shushed!"

Lucy's mother patted Johannah's hand.

"Maybe it's time for you to go, my dear. But come again tomorrow."

Johannah tried to cover her embarrassment. "Thank you, Mrs. O'Toole," she said with a slight curtsy. "Tea was very nice."

Johannah was not unaware of the feelings against her father on the estate. Often the tenants suddenly stopped talking when she arrived and more than once she had overheard her father's name spoken in anger when her presence was unnoticed. She had once asked her father about it, without betraying names, and also about The Great Disaster and the "English Devils."

"Such nonsense," he replied. "The tenants are jealous and greedy, some of them, and want what we have, but they're too lazy to work for it."

She had thought about her father's words and accepted them at the time, but she sensed it was not so simple. She saw how hard and long the tenants worked on the estate and yet their clothes were old and patched and it was rare that any meat was in their pot, only potatoes, and their kettles held only rough, thin tea leaves that were reused many times. Johannah certainly knew enough not to repeat Mr. O'Toole's word "thief" to her father, for it would mean trouble to Lucy's family, but a part of her wondered if there was truth in it.

As Johannah left the cottage, Lucy followed her outside.

"Sorry about my da," Lucy told her. "You won't say anything?"

"Of course not."

"Want to go for a short one?"

"Sure. Long as you want. Let me get on."

As they would often do this late in the day, Lucy hopped on Cuchulain behind her and they rode with the golden sun low in the sky, Lucy holding tight against Johannah's back and urging speed. Given her slight build, Cuchulain could gallop just as fast with Lucy on as with Johannah alone. Lucy usually hummed a tune like "The Croppy Boy" or "Irish Soldier Laddie" when they rode, her mouth close to Johannah's ear, her thin knees embracing Cuchulain's flanks, her hands locked around Johannah's waist. Almost always they would find themselves at the enchanted woodlot. Lucy and Johannah had secretly visited it since they were very young, for this modest copse was notorious in tales of the supernatural, the home of fairies and ghosts, a place of magic. Only a few years earlier, a young girl named Maher had wandered there and, despite a long frantic search by her family and the villagers, was never seen again. When a rag doll that she had carried with her appeared on her little bed at home, it was a sign, everyone knew, that she had been taken by the fairies.

Here, in this small meadow surrounded by tangled bushes and low, gnarly evergreens, the girls sat and waited to be taken. When they heard rustlings in the leaves and branches, Johannah's head said it was a jack-rabbit or weasel or grouse but her heart longed for it to be nymphs and fairies. They were sure they heard small voices, whispered conversations all around them, and Lucy impressed her by addressing them boldly.

"Creatures of the woodlot! We are Lucy O'Toole and Johannah Magee and we command you to come forward."

Whatever their reason, as with other days, the fairy folk chose not to obey. It was here in this woodlot Johannah and Lucy had made certain promises. They would have to approve each other's husbands. They would have numerous children and bring them up together, encouraging marriage between a few. However, first they would travel around the world, at least as far as China to see the Forbidden City, a name that in itself demanded their presence. And it was here they made grand oaths, swearing by the moon that their friendship would go on forever, even after death, when their freed souls would take each other's hands and fly up from the earth together to become two stars in the midnight sky.

The Poacher

ONE WARM SPRING evening about a week before the day of her confirmation, Johannah was setting out from Lucy's to Ballymore and made a slight detour along the hard-packed bridle path under the leafy canopy beside the mumbling stream. Like the woodlot, this was a special place she had always felt drawn toward. It was part of the estate and she and Raffy came here for picnics, to wade in the cold water and read, and it was here she had learned how to fish. So when she heard the clear notes of someone whistling a tune up ahead, it was an intrusion. She guided Cuch carefully and quietly into a clearing to find a boy standing near the stream, his back to her as he nonchalantly rigged up his fishing gear. She mustered a forceful authority.

"You there. These are estate lands. What are you doing?"

The boy turned toward her and she blushed to recognize him. He was Jim Donnelly, one of the tenant children, two or three years older than her, who worked long days in the fields with his father. Though she had known him all her life, she hadn't paid him much attention until recently, when she had spoken to Lucy about him. Jim was an altar boy at St. Patrick's. He faced the congregation and she had to admit she had noticed his sad smile and beautiful lips. She and Lucy had compared his dark eyes and face to the plaster statue of the Archangel Gabriel that stood in the dusty east chapel. And now here he was and they were alone together.

"You mean with this fishing gear, miss? Why, I'm picking wildflowers."

"You are poaching, Jim Donnelly! There are game wardens patrolling. They'll have you arrested, so they will."

"I guess I should just drown myself and get it over with, miss."

He turned away from her as if she were a dismissible irritant and tossed his baited line into the pool.

"You don't realize the trouble you could be in. I have a whistle I could blow. The warden'll be here in a minute."

"And just who gave you the right to these fish. They are God's free creatures to be caught by whoever they like. You go ahead and blow, miss, if you must. I need to catch some dinner so my family can eat."

Johannah hesitated, then looked down with interest at the deep pool in the stream where he was slowly bringing in the baited hook.

"That does look like a rather good spot."

She studied his back, brought Cuchulain a few steps closer and dismounted. She stood beside him in the tall grass, looking into the deep pool in the otherwise shallow stream. He tossed the bait again and it landed with a *plop*. She watched him critically.

"That wasn't the deepest spot."

"They lie in the tree shadows on the right," he whispered.

"You're still short."

"The current will take it there," he whispered again.

"And you should have more leader," she spoke at normal volume.

"Shhhh. They can hear you."

"That's what people say but only an eejit would believe that fish have ears."

"Shhhhh!"

Suddenly the line went tight and, as easy as that, Jim had hooked a good-sized salmon. He set the hook and struggled a little to bring it in.

"Gently! You're yanking it," she told him. "You'll tear his mouth and lose him. Here. Give it to me!"

"I caught the blessed thing," he protested.

"With my advice."

"Oh yes, your great wisdom."

She turned and glowered at his sarcasm.

"It's an estate fish. It belongs to me."

Jim resisted giving her the line at first but as they both struggled for it, he glanced over her shoulder and something changed his mind.

"As you like, my lady," he whispered, releasing the gear into her hands and sinking down into the high grass. Her attention was completely on the fish, for she had lost a few in her time at this critical point. She brought the catch in slowly, smoothly, letting a little go when he fought but keeping it tight as Raffy had showed her, then when he rested, bringing the line in, wrapping it neatly—no snags—around the spindle. The silver back fin of the salmon broke the surface.

"Oh look, he's a beauty!" she cried. As she brought the fish in to shore she was laughing with delight, lifting the big, flopping salmon up high and needing both hands and all her strength to do so.

"Look, I got him!"

As she turned around to show the catch to Jim, an older man faced her at the other end of the clearing with a shotgun raised. The Cavendish estate game warden. He, of course, immediately recognized her and lowered his weapon, embarrassed. He wore two pistols in his belt, from which also hung a pair of shackles. He approached her and spoke through a thick moustache.

"Oh, Miss Johannah! I'm so sorry. I thought you was a poacher."

"Poacher! Goodness, Ernest. Nothing on earth much lower than a poacher, is there? Lowest of the low!"

"I thought I heard you talking to someone, miss."

"Oh, just myself. I chatter away all the time."

Jim was concealed in the high grass near her feet.

"Glad to see you're doing such a fine job protecting our fish, Ernest."

"Yes, miss. There are plenty of fish thieves these days. We even get the women poaching out here. But that looks like a good one."

The fish was struggling and as the warden watched, Johannah chose a smooth river stone the size of her fist, laid the writhing salmon out in the deep grass a foot from Jim's head and clubbed the fish twice between the eyes until it lay still. Amused, Jim met her eyes for a moment.

"Your father ordered us if we see a poacher to shoot first. Have you seen any?"

"You know, I did hear quiet voices upstream not long ago. I might have scared them off."

The warden's interest was aroused.

"Those rascals. I best be after them, then."

"Good day, Ernest."

The warden headed quickly upstream and Jim extended his hand for a lift up.

"Thank you. You might have had me arrested."

"Hate to see you go off in shackles."

"Ernest didn't have much of a sense of humour."

"No. That's true. A man should have a sense of humour." She looked into his eyes for a moment. "I…I have to go now. I'm late for dinner. You can keep our fish for your family, then."

"Thank you, miss."

She mounted Cuchulain and smiled down at Jim Donnelly.

"Good evening, James. Nice to see you."

He stepped forward, reached up to take her hand in his and kissed it like a gentleman.

"Good evening yourself, m'lady," he said with his sad smile.

She laughed and guided Cuchulain's head around and rode off for the big house.

On the way home, and then alone inside the stable, Johannah's thoughts were all about Jim Donnelly. He was not bad to look at and had the wit to make her laugh. As she lit the lantern and loosened Cuchulain's cinch, she remembered she had once seen him shirtless, sweating, reaping barley in the fields. She definitely wanted to see him again.

She was sliding the halter over Cuch's ears when she heard her father's voice behind her.

"This is late for you to be out. I was worried."

"I'm sorry."

"How was the ride?"

She had felt her father's attention on her in the last few weeks. He would make small talk and watch her and listen to her as he had never done before. She was happy and made curious by his new interest.

"Good." She continued, enthused, "Cuchulain and I always take a path along the ridge when we go to Lucy's. It's beautiful up there when the sun is low. You should come with us, Da. Take Prince and see if you can keep up."

She surprised herself by making this invitation. He had not ridden with her in years, but she would enjoy it if he started doing so again. He moved closer to her, into the glow of the lantern. She could tell by the soft slur of his words he had been drinking whiskey, which could either soften his mood or make him angry.

"I hear you jump the stone fences at the bottom of the ridge. Bad girl." He said this with a smile and brought his face close to Johannah's.

"Just at the broken-down spots. We're always very careful."

"You ride that beast too fast."

"No faster than you ride."

"That's true. There's more of me in you than your mother."

He put the palm of his hand against her cheek. She moved her cheek against his hand, but then he smiled in a strange way and the intensity of his gaze did not feel to her like fatherly love.

"I would never want anything to happen to you. You're growing up. Becoming quite the lady. Quite the beauty."

He was more intoxicated than she had thought, the whiskey heavy on his breath. He drew his thumb slowly along the line of her mouth in a manner that made her feel ashamed and when Johannah went to back away, he took her arm firmly in his other hand to hold her close. For the first time in her life, she felt fearful of him.

"You're hurting me, Da."

"George. What are you doing?" It was her mother's voice. She was standing in the dark doorway of the stable and Johannah could not see her face. Her father immediately released his grip on her. Johannah backed away until she stood against Cuchulain. Her father calmed himself and turned toward his wife.

"Having a word with my daughter."

"Dinner is ready."

In cold silence, her father walked briskly past his wife and out of the stable. Johannah looked to her mother, who must have seen how close he had stood to her, his hand gripping her arm. She was badly shaken and so thankful for her mother's intervention that she wanted almost to go to her, to hug her in relief. But her mother remained in the dark doorway, stone still.

"Come inside and clean yourself up," was all that she said before turning her back to Johannah and leaving the stable.

The Ponies

JIM DONNELLY MADE his way home with the heavy salmon wrapped in his old jacket. They would have fillets tonight and good soup from the head tomorrow. He knew the route through the willows and around the peat patch where the warden would not spot him. However, his thoughts were neither on the fish nor the warden, but on Johannah Magee. The daughter of that son of a bastard estate manager, an arrogant horse girl riding around like a princess. They had lived near each other for all their lives but today he had the lovely creature all to himself, beside the stream, to listen to her voice and her laughter and feel the warmth of her body, inhale the sweetness of her sweat. He could have put his hands around her pale throat and choked the life out of her if he had wanted. Maybe even got away with the murder, sweet revenge against the man who had killed his father, destroyed his family. Lord knew he had for years harboured such dreams of revenge against George Magee. A life for a life.

Jim had been only nine years old. His father, Matthew Donnelly, was a proud man, the great-great-great-grandson of the famous chieftain Peter Donnelly, who was killed in battle by Cromwell himself, though Jim's family's small patch of earth and menial life was a shame to their noble bloodline. His father shared his conviction that they were not peasants, but rather poor noblemen who would one day be recognized and regain their lands and social standing from the foreign occupiers. Besides the family bible, Matthew Donnelly owned several books on history and philosophy and encouraged his children to read to develop their minds, gain a better comprehension of the world and prepare to reclaim their rightful place when the time came.

An old friend of Jim's father who had done well in horse trading had two sickly newborn Shetland ponies. They could not even stand. The mare had died and their chances of survival were slim. Being more pets than working animals, no one wanted them, but knowing Matthew Donnelly's affection for anything of an equestrian nature, the friend brought them both in a cart to Matthew's tenant house on the Cavendish estate and Matthew took them in right away. He turned them over to Jim with instructions. Every evening after a full day's work in the fields, young Jim would care for them. He nursed them for weeks with cow's milk, working their muscles until they could stand, walking them in a circle on a lead, brushing down their coats until they glistened. They graduated to a slop of oats and finally grass and hay. They were the prettiest little black and white ponies—Jim named them Salt and Pepper—and they became a great source of pride to the Donnelly family. Jim loved them as if they were his siblings. Then one day George Magee came to call at the cottage.

"Those are beautiful ponies, Donnelly. You've done a fine job with them."

"'Twas my son James's work, sir," his father told the estate manager with pride, but Jim could see his father was nervous.

"Fine. Well, I would like them for my daughter. I'm willing to make a good offer. I'll pay you ten pounds each. You should be pleased with that."

"They're not for sale, sir."

"Oh come now, Donnelly, that's a lot of money for you. It's my daughter's sixth birthday next week and I want them for her."

"Sorry, sir. They are not for sale."

"All right. Twenty each. Forty pounds, Donnelly! A fortune for you. Here's my hand. Let's make the deal before I change my mind."

Jim knew this was a lot of money but his father did not take the offered hand.

"I am so sorry, Mr. Magee. They're ours and we're keeping them."

"Why do you want to make trouble for yourself, Donnelly?" Matthew Donnelly remained silent. "All right. I want you to think hard about it. I'll be back tomorrow."

Jim tried to talk to his father that night. He loved the ponies, sure, but he didn't want his father to get in trouble. It would be all right. Maybe they could visit the ponies sometimes at Ballymore. But his father wouldn't hear a word about giving them up. The next day, Magee came and asked Matthew Donnelly if he had considered the offer.

"The ponies are not for sale."

"All right then. Fifty pounds each, Donnelly. One hundred pounds, man! My final offer. More money than you could save in ten years. You can move off the tenancy. Buy land. Build a house. You'd be a fool to turn me down. I want the ponies."

"I'm sorry, Mr. Magee."

Magee's eyes had blazed and he moved toward Matthew Donnelly as if he might strike him.

"I will not let you do this to yourself, Donnelly. I am coming early tomorrow morning for the ponies. I will give you one hundred pounds, which makes me a fool. You will be a rich man"—he looked around the yard—"by these standards."

That night, Jim brushed down the ponies' coats, fed them extra oats and talked to them about their new life at Ballymore. "You'll be spoiled rotten and a pretty little girl named Johannah will ride you both and you can learn tricks for her and maybe I can come and visit you."

Then Jim did what he would never do again. Making sure no one saw, he allowed himself to cry for the ponies until his face and hands were wet. That night, Jim listened as his mother tried to convince his father that the money would be a wonderful thing.

"We could have land of our own, Matthew. Have a cow—five cows! And pigs, too. We could even open a little shop in the village if we're careful."

His father spoke slowly. "For hundreds of years, that man and his kind have taken everything of value we have, anything and everything they want. We can't go on living like that, without honour or dignity. I have decided he will not have the ponies."

And Jim was proud of his father's stand. They would keep the ponies. But he knew his mother was the more practical one and her opinion was ignored at their peril. At midnight that night, Jim's father started drinking from a bottle of whiskey at the kitchen table. His mother put Jim and his sister, Theresa, to bed and closed the curtains. Jim had never seen his father drink like this and he could tell his mother was scared. She tried to get their father to bed but he refused. He stayed at the kitchen table with the lamp burning low, staring into darkness.

It was sometime in the night when Jim heard the outside door close and he was suddenly wide awake. He slipped out of bed carefully so as not to wake Theresa and made his way to the door. The bottle was empty on the kitchen table. Jim opened the door to a bright moon and saw his father walking unsteadily toward the little corral that held the ponies. There was something in his hand. Jim could make out the heavy sledge he used to drive in the fence posts and a small sound escaped him, more a moan than a shout.

"No."

Then he ran through the open door and he screamed "NO, DA!" and ran toward his father, who was now inside the gate with the sleepy ponies, which were oblivious to any threat. And Jim saw his father raise the heavy implement above his head.

"DA! DON'T!"

Matthew brought the sledge down on Pepper's head with a dull crack and the pony collapsed flat.

"NO!" Jim was almost to the gate. His father brought the thing down again, on the second pony's skull. Matthew was strong and precise with the stroke and Salt collapsed beside his sister. Jim threw his arms around his father and Matthew, possessed of some madness, threw him back against the fence and raised the sledge once more, this time over Jim. It wavered there in the air above his head in the moonlight and Jim saw his father's face turn to horror. His father let out a cry as the sledge was lowered and fell harmlessly into the dirt, then he turned and ran from his son into the night. A moment later, Theresa was at the ponies, crying hysterically, for she loved them as much as Jim. She was wild, trying to wake them up, pulling Salt's head up from the dirt and screaming until their mother took her up in her arms and carried her back into the house. As Theresa's cries became distant, Jim sat down beside the ponies and caressed the thick fur on Pepper's head and soft ears. Leaning back against the fence, he kept the dead ponies company until well after dawn as a slow, dangerous rage took hold inside him.

Jim did not get up from the ground when Magee arrived that morning. There were loud words spoken to Jim's mother. His father had not returned. Jim heard Magee's angry tone and his eyes went to the sledge where his father had dropped it. Magee only came close enough to assure himself the ponies were in fact dead, then mumbled "Bloody eejits!" and left in disgust. Jim remained with them all day until the flies began to swarm and Mr. O'Toole and Mr. Ryan came to drag them away for burial.

They promised Jim they would be gentle with them and they were. And Jim did not go to see them put in the ground.

That afternoon, a search was organized and Matthew Donnelly was found floating face down in a slough near the peat bog a mile from his cottage.

The memory of it all came flowing back to Jim as he made his way home from his encounter with Johannah Magee, the girl for whom the ponies and his father had died. His father had killed the things he loved and then himself.

Yes, maybe he should have drowned Johannah in the stream—for a dark moment when they were together it had in fact crossed his mind, a dangerous voice deep inside calling out for vengeance, a life for a life. But he doubted that Johannah even knew about the ponies. And, anyway, he now had a new and better plan for revenge against George Magee. A sweeter revenge than simply murder. He would make Johannah Magee his own.

Confirmation

LUCY AND JOHANNAH were to have their confirmation together and the next Sunday they found themselves side by side at St. Patrick's Church, kneeling in their white robes at the rail with four other children all about to become, as they were told, soldiers of Christ in God's army. Saint Pat's was a fine old church with three stained glass windows and a high-vaulted ceiling. In past weeks, the statues and pictures in the sanctuary had been draped for the period of Lent, the priest and altar boys dressed in purple and the lower windows covered to keep the inside dark, but now since Easter everything was light and bright, the drapes gone, the vestments white, generous bouquets of bluebells and lilies around the altar. Little Donald Murphy sang the Gloria.

But on the day of her confirmation, when she should have been occupied with holy thoughts, Johannah was focused instead on altar boy Jim Donnelly. Her heart beat a little faster just to lay eyes on him again.

The old bishop moved down the line, offering each of them a Latin prayer, a blessing and a gentle slap with three fingers on the cheek, hardly more than a caress really, to symbolize Christ's suffering on the cross. Johannah's father sat halfway back in his stiff-necked shirt, beside her mother in a high-waisted lace and velvet gown with her favourite pearl necklace. Raffy sat behind them. After the incident in the stable, George Magee had spent the week in Dublin and Johannah had avoided her mother. She felt betrayed by both parents: her father for his behaviour, which made her feel sick, and her mother for pretending it hadn't happened. It made her want to hurt them both, make them sorry.

When she looked up, Jim Donnelly was smiling at her. For Johannah's entertainment, he pretended to be falling asleep, his eyelids heavy, his head dipping. She stifled a laugh. Beside her, Lucy was aware of this silent interchange and gave Johannah a look and a playful nudge with her hip.

Then the bishop hovered before Lucy and spoke the Latin prayer. Lucy said her "Amen" and he touched her cheek with his three fingers and told her to go in peace. Then he stood before Johannah, whose attention he could see was clearly wandering. The bishop turned and glanced over his shoulder, but Jim stood looking away as solemn and serious as a carved saint. The bishop's disapproving attention returned to Johannah and he spoke the prayer, adding his "Amen," which she repeated. He put his hand to her cheek and gave her the ceremonial slap—she could have sworn it was much harder than slaps he gave the others—then he wished her peace and moved on.

After the service, when her father drew the bishop into one of his pointed conversations at the doors about how the estate should take over management of the common lands, or how the mandatory schooling of the tenant children represented a loss in productivity, Johannah saw her chance.

"Go on," Lucy told her. "He's probably outside waiting for you. Go!"

Once outside, Johannah looked up and down the road and scouted the horses and wagons, the bushes near the church and finally the cemetery, and that's where she found him. He was leaning against a large granite headstone with a kneeling angel on top, which was gazing heavenward in prayer. Out of his altar boy surplice, Jim was now in his patched, worn clothes. When he saw her, he assumed the devout position of the seraph on the headstone, his palms together in prayer, raising his eyes to heaven.

"Sure God's going to send a bolt of lightning for making fun of his angel."

"I'm quick."

"So is He."

"Come for a stroll."

There was a spot where the cemetery wall was broken down and they could find good footing to climb up on top of it.

"It's pretty high. Do you think you can do it?"

They made their way with care along the top of the cemetery wall, the mortar around the flat stones crumbling, Jim in his bare feet, Johannah behind in her fine leather boots, arms outstretched for balance like tight-rope walkers, placing one foot in front of the other.

The countryside beyond the cemetery was the rich dark green of the potato plots set aside for the tenants to use. Other rough walls framed pastures that extended high up the far hills where cattle and sheep grazed. They were approaching a spot where an extension of the wall formed a paddock and beneath them on their left stood an impressively large black Angus bull, eyeing their progress. Johannah really did not want to be this close to the bull but she was determined not to flinch. She told herself she'd be past the creature in a minute but halfway along the paddock, Jim stopped and turned back to her.

"Whatever you do, Johannah, don't fall in there or that's you done for," he teased. "He'll be on you in a heartbeat, tossing your bloody broken little body from horn to horn."

Johannah was not to be intimidated. She looked down and studied the seemingly docile bull. She had certainly been warned away from them and maintained a healthy respect, but she would never show fear in front of Jim Donnelly. She told him with a worldly nonchalance, "It's just a bull."

The animal watched them watching him. His big black eyes could have been those of a contented, uninterested bovine or of a committed killer about to strike.

"I believe he's killed three or four. Seems to like to do in the girl children best. The cailíní."

"I don't believe you," she told him.

As he looked back at her with that sad smile of his, he stumbled on some crumbling mortar, lost his balance, tried to right himself and then fell straight down into the muddy pen on his knees before the beast. The animal raised his head with a snort and pawed the earth. Jim got slowly up on his feet to face the enormous creature.

"Don't move, Jimmy," Johannah whispered.

The instruction was unnecessary, for the boy was frozen. Jim and the bull stared at one another. The creature pawed the earth again, his eyes awakening to this confrontation, a rage slowly building at this invasion of his pen. He snorted, lowered his enormous head and shook it at Jim. Johannah searched around for something to help and a few feet further along past the paddock, where the wall had broken down, someone had placed a long, rough board across the gap. She hurried to it, dragged it back to the paddock and dropped one end down beside Jim.

"Climb up, Jim!"

Jim's reverie was broken. He turned and scrambled up the rough plank just as the bull charged. His hands were on the top of the wall when

37

Johannah reached down, grabbed the seat of his trousers and helped haul his back end and legs out of harm's way. The bull's head snapped the board and butted into the stone and mortar structure where a split second before Jim had been standing, the horns crashing and damaging the stones of the wall on which the children were now perched. The two of them stood up, balanced on top of the narrow wall, holding on to each other, calming their pounding hearts.

"That was quite clever," Jim said and Johannah felt blood rush to her face. "You saved my skin." He extended his finger, touched the end of her nose and said, "Imagine that."

They laughed and she rubbed some splattered mud off his cheek, his face close to hers. With their arms around each other for balance, she felt the warmth of his slender body. She noticed the blue flecks in his brown eyes and the lines around his mouth and she felt a sudden impulse to kiss him on those perfect lips of his. It was an impulse he apparently shared as he leaned in toward her. And then, as one, they stopped just short of contact, both sensing they were being watched. They turned their heads to see her parents, the priest and the bishop in the churchyard, all watching them on the wall. Had they planned it, Johannah could not have staged a more perfect act of defiance against her parents. For Jim it was the opportunity to very publicly stake his claim to Magee's daughter. Johannah turned from the audience, leaned in and without shame kissed Jim on those perfect lips, and Jim kissed her back just as hard. For a moment they were both lost in the new joy of their soft, warm mouths. And for an instant the kiss was no longer for Johannah's defiance or Jim's revenge but the beginning of something else.

"Johannah!" The moment was severed by the fury of her father's voice. She and Jim reluctantly pulled away from each other and turned toward the churchyard to see her father coming fast toward them. Jim helped her down on the cemetery side of the wall and got down himself. He stood his ground as her father marched up to him.

"You filthy bastard!"

Her father swung his fist against the side of Jim's head and knocked him down onto the ground, then began to kick him with all his strength. Johannah had never seen her father so enraged, and it terrified her.

"Stop it, Da! It was not his fault!"

But her father kept kicking Jim until Johannah threw herself against him and he finally turned away from Jim to her, his chest heaving, face red. He grabbed her arm, pulled her toward him and slapped her face once, but as he raised his hand for the second blow, Jim was on him, his arm around his neck, pulling him away from Johannah. Her father let go of her, turned back toward Jim and again knocked him down with his fist. Jim got to his feet, ready to continue the fight, but her father had withdrawn a small pistol from his jacket and now aimed the weapon intently at Jim's heart. Raffy's voice cut through the melee: "NO!"

And Jim froze, the pistol an arm's length away. Johannah took a step toward her father.

"No, Da. Please—"

The bishop called out, "George! For the love of God."

Johannah's father spoke quietly to Jim. "Do you think if I shot you anyone would really care?"

Jim stared back at him in defiant silence.

Johannah's mother and Raffy swooped in on them then, the priest and bishop right behind them. Jim took a step back, holding his ribs, his fine mouth bloody and torn. Johannah's father loosened his grip on the pistol, then stood up straight, put the piece away and addressed Jim.

"Pack up your things and be off the estate by nightfall or I'll have you arrested. Do you understand?"

"I want to speak to your daughter."

"No. Never again."

Jim looked at Johannah for a moment, his pain apparent, then turned and began a limping walk back to his family cottage. As he left, it occurred to Johannah she truly might never see him again and it would serve her right. She had brought this on the boy with a kiss, to get back at her father. Who could blame him if he hated her for it. There was nothing to do but lock herself in her room for the rest of the day.

A week later, Johannah's father made an announcement at breakfast.

"Arrangements have been made, Johannah. You'll be going to Devoncroft Ladies' College in London. I do not trust the schools in Dublin, and in any case, you should spend time among the English. It will do you good to know something about the most powerful empire on earth."

"I won't go." Johannah turned to her mother. "Tell him I won't go." But her mother sat there in silence.

"Yes, you will," he assured her. The battle was lost even before she became aware of her fate. Whether she liked it or not, she was going off to London.

Johannah went for days without speaking to either of her parents as the date of departure approached. Raffy and Lucy were her confidants as ever and were as distressed as she was at the prospect of her leaving the estate, but opposed to fanning the flames of Johannah's rebellion, Raffy offered good advice.

"You must look upon this as your first adventure. Remember all the stories we made up? This is real. You will travel and see a part of the world as it is in the books you've read. It's what you always wanted, miss. Make the best of it."

On the day of her departure they were all there outside Ballymore House to say goodbye. The dancers Martin and Brid O'Day were kneeling in the grass by the drive and the twins Michael and Devon Ryan stood on the swinging gate, their glum expressions identical. Johannah's mother was to accompany her on her journey to London and they were ready in matching capes and bonnets. The servants loaded their cases into the open carriage. Little Donald Murphy sang "Molly Malone" for the occasion, in harmony with his blind sister, Maive, and Lucy stood beside Johannah, staring at her as if at any moment she might burst.

"What will I tell them at the enchanted woodlot?"

"Tell them I'll be back."

Even after her father's threats, Johannah held a sliver of hope that she might see Jim Donnelly one last time, that somehow he might find a way to say goodbye to her. But then, why would he risk violence at the hands of her father again? She had ruined his life, had him banished from his home and brought sorrow to his family.

When they were ready to leave, Johannah went around to say goodbye to each of her friends, ending with Lucy—who, like her, was losing her battle against tears. As her wide blue eyes were filling, she gave instructions.

"You must write to me every day and twice on Sundays."

They hugged each other breathless. Then she and her father faced each other for a moment and she relented enough to give him a short, cold kiss. Then last, Raffy hugged her hard and fired out her list of commands.

"You must keep yourself very clean and say your prayers morning and night and avoid ne'er-do-wells and always lock your doors! And don't start arguments but stick up for yourself. Don't eat uncooked vegetables or undercooked meat. Wear a scarf and don't let your socks get wet." Her diatribe went on, then ended in a bit of a sob. With a last powerful hug, Johannah left her and climbed up into the coach behind her mother.

Johannah took a final look out the coach window at the house and the estate that had been her world. She looked around one last time to the outbuildings and trees and bushes, but he was not there. The hope of seeing Jim was now extinguished and she left home with the conviction that wherever he was, he felt well rid of her. The carriage departed from the house with her father standing on the driveway, Raffy beside him. As they passed the gate, Johannah leaned out the window and for the last time waved sadly back at Lucy and the other children of the estate. She would take Raffy's advice and embrace this new and unexpected future as an adventure.

On that dark day, Jim Donnelly hid in the bushes near the barn, fearful of arrest, and watched Johannah Magee leave him. So much for his plan of revenge against her father, which had taken an unexpected turn. He had developed true feelings for this headstrong girl. They were young, it was true, he only fifteen and she younger still. But he had played his part too well. Did she know? She knew everything else to know in the world, or so she'd tell you, so she surely must have known his true feelings. And there was the kiss! What more needed explaining? That was the deal done.

Jim suddenly ducked down. Had they seen him? The manager had looked in his direction, but no, he was safe. Cowardly but safe. What to do about the plan, now that her father had sent her away? Jim was the great-great-great-grandson of Chieftain Peter Donnelly and the last male of that line. What would Peter do? Kidnap the girl? Slay her evil father? He could still feel Magee's fist pounding his head, boot connecting with his face, the barrel of the gun pointed at him. Jim had no horse. He had no weapons. He had no money or prospects. All he could do was to crouch down out of sight, hiding in the bushes like a thief, and peer out at her like a helpless fool. On that day, when the object of his sweet revenge left him for England, it felt like no less than the abrupt end of his short, disappointing life.

Exile

THE EARLY MONTHS at Devoncroft Ladies' College in London were not easy for Johannah. She deeply missed Raffy and Lucy and Cuchulain, although her little horse would have found the trails of Hyde Park an extreme disappointment. She pleaded in her short letters to her mother to be allowed to come home at Christmas and again in the summertime, but her father was adamant that she needed more time in England to break free from the base provincial life in Ireland and absorb a superior culture. As usual, her mother agreed. It was almost despite herself that Johannah's circle of friends grew at the school and in the city, and she became quite fond of her aunt Lydia, a relative on her mother's side who lived in Chelsea. She continued reading a great deal; in her letters to Lucy she compared her life to that of the literary characters in Peacock's *The Misfortunes of Elphin* or Dickens's *Oliver Twist*, and in the subject of philosophy, read and declared herself skeptical of Kant's transcendental perception of life. She did very well in history, geography and poetry and by the end of second year, her anxious yearnings for Ballymore began to ease. Except for the one persistent image that always made her a little heartsick, of a certain boy with a broken smile.

Johannah's mother visited her twice each year for a fortnight, once in late fall and again during the spring social season. Together they went to the theatre, strolled the museums and attended dances in London. With each visit, her mother's demeanour warmed toward Johannah, and Johannah could not help but warm to her as well. They were delighted each time a stranger mistook them for sisters. They joked about London men, with their blustery self-importance.

"How did you first meet Father?"

"He did cattle business with my brother in Galway. My brother arranged that we should meet at a friend's dinner party there."

"What was he like then?"

"Oh, well dressed. On his best behaviour. Dashing even. Of course, he had all his hair then and no belly to speak of. I was only eighteen. I was quite swept away, poor thing."

Johannah's mother had never spoken to her like this, as a woman to a woman. She stayed silent and let her mother continue her bittersweet story.

"I had mistakenly believed he was capable of loving me and the truth became clear not in any one moment or hour or day, but slowly, incrementally, as things do happen, and the years went by as the years will. And you came along and any vestiges of his love went to you."

"I'm sorry," she told her mother, startled by the admission of what she had suspected. But her mother smiled.

"No, no. Don't be. You were a lovely child, the only joy in my life."

"But…you didn't kiss me or hug me. I never really felt you even liked me."

"Your grandfather was Scots," she said, as if this explained everything. "But maybe…I could start to show you now."

In these times together, there began to grow between them a true and loving bond. In the quiet moments when they talked of the past, she heard in her mother's voice a distant note of apology for her behaviour.

Once Johannah turned seventeen, she began to receive invitations to teas and luncheons, small gatherings where she inevitably found herself in the company of single young men. After some discreet questions, she was shocked to realize that her parents, with the help of her aunt, were arranging these subtle liaisons. They were trying to marry her off! She was young and free and after seeing what marriage offered to her mother, spending the rest of her life with any of the men she had met was the last thing that interested her. The world was far too interesting a place to become indentured to an English husband.

In her fourth year away, Johannah came upon the pamphlets of Elizabeth Cady Stanton and Lucretia Mott, whose intent was to abolish slavery. Johannah had seen a black family of slaves for the first time on a London street, with the father in chains, and was astonished that human beings could be treated this way in a civilized society. She became a supporter of the cause and gathered with the crowd outside an anti-slavery meeting in London, which Mott and Stanton had helped organize, to hear her heroes speak.

What Stanton and Mott found was that they had been denied chairs on the stage. Their names had been taken off the speakers' list they had written and the moderator of their choice had been replaced. When one speaker, an Anglican minister with a melodramatic tremor in his voice, finished a sermon-like diatribe, Mott took the stage, holding papers up high.

"Ladies and gentlemen of this assembly...my colleague and friend Elizabeth Cady Stanton and I have drafted an amendment to the bill to abolish slavery within the United Kingdom in three stages. The first will be to create a foundation to guide, protect, house and give medical care to freed slaves and their children..."

"Next speaker!" A male voice called out. The new moderator turned to Lucretia.

"I'm afraid we don't have time for this, ma'am."

"Once the foundation is established," she continued, "and ready to receive newly freed men and women, then the abolition laws can be properly enforced so the transition is safe and organized..."

"Please, Miss Mott, we have men waiting to speak."

"Then let them wait! If you pass and enforce the anti-slavery laws without a plan, you will have chaos!"

"Next speaker!" another voice called out.

"Ma'am, I'm afraid slavery is far too important an issue to waste time hearing what women have to say!"

And Lucretia Mott was forcibly escorted off the stage.

This experience, and others like it, turned the efforts of Mott and Stanton toward increasing the rights of women—equal treatment under the law, equal education, equal property rights and most important, the right to vote. Inspired by their work, Johannah joined a small women's rights organization and skipped classes at Devoncroft to pass out pamphlets on the street that demanded the vote for women. She was insulted by many men and some women and called all sorts of names, all of which only served to invigorate her. Increasingly, the privileged and arrogant upper-class men of London she met, with their nasal accent, droll manner and dismissal of women's equality, did not attract her and the matchmaking efforts of her parents and aunt came to nothing.

Throughout this time, Johannah continued to exchange letters with Lucy, sharing the joys and tribulations of London life and hearing news from the estate. She often asked about Jim Donnelly, hopeful that Lucy was reading her letters to him. Her thoughts went to Jim more and more, given the selection of men she was encountering. She wondered if he had forgiven her. But Lucy reported Jim had left Borrisokane for Manchester and that was the last she had heard of him. It occurred to Johannah that Manchester was closer to London than Borrisokane and a flame of hope burned: Was he on his way to find her? But with time, the flame dimmed and then was all but extinguished.

Eviction

MORE THAN FOUR years after Johannah left for England, Jim Donnelly was given permission to come onto the estate again, but it was not out of any magnanimous feelings of generosity or forgiveness by George Magee. The tenants were being evicted from their lands—all the families. Jim was allowed to help his mother and sister pack up their belongings. His mother cried for much of the week they had been given to prepare. They had no bags or cases, as they had never moved before, and Jim found some rough sacks and borrowed an old beaten trunk in which to lay the utensils, the pots and pans, the few china dishes and the little crystal horse said to have belonged to the patriarch Peter, well padded in blankets and towels and clothing. Jim had found a wagon for the furniture, a table and cupboard, chairs and beds and a cabinet built and carved by his father. His mother and sister would share the tiny shed where Jim lived behind the grocer's on Clyde Street in town.

"It'll be fine, Ma. 'Tis a little tight, but it'll do until we find something better."

It was not his mother's sorrow Jim felt, but a heated anger as he surveyed the meagre possessions his family had accumulated over generations. This was everything they owned, a reminder of how they had been slowly sucked dry by the estate. And now this final outrage, to be thrown off their land for good. None of the other families were faring better.

George Magee had gathered the tenants together and explained to them they were only "tenants-at-will," meaning they had no rights to their houses or land and he could evict them at any time, which up until now, he assured them, he had been reluctant to do. He had four soldiers with him. As he spoke, there was the sound of hammers nailing eviction notices on the front doors of the tenant houses.

"The English armies must be supported and supplied in the years to come. They need salt beef, and the Cavendish estate plans to provide it to them. For the good of the empire, I am clearing the estate to make pastureland for cattle. You must all leave your homes by a week Saturday."

The tenants had listened to Magee in stunned silence. They had lived on the Cavendish lands for generations. Once, these lands had belonged to them, before the English army came. And now to support that same army, they were being sacrificed again.

Lucy O'Toole's father had shouted out, "Where are we supposed to live? What are we supposed to eat?"

The soldiers turned their menacing attention toward him.

"You have to make your own arrangements. You may take any personal crops, animals and tools that belong to you, but you must be out by Saturday. I urge you to do so peacefully. Any resistance will be met with force. God save the queen!"

It was a week of bitterness and tears. O'Toole spoke quietly of resistance and Daniel Murphy and Patrick O'Day went to the local magistrate, but there was nothing he could offer. They were legally tenants-at-will. And the laws—the English laws that went back to the days of Cromwell—were clear.

On Saturday morning, Magee brought in twenty well-armed soldiers to enforce the evictions. Jim Donnelly and his mother and sister sat outside their cottage with bags of clothing and mattress bales, the cart with furniture and the battered trunk. Jim had found a man with a second cart to take them into Borrisokane later that day. Most of the other families were out in front of the cottages with their possessions and a few animals. The families barely spoke to each other, their eyes cast down in mutual shame. Jim and his family watched as Magee arrived and inspected the O'Day house, two down from them, with four soldiers at his side.

Then the unexpected happened. One soldier lit a torch and applied it to the thatch of the O'Day house. It caught and spread quickly and everyone stared in shock. Any hope the tenants might have harboured that one day they'd be allowed to return to their homes was destroyed in the inferno that followed.

The soldier with the torch led the way, followed by Magee and his bodyguards. The Murphy cottage was next and then the Donnellys'. Jim and his family stared as the flames consumed their world. Jim approached

George Magee and watched his impassive face. The soldiers became aware of Jim and stood defensively with rifles raised.

"I hope you're proud of yourself, Magee. What d'you suppose Johannah would say?"

Magee studied him for a moment, then turned away without a word.

Patrick Ryan was away in town bringing a borrowed wagon back when the soldier with the torch approached the Ryan house. Patrick's teenaged twins, Devon and Michael, stepped forward from the cottage.

"Stay back!" young Devon shouted at the soldier. "You'll not burn our house!"

In Devon's hands, Jim could see the old blunderbuss that had been hanging above the hearth. The boy held it pointed toward the soldiers. One of them shouted out, "He's got a gun!"

As the soldiers raised their weapons to Devon and Ryan, Jim ran at them.

"Don't shoot! It's broken! It's harmless!"

Jim was able to knock aside the two closest rifles, but two more fired and Devon fell. One soldier hit Jim in the stomach with the butt of his weapon and Jim dropped to his knees, winded. Michael went to where his brother lay still and picked up the old broken weapon. Still down on his knees, Jim called out to him.

"No, Michael! Don't!" but his warning came out barely a croak. Two more shots rang out and the Ryan twins lay dead beside each other in front of the cottage.

With a shriek that sounded clearly over the roar of the flaming huts, their mother ran to them, throwing herself over the bodies of her dead boys, grasping them to her. Jim stared at Magee's stony face.

Jim heard another cry from the O'Toole house, sixty yards away. The little structure where the children had so often gathered was engulfed in flames. A face could be seen in the tiny window of the attic. It was Lucy.

"You said the houses were cleared," Magee growled at the officer.

"They were, sir."

Jim stumbled to his feet as Lucy's father made a run for the door. Two soldiers blocked O'Toole's way and held him back from entering the inferno. He struggled and shouted and they had to wrestle him to the ground to stop him. Lucy cried out again and then there was silence as the flames consumed everything. Mr. O'Toole sobbed in grief.

Jim caught Magee's eye. "God forgive you, Magee. But I never will," he told him. Then a soldier's quick rifle butt to the head sent him into unconsciousness.

The Whiteboys

Jim Donnelly spent two days in the Borrisokane lock-up for threatening George Magee and passed them thinking up ways to make Magee suffer for his sins. Murder was too easy. It was here he met a colourful young man named Mick Tooney—in for vagrancy—who had grown up in Dublin and moved to Tipperary. He was a handsome young man with long lashes and an ironic smile, almost pretty, and wore a tattered waistcoat and ancient top hat. He had attended classes at Trinity and spoke like an educated man, and he had some interesting political ideas Jim had never heard before about the struggle of the classes and the reform of politics.

"One man alone can't do anything, Jimmy. We must be organized to fight the oppressors."

When the charges against each of them were dropped, Mick and Jim were released together. Mick took Jim across town and introduced him to his collected assortment of mates with empty bellies, who shared his interests. They called themselves the Whiteboys and their home base, as it were, was the Unicorn Tavern. Jim joined them with enthusiasm and in the following months he would quickly rise up to become Mick's second-in-command.

The Unicorn was a rough little pub in the darkest, most crowded part of Borrisokane, near the filthy canal off the Ballyfinboy River. With its cheap ale, it catered to farmers, common labourers and various ne'er-do-wells of the region such as themselves. Ryan, the bartender, wore a wild and particular hairpiece that looked as if it might come alive at any moment. He often cleaned his fingernails with an enormous bowie knife, a "bear-killer" he called it, imported all the way from America. A young boy swept the floor with strokes as slow and studied as those of a fine artist. Paddy, an aging patron almost permanently installed at the bar, spoke the same eulogy after each pint he finished: "There's another the English won't get."

The Unicorn could be quiet, as customers communed with their drinks and dreamed of bad ends for their enemies, but Mick and Jim and friends livened up the place. They knew they had no authority or right beyond their own minds, but once they'd had a few, their credentials and worldview expanded. Quoting his father, Jim would tell them that they must see themselves as the impoverished knights of the Irish realm who opposed not just the English Protestant land holders who had stolen most of Ireland in the time of Cromwell and ever since, but the "Blacklegs," any Irish Catholics who were friendly to or did business with them.

They had adopted Mick's looks, shabby but flamboyant, with waistcoats, high boots, scarves and canes. When they entered the Unicorn, they smiled and called out greetings to several of the patrons, patted the backs and shoulders of some and generally behaved as if they owned the place.

"Hello, Paddy! Ryan! James! God bless this house," Mick offered. "Are the constables about?"

"No, you're fine."

"Andy, watch the front," Jim ordered and the sweeping boy took his place at the window as lookout for snitches, traitors and Blacklegs, for some of the Whiteboys had a price on their heads.

"Ryan, a round for the boys and one for the house," Jim demanded.

"You still owe me for the last two."

"Ah, be a grand lad now, Ryan," Jim told him. "We're good for it. We've got a fine business deal coming up."

Ryan began to pour small portions of beer for them.

"You mean a fine tip on a horse."

The Whiteboys went to their table near the bar. Mouths watering, they trimmed the mold off a fair chunk of corned beef Ryan donated to them, divided the good meat and tore up a loaf of rye one lad had stolen from the baker, sharing it equally, a silent savouring, to keep them going another day.

Paddy turned toward their table. "Boys, did you see? They've started loading the barges."

Jim offered Paddy a crust but he refused. He seemed to survive on ale alone. Ryan served them quarter-full mugs of beer from a tray as Paddy continued.

"The finest meat and meal all bound for England and to line Cavendish's pockets."

"Good Catholics starving and the priest giving his blessing to it all."

"And that son of a bitch Magee."

"The worst of the Blacklegs."

Andy at the window alerted them.

"Jimmy?"

A moment later, Stephen Feehley entered, a skinny man with small eyes and the look of a travelling rat. "Speaking of Blacklegs." They gave him the once-over from the table.

Feehley went to the bar and gazed around with a smile as innocent as a kitten and shone this benevolent countenance on the bartender.

"Ryan, old love. Give me a pint, sir."

"We just ran out, Feehley."

Feehley's smile wavered. "You have no call to be like that, Ryan. I've got money."

"We know you do. And where it came from."

Feehley looked around at the others. "I don't know what you're thinking."

Paddy raised a glass.

"Here's to England...and the day she sinks beneath the waves and takes all the filthy Protestants and their lackeys with her."

Everyone with glasses in their hands drank with enthusiasm. It was then Feehley saw Mick and Jim and the Whiteboys, who had now turned toward him, watching him from their table. Feehley's smile left him and his face went pale. He called out, his voice unsure.

"Hello, Mick...Jimmy. Didn't see you there."

Two of the Whiteboys stood and walked past Feehley to the door, effectively blocking any exit. Among all the patrons, Feehley could see only accusing eyes. Mick and Jim rose and moved toward him.

"Now what kind of fool would come in here after what you've been up to?"

"I don't know what you're talking about."

"Oh, I think you do."

Mick picked up Ryan's bear-killer and began to clean his fingernails in the manner of its owner. He studied Feehley. The Blackleg backed away from him, and then suddenly turned and made an attempt to run but as he tried to push past the two boys at the door, they grabbed him and held him firmly.

Out in the dark alley behind the Unicorn Tavern, one of the boys had an armful of wilted, long-stem rose briars, their thorns prominent, with which he was lining the inside of a large beer barrel. With the "rose barrel" prepared, the two Whiteboys brought out their captive. Feehley was gagged, shirtless, his hands tied behind his back.

"So Feehley, you were warned now, were you not?" Mick told him.

"You don't go selling your cow to Magee," Jim explained, as if the man did not know. "And this was the second time."

Feehley stared at them, whimpering through his gag. Three Whiteboys lifted him and placed him into the barrel feet first, but he didn't go easy and so even turning him head down, it was all they could do to gather and force down his resisting arms and kicking legs, stuffing them below the rim.

"No. Nooooooo!" Feehley grimaced, muffled by the gag. He tried to call out to bystanders. "Help! Help me!"

When the Whiteboys had secured the barrel top, they turned it on its side and two of them started rolling it out and around the square in a widening circle. As the speed of the barrel increased, Feehley's muffled screams could be heard inside, his body speared a thousand times by the thorns. Some curious onlookers came out to watch "a Blackleg getting his due," as it was explained to them, and this was met with general acceptance.

"I think the lesson's over," Mick told Jim quietly after the second roll by.

"Truly?" Jim was surprised. As the barrel came back around the square, Mick stepped out onto the road, put his foot out and stopped it.

"That's all? Two rounds?"

Muffled moans came from inside.

"'Twas only a cow."

Jim studied him for a moment. "You're not going soft on us, Mick?"

"Don't be a shite. I just don't see this as a major help to the cause."

"Fair enough," Jim said, still looking pointedly at Mick. "Let him out, lads. Today's lesson will be one of compassion."

The Whiteboys righted the barrel and took the lid off. Feehley fell out among the blood and roses on the muddy cobblestones.

With this good work done, Jim and Mick turned to go back inside to finish their drinks. Mick held the door for Jim, glancing left and right outside for enemies before entering. When they were back at the table, Mick shared some news.

"Speaking of Magee, Jim, did you hear his wife passed away?"

Jim almost spilled the small amount of ale in his mug. "Magee's wife, Mary?"

"Did he have more than one?"

"Don't be an arse." He was anxious for answers. "She's dead, then? When?"

"Just a couple of days ago. It was sudden."

"Did they bury her yet?"

"No. Don't think so. They're waiting for family to come. It'll be private though. Magee has too many enemies for a public funeral."

That's for sure, thought Jim, but his mind was not on Magee or his poor wife. His thoughts were on Johannah. She would be coming back for sure, he realized. Imagine that. All of these years. How would she look? Would she even remember him? Of course she would. She better.

Johannah's Return

JOHANNAH STOOD BESIDE her father over her mother's grave in the cemetery at St. Patrick's and threw wild roses down on top of the casket as it was slowly lowered on ropes by four men from the village. Johannah had been wearing black since she heard of her mother's death, throughout the four-day journey from London by carriage, ship and stagecoach, and would remain cloistered in black for another day of formal grieving.

"God our Father, Your power brings us to birth, Your providence guides our lives, and by Your command we return to dust."

Her mother's final descent into the cold ground brought Johannah a sudden panic. She glanced over at her father's face beside her, hardened, his jaw clenched tight. He did not look at her.

"May she rejoice in Your kingdom where all tears are wiped away, unite us together again in one family, to sing Your praises forever and ever."

The priest continued his eulogy for a woman who had been "dignified and kind." By then, Johannah's eyes were again full of tears and her chin trembled. Ever since her mother's death—a sudden ailment of the heart and she was gone—Johannah had felt a powerful grief she had not expected. A huge black hole had opened in her life, one she could not get around or through.

She and her mother had grown closer than she thought possible in the last few years. She had hoped for many more years with her, and her sorrow was tinged with bitterness at the loss of a friend that had just been found.

The funeral party was remarkably small, with Raffy, two of Johannah's second cousins on her father's side, three graziers who looked after the twelve hundred head of cattle now on the estate and two elders of the church and one of their wives. But where were her old friends? Where was Lucy? She had not received a letter from Lucy in over a year and a half and even her own mother, on her last visit to London, had been vague, pretending to not even remember who Lucy was. Johannah had expected at least some of the tenants to be here, but her father said they had moved too far away to return. She would have invited the world but, inexplicably, her father wanted the ceremony small, just family and a few friends, and of course the four soldiers who would stand guard. Her father had said there had been trouble with thieves and hooligans and the soldiers were a precaution. Soldiers at a funeral. Johannah wondered again what that was about.

She had arrived the day before, and it was so strange to be home after almost six years away, especially under these terrible circumstances. Her father seemed older and weary but his edge was not gone, nor his anger.

At supper, she had told her father a little about her life in London. But when she asked about Lucy and the others, he seemed unclear about where the tenants had gone and Johannah felt just too tired to push the matter.

The question she didn't dare ask of anyone yet was the whereabouts of Jim Donnelly. Was he still in Manchester, as Lucy had written? He had stayed persistently at the back of her mind, with his perfect lips like the plaster angel. He was the only boy she had met who could truly make her laugh. He would be a man now. She had kissed other men and done much more than that in London, but no kiss had excited her as much as the forbidden one on the churchyard wall.

Now, as the first shovelful of earth boomed down on the casket, Johannah's eyes strayed to the old wall they had walked six years before, the spot they had kissed. Her fingers went to her lips. She became aware of the sudden silence in the service. Everyone was waiting for her. Her father held out the loaded spade and she blushed at her wayward thoughts. How could she think of Jim at this moment?

She took the shovel and spilled the earth down on her mother's casket as gently as possible. The filling in of the grave was such a final act and the tears came again and they felt good and full, a tribute to the woman her mother had tried at the end to be.

Had Johannah looked a bit higher, just beyond the cemetery wall, she would have seen him up in the branches of an oak tree. From that safe distance, Jim Donnelly watched the proceedings. He could have been down in the cemetery—they could not have stopped him—but it would have been awkward with Magee. He respected their grief and he had wanted to see Johannah before she saw him. *My God*, he thought, *the skinny young girl has butterflied into a full-blown woman, with beauty and confidence.* He suddenly felt intimidated and diminished hiding in the oak tree like a shy, curious child. If she were to see him like this, he would certainly be mortified, but the important thing was he was not disappointed by the present Johannah. She was breathtaking. His memory and his old desire for her remained true. The desire for her and the desire for retribution against the bastard beside her.

On the day after her mother's funeral, Johannah changed from her black wardrobe into a riding outfit and decided to escape the gloom and grief of Ballymore to do a short tour with Cuchulain. The glistening milk-white boy with his combed-out tail and mane had been well cared for by the one remaining groom. The horse knew her immediately, as if they had ridden together the day before. Their years apart dissolved to a moment as they took their old route across the glen and up along the ridge where she could see the Ballyfinboy River wandering through the fields toward the Shannon and the sea. They cantered through the enchanted woodlot—Johannah could almost hear Lucy singing in her ear—and they ran down again well clear of the bog and then along the shaded path by the fishing stream, where horse and rider slowed down to cool themselves and strong memories of Jim Donnelly came to her again.

Johannah soon found herself standing on the edge of the rich green pasture where the tenant houses had once been, full of life and activity. It was as if she were in some sort of dream now as everything lay in ruins, all of the roofs of the cottages gone, the scorched stone walls crumbling, the silence overwhelming. Her body felt weak as she dismounted, dropping the reins and walking over to stand in front of what remained of Lucy's old cottage. Hers was only one of several within sight around the pasture, all gone, burned-out foundations left overgrown with deep green grasses and ferns, liverwort and thistle, blue-eyed flowers and vines, nature's attempt to soften the shock of the human absence in these once lively places. She had been told some of the tenants were gone, but they were all gone. And why this burned-out devastation?

She reached down her gloved hand to gently pick up a broken tea cup, the delicate curved handle still intact, which lay amid the ashes and mud, and gave it close inspection. This fragment of the past had a blue rose pattern—there had been three such cups—that held a memory for her of tea with Lucy's family. What had happened here? She looked beyond to the many fat cows grazing nearby as if for answers. Then she gently placed the remnant of the cup back into the ashes and mounted Cuchulain. Wheeling his muscular body around, she rode off toward town to find out, scattering the fat indolent cows like so many pigeons.

Ruins

At the Borrisokane canal outside the Cavendish warehouses, on the edge of the town square, Jim, Mick and their boys stayed undercover and watched as men loaded a barge with rough crates and barrels of meat and other foods for export. That year's poor potato harvest had been made worse by a strange fungus affecting in some cases as many as half the plants. Nearby a soup kitchen serviced a long line of the poor who had come in from neighbouring lands, the people in need, some desperate, approaching a single monk in robes who distributed the thin soup in measured portions, ladled from an enormous iron vat. On the river's edge, not far from the soup line, huge pallets of salted meat, sacks of oats and barley, crates of turnips and apples and barrels of whiskey and ale that came from a warehouse alongside the wharf with the name "Cavendish & Company" awaited loading. The manager of the Cavendish estate, who oversaw all of this injustice, was the man Jim hated most: George Magee. With a passion equal to what he felt for Magee's daughter, Jim loathed this man, for all his sins. Magee rode a black mare, as fine a horse as any in the township, and he wore a pistol on his hip and retained five armed soldiers to stand guard as the food was hoisted by crane on board the barge for Dublin, where it would be transported to Liverpool and on to London, away from the mouths of the starving and onto the tin plates of the soldiers of the English army. The English were bad enough, but the man who betrayed his own country, his own people, was evil indeed. The soldiers guarding the shipment were led by a young English corporal on horseback, monitoring the docile crowd to be sure they stayed that way. The Whiteboys' job was to see they didn't.

"All right lads," Mick murmured. "Nice and casual like, keep smiling, a nod to the ladies, move to your positions and watch for my signal."

Jim, Mick and two other boys made their way slowly through the soup line crowd toward the barge, twirling their canes and smiling cheerfully at one and all. They kept a careful eye on Magee and the soldiers. The crane hoisted and swung another pallet of salted meat half the size of a tenant house aboard the barge. George Magee was ever watchful of the men working as the vessel was slowly filled, and his presence kept the soldiers vigilant. Three stevedores took a barrel of salted beef, one of ale and a crate of fresh vegetables to the side door of St. Patrick's rectory across the square. They pushed them forward as the priest held the door, pleased with the offering. Jim glanced at Mick, his voice quiet. "Look. Beef and ale for the priest. But for the sinners, that thin gruel the church is spooning out."

When all was safely inside, the priest quickly closed the door.

The boys spread out and continued to make their way across the crowded square to the loading dock. They had done a few minor jobs like this before. They couldn't just do nothing. Jim whistled his favourite little Limerick tune, "Oyster Nan." Then while he was standing there, watching the crane, who should ride into town but Johannah Magee.

He studied her as if she had suddenly descended, an angel from heaven, or a ghost or a goddess, and now in this moment all his buried feelings for her rose up, strong and fresh. She was not merely a pawn in his plans of reckoning, and any attempt to control his feelings for her was a ridiculous fraud. He watched her with the horse, as he had done many times from a distance in their youth. She was now even more the competent and impressive horsewoman, carefully making her way through the crowd toward her father, his enemy George Magee. He hoped Magee loved her deeply, for he was soon to lose her.

Her electric eyes swept across Jim's, passing without recognition, and he suffered a pang of heartache. She was haughty, direct and lovely as she rode right past him.

Jim steadied himself and calmed his breathing as he watched her lean forward to speak to her father. She seemed preoccupied, even upset.

"Da."

"Good morning, my dear."

"I rode out to the O'Tooles' and Donnellys'. The cottages are destroyed. There is no one left. What happened to them?"

Her father looked at her blankly, then suddenly, distracted, he turned and called out to the stevedores loading the barge.

"No, no you fools! I said meat barrels and crates at the back! All together!"

As her father rode away from her to direct his men, she studied the ragged people in the long soup line with a sudden alarm. When she left, there had been a level of dignity and health among even the poorest of the tenants and townspeople, but here she was presented with ragged clothes and gaunt faces and a new aura of desperation in their eyes. She had heard no reports in London about any change in Irish fortunes, nothing in the papers save a reference to a poor Irish crop. Her mother had never spoken of such things and yet the transformation of a hundred local souls was shocking. What could have happened?

Jim had to turn away from the distraction of Johannah's presence to get back to the mission at hand. He made his way toward the crane while Mick manoeuvred himself near the front of the tightly packed soup line. Mick backed hard into an old fellow who tumbled against another and almost knocked down a thin young woman with a fussing baby. This started a pushing match in the soup line with recriminations flying.

The English soldiers turned all their attention toward the fray. One snarled at the surging crowd, "Stop it! Or you go to the back of the line!"

The peasants glared at the soldiers and settled. Mick crouched down behind them and called out in a projected voice, "English shite! Dirty Protestant!" then moved smoothly away.

"What? Who said that? You!"

The soldier grabbed one man with a goiter on his neck the size of an apple and dragged him out of the line. The unfortunate struggled to get away.

"Wasn't me, sir! Wasn't me!"

Two of Jim's boys had worked their way into the crowd and called out to the soldiers, "Leave him alone! Cowards! British bastards!" then hid themselves.

The soldiers grabbed others, trying to identify the name-callers in the line. The innocent ones resisted and feelings turned hostile toward the redcoats. All eyes, including those of the bearded man operating the crane, were on the scuffle in the line when Jim pulled up a kerchief to mask his face, moved to the base of the derrick, withdrew his sheath knife and quickly began severing the rope, thick as a child's wrist, that suspended the substantial pallet of food high above the dock.

While all other eyes were turned away, one soldier several yards across the crowd saw him at the rope. "You! What are you doing? Get away from there!"

Jim ran the sharpened blade two more times across the thick, taut hemp. The rope strands separated cleanly, the end flew through the block and tackle, and the huge suspended pallet came crashing down, splitting open sacks of barley and crates of turnips, and breaking open barrels with slabs of salt beef cascading onto the dock in a very satisfying manner, like a grocer's display open to the public. His face still covered, Jim made his escape from the soldier, who could not get to him through the thick crowd and dared not use his rifle. People in line had heard the crash of the pallet and now turned, leaving the promise of only thin soup to rush forward and claim the glory of spilled meat and meal. They filled their pockets with grain and their arms with turnips and grabbed the raw beef in their hands.

The soldiers ran in the direction of the shattered pallet to fight them off, shouting, pushing and threatening with their rifle butts, but the hungry crowd would not be dispersed. With the people now pushing back, threatening the soldiers who tried to protect the spilled food, the situation quickly descended into a riot. The Whiteboys had accomplished their simple mission and Jim saluted Mick and his mates over the heads of the crowd, pleased with the results.

Jim moved quickly through the fray toward the bounty, spurring the people on. "Grab it now, my friends. Take it away!" He placed two big beef tenderloins in the arms of an old woman, tossed a sack of oats to a burly plowman. "Come on, now. Take it all and run!" He put an unripe melon in the hands of a skinny, excited boy.

George Magee bellowed to the young corporal leading the soldiers. "Stop them!"

The corporal moved into the crowd on horseback in a vain attempt to separate the people from the spilled food. He had a long sword to threaten them with, but he did not use it.

In the melee, Johannah was caught up in the dense crowd, and two rough men took the opportunity to try to steal her horse. She beat them back aggressively with her riding crop as they attempted to pull her off the saddle. Seeing this, Jim charged over. She was bellowing at her assailants, "Get away! Get away, I said."

Cuchulain reared up. Jim arrived and though his first punch landed well, the men almost overwhelmed him. With skilful use of his cane, he finally knocked one unconscious and drove the other away. He grabbed hold of the horse's reins to lead Johannah through the surge of people toward the safety of an empty alley, but with his face covered, she must have thought him one of her assailants, for she hit at him with her crop, striking him across the head. He was amazed she didn't recognize him despite the handkerchief, for he knew her in a moment and would have known her at a thousand yards. Still, he was reluctant to identify himself to her just yet.

"Get away, I said!" she yelled at him.

He put up an arm to defend himself from further blows as he led Cuchulain away from the crowd.

"I'm not kidnapping you. Just trying to save your arse."

"I can save my own arse, thank you all the same."

They arrived at a quiet place of safety in the mouth of the alley, away from the canal and the spilled provisions. Jim felt Johannah's curious eyes settle on him as he saluted her, then turned back and re-entered the fray.

The people were still scrambling for food. It was all going well, Jim thought. Magee's whip had little effect. The food from the broken pallet was fast disappearing. Then the estate manager called out to the soldiers, "Fire at them!"

The soldiers were rightly fearful of the repercussions of firing on a crowd that outnumbered them thirty to one. They looked to their commanding officer for orders. Magee glared at the young corporal.

"Did you hear me? Shoot the thieving bastards!"

The soldiers pointed their rifles at the crowd and waited, unsure.

"Over their heads! Squad One…" Half the soldiers raised their muskets.

"FIRE!"

The volley of musket fire almost immediately achieved the desired effect: the peasants cowered and retreated. The other half of the soldiers prepared to fire again while the first squad reloaded, but it was not necessary. In a moment, control was resumed. A few members of the crowd who were hurt in the scramble lay suffering on the ground. The soldiers let others, the Whiteboys among them, help the injured retreat or carry them away. Somehow the vat of thin soup had been overturned.

With the square now deserted and still, a few rolling turnips meandered slowly down the cobblestone grade. A young boy grabbed one and made his escape. Magee called out to the stevedores, "Come on, come on. Clean this up! Keep loading."

Jim watched Magee from behind an overturned cart. How he yearned to drag him off that horse and find some satisfaction. Instead, for now, he withdrew from the scene.

In the saddle atop Cuchulain, from the mouth of the alleyway where the kerchiefed man had led her to safety, Johannah watched her father dealing with the soldiers and the workers returning to loading the barge. She had seen the desperation in the faces of the people as they ran for the food and seized it in their hands, even with the soldiers' muzzles trained on them. How had it come to this? When she was a child, there were no soup lines, no ragged clothes, no surrender of dignity. What had happened? She turned Cuchulain around and made her way back to the estate.

Raffy

THE CLOUDS MOVED in that night and brought periodic showers with spears of lightning in between that flashed through the tightly closed windows of Johannah's bedroom, made cozy by a blazing fire that Raffy had set and lit. She had enthusiastically taken over Johannah's care again, as if she had never left, as if she had never grown into a young woman, and Johannah let Raffy treat her and fuss over her as before. They had dinner alone, which Raffy cooked and served, for the fortunes of the estate had taken a downturn—this her mother had mentioned on her last visit—and Raffy was the only waitstaff left.

"Raffy...I went out to the tenant cottages today to visit. They're gone! The buildings have been burned. What happened? Where are the O'Tooles and the Donnellys?"

Raffy's expression revealed this to be dangerous ground, and she responded carefully. "It's your father you must be asking about that. Not my business." And she would say no more.

Johannah's father was working late at the Cavendish offices and warehouse and was still not home as she prepared for bed. This was her third night back and she had spent hardly any time in his company. He was the last of her family. Though he was not an easy man, she wanted to think better of him, even to imagine that his behaviour that night so many years ago had been an aberration. Or perhaps even a misunderstanding.

Johannah stood in a bathing pan wearing a very loose cotton nightgown with her arms raised. Raffy used a soapy cloth to quickly, roughly clean her arms, back and neck, reaching under the gown so Johannah wouldn't get a chill. It had been their nightly ritual years before, resumed as if from only yesterday. She was too old for it now, she thought at first. In six years, her body had changed from a skinny adolescent's to that of a full woman. And recently in London, she had proudly let a very few selected others touch that new body. Now, strangely with Raffy, for a moment she felt shy. But Raffy began scrubbing and the years dissolved and it all felt very natural again.

Johannah noticed on the wall in front of her an unfaded square of wallpaper where a painting had hung. It had been a landscape by the Englishman Turner of a sunny pasture with highland cattle grazing. As a child she would stare at it, become lost deep beyond the precise brush strokes that created the illusion of that gentle world. There was another unfaded square near the bed, another favourite painting of hers, a young girl of title with kittens and a white bow in her hair by a portrait artist who specialized in the children of the European aristocracy. Where had these paintings gone? She had noticed other furnishings missing and asked Raffy, but Raffy was firm that these were questions she must ask her father.

Now, Johannah told Raffy about her day and the trouble at the soup line. "I just don't understand how things could have changed so quickly. To watch those people scramble after that food."

"An empty belly'll do that, miss," Raffy offered, frowning. "It's the second year the potatoes have been diseased. Do you not hear of these things in London?"

"No, not really."

Raffy put down the washcloth, picked up the small brush and began to clean Johannah's teeth as if she were six years old, holding a bowl under her chin. Johannah spoke through a mouthful of tooth powder suds.

"Can't they grow different crops?" But she was thinking that after what she'd seen that day, there could be no simple answers.

"Spit, my love."

She did so and Raffy put the bowl away. Then the heavy woman's joints cracked as she knelt on the floor.

"I can do my feet, Raffy. Please, there's no need."

"Let's get the whole job done. Clean as a whistle."

She began with the washcloth on her feet, Johannah steadying herself with a hand on the bureau as Raffy scrubbed between her lifted toes.

"Father seems so tired…"

"It's good you've come home, my love. Maybe it'll take the edge off him. You liked it then, England? Mightn't you go back?"

Johannah considered this question for a moment. What would she do now? She had not realized how much the death of her mother meant to her. She had completed almost six years at Devoncroft and beyond the real subjects of history, geography, elocution and mathematics there were courses on household management, with a staff below and a husband above, on the social graces of dinner parties, on gift giving and, in certain cases, matchmaking. After the excitingly raw and fresh politics of the feminists Mott and Stanton, she realized she could not go back to Devoncroft. The school had nothing to offer her. But did she see herself continuing in the life of an abolitionist or women's rights advocate? Maybe.

Raffy was waiting for an answer. "What did you think of London, my love? I've never been. What did you learn?"

"Well, one thing I learned was you don't have to simply put up with the way things are. There are people out there who fight back against slavery or injustice or for women's rights. I believe soon, Raffy, women could have the vote!"

"Good heavens! Anarchy!" They both laughed.

"I believe Mrs. Mott and Mrs. Stanton will eventually get their way."

"So will you go back?"

Johannah hesitated. "Well, London is the centre of the world," she said with a bit of sarcasm, "or so they have convinced themselves...civilized and proper. The museums and art galleries...music...everything very 'à la mode.' So, exciting and all, I guess, except"—Raffy paused in her ablutions to listen—"the gentlemen. They're all so boring. Just boys, really. Full of themselves and their fathers' money and who they know and their nasty little circles of friends and enemies. Not one of the boys I met took me seriously. Not one I could be serious about."

"You always had such 'lofty' standards, miss."

Johannah looked at her, catching her own sarcasm, and laughed again as Raffy picked up a towel and dried her feet, one then the other.

"Yes...these standards of mine. They've left me stranded here, Raffy, on the shoals of spinsterhood. Aged, loveless..."

"How will you ever find the strength to carry on, my love?"

Johannah looked at her as they warmed to each other even more after so long apart. She took Raffy's big face in her hands, leaned down and kissed her on the cheek. Raffy smiled up at her and her joints creaked again as she rose to her feet. Johannah stepped out and away from the wash pan onto the cold bare floor and she wondered, hadn't there been a Persian rug here, blue, with men hunting tigers? Intent on further explaining her heart to Raffy, she dismissed the question of the absent carpet and stepped onto a towel.

"Do you know what I want? I want to have some adventures, Raffy. London is all very well but it is so staid, so conservative so…circumscribed and safe. I want to travel to places far away and live by my wits. I want to meet interesting people I would never normally meet. I want to see the orient like Captain Edward Belcher, or explore Africa by safari like René Caillié and find the source of the Nile, or sail with Crozier to discover Antarctica. Life is passing me by, Raffy. Do you understand?"

"I do, my love. Sadly, it sounds like Borrisokane is not your future."

Later, sitting on a settee before a full mirror in an elegantly carved cherrywood frame, Johannah appraised her own young face as Raffy combed out her thick, dark hair. Outside the window, lightning continued to flash and the long, distant rumble thundered a few seconds behind. Johannah held out her palm.

"Tell me my fortune, Raffy. Not just the old stuff."

Raffy smiled, hesitated, put down the brush and took her hand, holding it to the candlelight, studying the lines with practised skill. As she ran a finger down Johannah's life line, Raffy's face clouded as outside the distant thunder cracked and grumbled again.

"What? What did you see?"

"Nothing…" Raffy let go of Johannah's hand. She picked up the brush and continued brushing Johannah's hair.

"Really, what did you see?"

"Nothing, miss. I…I don't have the knack tonight."

"I don't believe you."

Before she could insist, there was a knock at the door and a moment later, her father entered. He gave her as warm a smile as he could muster.

"Johannah. I was awful worried about you this afternoon. You were fierce brave today and I was proud of you, my dear. I don't know what I'd do if anything ever happened to you."

He turned to Raffy. "Good night, Raffy," he said, dismissing her.

She hesitated, looking from him to Johannah. Magee stood watching until finally, under his gaze, Raffy picked up some laundry and left the room.

"There are some things…I should tell you." He was moving about the room without looking at her. "The estate has been suffering, financially.

I have tried hard, but the world is in depression. And I have made some investments that proved ill-advised."

Her father raised his chin to show he was not in defeat, then removed a flask from his pocket, turned away from her to look out the window and took a long drink.

"I was cheated. We owe a lot of money. I had to sell some things."

"So I see."

"It's worse. Many of the things belonged to Cavendish."

"Oh." This was unexpected. She had always assumed her father was a good and honest manager.

"And I will not be able to send you back to Devoncroft."

"This is not a misfortune," she informed him.

"Good. But still, beyond the cruel loss of your mother, I am financially in trouble."

"Well, I'm sure it will all work out. Cavendish knows how good a manager you've been for him."

"Yes. It'll all work out. I'm glad you see it so. You have my optimistic spirit."

Her father sat down on the settee close beside Johannah. Unconsciously, her hand went to touch the fine silver locket that was hanging from her neck. Her father raised his hand and took hers and the medallion in his own fingers.

"It keeps me safe," she told him.

"Yes. I gave her that…"

"…on the day I was born. She gave it to me the first time she left me at Devoncroft."

Her father looked into her eyes and tenderly traced the soft side of her face with the back of his fingers. "Now that you are a woman, you have her face. Extraordinary. So beautiful."

She looked into his sunken features, smelled the whiskey on his breath and sat back from him.

"She said you never loved her."

"That was a lie. I loved her in my own way."

"With the back of your hand?"

Her father froze for a moment. "She was not an easy woman. But you're not like her. You're like me. I have been so very lonely, Johannah."

Her father turned his hand over and ran his finger along her mouth, tracing her lips, and the icy memory of that confusing and fearful moment in the barn six years before rose up fully within her. She gave an involuntary shudder and pulled away from him again.

"Don't touch me."

She stood and took a few steps toward the window to look out and calm herself. She felt ill.

"What is wrong, Johannah?"

She would not let her father's behaviour distract her from the questions she needed to ask. She turned back to him.

"Tell me the truth. I took a ride today out to the tenant houses. The Ryans…the O'Tooles…the Donnellys. What happened to them? Where is Lucy?"

George Magee's face hardened, his emotions as tight and controlled as they were at his wife's graveside.

"We had to make changes. The markets forced us to produce meat for the British armies. It was Cavendish's decision. We had to convert the grain fields to pasture. There was no call for labourers. The tenants moved on."

"The houses are burned out."

"Yes. It's sad. But there was no need for them. We didn't want squatters occupying them. Taxes have to be paid on any structure with a roof."

"Where did they all go?"

"They moved on into town or up to Limerick or into Dublin."

"But I've heard nothing from Lucy. I was going to send her money to visit me in London."

"I don't know anything about that," he said, looking perplexed. "They will have found work somewhere. Darling, the only constant in this world is change and we must change with it. We are caught between the peasants and the wealthy classes. It's our responsibility to lead. It's not easy."

After a moment, he came toward her and took her arm, staring into her eyes, drawing her closer. "So like her," he murmured, gazing steadily at her. "But with spirit."

Johannah tried to pull away, but he held her firmly.

"Let go of me."

She turned her face from her father's burning eyes, but he continued to hold her close to him with a strength that exceeded hers. She could feel the heat of his body through the light cotton of her gown.

"I need you."

As her father kissed her neck, she stood frozen and tried to calm the panic from her voice.

"I'm very tired. I need some sleep…Daddy, please!"

At this endearment, the fire suddenly left his gaze and he stepped back and released her arm. His expression became troubled and confused.

"Yes. Yes, you've had a long day."

"I have. So good night, Da. Go now."

"Yes. Good night, sweetheart."

He turned, then, and lurched unsteadily toward the door. He pushed it open wide and continued on toward his own bedroom.

Johannah stepped out into the hall and was about to pull the door closed to lock it when she noticed someone in the shadows behind. Raffy was standing there, quiet and still. She looked at Johannah without a word. In her hand she held a small pistol, Johannah's mother's own little weapon. She was breathing hard. When Magee was gone down the hall, Raffy uncocked the hammers and folded the two triggers back into place. She then wrapped the little pistol in her shawl and, without a word, made her way back across the hall to her own room. Johannah went back into hers and sat on the bed, thinking about what had just happened, knowing she could not live at Ballymore House anymore.

Oyster Nan

JOHANNAH PLACED A bouquet of wild roses on the fresh dirt of her mother's grave in St. Patrick's crowded little cemetery. The headstone read "Mary Elizabeth Ryan Magee." She had taken the silver locket from around her neck and held it in her hand, tears misting her vision as she gazed at the tiny daguerreotype of her beautiful mother. Already, shoots of grass and clover were coming up through the rich earth. She longed for her mother's company. She imagined she could hear her mother's voice in the gentle wind, the words almost discernible, but not quite, and this only made her feel more alone.

Johannah entered the darkened, empty church, knelt at a side altar, struck a match that briefly illuminated her spot in the sanctuary and lit a candle for her mother. She carefully placed it among the few others and said a little prayer to the angels for solace and for guidance. After a few moments, she felt no answer. She was not a patient young woman. She rose, genuflected to the altar and went out for a good ride on Cuchulain.

Across the wide green pasture, scattering the damn cows again, she drove Cuchulain at a full, furious gallop, trying to escape her grief, riding off the fear and disgust she felt toward her father's attentions. She felt truly an orphan. What could she now do with her life?

On the hard-packed bridle path under a leafy canopy beside the mumbling stream, Cuchulain made his careful way. Johannah's emotions were calmed beside the flowing water. This was a place she would come to very often as a child, most times alone, to dream, to read. It was a place of contemplation, sanctuary and solitude. What would she now tell that young girl, if she could? What would that girl now tell her?

And then she remembered the day fishing with Jim Donnelly and the encounter with the warden, and she smiled at how Jim had made her laugh. She remembered the place, a pool in a bend in the river just ahead. And then, as if God were conniving to re-create His little play, she swore she could hear whistling, the clear notes of someone up ahead. It was Jim Donnelly's tune and as she drew closer on the winding path, the whistler began to sing in a clear, warm tenor that was much deeper than she remembered, but still, there was no question.

"As Oyster Nan stood by her tub,
to show her inclination…"

Johannah rode quietly into the clearing, and there he was, standing near the stream, his back to her, nonchalantly rigging up his fishing gear. She had the distinct feeling she was expected.

"she gave her noblest parts a scrub,
and sighed for want of copulaaaaaaaaation…"

Johannah blushed at the lyrics she'd never heard before, but only a little. Jim glanced over his shoulder as she approached. Johannah was delighted. "I'll be damned," she said out loud. "Jim Donnelly."

Neither could hide their pleasure at seeing the other. And in the interest of restaging the scene from almost six years before, Johannah mustered a forceful authority. "You! Peasant! These are estate lands."

She rode a little closer to him. "What are you doing there?" she continued in her affected upper-class accent. Jim joined the game, holding up his fishing tackle. "You mean with this fishing gear, my lady? I'm picking wildflowers."

"You're poaching! I'll call the game wardens. They'll arrest you!"

She drew a little closer to him.

"Why don't you just toss me a rope, my lady, and I'll hang meself right here?"

"You don't realize the trouble you're in, sir."

"Maybe not. But I'm willing to find out."

Smiling at him, Johannah went to dismount and Jim dropped his gear and stepped closer to help her down. As her foot touched the ground, she stumbled and steadied herself against his shoulder, then regained her footing and stepped back to have a look at him.

"Well…Jim Donnelly? Are you sure? He was a homely, skinny runt with crossed eyes and a bad attitude!"

He offered her his sad smile. "So were you."

They stood face to face for a moment, a passing awkwardness between them that was quickly dispelled, and Johannah could not stop smiling back at him.

"You! It was you at the riot! The masked man who helped me." It was the voice. His voice had changed to a deeper register and with his face covered, she had not recognized Jim Donnelly in the helpful stranger.

"I plead guilty."

"This is wonderful, Jim. I didn't expect to see you. Lucy wrote to me years ago that you had left. That you'd moved to…Manchester, wasn't it?" She asked the question coyly, though she knew this well.

"For a couple years. I was looking for you. Manchester was as far as I got."

"You were looking for me?" she asked, surprised. "I thought you'd had enough of me."

"Some nights after dark, I would head over to the estate, bring a little food to my mother and sister and go by Lucy's house, and she would read your letters to me: the things you were doing and the new people you met, the stupid teachers, how they made a skit of the way you talked."

"They were the ones who talked funny, with their accents like donkeys."

"You wrote about the fashions and the fine horses you rode, and then later the handsome young fellas you were introduced to, until I could barely stand it. So I decided to go and find you."

"You did?"

"Surely. I made my way to Dublin and then across the sea to Manchester. What a city, with so many huge ships coming and going and three, four, even five-storey houses and ten times more people than I'd ever seen in one place, even in Dublin. The people seemed friendly at first. Three men bought me a drink and I thought *how lovely these Englishmen are* and that's all I remember until waking up next morning in the street to find they had drugged me and relieved me of the coins in my boot, and of the boots themselves, and my pack with my second shirt. I can tell you this now, Manchester is not a friendly town to a man with an Irish accent and no money."

"Oh no! What did you do?"

"Well, I found mule work in a steel foundry on Wood Street, didn't I, and lived under a bridge off Cupid's Alley—a filthy little boulevard—for a few weeks to save enough for a clean shirt and a ticket to London to find you."

"I didn't know any of this!"

"There was a foreman at the foundry, Bradwell, took a dislike to me and I took it all until the man cuffed me once on the head so I knocked him down and put the boots to him. I knew by then this would go badly for my fortunes."

"Were you arrested?"

"That I was. The judge was no kinder to me than the other English I'd met and I spent some months in a stinking jail cell with six other men, four of them Irishmen, close enough to the docks to be a right playground for vermin. I began to prefer the company of the rats to that of my cellmates.

"I still planned to go to London and find you, but when they let me out after a year for good behaviour, the constables put me aboard a ship back home to Ireland warning that if I tried to come back to England I'd get more prison time."

"You poor thing. You did all that to find me?"

"Didn't get very far, did I?"

"Well…maybe not, but…so…here we are."

"Yes. Imagine that."

Jim raised his hand, extended his index finger and touched the tip of her nose.

"I have caught a nice fish here. Let me cook it for you, my lady, and you can tell me more about your adventures."

"What if the warden comes?"

"You can save me again, sure."

Jim took her into the high grass beside the stream, sat on the bank to show her the fine salmon he had caught. She took his hand and he gently assisted her down into the soft cushion of the grass to continue their conversation. They lay close and studied each other's faces, the years slipping away.

"That old bull isn't still around here anywhere, is he?" she asked him playfully.

"No. Just me."

"I said bull, not bull shite."

He rolled his eyes at her broad humour.

"You're too easy to take the mickey out of," she laughed at him.

Jim gave her a tentative, gentle kiss on her lips. She did not withdraw. He took the silver locket and held it for a moment, rubbing it between his fingers. So she kissed him back but kept it short.

"You know I've waited all these years to do that again. Wondering what it would be like."

"And what do you think?"

She smiled, put her hand on his face and drew him to her, kissing him a second time, with force and passion full on his mouth, and their breathing quickened. Then they pulled back and stared at each other, amazed and excited. Jim broke eye contact and looked down. They brushed foreheads, then laughed. Jim placed one hand softly against her cheek and she pushed gently into it and looked up into his eyes as he whispered, "I have thought of you every day of every year. I thought you would have forgotten me."

"I have not forgotten."

He leaned forward and kissed her again, long and soft. It was the moment of choice and neither of them had anyplace else in the world to be. Holding their kiss, they began to loosen each other's buttons and belts with equal and growing enthusiasm. She pulled off his shirt and admired what was revealed. He helped her off with her jacket, then her blouse and camisole, and she faced him proudly. He was breathless as he gently placed his hands on her breasts and held their soft weight.

"My God, Jo. You've become magnificent." He moved toward her but she pushed him hard with both hands back onto the grass and came to straddle him.

"I prefer to ride than to be ridden," she told him.

She quickly undid his belt and the buttons to give him release, then pulled back her pleated skirts and mounted him with a sudden joy at the rightness of it all.

Awakening

IT WAS THE golden hour of the afternoon, the sun low but still vital, fil-
tering through the trees below an azure sky. They had a small fire burning.
The second half of the fish was cooking on a stick. They were in that happy,
affectionate aftermath of lovemaking, their clothes on in case a warden or
poacher might happen by, but loose and untucked and uncaring as they ate
the first half of the salmon with their fingers. Johannah was purely enjoying herself, stealing glances at Jim, wiping the grease from her lips, as he
did, with the back of her hand. How right that they should make love like
this in the wild, suddenly, instinctively, with a carnal passion she had never
experienced before. She had taken lovers, three exactly in the last three
years, all young gentlemen and with a gentleman's mundane protocol. To
call it lovemaking was attaching too much sentiment to it. With all three,
it was merely sexual relations. But with Jimmy she felt such forbidden
excitement, giving of herself completely. Now this was lovemaking, and
she wanted more very soon, as soon as she finished eating his illegal fish.
As he studied her, she raised her greasy index finger and touched his nose.

"Imagine that," she said aloud.

She then took another big bite of the pink flesh and spoke with her
mouth half full, in happy contradiction of her etiquette classes.

"So, Jimmy…what do you do when you're not poaching salmon?"

He brought his face close, as if he might kiss her again, and they continued that way.

"This and that."

"I mean what line of work are you in?"

"I'm a gentleman, for now. I'm looking for opportunities. I'll see what
comes up."

"If all your stars were to align and opportunities present themselves,
what would you like to do?"

Jim thought about this for a moment. "I would have land. A farm to keep animals and grow things. A man is nothing without land. But the land is all taken here by the rich or the church. It would take more than stars aligning. Would take a revolution before I could afford land here."

"Do you keep in touch with Lucy O'Toole? Maybe her family has found a better situation. That bad girl stopped writing to me ages ago, so I've no idea where she ended up. Do you?" As she wiped her mouth with the back of her hand, she added, "We're due for a long visit."

Jim was silent for a moment, his expression grave. "You should ask your father about Lucy."

"My father? Why does everyone tell me to talk to my father. What about Lucy?"

Jim just shook his head and looked away, which infuriated her.

"What happened? Is she all right? Tell me!"

"It was when the estate was cleared."

"My father said the tenants decided to move on, find other work."

Jim gave a thin smile and shook his head again.

"They moved on all right. At the barrel of a musket. You don't know this?"

She shook her head.

"Your father brought in the soldiers. Threw everyone out of their homes. The Ryans, O'Tooles, O'Days…everyone. Beef cattle. That's what your father replaced us with. We were worth less than cows!"

"What about Lucy?"

"Your father ordered the soldiers to burn the houses on the day. The Ryan twins tried to defend the house. Dragged out that old blunderbuss from the mantle. The soldiers shot them both dead."

"No! Oh my God," she stared at him, trying to comprehend.

"And then…that's when Lucy was killed."

"Lucy is dead?" Johannah's lips trembled.

"We didn't expect them to burn the houses. The thatch went up like the fires of hell. Her brother said she had hidden some letters in the attic. She ran back inside for them. She never got out."

Johannah felt dizzy. The letters. For a moment she couldn't move. She threw down what was left of her fish and stood up, wiping her hands on her skirts.

"Swear to me this is true. You're not lying?"

"I wish to Christ I was," he said, getting to his feet. "I saw it all, Jo."

"Lucy's dead," she repeated numbly, letting it sink in.

"Yes. I'm sorry…"

She felt her eyes tearing up, struggling to accept the story, her thoughts in all directions, tucking in her clothes. Jim tried to embrace her, but she stepped back and would not let him touch her.

"I have to go."

As she grabbed the trailing rein of Cuchulain, Jim gently took her arm. "Johannah…"

She turned back to him.

"I love you," he told her. Her pained expression softened slightly. She mounted her horse and galloped off down the path without a word.

As he began the long walk back to town, he hoped she would be all right with this new burden of truth he had given her. The angry memories of his family's expulsion from the house, the shooting of the Ryans and the tragedy of Lucy's death—all of the bitter memories that had been stirred up with the telling, and how Magee would pay—settled down again as he remembered the passionate, angry figure riding off in the distance, erect, stirrups stretched long, in perfect balance as she and the animal moved as one. He had never seen anyone ride a horse like Johannah and the image excited him, and his thoughts returned to the feel and sound and power of their lovemaking.

Later that night on a dark street in Borrisokane, Jim noticed the three-year-old girl with long, unkempt hair and eyes big enough to melt any heart standing alone and unsupervised on the narrow sidewalk, and his anger returned. He watched as, perilously close, the heavy wheels of cargo wagons and the tree trunk hooves of Clydesdales thundered by. He was walking with two of his Whiteboys down the far side of the street when he saw the child.

"I'll meet you at Ryan's, lads."

Leaving the others behind, he quickly crossed over and approached the little girl. He came up beside her and scooped her up in his arms and danced her around and she laughed at the sweeping ride.

"Bridget, you little scamp. What you doing here, girl?"

"Being good."

"Where's your ma, darling?"

"In there."

Bridget pointed to a hotel tavern beside them. He gave her a smile to hide his frustration with her mother, Jim's sister, Theresa.

Just then Theresa came out of the hotel, straightening her clothes. A well-to-do Protestant in a brown wool suit with a full moustache followed her out. Jim grabbed her by the arm.

"So here you are, sister. Are you cracked, leaving little Bridget wandering in the street?"

"I told her to stay inside. Give her to me."

Theresa held out her arms to Bridget and Jim gave her up reluctantly.

"By God, you're an unfit mother. Unfit for anything but"—he eyed the suit— "pleasuring filthy Protestants."

The man took a step toward them. "Now just a minute. You can't…"

It was Theresa who turned on her client. "Mind your own feckin' business. You and I are done. Get out of here."

"I say…it really is uncalled for to…"

Jim had to punch the client in the face and he went down hard, then he started to kick the man on the ground.

"Stop it," Theresa told him, on a more practical than compassionate note, and he backed off the unconscious Protestant. He found he had little heart for fighting these days. It gave him little pleasure. His sister shoved him farther away with the heel of her hand.

"You'll just cause me trouble."

"You bring it on yourself."

"You have no right to criticize! I'se the one keeps the family going while you're off with your mates! You owe me plenty but I never see it. When was the last time you earned a decent wage?"

"You call the money you make decent?"

"I does what I have to do! For Ma and Brid, so we can eat. If we counted on Your Highness, we'd all starve to death. So you can just clear off. Where's the shilling you owe me from last week? Where is it?"

Jim hesitated. "I'll get it."

Theresa offered a snorting laugh. "Aye, not in a month of Sundays."

Jim remembered the remnants of the fish he had wrapped in his pocket and offered it to her. She hesitated and then took it.

"Was a nice salmon."

Theresa inspected what was left of the fish and laughed again, and the truth hit Jim at that moment of how little he had to offer Johannah. No job, no land, no prospects. How impossible it was that she would ever become his wife.

"I'm sorry, Theresa. You're right. I just want us to have a little dignity."

She smiled sadly at her brother as she bit into the pink flesh and spoke with her mouth half full.

"Jimmy, this is our life, such as it is. Our family's life. We're cursed, don't you know it? It's in our blood. Right from the great Peter Donnelly, with Cromwell's sword in his gut, on down. We can't be putting on airs. And the sooner you realize that, you'll see our life as it is makes all the sense in the world. All we can do is make our way through the shite, best we can."

Theresa was still holding Bridget, who began to cry. The client was moaning on the ground.

"We're cursed, Jimmy," she repeated very quietly. "Every last one of us."

As he walked away, Jim turned her words over in his mind. A family curse. Sadly, the notion rang true. But he would fight it as he fought the other forces aligned against him. When you stop the fighting is when you fade away.

The Troubles

UNDER THE LIGHT of a full moon, Jim kept watch on Magee's warehouse from a nearby alleyway. Four soldiers stood guard outside the massive building, with the corporal patrolling on horseback. Behind Jim, deeper into the alleyway, six Whiteboys readied themselves for the evening's activities. The boys helped each other blacken their faces, and put on kerchiefs and wigs, a well-accepted fashion of rebellion on missions like this, as much honoured ritual as disguise. Some, like Mick, dressed as women. Four held unlit torches.

"You look lovely, darlings," Jim told them. Resuming his watch on Magee's warehouse, Jim mused on the irony of all this, that he could feel such different emotion for two people bound in blood: such hatred for the father, such love for the daughter. But he knew he must put those distracting thoughts behind him. This was their biggest mission yet.

Two blocks from Magee's warehouse, Mick lit a rag in the neck of a bottle of coal oil and tossed it through the glass window of a small law office that worked with English banks. A fire ignited inside and the flames grew quickly. Jim saw Mick running back to join them, favouring the shadows, his white teeth showing in a triumphant smile.

A soldier up the street spotted the distant smoke and alerted his superior. The first licks of flame could soon be seen and they could hear the corporal directing his men.

"Williams! Shaw! Get those buckets and fill them. Let's go! All of you! Quick step!"

The soldiers put their rifles over their shoulders and grabbed the fire pails nearby, filling them in a watering trough. All four soldiers and the corporal hurried down the street away from the warehouse to fight the fire.

Jim whispered to his men as they lit their torches, "Off we go, gentlemen! Bring in the wagons!"

With the soldiers gone, and happy with their easy success, Mick, Jim and the Whiteboys headed across the street. Jim cracked open the lock with an iron bar, opened the double doors and they entered the massive warehouse, their faces illuminated in torchlight. Two heavy wagons were quickly backed into the doorway. The boys rucked up their dresses and began breaking up the crates and loading the wagons with barrels of meat and smaller crates of food. They worked quickly and soon the two wagons were packed high, enough to feed hundreds for a few days in the poor huts on the river.

"All right, lads. That's all we can hold. Get the wagons out of here!" Mick ordered. Two Whiteboys were at the reins and the full wagons charged out of the warehouse, rumbling off toward hungry mouths down the river. Jim gave Mick a look.

Jim picked up a can of coal oil and heavily doused a nearby crate.

"Are you sure you want to do that Jim?"

"Why not? If we can't have the rest, neither can the English!"

He lit the crate on fire with his torch.

"Such a waste."

"It's a war, Mick!"

Jim began moving up and down the aisles, pouring coal oil on everything in the warehouse until the can was empty. One of the Whiteboys followed him with the torch, lighting fire points that grew and joined each other. The warehouse would soon be an inferno. Feeling the heat on his face, Jim was suddenly standing before the tenant houses as they blazed before him and George Magee looked on. Lucy's screams were in his head. Then the image of his father's body floating face down. He was satisfied this food would never see England.

Johannah sat very still in the generous winged chair, the chair on which she had climbed as a child, one of the last pieces of furniture left in the once-lavish parlour after her father's debtors had finished with it. She had once enacted exotic adventures here in this room under the Broadwood and Sons piano that her mother so loved and played well. Those times, along with the instrument, were now gone. The paintings by Wilson and Constable, scenes in which she would lose herself, had been taken like the ones in her bedroom, the faded outlines on the wallpaper their only traces. There had been the gilded books of classic English and French stories she could read at an early age—she remembered names from far-away places, like Timbuktu, Siam, Xanadu and the Amazon River, but the shelves were now empty, the promises of other worlds beyond hers now gone. What was once a room of cultural enlightenment was stripped bare.

Johannah had decided she must leave Ballymore as soon as possible. She would arrange for a coach the next day to take her…where? And what about Jim? The rediscovery of their love had been so sudden. Would he come with her? To Dublin or back to London? She would need to make an income—she would take nothing from her father—she could teach or perhaps become a nurse. She had to get in touch with Jim. But that was for tomorrow. Tonight she would confront her father one last time.

She sat in near darkness, choosing not to light a lamp, watching as the shadows grew longer in the room, the colours flattening and merging into an imperfect darkness, which suited her mood. It was deep into night when she heard her father arrive home, his footsteps echoing in the almost empty house. He carried a lamp into the parlour, placed it down on a small desk and poured himself a substantial drink of his whiskey, a now much cheaper brand. He finished half in a swallow, put down the glass, then turned, startled to see Johannah in the chair facing him.

"Johannah. What are you doing sitting in the dark?"

"Waiting for you."

"What is it?"

She studied his face for a moment in the lamplight.

"Is it true? You drove the tenants off the land and then burned down their cottages so they couldn't return?"

She could see he was caught off guard. He took a moment to regain his bearings.

"I asked the tenants to leave. I had no choice. The estate was losing money fast. Beef prices had tripled in England. Cavendish gave me his orders. We needed the pasture land."

"So it is true." She stared at him bitterly.

"Most of those families hadn't paid their rent in a year. They had to go. I didn't want to bring in the soldiers. They left me no choice."

"You burned them in their houses. Your soldiers shot the Ryan brothers!"

"They had a gun."

"You killed Lucy!"

"The cottage was already burning when she ran inside."

"You killed her."

He came toward her, his voice taking on a new bloodless tone. "Now listen to me. I wasn't going to let a gaggle of pig-headed peasants hold me ransom, breeding like rats. It was them or us."

Johannah now stared at him with loathing. "Don't include me in your disgusting cadre."

"Oh you are very much a part of this. You were born into privilege and enjoyed the benefits. Everything has a price."

He studied her and Johannah could see his rising emotions shifting to what she had seen in him before. He moved toward her as a predator toward prey and she felt fear. Then his eyes were suddenly diverted by something out the window. She turned to see a glow had appeared in the sky like a late sunset. Her father stared in shock at the distant flames and spoke beneath his breath: "The warehouse."

For a moment, he stood frozen by the image of the flames. Then he turned and ran from the room. It took Johannah a moment to catch her breath, free of her father's toxic presence. She moved to the window. The distant smoke and flames were rising above the warehouse and for a moment she savoured the sweet justice of her father's tragedy.

Inside, the warehouse was becoming a very satisfactory inferno with barrels and crates engulfed and flames travelling up and beginning to consume the roof beams. Jim was admiring the results of their efforts.

"All right! Let's go!" he called to the others. "The soldiers will be out front. Out the back way."

The rest of the Whiteboys headed for the back exit where they lifted the bar, opened the heavy door and scrambled out of the burning warehouse into the back alley. Just as Mick and Jim were about to join them, they heard the first animal screams. Somewhere, there were horses trapped.

Mick grabbed Jim's arm. "Come on! Too late!"

"No. We can't leave them." Jim pulled away. He ran back inside with Mick's voice in his ears. "Jimmy! For Christ's sake!"

In an extension at the back of the flaming warehouse as yet untouched by the flames, Jim pushed open a wide gate and went inside the stable to find half a dozen agitated horses in three stalls. The smoke was growing thick and the horses were panicking as the roar of the fire grew louder and the flames crept quickly toward them. Jim stayed low under the smoke and kept his voice calm.

"Easy now, beauties. It's all right. You'll be fine."

He slid the wooden bolt and swung open the door of the first stall, then the second. The horses reared back, hesitant at first, but he entered each stall and chased them out. Four horses ran off through a wider door, out into the night. Jim went to the third and last stall and slid the bolt, but before he could open the door, a figure appeared in the open doorway through the heavy smoke. It was George Magee with his pistol drawn.

"Who's there! Come out, you bastards!"

He fired a shot that splintered the wood a foot above Jim's ear.

Jim opened the last gate as Magee prepared to shoot again through the smoke. The final horse left alone was a fine black mare and as she headed toward the open doors, Jim grabbed hold of her mane and was able to hoist himself up on her back. Slung on the opposite side of the horse, he rode out of the inferno past the furious Magee.

"You dirty blaggard! I'll send you to hell!"

Magee took aim and fired two shots over the horse at where Jim's hand and leg grasped hold and missed Jim by inches as horse and rider galloped out of the stable.

Now free and away in the cool dark of the night, Jim guided his fine new mount down the street toward safety. Looking back, he could see a furious Magee emerging from the flaming warehouse, signalling to the soldiers in front of him.

"Shoot him, damn it! Don't hit the horse!"

Three soldiers stopped to aim as Jim rode past, his body a low profile hanging off the opposite side of the mare. Following Magee's instructions, the soldiers all fired high and missed both man and horse. Jim caught a glimpse of Mick watching from a darkened doorway, giving him a half salute as it appeared Jim's escape would be made good.

Now well past and away from the soldiers who were reloading their muskets, Jim sat up straight on his mount and guided the horse toward the buildings at the end of the block and the entrance to a side street, sure that once he was round the corner he would be free and clear. But as he leaned into the corner, a soldier suddenly leapt out—he barely saw him— and swung his musket well, hitting Jim in the chest and knocking him off his mount onto the street. He landed hard, his head bouncing off the surface, and lay half conscious on the greasy cobblestones as the soldiers arrived and gathered around him, muskets pointed at his heart. Magee ran up to have a look at him.

"I know this man. Tie him up and get him to the lock-up. He'll hang for this."

Jim cursed his bad luck. He turned his head around to study the warehouse one last time. The two wagons of meat and food would have had time to get to the poor huts. They accomplished their goal. Although a wagonload of firemen had arrived and were dousing the buildings on each side, the flames that now swallowed the warehouse would guarantee the total destruction of Magee's exports. Jim was happy. He hoped Mick and the boys had finished making their escape—this was his last thought before he passed out.

The Borrisokane lock-up was off the town square, built from thick limestone blocks, with four cells, all four by six feet, with windows so tiny they were almost not worth the bother. Though the jail was run by constables, two soldiers had been ordered to stand guard outside. Inside, Jim lay recuperating in one of the cells on a narrow, stinking straw cot. On the rough wooden walls separating the cells, seen in the dim light, there were crude markings of skeletons, hanging men and hundreds of cross-hatchings counting long days in the lock-up. It was not his first time here but never for troubles so serious. He stared at the wall and thought of Johannah.

His head ached and his ribs gave shooting pains with each breath where the butt of the musket had cracked them. They had used that wound during questioning an hour after he was arrested. Two soldiers had held him up while a burly third had punched his wounded ribs and the corporal demanded the names of the other Whiteboys. They only stopped when he spit up blood and passed out again. They promised to be back in an hour for the names. Jim would give them up, sooner or later. He closed his eyes and tried to rest his aching brain. He wondered if Johannah knew he was arrested. To have found her again and then so soon after, this misfortune; the Donnelly curse was alive and well.

Just then, he heard the sound of the heavy outside door opening. *They have come again,* he thought. It hadn't been an hour. He was not ready. He worried that he might not have the strength to resist. But then a familiar voice was speaking to the constable in the outer room and Jim was suddenly alert.

"…even the dregs of society must have a chance to save their souls. It is what our Lord would want." The voice called out to him. "Are you ready for your confession, my son?"

He could not believe his ears. It was Mick. Was there still hope? Might he still hold Johannah again? As they entered the cells, it was all Jim could do to play along and not give Mick away.

"Thank goodness you've come, Father," he called out evenly. "I want to confess."

"Open the door, now. I want to see his eyes so I know this poor wretch is sincere."

Jim wondered if there was any chance the constable would actually allow this. After a hesitation, to his surprise the young policeman inserted his big key, turned it and opened wide the cell door. Jim squinted into the light. There stood Mick, serviceably dressed as a priest in white collar with the guard behind him holding a lantern, his musket casually under his arm. When Mick winked, Jim had to stifle a laugh and play the serious penitent.

"In the name of the Father, Son and Holy Ghost…may God forgive me."

Mick turned, pulled the musket from the surprised policeman and with a quick, clever upward movement, hit him in the side of the head with the heavy barrel. The constable fell, unconscious. Mick whistled his signal to the boys.

Outside the lock-up, four of the Whiteboys came out of the shadows and clubbed the two soldiers on duty. They dragged their unconscious bodies back into the shadows beside the building. Inside, Mick and Jim quickly tied up and gagged the semi-conscious police officer. Mick locked him in the cell and took his pistol.

"Sorry, my son. God bless you."

Mick and Jim burst outside onto the deserted street to join the four other Whiteboys. A dog barked in the distance, but otherwise they were undiscovered.

"Thanks, boys," Jim told them.

"Split up and let's get out of here," Mick ordered.

As they were about to run in different directions, Jim looked back to see one soldier, who had been unconscious on the ground beside his musket, was coming to. The boys had not tied him and his hand found the weapon. He scrambled groggily to his knees, raised the barrel and fired a shot at them, missing them all. Mick turned, raised the pistol without aiming and fired back in retaliation. The ball hit the soldier between the eyes, tossing him backwards. For a moment they stopped and stared with shock at the smashed face, the body so suddenly still and flat—the first man they had killed, and an English soldier at that.

They heard the sound of boots on cobblestones—a large patrol approaching at a run, a sergeant's voice shouting them on. Jim's eyes went back to the dead soldier for a moment. They had not wanted this, to take a life. Musket fire hit the lamppost and the brick wall beside them. The soldiers moving up the street could see them now and were within range.

"Jimmy! Come on!" Mick called out. "For the love of God."

Jim turned away from the dead soldier. The Whiteboys divided into pairs with Mick and Jim together and they all made a run for it.

The Plan

THERE WAS A pounding at the door and Raffy and Johannah opened it together. The young corporal she had seen at the soup line stepped into the foyer to report to her father. George Magee took the young man into his study. From the large panelled dining room next door, Raffy and Johannah listened to the description of the murder of the soldier and the escape of the Whiteboys. She glanced through the door to see her father's red face about to explode as he took it in.

"At least we had the ringleader, Donnelly. Now we have nothing!"

At this, Johannah froze. He was talking about Jimmy! She would have been naive not to suspect that Jim was involved with politics, and even maybe the Whiteboys, but arson and murder?

"How could you let him escape?" her father went on. "They have ruined me. I have lost everything. I want them all, dead or alive."

"A mounted regiment from Limerick is on its way, sir."

Magee put on his coat, buckled on his pistol belt and headed for the door with the young corporal on his heels.

"Come on. We can't wait. We'll hunt them down. Every one!"

"It's only a question of time, sir."

After the men had passed without a word and left the house, Johannah turned to Raffy.

"I have to help Jimmy."

"You best stay out of it."

"I can't, Raffy!" She held the older woman's eyes for a moment. "I love him."

They could hear Magee and the corporal ride off into the night.

Raffy studied her gravely. "And when did all this come about?"

"A couple days ago. All my life."

Raffy thought for a moment. Johannah watched her face anxiously.

"You love the boy? You're sure?"

She nodded, her eyes wide. "I've never been so sure."

"And he loves you?" Johannah nodded and Raffy sighed deeply, considering the problem.

"Well, there's no life for him in Ireland now. He has to get out. Even England won't be safe. There are ships leaving Dublin every day."

"All right. Let's help him. But how can we find him?"

"I can get word to him."

Johannah stared at her in surprise.

"You know the Whiteboys?"

"A nephew."

"Then do it, Raffy, please!"

In the streets of Borrisokane, small patrols of soldiers moved swiftly along the cobblestone streets through the town searching for Jim and Mick. The other Whiteboys had dispersed. Their chances were better alone. Jim had thought of going home to say goodbye to his mother and Theresa and little Bridget. No matter what the future held, he would not see them for a long time.

"You must be daft, man," Mick told him. "You can't go home. The soldiers'll be crawling all over the place."

Jim realized of course he was right. His mother would be weeping at these new troubles and Theresa would shaking her head at him.

It was Ryan's boy Andy who found them hiding in a blind alley they often frequented and delivered the surprising message.

"The lady wants to help you. She wants to meet," the boy told them.

"Magee's daughter?" Mick exclaimed. "This is madness, Jimmy."

"She loves me. She'll not betray us."

"How can a lovesick pup know that? It's a trap for sure or I'm the Pope."

"What other chance do we have?"

Alone now, keeping to the shadows, Mick carrying the musket, they crossed a street, ran across the commons and the pastureland beyond. Twenty minutes later they came to a stone wall bordering the Cavendish estate lands and climbed over. At the second building, the main stables, they came to a window with unlocked shutters. Again the concern of entrapment came to Jim, but is this not the last place the soldiers would look? It was smart on Johannah's part and, either way, he surrendered himself to her mercy. He and Mick slipped through a window into the stable.

A moment after they entered, a lamp was lit in an open stall and Jim and Mick found themselves standing before Johannah Magee in a hooded cloak and her housekeeper, Miss Rafferty. Jim had known Rafferty as a forthright woman, an aunt of one of his boys, and although she worked in Magee's house, he hoped and assumed she could be trusted. There were two horses, one of them the milky Cuchulain, saddled and waiting. The lantern burned between them and Johannah's beauty distracted Jim for a moment as she came closer.

"You were right about my father and what he did to the families. It was just as you said."

"Yes."

Johannah put her arms around him and they embraced each other tight and kissed to prove their love and Jim felt such joy, made less only a little by their current circumstances.

"Jimmy, you have to run," she whispered to him. "They're after hanging you all now for killing the soldier."

"I'm sure they are. We can fight them."

"No, you can't. Half the Limerick regiment is on its way."

"There's only one chance," Raffy asserted with authority. "You have to get out of Ireland. You have to get on a ship in Dublin."

"I can't go to England. They'll arrest me. There's Europe but I don't speak French."

"Then America. Or Canada," Raffy continued. "Ships leaving every day."

"Canada?"

"If you stay here, they'll hunt you down and hang you, Jim," Johannah agreed. "You and Mick both. All your lads if they can. You can just make it there tonight."

Mick agreed. "She's right, Jimmy. We have to go."

"I can't." He turned to Johannah. "I can't leave you. You've just come back into my life again, Jo. You're all I think about. I can't lose you again."

"Then I'll come with you."

Jim stared at her.

"No." Raffy appeared stricken.

"Would you really come with me?" Jim asked softly, searching her eyes.

Johannah stayed quiet for a moment as she weighed the idea. Her face flushed.

"A new life together in America. Yes. Yes, I will come."

Johannah looked to Raffy. The old woman turned on Jim.

"And just how would you propose to keep her? You who can't hold a job. All very clever with your tricks and ideas but in the New World she needs a real man, an able one."

"I will provide for her. I promise you that."

"And what about your violent ways? Sure you'll get there and have a temper and someone'll beat you senseless or dead and then what will she do?"

"I promise her…" Jim turned to Johannah. "I promise you, I'll never fight again if you'll have me."

Johannah looked again to Raffy. Tears filled Raffy's eyes but her face remained stern as she asked Johannah the question. "Tell me again if you truly love him?"

Johannah went to Jim and took his hand and answered without hesitation. "Yes, Raffy. I do."

"Then you should go."

"And you promise there'll be none of this fighting over there? We'll leave all these troubles behind, yes?" Johannah asked him.

"Sure. Over there, what could there be to fight about?"

"Promise me!"

"I swear it," Jim told her with all the gravity and conviction he could muster. Then he smiled into her eyes. His dreams were within reach. "Come with me, my love. We'll make a life in the New World."

"All right, then."

Johannah turned to Raffy and embraced her with all her might, suddenly tearful.

"Thank you, Raffy."

"God's speed, Miss."

"Cuchulain can take us both," Jim reasoned. "Mick, you on t'other."

As Johannah was about to mount, a figure appeared in the open doorway, a silhouette confronting them again in the moonlight. Magee held a double-barrelled shotgun in his right hand and his pistol in the left. The shotgun was aimed at Jim.

"Donnelly! Murderer. You have taken everything else from me. You won't take my daughter."

Mick swung his musket up to fire but Magee's shotgun moved and exploded first, hitting Mick squarely in the chest, blowing him back against the gate, his body collapsing limp on the stable floor.

"Mick!" Jim made a move toward his friend, but Magee had the shotgun and the pistol trained on him again.

"Leave him!"

Jim froze. Johannah was remarkably calm.

"Da. I can't stay here with you. I'm going with Jim to America."

"Never."

"I love him, Da. I have to go. I'm strong. I'll be all right."

Raffy warned them, "The soldiers could have heard the shot."

Magee turned his attention and the barrels of his guns toward Raffy, furious.

"Shut up, you stupid cow! You're a part of this, aren't you?"

Johannah stepped in front of Raffy, facing her father in defiance.

"Da, there is nothing here for me. I'm leaving now with Jim. If you have any love for me, you'll let me go."

Magee turned his attention to Jim. "Well then, there seems a simple remedy for this situation. I should have done it six years ago."

Prepared to fire, he raised his shotgun and aimed at Jim's chest, but before Magee could pull the trigger, a pistol shot rang out. In Raffy's hand, the little pistol was smoking. A small flowering of crimson blossomed from Magee's chest and the shotgun fell from his hands to the stable floor as he stared at Raffy in disbelief. His body crumpled and he collapsed on his side.

"Da!" Johannah went to him and fell down on her knees. Magee stared at her in pain and panic. Then his features calmed as she held his head and brought her face close to his. "Da, I'm so sorry."

Her father raised his hand and touched her cheek. His lips moved, but then his body went still. Johannah offered silent tears. Raffy beheld the body of her master in confusion for a moment. Jim stared down at Magee, for so long the object of his fevered hatred and desire for retribution, now gone. His death left Jim strangely empty. But then the image of the grieving Johannah transformed his former hatred into a greater love and he had the overwhelming desire to survive.

"We have to go, Johannah. The soldiers will come now and we'll lose our chance."

Johannah nodded tearfully in her grief and with a gesture of determination, she stood up from the body. Raffy bent down, her joints cracking with the effort, and put her little pistol in Mick's dead hand. She looked to Johannah for endorsement and Jo nodded through the tears at the practical choice. Johannah ran into the house to quickly grab a bag of clothes and personal items and her mother's string of pearls, some odds and ends, before she left Borrisokane for good, then returned to the stable. Raffy guided her up onto Cuchulain and Jim mounted the second horse. Raffy opened the stable door a crack to see if the way was clear, then pushed it wide open to let them out.

"I'll tell the soldiers you were here and that you rode west to Galway."

"Thank you, Raffy. Thank you for so much." Johannah leaned down and kissed her. As Jim watched, the sacrifices they were making on his behalf were not lost on him.

"Wait one moment," Raffy stepped out into the yard where smooth flat river stones had been brought from the Ballyfinboy and spread as gravel to keep the earth firm. She bent down and chose one she could just enclose in her palm, cleaned it off on her skirt and gave it to Johannah.

"A piece of home for you, so you won't forget."

"I won't ever forget, Raffy."

In the distance from the north beyond the rise of the road came the sound of approaching horsemen.

"Go!" Raffy commanded.

As Raffy watched them in the moonlight, they rode abreast out of the stable. Then they were away to the southwest, the nimble hoofbeats of their fresh horses sounding as one on the road to Dublin.

Jim and Johannah stopped twice that night to rest and water the horses, saying little to each other. Never once on that long ride did Jim see Johannah's determination flag, or a sigh escape her, nor was a second thought betrayed on her pretty, resolute face. And that night, considering all the demands he was making of her, the life she was sacrificing, the lot she was throwing in with his, he fell into such love with her all over again and swore that he would rise to deserve what God had given him.

The Voyage

Jim and Johannah left Borrisokane with little in their pockets, then sold the horses and saddles to a Dublin livery for a small fraction of their worth and could only afford steerage fare on an aging barque named the *Naparima* that was to sail that day. Johannah needed to steal herself to say a quick goodbye to Cuchulain, hugging his strong neck for a moment, knowing she would never see him again. On that day they sailed from Dublin, they stayed as long as they could at the railing on the undulating deck, breathing in the salty air, hearing the unfamiliar cries of the wheeling gulls, still holding firm to the promise of freedom in the new life they had entered into, as the grey North Atlantic stretched out before them.

It was hardly the grand adventure Johannah had always imagined such a trip to be, the triumphant leave-taking to spite her father and fulfill her dreams. It was more a desperate escape, with her father dead and herself a fugitive, aboard an old ship in dire need of refitting. In brief moments her resolve failed, when thoughts flooded in of her father's body on the stable floor, and she had to fight back her grief and shame. She leaned into Jim harder and they watched in bittersweet silence as Ireland's darkening shore fell away behind them and Jim slipped an arm around her waist to hold her tight.

In her pocket, Johannah felt the smooth river stone that Raffy had given her. She took it out to inspect it and found it was gray with flecks of green, gold and red pyrites. She held it out for Jim's perusal.

"There are colours."

"Yes, the green bits for Ireland, I guess, and the gold for our fortunes and red ones...for the bloodline you and I will begin," Jim told her.

"This stone is a million years old and will last a million years more after we're gone."

"Johannah...you're a brave girl coming with me. You must love me after all, or think you could. I'll do everything I can to make it up to you."

Johannah put her hand on his cheek and caressed the edge of his sad smile.

"We're in it for good and all, Mr. Donnelly. Our grand adventure together has begun. No turning back now."

"No turning back."

And they kissed each other with a passion that matched their first kiss on the cemetery wall.

When they finally took their few belongings into the gloom below decks, the hatches were closed tight for the night and the stench of smoke, mildew and human bodies hit them like a tangible wall. Johannah held a handkerchief over her mouth and nose as they ventured deeper into the hold, trying to keep their balance with the movements of the ship, lit only here and there with a few thin candles. There was a narrow corridor with rough boards forming little "pens" against the curved damp hull, each filled with bodies, faces watching them pass. Two babies cried in exhausted protest. A woman was whimpering, but most were very quiet—eerily so, for the entire hold was packed with people and stunned faces looked out in tiers two storeys high, and yet all was quiet. Johannah had stopped and stared around in shock at what appeared like the image she had imagined of Dante's hell. She was here and must deserve to be here.

"Come on, Jo. We'll find some room."

Jim led them deeper, past the silent faces, to discover a couple of feet of space behind a bulwark near the bow, against the thick hull timbers of the old ship. Here and there, sea water seeped through the broken deck boards into the bilge below. People shifted away a little to give them room to slide in, all joined together in the misery of their first night on what would prove a very long voyage.

After midnight the wind increased—they could feel the power of the rising north Atlantic swells and the ship began pitching violently, fighting a growing storm, the planks of her hull beneath their bodies creaking under the strain. Jim and Johannah sat holding onto each other in the oppressive darkness with only a frugal candle burning. She looked around again to glimpse the sick and fearful faces, men, women and children huddling in small groups. Many of them had not seen the sea before, let alone been at its mercy, and the full storm began to rage outside. The crewmen made sure the leaking hatches were as secure as possible, while others worked the long levers of bilge pumps. The ship rolled brutally and people gasped and groaned. A few began to be seasick and threw up in the few available buckets. Many missed as the ship plunged, or sometimes a bucket tipped over on a rolling wave, and the floorboards were soon awash in vomit. Despite Johannah's initial refusal, she finally made use of a bucket nearby. Children were too traumatized to cry and men cursed in helpless frustration as the vessel pounded against the northwest waves. There was nothing they could do but hold on for endless hours in the filthy, crowded, suffocating hold.

The first tempest lasted three days. On the third day, when the storm's heaving abated long enough to move around without being knocked off one's feet, Jim ventured from their spot. He found and paid for a better spot for them near the stern, where the vessel's pitch was felt less, a small berth on a platform. He was anxious for Johannah, who had not eaten and had drunk very little. He held a tin bowl of clear fluid over a candle to heat it and then presented the broth to her.

"Try a little. If you get it down, it'll settle your stomach."

Johannah turned away from it. He held up a second cup.

"There's still a bit of the water ration left."

When Johannah didn't respond, he held the cup to her lips as if she were a child or an invalid. She took some then and some ran down from her mouth. He scooped the drops from her chin into his own mouth and searched his imagination for any words of encouragement to help her.

"Storm can't last much longer, Jo. We'll get through it," he offered again lamely.

Each time the ship heaved and the sound of moaning and retching increased, Johannah could not shake the image of the hungry sea about to swallow the vessel whole. She imagined the waves closing over them as the ship with all passengers and crew left the sky behind and began the rapid decent to the utter darkness of the ocean floor. And maybe that wouldn't be so bad. She closed her eyes and hung on to face another night.

By the morning of the fourth day, the storm had passed and the sea, though still troubled, was kinder to them and the old vessel seemed to finally be making decent headway. Johannah found herself sitting up staring numbly at the deck boards in front of her, but with the calming of the storm she could relax a little. Jim slept quietly beside her. She began to look around at the other passengers, as if for the first time. Most were asleep and there was a chorus of multi-registered snoring. Nearby, a sallow-faced mother tended her two little girls, both of whom appeared feverish. The mother held a damp cloth against their cheeks and whispered little stories to them. Across the hold was an old woman with desperate eyes looking after her weak, aged husband, his breathing ragged, who also exhibited signs of fever. Nearby was a grubby young boy about fifteen lying on a stained pallet, semi-conscious and alone. They were all ill and a new fear of fever came over Johannah. And though she tried at first to resist, her thoughts went to the comforts of her home in Borrisokane, the warm affections of Raffy, her school chums in London and the parties and social affairs she attended there.

What would they all think of her now? How had she come to this state, living among these people? Even Jim. She watched him sleeping beside her and despite all her valiant words to the contrary and her declarations of love, doubts began to emerge and grow heavy. Was she a complete fool? Could this man provide for her? Protect her against evils? Apparently not. Perhaps this was all a terrible mistake. She withdrew from everyone around her, all of them, in disgust, forcing herself into a narrow space behind a bulwark, trying to avoid breathing their air, or touching or even looking at them.

Suddenly Johannah winced and examined her shoulder, where she felt an unusual pinprick. Her hand slipped inside her bodice to her collar bone. There was another pinprick on her breast. Holding her shirt open, she looked down to discover tiny black specks on her skin and tiny pink bites all over her chest. She gasped, stifled a scream and pulled her outer blouse off her shoulders and started to undress, mindless now of those around her. Jim woke up.

"What? What is it, Jo?"

"I don't know. What is this?"

After a brief inspection Jim told her, "Fleas."

She fought not to become hysterical.

"Fleas? I have fleas!"

Jim attempted to cover her from the others as she took off her outer blouse, loosened her undershirt and took off her skirt. He pulled the sheets around them and tried to help her be free of the infested clothes.

"Don't touch me!"

"I'll get water…soap…"

Jim left their berth and hurried up on deck to find what was needed. Clothed only in her light undershirt and slip, Johannah put her hands over her face and collapsed in tears.

"What have I done?"

After a few moments, Johannah stood up. She moved to the gangway and climbed to the deck level. Though it was not the time allotted for passengers to come up on deck, she walked with determination across to the railing and looked down at the troubled surface of the sea, mesmerized. What did the poets call the ocean: The cradle of life? Life and death in equal parts? It is all the same. And her mind kept flashing to images of her dead father's body. She missed her mother. She did not belong here.

She put her hands on the railing and looked for footholds to climb. She put one leg over and then the other and sat on the railing, staring down at the water below. It would be so easy to simply let herself fall into the sea. Jim would be much better off on his own. They would never find her in the waves. Would they even turn the ship around? She would sink into the dark depths in a welcome sleep without pain or guilt or misery.

Jim had negotiated for hot water and soap in the upper galley for tuppence and was on his way back to her when he spotted her at the railing, her body poised. He approached slowly, not to startle her, trying to calm his own pounding heart.

She was drawn out of her reverie by Jim's voice.

"Johannah? I'm here."

She stared at the waves.

"Johannah. Give me your hand." She did not move.

"My love? Please. Give me your hand." She did not move.

"If anything happened to you, Jo, it would kill me."

At this she raised her eyes and held his for a moment. Then, still considering her option below, she slowly took her hand from the railing. She held it out. Jim dove forward to grab it firmly and then he could breathe again. He put his arms around her and lifted her up off the railing and set her down on the deck. He placed a bucket of hot, steaming water before her with a cloth and bar of lye soap.

"Look my love, you can wash. Nice and hot. Come on, darling. It'll be all right."

Slowly she gathered herself and knelt beside the bucket. Jim helped her as she soaked the cloth, rubbing it hard with soap. The crewman on deck turned discreetly away. She began to clean herself under her shirt, arms, shoulders, breasts. She began to scrub with the determination of a survivor, and after she was fully clean, Jim brought a second bucket of hot water and helped her wash her hair with lye soap. And after that, wearing her second dress that her inspection had found without fleas, she washed and scrubbed her clothes in a tub. In the clean dress, combing out her long hair, she was calm now. It was all right, and she resolved that she must not ever lose control of herself like that again. She had to be stronger than that for Jim. She smiled and touched Jim's worried face beside her.

"I'll be all right now," she told him. "As long as you're here, I'll be fine."

By that evening, the old man who had been ill was dead, his blank eyes staring upward. His wife was holding him, whispering to him as a mother would to her child, as if he were still listening. Johannah could see the pretty young girl deep in the woman's aged face, a girl once newly in love, now an elderly woman in grief. This old couple's lifetime together had just ended. Jim and Johannah had watched the soul depart. Though neither spoke of it, both thought about how this time would one day come to them.

Jim whispered to Johannah, "I should tell the crew."

"Give her a little more time with him."

But the situation had been reported and the second mate and two crewmen came, with handkerchiefs over their mouths against the fever, to take the body away. The old woman resisted.

"No."

"He's dead, ma'am."

"No, no! He sleeps sound. Leave him for a bit."

Jim and Johannah and their neighbours witnessed the scene.

"He's dead. I know a dead man, ma'am," the mate repeated.

"No, he can trick you. He's fine. Leave him. Don't take him yet. Leave him with me. Please. I tell you he'll be all right!"

"Sorry, ma'am." He gestured to his crewmen. The woman began to howl as they gently but firmly extricated the corpse from her arms and put him on a stretcher to take away. Jim and Johannah and the others watched sympathetically. On impulse, Johannah went and put her comforting arms around the old woman, who cried and keened and Johannah cried with her and the woman held onto her as would a child.

Jim watched his wife and his heart was lightened. Yes, she would be all right.

Headway

THE OLD MAN was not the only one to die aboard ship during those first terrible days at sea. Some had boarded in a state of illness and starvation, so several more deaths had occurred. Their burials took place one calm morning. The passengers, those physically able, were allowed to assemble on deck for the service. There was not the complete pall of gloom one might expect at such a ceremony, for if one could attend, one had survived the storm. And if one had survived, one was alive and very aware of the sun on one's face, the murmur of human voices and the sweetness of the sea air in the morning. The captain was a thin man, scholarly in appearance, but with the broken hands of a crewman. In the absence of a priest on board, he conducted the service and, although he held the book of prayer open, he spoke the service entirely from memory.

"Forasmuch as it hath pleased Almighty God of His great mercy to receive unto Himself..."

There were seven bodies, each wrapped up in thin canvas—four adults and three children, one a tiny infant—all lying parallel on smooth boards, feet to the sea. Even though they were arranged on the lee side so the odour of corrupting flesh would escape downwind, a waft would occasionally come to the passengers and several had handkerchiefs to their noses.

"...the souls of our dear brothers and sisters here departed. From dust we come and to dust we surely return. James Flynn, Marguerite O'Halleran, Michael Reilly, Robert O'Connor..." The old woman could be heard tearfully grieving her husband as his name, John Hodgins, was called.

The first mate placed spoonfuls of Irish earth from a ceramic jar, brought for the occasion, on the chests of each of the dead. Two crewmen lifted up the end of the first board and the body slid smoothly into the sea. They went to the second and did the same.

"… Maggie Tooley, Pat Rouke and little James Connell, stillborn."

In this way, one body after the other went down into the sea, the slide a silent moment, a distant splash below marking the sound of the water's embrace.

"We look to the life to come, through our Lord Jesus Christ. We therefore commit their bodies to the deep and look to the resurrection when the sea shall give up her dead. Blessed are the dead that die in the Lord, for they have rest from their labours."

Johannah suddenly put her arms around Jim and hugged him as hard as she could. She looked into his eyes and told him quietly, "I am not thinking of the next life to come and I don't want to rest from my labours. We will make a good life out of this one."

"Yes, my love. We will. Nothing will stop us."

During the past days, Jim had been thinking about what his sister had thought of him, that he was all talk without substance, and about the family curse.

"I'll work and make some money. Then we'll find some land and buy it," he said now. "Somewhere between fifty and one hundred acres should do. With some water on it and close to a town."

"And a church. I'd like to be close to a church."

"Of course. And I'll build you a house and there'll be friendly neighbours all around that will welcome us. We'll have animals. Pigs and chickens."

"And horses."

"Yes, of course horses."

"And children."

"Them too."

When the other passengers had returned below, Johannah approached the second mate and showed him her string of pearls.

"Mallorcan. Finest quality."

She broke the string with her teeth and counted out three pearls into his hand. She would save the rest for Canada. He went down below to his personal larder for her and brought back an impressive offering of cheese, several oranges and bread.

Below again, she went to the two feverish young girls and gave the very thankful mother an orange and a half, a half loaf of bread and an extra ration of water. Next she went to the old woman who had lost her husband and gave her half an orange and extra water. She arrived next at the grubby boy who was alone and feverish. She cut a slice of the orange and put the piece between his lips. He sucked the juice hungrily, then chewed the flesh. His blue eyes opened briefly to look up at her and attempt to focus. She cooled his sweaty forehead with a damp cloth and gave him an encouraging smile.

"We'll get you through this, lad," she told him, and the boy stared intently up at her and then simply closed his eyes again and fell asleep. Johannah returned to Jim.

After six weeks at sea, Jim and Johannah stood at the starboard rail. The early storm had blown them two weeks off course but the weather had stayed agreeable since and passengers were allowed up on deck in regular shifts. The grubby boy to whom she had given the orange had recovered from his fever and it was good to see him now conscious and upright, playing ball on deck with his friends. Two or three days after Johannah's ministrations, his fever had passed and he had made his way above decks and approached them with surprising vigour. He had washed himself, combed his hair and turned into quite a handsome young fellow.

"There she is! My beauty of the night. I could have sworn you had wings." He had held out a hand of introduction to Jim. "Vincent Matthew O'Toole. But you can call me Vinnie. You know, of course, you're married to an angel."

Jim kept an arm protectively around Johannah at the enthusiasm of this starry-eyed youth, but he addressed the boy with good nature.

"I do, Vinnie. I'm Jim Donnelly and my wife is Johannah. Glad to see you recovered. So...what is it you're hoping to find in Canada?"

"Oh, I've got big plans. Big plans. I'm heading west through the deep forests and across the Great Lakes and over the Prairies to the Rocky Mountains."

"What'll you do the day after that?"

"I know it'll take more than a day. But I've got to see the Rocky Mountains."

"Can't farm mountains."

"I want to see 'em first. Then I'll decide what to do with them. See, what I'm thinking is that first I'll build a rowboat, 'cause I have it on good authority there's lakes and rivers all across the deep woods. Then when I gets to the Great Plains, I put wheels on her and a big sail 'cause, I have it on good authority there's no trees and plenty of wind there to sail across the Prairies, ha?"

"But then what good is a boat in the mountains?"

"Snow runners on the bottom, of course! A sleigh! Hard going on the way up, it's true, but just think about the coming down!"

And they laughed, enjoying his enthusiasm. "It's good to meet someone who has it all figured out." They remained good friends with Vinnie from then on.

As Johannah and Jim watched Vinnie playing ball with his friends, she took his hand. She guided him down the starboard deck under the boom of the mainsail away from other passengers and they looked out over the calm sea.

"I have something to tell you."

"What is it, Jo?"

"You've gone and done it now, Mr. Donnelly."

"What?"

"My time has come and gone." She placed his hand on her belly and looked at him.

She gauged Jim's surprised reaction carefully as he paused to assess this news.

"I don't want to have her aboard ship."

"We'll be on land long before it comes, Jo. It'll be fine!" He broke into an enormous grin. "A baby! Oh, sweetheart, this is wonderful! A new land and a new little soul."

Johannah allowed the relief to flow through her at Jim's reaction. "I think it's a girl. A little girl, can you imagine?"

"We'll be all right, Jo. We'll be fine."

"Are you sure?"

"More than anything. It's more than just us we'll be working for now. Thank God we're not in bloody Ireland."

She embraced Jim's attitude. "Yes. Thank God. We'll be all right."

With the cry of "LAAAAAAND!" everyone crowded the deck, struggling to contain their excitement as they squinted toward a distant dark line on the edge of the horizon, their first glimpse of the new country. Over the next three days, the *Naparima* tacked her way slowly against the current into the mouth of the broad St. Lawrence River, which drained a huge portion of the continent. As they drew into it, they could see the long, parallel verdant strips of farmland on either side of the river, each coloured with different crops: golden barley, purple clover, the green of feed grass coming down to the river's edge, to the shore where the posts of makeshift docks leaned east from the current. Small cat boats could be seen skirting the north shore between the villages. Here they spoke French, the passengers were told, and Jim, Johannah and Vinnie stared hard at the shore, trying to spot the exotic people in this new land and wondering what they would be like. Vinnie had become a close friend, like a little brother to Jim and Johannah, and they decided they would all stay and travel together.

Their first landfall was Grosse Île, a quarantine station still thirty miles downstream of Quebec City in the Province of Canada where they had been told they would have to stay until it was proven they had no illness and their numbers could be absorbed into the country. Other ships were anchored off the island. It all seemed almost idyllic from a distance, a pleasant green island in the river, a portal to a continent. The island was a high fist of granite, two miles long and half a mile across, punched up through the middle of the river with a rocky highland to the west tapering off downstream to provide fields enough for modest cultivation. Once the ship anchored in the current of the river, Jim and Johannah, along with fourteen others in the first party, disembarked into rowboats and broke away from the dreadful confines of that vessel, one step closer to the Promised Land. Dropped off on the island, they hauled their few belongings up from the docks and made their way toward a disorganized collection of customs houses and large sheds near the shore, overseen by soldiers and uniformed officials. Most, with Jim and Johannah among them, were slowed in their walking by the heaving of the earth under them as they tried to get their land legs back after so many weeks at sea. Yet Johannah could not contain her relief and excitement to be taking in the sights and earthy smells of this island. And just across the wide river was the new land that would be their home. They were nearly there.

As they approached the closest building, customs officials, wearing masks for inspection, began shouting at them in French and English:

"*En trois lignes! Tout droit! Trois lignes!* Three separate rows!"

Three long lines of immigrants from other ships, complete with worldly possessions and an abundance of children, stretched out and worked their way slowly toward the tables. Jim tried to be patient. Two French-speaking nuns were identifying and ministering to the sick. A masked English official worked his way down the line with a clipboard.

"Name and town of origin?"

Jim noticed that at the end of the line, all the passengers were going into a wide fenced area with a row of large sheds and a sign that read "Quarantine Camp." As the official came closer, Jim addressed him.

"How long do we have to stay here?"

"'Til spring."

"Spring! We were not told this!" Jim almost shouted at the man. "My wife is having a child. We have to find our land before winter!"

"There is a backup of you on the mainland. They want to keep you here for a while." And the official moved quickly along to avoid further argument. They were ushered together with the other families into one of the huge dormitory sheds. Inside, their hearts sank. The shed had rough walls on the perimeter and mud-stained canvas dividing sheets for privacy, and the structure went on forever. It was filthy and already overcrowded, many of the occupants showing signs of malnutrition and illness. Jim's anger was simmering.

"God. This is worse than the ship!"

"At least it's not moving," Vinnie offered brightly.

"I am. I feel I'm still at sea," Johannah remarked, losing her balance and almost fainting as Jim caught her. Jim held her tight as they watched two men wearing cloth masks hurry past them with a covered body on a stretcher.

They found a small section of floor available between a roof pole and a gloomy family, the Kellys from Sligo, four children under nine with identical frowns of exhausted desolation. But they dutifully made room for Jim and Johannah to sit, and for Vincent too.

"We'll get through this too, Jo. We will."

"Yes, my love. We will," she whispered.

Quarantine

AFTER TWO WEEKS on Grosse Île, they had settled in as much as was possible. There was little to break the monotony. Though the island was large, with the coastline visible through the trees, they were not allowed outside the fence to walk in the woods or on the rocky beach. It was fall now and the cold nights foreshadowed the winter they would face in the open wooden sheds. The officials installed a small woodstove at both ends of each shed for warmth and supplied hardwood to keep them going all night, but in the mornings they could still see their breath. Nuns in their black habits, silent and grave, came among them to distribute thin wool blankets.

When word had circulated, they suspected through Vinnie, that Johannah was pregnant, a gnarled grandmother offered to determine if she was carrying a boy or girl. The woman held a ring on a thread over Johannah's belly. The ring swung first in a straight line but then swivelled and began to swing in a circle. The fortune teller declared the "child" was both. Johannah was having twins! Johannah was immediately convinced it was true, though she was not without worries.

"Two times the fun!" Jim declared in the face of Johannah's apprehensions and she tried to embrace his rosy optimism. Johannah was confident the old woman was right and there was a babe of each sex growing inside her. She spoke to them often with words of encouragement, and of her impatience to meet them—but only when they were ready. She sometimes whispered a Celtic chant Raffy had taught her to save their little souls from evil. And she whispered things to them she would tell no one else, the truth of her own hopes and fears. It was bad luck to say a child's name out loud before it was born but Johannah had always thought "Lucy" was a beautiful name and whispered it sometimes. Lucy, Luce, Lucille. The boy? Well, no rush to decide on a name there. It was a guilty truth she spoke more to the girl than to the boy, for girls had to be smarter in this world and her dreams were already caught up in her daughter's future. She could see her face, feel her touch, almost hear her voice. Her only regret was that the baby's grandmother would never meet her.

One night after they had been trapped in the quarantine camp for several more weeks, Jim waited in the food line in the mess tent to get some dinner for the others while his anger began to rise. This was a fine thing, stuck on this godforsaken island in the middle of this grey river, with his woman only short months away from giving birth, surrounded by desperate souls and contagion on every breath and no progress from day to day to day. As the bitter winter weather advanced, numbers taken by fever grew, usually the very young or very old, and his concern for Johannah and the lives she carried fed his humiliation and feeling of helplessness. As he came to the servers with his three bowls, he faced the usual thin soup and dry biscuits, handed to him by the surly staff. Jim appraised the offering and glared at the server.

"Is there no meat? No fruit? My wife is growing two babies inside. Is every meal to be soup and biscuits?"

A server looked at him and replied dryly as he filled the three bowls, "No. Tomorrow, just for a change, we'll have biscuits and soup!" The servers all laughed at the stupid old joke, but Jim wasn't laughing and it was all he could do to keep his fist from the man's rancid mouth. At the mess tent door, Jim confronted one of the senior guards, well fed and holding a baton to discourage the greedy.

"If we can't get decent food here to keep our strength, let a few of us go to shore, to the towns along the river, to find work and pay for it ourselves."

"You are in quarantine. You don't go off the island. You will be shot if you try," the guard told him, hefting his baton and glancing at a British soldier standing near them. The soldier had overheard them and added his unrequested opinion. "You people are full of diseases."

"I'll give you a disease, boy," Jim told him.

The soldier unslung his rifle and made a move toward him. "You get back inside and behave yourself, Paddy. You make trouble, we'll put you in the stockade."

Jim stood his ground, barely containing his temper. The uniform was like a red flag in his face. British soldiers in Borrisokane, the damn Protestant British soldiers here in the new world. Was there no escaping the sons of bitches? But finally he looked down at the bowls of soup in his hands and backed down. He returned to his tent.

That night Jim went to have a quiet talk out beside the latrines with a couple of men who had been quarantined on Grosse Île longer than himself. He had discussed Irish politics and history with them and they knew how things worked around the camp. Jim explained to them his need to get off the island and they introduced him to a third man, a Frenchman named Drapeau who did maintenance on the island through the week but lived weekends with his large family across on the north shore. They met outside the latrine where the stink discouraged any eavesdropping lingerers. Thankfully the man spoke English.

"I can have a boat here to take you, but how will you get past the soldiers?" Drapeau asked him. "They patrol the fences all night and will shoot if you try to climb them or dig underneath."

"You leave that to me."

"All right. I will send a boat two nights from now. She will come in on the north shore of the island an hour before dawn. The weather will be calm. Half an English pound to me now, another half to the boatman when you meet."

"Agreed."

Jim gave Drapeau what was almost the last of their money and the Frenchman walked away inspecting it.

Later that night when they were settled in their small patch of hard floor in the quarantine shed, as another covered body was taken away and a wife and child cried in grief, Jim turned to Johannah and Vinnie, pulled the paper-thin curtain around them and spoke with quiet determination through the din of outside conversation.

"I'm wasting time, Jo. I have to get out of here. You need some decent food, meat and fruit for the babes. And I have to make some money so we can buy land when we are free."

"And just how d'you plan to do that? You can't even swim," she pointed out. It was a fair question.

"I met a man who's going to help get me to shore. In a boat."

Jim glanced out through the curtains, worried he had spoken too loud.

"When is this?"

"In two days."

"I'll come with you!"

"No, it could be rough out there. You stay here and grow the childer. I'll make some money and be back."

"How long would you be gone?"

"Shhhhhhhh," he cautioned her and continued in a whisper. "It could be some weeks, but I'll be back before the babies come."

"Oh, Jim. I don't know..."

"You've got Vinnie here to help you."

Vinnie nodded encouragingly. Johannah looked into Jim's eyes.

"Will you be careful? Will you keep yourself safe?"

"Yes. I will, love. I'll be very careful."

"All right. If this is what we must do, I'll be fine."

"Good girl," he told her.

"Just be back before the babies come."

"I promise."

Two days later, late in the evening, as others around them were sleeping, Jim kissed Johannah a final goodbye. Vinnie was awake but turned away to give them a vestige of privacy in this moment. Johannah took Jim by the shoulders and gave him a little shake.

"Be careful. Remember your promises. No fighting—you swore it—and be back before the babies." Her eyes were shining, imploring him.

"I'll remember."

Jim touched Vinnie's shoulder and the boy turned back to them. "You'll take good care of her."

Vinnie nodded. Jim held some old burlap bags and waxed thread.

"All right, then. Get me ready."

It was cold, near midnight when two men in cloth masks entered the shed carrying a stretcher. Vinnie had gone to inform them of Jim's demise. They always took and buried the bodies at night if they could, so the immigrants would not know the growing number of dead. They arrived at the cubicle and pulled back the sheet to find Johannah sitting beside Jim, weeping convincingly. Vinnie was sewing up the last few stitches of a burlap shroud around his still body, face last. The men waited, bored. Vinnie finished up his stitching, loosely covering the face, leaving a vent.

"Terrible thing, a man such as this, noble and kind, cut down in the prime of his life. Yes, a noble man…could be rather pig-headed at times but it's a great loss. May the Lord have mercy…"

Vinnie tied the knot and bit off the thread. The men placed Jim's body on the stretcher and took him away.

The burial crew was excavating graves by lamplight for the newly dead in the quarantine cemetery outside the fences. Four wrapped bodies had just been laid side by side a short distance from the woods, awaiting burial. Jim's body was on the end.

Through the vent in the burlap and through the weave of the sacking, he could see men a short distance away labouring on behalf of his mortal remains, digging a long trench in the pasture beside the woods, one that matched in size a dozen long parallel mounds filled in beside it. He tried not to shiver noticeably in the cold. With a slight cock of his head he looked back toward the camp and saw Vinnie at the wire fence, a blanket over his shoulders against the cold, keeping an eye on him. Jim could see Vinnie's breath in the chilled air and he suddenly worried that the same could be true of him. Could a puff of vapour betray him to the soldiers? Could they catch Jim breathing, when as a corpse he had no right to be doing so?

The soldiers were facing away from Jim, the diggers were intent on the difficult task of breaking the frozen ground and he still had the cover of darkness. The time was right for him to make his move. He rotated himself slightly onto his side, settled back, then rolled again right over and kept on going. His body began to tumble down the incline toward the woods. The ground was earth and stones and would cause him some bruising but no one noticed as he continued to roll into the rough bushes and finally came to lie still and hidden in the brush. Standing near the fence, Vinnie had seen Jim's successful escape and it was all he could do to stop himself from laughing out loud.

Jim trusted no one had seen him and now that he was concealed in the dark woods, he took out his knife and sliced open the burlap from within. Staying low, he emerged from the sacking, kicking it into the bushes, then looked through the brush toward the soldiers and the gravediggers. They were still facing away from him. They had not noticed they had lost one of their dead. Jim stood and scrambled deeper into the trees and, with the aid of the light of a thin moon, began to cross the wooded island, less than a mile to the other side.

Down at the rocky north shore, a fair-haired young boy in a very small rowboat waited for him, the boat's nose secured into the pebbly beach, stern bobbing gently in the river's current. Jim looked up and down the shoreline, then turned around to look behind him for sentries. He had not been spotted. The boy called to him with a cheery smile.

"Allez, Irlande. On n'a pas toute la nuit!"

Jim approached the boat, slipping a little on the icy rocks as the river tide was out. The boy did not speak English but gestured to him to come quickly and Jim climbed aboard. He gave him the half pound. The boy smiled again at him, then, releasing the painter and using one oar, he pushed the boat out into the current, placed the oar back in its lock and started to row for the north shore of the river. Out in the middle of the wide blue-grey St. Lawrence in the tiny boat, Jim held on anxiously to the gunnels, terrified of the water, as he could not swim, but his fears were overridden by his determination to get to the mainland and make some progress for the future of his family.

The New Land

ONE COLD WINTER morning, when Jim had been gone for nine days, Johannah and Vinnie waited, as they did twice a day, every day, in the food line with the others at the kitchen tent on Grosse Île, for the thin soup to be ladled out as usual by the server into cold tin bowls that took any heat away from the gruel in a moment. Johannah was growing bigger each day, almost alarmingly so. She had suffered a few bouts of morning sickness. Thankfully that had passed, but her feet were swollen and the long food lines were hard on her. Soon Vinnie would have to bring her meals to her. But this morning, the French server noticed her and stopped them.

"Donnelly?"

Johannah nodded and he reached under the table for a burlap sack and gave it to her, keeping it low and passing it without flourish in front of the others. He told her it was from "*votre mari*," and this was no sooner done than he ignored Johannah and Vinnie totally to keep spooning his anemic offering to the others.

Knowing that Jim was safe, she wanted to shout with relief. But knowing that discretion was in order, Johannah made little of it, put the sack under her shawl and returned to their lodgings.

"He's all right!" she whispered as they left the tent.

Back in their own space, she and Vinnie pulled the curtains across and, opening the sack, pulled out their prize. A full roasted capon chicken! And also some cooked potatoes and carrots and a small loaf of oat bread, plus a short sharp knife with which to cut it.

"Such wonderful things!" Vinnie exclaimed for both of them.

"Oh my God, we will feast like royalty."

And their conversation was reduced to moans and sighs as they ate well beyond their fill.

Throughout the next month, the special food came to them in the small sacks, a small roast of beef or leg of lamb two or three times a week, and they found private places behind the sheds or in the latrines to eat unseen. No one questioned them about it, but both of them stayed healthy and strong and Johannah's belly continued to grow.

A few more miserable ships came into quarantine before the river froze. Though in constant conflict with filth and contagion, the camp's inhabitants found a routine of life and with occasional acts of kindness they were kept, all of them, just above desperation. Vinnie played football with some mates he had met on the ship and others found in quarantine, and when a large puddle froze on the flats, local workers showed them how to set up goals and knock a stone around on the smooth icy surface with sticks. Johannah was able to borrow books to read from women with whom she made friends. They commented kindly on her swelling belly and she told them her husband had been able to go on ahead and she would join him after quarantine. She even found paper and a pencil and began to draw designs of the house she hoped one day to build with Jim. She quietly described it to Lucy inside her and promised to keep the pictures to show her when she decided to join them on the outside.

It was a lean Christmas in the camp but spirited in that so many of the immigrants were devout, and the passengers of the *Naparima* were that much closer to the end of quarantine in the early spring. They had the crossing of the sea behind them, like Moses and his people, and before them was the future of a promised land.

Late that fall and into the winter, a hundred men had worked on the railway bed that cut through the Quebec forest and would soon open western land to settlement. Jim had arrived and joined the line of labourers looking for jobs and they approached a young hiring clerk in a waistcoat and old top hat who reminded him for a sad moment of Mick. The clerk sat at a table near the end of the track, writing down workers' names, hiring some on the spot and telling others to come back, but there was never an argument. Most of the navvies in line were older, hard-bitten men, Irish and French. In the distance, the team was laying down track. Jim had watched them with interest, having never seen rail track being laid before. He was about to know the process intimately, though, for the clerk hired him then and there.

Construction of the regional rail line continued through the bitter winter, like no winter he had ever experienced in Ireland for cold and snow, needing pick axes more than shovels to break the diamond-hard ground, but the pay was 20 percent higher at that time of year and they lived in crowded but cozy log cabins. The monotonous process was to create the elevated bed, lay cross ties and fill, then ten men would pick up and drop each long rail onto the ties, and it would be riveted to the last one. Then twenty spikes each side of the rail, one man holding, one man hammering them down with a sledge, three or four blows to drive them to the hilt tight against the apron base of the rail.

"Sure you've a keen eye, Quinn," Jim complimented his partner at the end of an hour's labour—not once had the hammer missed the nail head or grazed his hand. Quinn was a big man, grizzled and red faced. Despite having worked there for five weeks, Jim had never teamed with him before.

"Doing it so long I can do it in my sleep. Where you from then, Donnelly?"

"Borrisokane…Tipperary."

"Really? I'm from Birr!"

"Birr! We were neighbours. Well, good to meet you."

They shook and the man from Birr's hand was like a vice. An acquaintance of Quinn's came up to them. He was a large mean-looking piece of work, even bigger than Quinn.

"Donnelly. This is Kavanaugh. He's from across the county line in Limerick. Hey Kavanaugh, the lad's come for the three wishes and the treasure. He's from Borrisokane."

"Borrisokane? That shite hole? You poor bastard."

It was Quinn who took offense. "You can't talk to the lad like that, so far from home."

"What's it to you? I'll talk to him any way I want."

"You're an awful rude bollocks."

"You just found out? But I always knew you were an arsehole."

Quinn swung a seriously deadly shovel at Kavanaugh, barely missing his head and almost clipping Jim. Kavanaugh moved in and punched him in the face. The two men got into a clutch and went at it, wrestling and pounding each other's faces with their fists. Despite the frivolity of this encounter and the question of where the men got the energy for this contest near the end of a hard day, Jim felt his blood rise, for it had been a while since he had been in a good fight.

"Gentlemen. They'll fire you," Jim tried to tell them, but they were hearing none of it. As Quinn began losing badly to the bigger man, the French foreman and two burly assistants approached.

"*Separez ces putains de Paddies! Virez les deux!*"

With substantial effort, the assistants pulled Quinn and Kavanaugh from each other's embrace and dragged them off. The foreman studied Jim to gauge the level of his involvement in the skirmish, if any. Jim lowered his eyes and went back to work with great enthusiasm, keeping to himself.

It was one of the first mild nights of late winter when a gentle southwestern breeze began to soften the snow on the ground and Johannah could hear the water under the river ice around Grosse Île and catch the first muddy scent of spring, which would mean their release from quarantine. Close after midnight, she had her first hard contraction. It was much too soon—she wasn't due for several more weeks—but her water breaking confirmed it was true. Vinnie lay on his mat on the other side of their small pile of belongings.

"Vinnie. Vinnie? I think they're coming."

Vinnie awoke terrified. "The babies? What do I do? All right. I'm here. You'll be all right. Jesus, save us."

"Vinnie. Listen to me. The babies are too soon. We need to find the doctor."

The Catholic doctor, a hurried little man with a Sligo accent, had examined her very briefly when they first arrived, declaring all was well.

"Right!" Vinnie hurried out of the shed.

Through increasingly strong contractions, Johannah's hands gripped the edge of the pallet with all her might. They were coming faster now, and stronger, and she cried out and attempted to push the children closer to freedom. Where was Vinnie, where was the doctor? And why was her man not here?

Finally, the sheet was pulled back from outside their enclosure and Vinnie's face appeared. Behind him was a tall grey-haired man with a trim beard carrying a medical bag. Vinnie looked worried as he spoke.

"Johannah? This is Dr. Davis. I'm sorry, Johannah. I couldn't find the Catholic doctor."

"Doctor. It's too soon. I'm not due yet."

"Babies usually know what they're doing, ma'am. You look healthy and strong. You'll be fine. I'm sorry I'm not of your faith but I've asked Sister Patricia to assist me."

He placed a towel as a pillow under her head and gave her a reassuring smile. Johannah cried out as another contraction hit. Inside the sheeted enclosure, Dr. Davis spread out a towel and unpacked his bag. The nun came to assist him, bringing hot water, towels and a warmed blanket. Vinnie waited outside.

After the doctor had examined Johannah, he spoke to her calmly, firmly. "Johannah, you are fully open and ready to give birth. I know it's early but it'll be all right. We need you to push now."

And she did so with all her might. The first little head crowned and then came out fully and stopped there. The child would come no farther. Dr. Davis ran his fingers around the head and down the neck.

"Stop pushing now, Johannah," he told her and with great effort she tried to hold back. "Johannah? Listen to me. The cord is around the baby's neck. I can free it if you release the pressure. You have to stop pushing. Understand? I know it's hard. Let the baby move back."

Johannah found the only thing harder than pushing was not pushing, but she held back against all her instincts, breathing in and out until she saw stars. The doctor worked his two fingers down the back of the head of the child and was able to take hold of the umbilical cord between them and pull up enough of the loop to slide it over the child's head. The cord went back inside and the child was now freed from his constraint to continue his earthbound journey. Johannah was free to push and the birth proceeded quickly. A moment later a strong little wavering voice announced its owner's arrival.

"The first one is a boy," Dr. Davis informed her as he tied off and severed the cord with a scalpel. Johannah saw him lift the tiny infant, not much bigger than one of the doctor's strong hands, and pass him gently to Sister Patricia, who wrapped him up like a silkworm in a warm sheet. The nun handed the baby to Vinnie outside the curtain.

"Good, Johannah. The second is coming well. Push. That's it."

As if it came from another person, Johannah heard her final groan and the gasp of birth.

"Well done, Johannah. It's a girl."

She was delighted to hear this confirmed and she listened for Lucy's first cry.

"Already a good head of red hair," Dr. Davis told her.

Another moment went by and another. Johannah turned her head to see Dr. Davis working on the little grey wet child, carefully holding her upside down, patting her bottom, then turning her over, massaging her tiny chest, blowing into her face.

"Come on, little one. Breathe in for me. Breathe."

Dr. Davis blew into the miniature mouth and nose, the opening no larger than his baby finger. But only silence continued. He turned the child away from Johannah and kept working.

"Where…? What is it…?" she asked breathlessly.

After a few more moments, her mind and body went numb as she heard the sombre voice of the nun reciting a prayer.

"Lord God of all creation, receive this life you created in love and comfort your faithful people in their time of loss…"

"Damn it, sister, wait." And Dr. Davis worked on. "Come on, little beauty. Live."

But the baby did not cry, and a minute later the nun continued.

"In the pain of sorrow there is consolation, in the face of despair there is hope, in the midst of death there is life…" This time Dr. Davis did not interrupt.

No, this could not be, Johannah thought. Where was her Lucy? Her breasts were full. Lucy would be hungry. Johannah called out for her and she saw Vinnie bow his head. After that, Johannah was quiet and all became a blur of anguish.

The next hours or days, she lost track, were as if Johannah existed in a guilty nightmare from which she could not awaken, one that included the ghosts of her father and mother along with this new little soul she had failed. Somehow she understood that the stillborn child would be buried immediately and Vinnie was sent to find a priest. Dr. Davis said she did not have to be present but of course she did have to and so, though she was weak, Dr. Davis made arrangements to have her carried in a chair by two men to the site. In years to follow, Johannah's memory of the quarantine cemetery was vague and she was told later that Vinnie held the other, the boy, in his arms during the burial of his sister. Dr. Davis had provided a bottle of goat's milk and the infant had taken to it easily. The priest, who had first baptized the dead child, then spoke the words: "O heavenly Father, whose face the angels of the little ones do always behold in heaven, grant us to believe that this child hath been taken into the safe keeping of Thy eternal love..."

Johannah stared down into the small open pit as if under a spell. Vinnie asked her if she was all right, but she could not answer. She looked out over the few rows of thin white crosses, then looked up to see out across the field where there were hundreds more, even a thousand. A thousand and more thin white crosses. A thousand and more graves. So many had made it this far only to fall here on this cruel little island. Now including her own daughter, who they put into the cold ground that day and if there had been any way that she could have crawled down in beside her to hold her, she would have done so.

Johannah lay on her mat bed for days after that, her eyes glazed and staring. Vinnie held her other baby, who was fussing and hungry in his arms. Dr. Davis had monitored the vital signs of the tiny child and, though he had come far too early, his heart was strong, lungs clear. Johannah too was medically fit. There had been little bleeding, the births went well and the single placenta was delivered intact. Johannah came physically through it all just fine. But it was the second child, the girl, who refused to breathe. Vinnie told her what she had seen: how Davis had massaged the tiny chest, blown on the little face, spoken to her. But then he told her what she had not seen: the child's eyes did open for a second, and that was all, as Davis worked on and on to try to save her. Lucy had seen the world for that moment, that flicker of life and consciousness, and then it passed her by. A whole life in an instant. The image of anxious faces—was Johannah's among them?—a blurry memory of earth to take with her to heaven for all eternity.

Johannah lay there with her long stare, with no interest in the surviving child, and a deep lethargy far beyond the exhaustion of childbirth. Dr. Davis took the baby from Vinnie, held him toward her and spoke gently.

"Johannah, you'll have other daughters. Daughters and granddaughters and great-granddaughters. Will you try with him? He's a fine wee tyke. Got a little crooked foot but otherwise strong as a goat. He needs you, Johannah."

She turned her back on them. Vinnie whispered to her.

"Jim'll be back soon. He's been sending the food. Was only since the babes came early he wasn't here. He'll be back for sure! This one's so hungry."

But Johannah wasn't really listening. She was thinking of that moment of life when Lucy's eyes opened and then closed forever.

Before he left, Dr. Davis gave Vinnie a warmed bottle of cow's milk with a rubber nipple and, in the absence of Johannah's willingness to nurse him, the boy fed the tiny surviving twin himself.

The Wager

Jim sat with his back against the wall of the tavern at a small table, nursing a ten-cent glass of bad whiskey and counting again the small pile of currency he had accumulated in the two and a half months he had been working. After bed and board, and sending the food packages to Johannah, he had six pounds, five shillings and four pence saved. He spent a moment admiring his calloused hands, the pads thick and the lifelines deep. He could drive a spike firmly into a tie with only three blows of his sledge, and he was now a valuable man on the line. He found satisfaction in the miles of track he had helped to lay. What a long way he was from his poor dandy boy days in Borrisokane when his hands were soft and his pockets empty. Raised on the estate, he was never shy of hard work and felt he had recaptured a certain righteousness in it again. He thought of Mick and how good it would be if he had lived to come with them, and what he would have thought of this new world.

The tavern in the village near the railhead was a cramped rough log affair with a boisterous crowd taking up the extra space of men used to spending most of their days outside. A massive bald bartender with a stained apron and enormous hands kept order among the jostling drunks. In a tiny open area across the bar where the tables had been pushed back, there was a semi-organized boxing contest under way. A serious man with steel-rimmed specs was taking bets at a battered table. The elbows and knees of the fighters struck as many blows to the audience in the close press of bodies as to the opponent, but there was no room to give.

"You will wear it out, *mon ami*."

Jim looked up at the bartender's remark.

"The money," the burly Frenchman clarified, pointing to his meagre treasure. He put down another glass of whiskey. Jim carefully slid him a shilling but the man didn't take it.

"*C'est la tournée du patron.*"

Jim slid the shilling back into his little pile.

"Thanks. Yeah, not much for two and a half months' work," he concluded. "What do you think land would go for around here an acre? Good farm land now."

"Here, three or four pounds maybe." Jim covered his shock. "But I heard there's land to the west, in old Upper Canada you can buy there for ten shillings an acre, maybe."

"Ten shillings. That's good, but at this rate it'll still take me five years to buy a decent-sized farm."

Jim watched the punching match across the bar for a moment. One of the fighters seemed familiar and he realized it was Kavanaugh, the bully from Limerick. Jim could tell he was toying with his opponent, threatening with his right. Then suddenly with a powerful left hook, Kavanaugh laid the other man out cold on the plank floor. The ten count by the bartender went quickly. There were cheers and groans and people collected money from their wagers. Jim looked around at the betting action. Mick would have enjoyed this and found some opportunities here. Kavanaugh was strutting about in triumph, pounding his chest with his bloody cloth-wrapped fists, jeering at his opponent as two men slapped the man into consciousness, got him groggily to his feet and half carried him outside.

"Go home to your mammy, you pansy harp. Who's next? I just begun."

Jim saw that Kavanaugh was looking at him, his fists up, shifting his weight from one foot to the other.

"You there. It's the Borrisokane boy. You don't have Quinn to hide behind. Come for a little slap and tickle. I'll be easy on you."

Again Jim's blood was stirred by the offer, but he had promised Johannah not to fight. He could not afford a feud or to jeopardize his job with broken bones.

"I don't fight."

"Ahhhhh. He doesn't fight. Are you a priest or a molly?"

Kavanaugh came up to Jim's table and suddenly gave him a stinging slap across the face. The bar fell silent. It took everything Jim had not to go for the man's throat but he had made his promise to Johannah and it stopped him short.

"I told you, I don't fight."

"Everyone'll fight for something. What'll you fight for?"

Kavanaugh slapped him again hard across the face and this time there were cheers and shouts of encouragement to Jim. What would Mick do? No question there.

Jim stood up and stepped out from his table, his face burning. Kavanaugh was a head taller and fifty pounds heavier. Jim thought of his promise and began to negotiate a bit with himself. It's true he had promised not to fight, to keep the peace and not raise a hand, but wasn't this merely sport? It didn't really count, did it? This was not serious fighting, not real fighting. There would be no later recriminations, no revenge. Jim looked down at his paltry pile and thought of Johannah. He scooped up the money and took it to the bookmaker nearby, who was holding a fistful of bills, his steel glasses askew from the jostling of the onlookers.

"What are my odds?"

The bookmaker looked him up and down, then glanced at the substantially larger Kavanaugh.

"Ten to one."

Jim frowned a moment at this insult, but the odds were good for him. "Done."

Jim gave him all his money. Other men were actively betting on the side. Jim took off his jacket, giving it to the bookmaker, and began talking quietly to Kavanaugh.

"So you'll be gentle with me then and not…?"

As he turned toward Kavanaugh a huge fist slammed into his face, knocking him back against a table and spilling the beer of several patrons. The supporters of Kavanaugh cheered while those taking a long shot bet on Jim groaned. Jim felt his jaw and spit out a broken tooth and some blood from the sucker punch.

"No, hah?"

Kavanaugh came at him again in the cramped ring with fists flying. Jim recognized the left hook that had taken out the last man and was just able to dodge it and two more mighty punches. All three were left hooks—his opponent had little imagination and could be anticipated. Jim held up his hands, stepping back from the big man.

"Wait, wait, wait, now," Jim appealed to all present. "Let's be clear. Are we playing Tipperary rules?"

Kavanaugh stood straight up and lowered his fists, perplexed.

"Tipperary rules? What the hell are Tipperary rules?"

Jim looked at the bookmaker, backing closer to Kavanaugh.

"Well…first, you can't do this."

Jim suddenly turned and with great momentum rammed his forehead into Kavanaugh's nose, breaking it with a satisfying crunch. Kavanaugh stumbled back groaning, hands to his beak. Blood started to flow down his chest.

"And you shouldn't ever do this."

Jim gave the distracted man a kick in the crotch so powerful that it lifted him up off the floor. Kavanaugh bent over holding his privates, moaning, totally vulnerable to Jim's further ministrations. Jim began to enjoy himself.

"But…you *can* do this."

Jim swung his fist, hardened by many weeks of driving spikes, with all his might up into Kavanaugh's fleshy face and, as onlookers scrambled out of the way, knocked him over onto his back on the filthy barroom floor. Half the tavern cheered.

"One…two…three…four…"

Some losers began to argue with the bookmaker over Jim's technique but the original sucker punch Kavanaugh gave Jim had established protocol. Kavanaugh lay semi-conscious on the floor as the bartender continued the count.

"Five…six…seven…eight…nine…you're out!"

Nursing a raw, bloody fist, feeling for any broken bones, Jim retrieved his jacket and his winnings from the disgruntled bookmaker. He gave the bills a rough assessment (now was not the time to dally) and it was well over fifty pounds! Jim gave the rowdy house a bloody gap-toothed smile, extended his arm in a victory wave and took his leave before any man seriously disputed his victory.

Jim stepped out into the cold night air and thought of Johannah and the broken promise. But it was only a temporary lapse and she needn't know, and now they had money for land. It was well worth it for the greater good.

Johannah lay on the mat in the quarantine shed, her face to the wall. Though her breasts ached with milk, when anyone presented the surviving child to her, she just couldn't bring herself to do what she should be doing. How could she hold and feed her son when her daughter was dead? She had failed to give Lucy life and each day was dark with guilt and remorse and she just could not find her way out.

Vinnie would come to her, sweet Vinnie, and tell her about how strong the boy was growing on the goat milk and how spring was almost with them, and the quarantine period was almost over, and that Jim would be back any day to take them off the island and to the new land and a new life. Vinnie would tell her every promise and dream he could think of and still, Johannah would hear the voice of her mother or see her father, his body contorted on the stable floor, or imagine the face of her stillborn child, and she could not find her way out of the darkness.

Some nights were so still and quiet that she thought this was what eternity could be like and it was not so bad. On one such night, she held in her hand the small, sharp knife that Jim had sent with the first sack of food. She had had it with her for three days. She set the blade against her wrist and thought the plan was quite tenable to cut herself deep, for Vinnie was sound asleep on the other side of the pile of belongings and they would not find out what she had done until morning, when it was too late. There was a bright moon shining through the cracks in the shed wall and Johannah had bolstered her courage to the point of doing it. She hoisted herself up on one elbow to brace herself and apply the knife when a little weight shifted in her pocket and it was the river stone she felt. She took it out and looked at the red and green flecks and held it tight in her hand. She put the knife aside and fell into a light sleep. She was awakened a couple of hours later when she heard something: a few faint whistled notes of a tune, lost in the still air, perhaps only imagination. But the tune...wasn't it...? It was "Oyster Nan." She sat up, her heart beating faster. Was it another dream? But then she heard it again and she saw his silhouette come through the door and then Jim was there beside her.

"Miss me?"

She hid the knife and threw her arms around him and embraced him with all her might, burying her face in his neck, shaking, holding back tears. He held her tight, sensing her deep need, and did not let go. Vinnie woke up, rubbed the sleep from his eyes, then grabbed Jim's hand to shake and rubbed his shoulder in greeting, and whispered so as not to disturb those asleep nearby.

"I knew you'd come soon, Jim. I told Jo. I knew it."

As Vinnie lighted their nub of candle, Jim pulled back from Johannah to look at her, to see her slim body, a little alarmed at her tangled hair and haunted eyes.

"The babes? You've had the babies?"

"They came early," Vinnie explained.

Vinnie picked up a sleeping bundle almost hidden next to him, folding back the thin blanket to show the pale face in the candlelight.

"Here he is, a strong little thing. Here's your son."

Gently, Jim released Johannah and reached out as Vinnie passed the child over to him. Jim took and held his new son with reverence and stared down into his little face. The boy looked back calmly with interest and made gentle noises to his father.

Vinnie explained, "There was a Dr. Davis. A Protestant, but he was good and between the two of us, we did the job."

Jim remained silent for some moments, staring into the child's blue eyes. "He's beautiful." Then he looked around them in their curtained area. "And just the one, then?"

Johannah looked up at him as the tears began, "I'm sorry, Jim. I'm so sorry." She looked away in shame.

Vinnie explained, "Dr. Davis did all he could for the other."

"A girl, was she?"

"Yes."

Jim nodded sadly at this information, then turned his loving attention back to the boy.

"Well, it's all right, Jo. It's all right. Look, he's a handsome young lad, this one. The identity of the father's no mystery. He's beautiful, Jo! What's his name?"

Vinnie looked at Johannah, embarrassed. Johannah would not raise her eyes.

"What? No name? You can't be calling him, 'Hey, you!'"

"We...Johannah thought she should wait for you for the naming," Vinnie told him convincingly.

"The doctor was so good to us, Jim," Johannah raised her eyes to him finally. "Maybe his name..."

"The Protestant?" Jim frowned about this for a moment. "Oh, I don't know about that. What's his name?"

"Dr. Davis. William Davis."

"Well, maybe. William. Will, then. A good, durable name. I'll think on it. Now, let me show you something."

Jim emptied his pockets of the winnings, pound notes and coins piling forward on the mat as he balanced the baby in one arm. He spoke in excited whispers.

"Sixty-eight pounds! We can buy a hundred acres!"

She touched the currency and then noticed his bruises in the candlelight, and the missing tooth. "What happened to your face? You weren't fighting?"

"No, no. I…fell off a mule." He moved quickly past the lame ruse. "So when we get out—its only two more weeks and we're free—we're going to go west. Lots of land there. There's too many Irishmen here in Quebec already. And we've got enough money for seed and tools, an animal or two and food for a year!"

Jim looked at the baby again with great satisfaction. Young Will gurgled and smiled up at him.

"And the next thing to do is save this little one from being a bastard! What do you say, Jo? Will you marry me? You better say yes."

Jim took from his pocket a small silver ring and gave it to her. She held it in her hand.

"Jo?"

"Yes, yes, I'll marry you. When?"

"The sooner the better. Vinnie, you can be our best man. And when we leave, you'll come with us, won't you? You're going west anyway. We could use some help to find land and get settled. What do you say?"

"I guess I could come and stay for a bit. The mountains can get by without me a little longer." Will had been fussing and now began to cry. Jim noted Johannah made no move to take him.

"I guess it's supper time."

Jim looked to her expectantly for a moment as Will's cries became more insistent, but Johannah remained still and Jim began to regard her with concern. Vinnie stepped in.

"I can take him," Vinnie held out his hands. He had the bottle of milk ready. But Jim did not surrender the child.

"Johannah will do it. Won't you, Jo?" He held Will out to her. "Our son is hungry."

Johannah looked at him and at the baby. The baby was crying now for her.

"Johannah?" Hesitantly, under her husband's look, she reached out for him. Jim put the child firmly into her arms and his crying eased as for the first time she stared down into his eyes.

"He's beautiful, isn't he, Jo?"

Johannah studied the child a moment longer.

"Yes. Yes, he is."

"Will is a good name for him if you like it."

Will began to cry again with new force, knowing that sustenance was near. Johannah turned her back on them and slipped down the shoulder of her dress to feed her son, pulling her shawl around to shelter him, worried she might not now be able, she had waited so long. The baby—he had a name now, Will—found her breast and in a moment was feeding hungrily as if this was nothing new, as if she had not spurned him, as if all was forgiven. He put up a tiny hand and patted her chest gently, with affection, and suddenly all the grief and guilt was washed away in the flow of milk and she felt such love for this little creature who wanted and needed her and knew she needed him. Johannah's eyes filled with tears of relief that her milk was still ready, in fact bursting to be taken and she was able to give what was needed and she would never deny it again.

By what they had told Jim, Dr. Davis had been good to his family. But it was hard for him to get his thoughts in tune with it. Help from a Protestant. It made no sense. He caught up with Dr. Davis on his rounds.

"Johannah told me all you did for them," Jim said to him. "I've never known a Protestant to help Catholics like this. I want you to know how much we appreciate your kindness. You know we've named the babe Will."

"Yes. Thank you. I'm deeply touched. The lad will be lame, but I can tell he will be strong in other ways."

"The strength of his mother. We hope he will be the first of many."

"There is no reason to doubt it."

"Doctor, Johannah and I are getting married tomorrow and we'd be honoured if you came."

"It would be my pleasure."

On a beautiful spring day on Grosse Île, Jim finally stood beside his Johannah in the open field outside the fence above the broad river facing west, holding hands before the priest. The blue-grey surface of the St. Lawrence was visible on both sides of the island from this elevated place. With the river current flowing past, so smooth and steady, Jim had the impression that it was the island that was moving and the river that was still; the island like some great granite vessel moving west, carrying them deeper into the land and the future they would share.

"Forasmuch as Jim and Johannah have consented together in holy wedlock and have witnessed the same before God and pledged their troth either to the other…"

Vinnie stood beside Jim as best man, holding little Will. Dr. Davis was beside Johannah. The rows of white crosses stretched out into the distance, an army of silent, benevolent witnesses to their hopefulness.

"…and by joining hands; I pronounce that they be man and wife together, in the name of the Father, Son and Holy Ghost. Amen. Kiss the bride, man."

Jim kissed Johannah with a sudden heat that he realized embarrassed her in front of the priest, but he didn't give a damn. Vinnie applauded, then laughed, little Will yowled happily, and the deed was done.

After the brief ceremony, Dr. Davis congratulated them both and kissed the bride.

"You know, I've been thinking. My home's in Biddulph Township, six hundred miles west of here. A town called Lucan. My family helped settle it, but there's lots of Catholics. Lots of land and good soil. When you're released, why don't you go there and see if you like it. You can clear a farm, raise a family. I'll be back in the fall when my stint here is done."

"Is it green there?"

"Green rolling fields. Spring and summer, there's no greener place on earth."

"And churches? Are there Catholic churches there?" Johannah asked.

"A fine new brick one. St. Patrick's."

"We had a St. Patrick's in Borrisokane!" Johannah told him.

"It's only a couple of years old, quite impressive. I've never seen inside, of course."

"I'd like to go there," Johannah said and glanced at Jim. "Lucan, is it?"

"Yes. You'd be welcomed," Dr. Davis replied. "You decide what's best for you."

"Thank you," Jim told him, shaking his hand, still surprised that a Protestant could be a man of honour. He looked the English soldiers nearby in the eye so they understood that even though he was an Irishman, he was good enough for a Protestant doctor to shake his hand.

A week after the wedding on another sunny early spring day, Jim, Johannah and Vincent were released from quarantine. They stood on the shore of Grosse Île, Jim with his arm around Johannah holding the sleeping Will, Vinnie all full of anticipation, their meagre belongings at their feet, waiting for the longboat that would take them and a dozen others across the broad river to the village of Bearer on the north shore and into the next stage of their lives.

A Piece of Heaven

THE ROUGH PAINTED sign on the side of the dirt road came to them as a surprise, saying "Welcome to Lucan."

"We're here!" Vinnie announced with weary delight. "We made it!"

They stopped the pony cart to savour the moment. The Donnellys had been travelling for several weeks now. From Beaupré they had journeyed along the north shore of the river to Quebec City, where they bought a pony and cart and provisions, bread and seed, utensils and farm tools, from friendly hand-gesturing people who spoke no English at all. Vinnie and Jim walked alongside while Johannah and baby Will rode in the cart, to the sound of the creaking cartwheels turning, pots and pans hanging off the side chiming lightly to the vehicle's ambling progress. Their path was a dirt and gravel road cut through the trees along the huge river, negotiating other coaches and wagons, skirting past the old town of Montreal and then along the north shore of Lake Ontario. They had a small canvas tent for Johannah and the baby, but the weather was often fair enough for them to sleep under the stars and the mild nights reminded Jim of the need to get seeds in the ground. They walked through the busy sprawling town of Toronto, with its multi-storied buildings on Lake Ontario. Then they headed west into rolling countryside. A few days later, their anticipation growing steadily, they passed through the busy inland market town called London.

"I finally got to London!" Jim declared as they made their way along the Thames River. "I wonder if they have a Bridge and a Tower." From what they could see passing through the town on Richmond Street, the emulation of the British namesake had a way to go. But their destination still lay miles ahead.

Richmond Street became a "corduroy" road made of logs laid side by side with sand and gravel on top, leading north from London into

Biddulph Township, where the hills had relaxed and they faced a flat plain of forest. The small town of Lucan was in the middle of this township, with clear pasture on each side and buildings up ahead, including the church of which Dr. Davis had spoken.

"Look, it's St. Patrick's. Beautiful!"

They stopped to admire the church, only three years old, which stood at a crossroads between the far east end of Lucan's main street and the Roman Line running north and south. It was a substantial yellow brick edifice with four tall, narrow windows of coloured glass on each side. But its most distinctive feature was a sharp, almost needle-like steeple jabbing aggressively toward heaven, visible for miles around.

"Well, thanks be to God for getting us here safely."

"And to your Dr. Davis for directing us here. Our new home, Jo!"

"What are we waiting for?"

Their pony cart with Johannah and Will as passengers rolled down busy Main Street among horses and carts and wagons and past several new wooden storefronts: a tavern, a general store, a blacksmith and a hotel with another tavern, outside which two men were arguing. As Jim and Johannah's cart passed, they began to scuffle and other men pulled them apart. The cart finally stopped outside the post office with a new-looking sign that read "Land Registry Office" and Jim glanced at Johannah with no small degree of excitement.

"You see that, Jo? Land!"

Inside the post office and land registry, a map was spread out before Jim, Johannah and Vinnie by the postmaster and town clerk, Mr. Porte, a friendly and deliberate man, thin and almost completely bald, whose mother was from Kilkenny. He had told them a little about the makeup of Lucan, where everyone west of Princess Street was Protestant and connected to the Holy Trinity Anglican Church, and everyone east, in St. Patrick's parish, was Catholic. Now he had the map out and gestured to the parcels of land around the town.

"The ones marked in red are for sale."

Jim was ready with his money in his hand as he stared at the offerings before him.

"I'd like it close to town, you see, but not too close. At least a hundred acres. We used to plow that much each year on the estate. Yeah. A hundred acres sounds just right. And some of it cleared would be nice, but I'll be needing trees, too, to build. And maybe a creek going through it with a pond. What do you think, Jo? A nice deep pond would be fine."

Porte studied them through his thick glasses, then pointed to some red markings on the map.

"All right. This one's a mile out of town, but it's only fifty acres."

"Not big enough. How much is it?"

"One thousand pounds."

Jim went pale. Johannah looked at him, very worried. Jim stared at the map in silence.

"Farther out, they get cheaper. Here's one six miles north of town. Sixty acres. Six hundred pounds."

"No, no, I want to see the ten shillings an acre farms I heard about. Where are they?"

Porte laughed dryly.

"That was a few years ago, my son. The good land 'round here has all been bought up by the Protestants, the English and Scots. They'll try to sell you the "Irish land" up north, but it's no good. There's no topsoil."

"I've only got sixty pounds."

A sympathetic tone came into Porte's voice. "You'll need a mortgage."

"We can talk to the bank, Jim," Johannah suggested.

Jim's heart was racing as he tried to control his anger and frustration.

"I'll be owing nobody nothing. I've been told about the banks. Protestants, all of them! I won't be under the thumb of those devils in suits. I've heard they'll cheat you every time! I thought the land was cheap, that you bring your family all the way over here and you can buy land at a reasonable price!"

"It's been twenty years since there was any land sold that cheaply. Maybe out west on the prairies."

"I like the look of the land here. This is where we want to be," Jim told him. He knew he sounded petulant and was embarrassed again, and Johannah was embarrassed for him and he knew that too.

Porte studied him for a moment.

"Well…there is a law. Some people have used it with success," Porte told him. "Says you can squat on land and work it and in time you get to keep it."

"Squat?"

"Yes. You become an official squatter. You find a section of wild land that's not been improved. Even if it's owned by someone, they have to work it, improve it, or they lose it. That's the law here. You move onto it and improve it, clear some of it, plant some of it, and in seven years it becomes yours. A man named Toohey did that with seventy acres on the Granton Road and got his deed last year."

Jim was excited by this idea. But he could see Johannah was not.

"I don't like the sound of it, Jim. We don't own the land for seven years? And maybe not even then. Let's talk to the banks about a mortgage, see what they say."

"But if we squat, the land is free and I could use the money I have for more equipment and seed and another animal or two. We just have to be smart about it."

Studying the map, he pointed to a hundred-acre parcel four miles from town with "uncleared" handwritten across it.

"What about this? Uncleared. It has a stream through it."

Porte brought out a thick heavy book bound in black cloth and placed it on the counter, then opened it with effort and leafed through to the registration number of the parcel of land indicated on the map.

"Yeah. It's north of town here on the Roman Line road. That's for Roman Catholic. Pretty well all Irish out there." He found the number. "It's registered to Patrick Farrell. I know him. He went to the States."

"Did he clear any of it?"

"Don't think so."

"Then I can claim it, right?"

"Yes. You can do that. Just hope Farrell doesn't come back within seven years and claim it back."

Johannah studied the various parcels marked in red. "I don't like this, Jim. It's so uncertain. I want to own the land. Could we buy forty acres, farther out from town?"

Johannah pointed to a small patch some nine miles west of Lucan.

"Look at this little one here."

"No, too far. I like the sound of this hundred acres. Why don't we just go and have a look at it? Get an idea of what's available."

Johannah glared at him. "I think we need to buy."

Jim ignored her. Vinnie held his peace.

They piled Johannah and Will in the cart and headed back out of town, out past the church and north along the Roman Line toward the land, four miles distant, excited anticipation giving a lightness to Jim's step.

"Can we just ask about a mortgage, Jim? See what they say."

"I know how that works with banks. It's the game they play. One missed payment and they take the farm away and sell it to the next man. But this is our land for the taking, Jo. Free land! Earned with our sweat."

"I'm not sure, Jim…"

"I'm sure," Jim told her. "I've never been so sure."

Johannah could not deny her misgivings; to claim someone else's land on a legal point, there were so many pitfalls. But on a beautiful day in early summer, passing fields of optimistic green with lofty trees towering overhead and the mesmerizing blue sky beyond, everything was possible, and God could not help but smile on their endeavours. And very soon they had arrived at the acreage.

"This is it!"

"The Farrell lot," Vinnie said, studying the map, impressed.

"The Donnelly lot, lad. Get it straight."

It was a most verdant time of the year and everything was lush, very green, a wall of trees, all they had dreamed of.

"Oh Jim. It's…beautiful."

Jim could hardly contain his excitement, looking at what would be their land. Was their land, from this day on. With an elaborate bow, he extended a hand to Johannah to help her from the cart.

"M'lady! Welcome to your kingdom."

Johannah laughed, took his hand and stepped down, holding Will in one arm.

"Thank you, m'lord."

She stared breathlessly into the wilderness they would tame together.

"There are a few trees, Jim."

His enthusiasm was not to be diminished.

"Ah, only a handful. Clear them out in no time, won't we, Vinnie?"

"Before you can turn around three times," Vinnie offered, trying to match his enthusiasm. "And we need the logs anyway."

From up the road, the squeak and rumble of wagon wheels long preceded the arrival of a grizzled, bare-headed young man in dirty overalls who was driving a team of oxen down the Roman Line. Jim waved to him and the man hauled back on the reins and brought the huge beasts and the cargo rig to a stop.

"Isn't it a beautiful day, sir?" Jim asked him, his heart made light with the finding of the land. "And that's a fine pair of animals you've got there."

"Thank you. Yes, they are."

"You got a farm close by then?"

The man gestured over his shoulder. "Fifty acres, one concession back."

"Good. Then we're your new neighbours. I'm Jim Donnelly, this is my wife, Johannah, and our friend Vinnie O'Toole. Oh, and young Will, the sprat."

The man stayed on the wagon seat but when the others came forward, he reached out enthusiastically to shake hands all around.

"James Keefe. Welcome to Lucan. So you bought Farrell's place?"

"It's mine now."

"Good. Never liked Farrell much. You got a couple trees there to keep you busy. Might want to borrow my beasts for moving logs and pulling stumps."

"I'd be much obliged."

"Come over when you get settled and need 'em. I own the farm out here and my brother owns the hotel across the way from St. Patrick's Church down the Roman Line, so you needn't be a stranger in either place. Good luck to you."

Keefe waved, gave a grunt to the oxen, a flick of the reins, and continued on his way.

"You see that? Only the first of many new friends. What do you say, Johannah, my love? Are we home?"

She could not resist his contagious enthusiasm and her smile confirmed that he had her.

"Let's make it so," she told him.

Beaming, Jim selected a new axe from the cart and strode across the ditch and up to a fine elm the width of a man's head. He glanced at the others with a significant grin, spit on his hands with no less reverence than a priest preparing the Mass, raised the blade over his shoulder and with a mighty swing, followed by the applause of Vinnie and Johannah, sliced deep into the first tree.

To Your Good Health

INSIDE KEEFE'S HOTEL was a line of shot glasses on the bar touching rims and filled by one long pour, with remarkably little spillage, and consumed almost as quickly by a line of patrons and the glasses replaced just so for another round. Jim and Vinnie were introduced by James Keefe to the tavern's owner, his brother Michael. The neighbours, all Catholic of course, gestured to them, each with beer or whiskey in their hands, greeting them with friendly faces while James Keefe went on introducing other patrons for the benefit of Jim and Vinnie.

"…these two ugly lads are the Feehleys, Pat and Joe. This individual is a Hogan by the name of Robert. The wee fella there is John Purtell and over there are the Kennedy brothers. The Kennedys breed like rabbits. No one can remember all their names. They're starting to give 'em numbers."

Jim was delighted to meet the men he would live among. He and Vinnie smiled, nodded and shook some hands.

"Jim Donnelly. Pleased to meet you all."

"Vincent O'Toole. How do you do?"

Just then a big red-faced man, John Carroll, came up to them. He had two men with him and Jim noticed that Keefe deferred to him, stepping back a little.

"Evening, Mr. Carroll."

"Hello, Keefe. Who's this, then?"

"Jim Donnelly, just over from Tipperary. And his friend Vincent. Bought the Farrell place."

Carroll shook Jim's hand, sizing him up.

"Really? The Farrell place. Good for you. Nice chunk of land. Did Pat give you a good deal?"

"Yes. A good deal."

"What would that be? Under eight hundred pounds?" he asked pointedly.

"Maybe."

Carroll studied him, then suddenly gave a generous laugh. "A man who doesn't want his business public. I respect that. Good luck to you with it. Let me know if I can ever help you out."

"Thank you."

A small, wiry man with a heavy moustache and a canvas cap walked into the bar. Carroll noticed him, gave him a moment to walk deeper into the bar and called him out.

"Thomas Dunn. Just the bollocks I was looking for."

Dunn looked up at Carroll in shock, then searched around for an avenue of escape, but Carroll's two men had stepped around behind to block his way. Dunn turned to face Carroll. In front of the other men present, Dunn stood up straight and assumed a level of dignity.

"You have no call to talk to me like that, John Carroll."

Carroll slapped him across the face with the back of his hand.

"Oh but I do, you see. You've been stealing my firewood again, haven't you?"

"No, I..."

"Don't lie to me, 'cause I found out what you done with it. That's the worst part. You sold a wagon load of my wood to that Protestant blacksmith, McBain."

"I didn't know he was Protestant..."

"With a name like McBain? You're a lying Blackleg!"

Jim had the strange feeling he had been through all this before, several thousand miles away, a Blackleg called out in a tavern.

"And you know what we do with Blacklegs. It's time for the barrel!"

Dunn's face went white. Carroll's two men grabbed him by the arms. Jim was strongly hoping that this wasn't what he thought it was. Vinnie looked at him askance.

Carroll turned to Jim. "Donnelly. Come out and see the fun."

Jim hesitated as Carroll waited for him at the door, but then in the interest of diplomacy, Jim followed him with Vinnie behind.

On the road outside the tavern, Jim's apprehensions were realized. The practice had been imported here in all its cruel detail, the punishment Jim and the Whiteboys had employed with such righteous enthusiasm in

Borrisokane. Carroll's men used the last of an armful of wilted wild rose briars with numerous long thorns to line the inside of a large beer barrel. Carroll's men escorted Dunn out, gagged, shirtless and with his hands tied tightly behind his back.

"So Dunn, you were warned, now weren't you?"

Dunn could not hide the terror in his eyes as Carroll's men forced him inside the barrel, quickly put the barrel top in place and began to secure it.

Despite himself, despite the promises made to Johannah, the rose barrel opened up the anger that still lived deep inside him. That anger he once focused so intensely on Magee, that deposit of hate bequeathed to him by all his forefathers since the days of Cromwell. Despite the prospect of a new life here, despite the love of a good wife and a child, despite having no real quarrel with any man in this country, least of all the poor wretch in the barrel, the desire to fight or to cause someone pain still stirred his blood. He was ashamed of it.

Carroll was watching him. "Have you seen this punishment before, then?"

"No," Jim told him, for it was none of Carroll's business if he had.

"It's rather poetic with the lovely, sweet-smelling roses causing such pain by the thorns, don't you think? Rather like a woman."

Carroll was pleased with his metaphor. Jim remained silent. Carroll's men turned the barrel on its side and they started rolling it down the dirt road. Dunn's muffled screams and curses could be heard from inside.

Vinnie turned to Jim, saying quietly, "This is horrible. So it is."

The patrons from the tavern watched the barrel roll, some grim, some amused. A short distance down the dirt road, the men turned the barrel and rolled it back. Jim exchanged a look with Vinnie. As it approached, the screams now reduced to moans, Jim stepped out to stand in the barrel's path, caught the rims in his hands and brought it to a stop. The men rolling it looked at him in surprise.

"What do you think you're doing, Donnelly?" Carroll asked him.

Just then came the sound of cantering hooves and Jim turned to see a substantial figure in a black constable uniform ride up to the men on the road. Jim watched them all shy away. They feared the newcomer. The big policeman, whose name Jim would find out was Constable Vincent Fitzhenry, dismounted.

"What's going on here?" He was a head taller than most of them. "Who's in the barrel?" He looked askance at the other witnesses. "Carroll? Kennedy?"

No one faced up to him. He stepped over to the closest of Carroll's men, took him by his shirt, twisted it with one gloved hand and pulled his face up close to his own.

"I asked a question."

The man gasped for breath. "It's Dunn." Muffled moans could be heard from inside the barrel, lying on its side. The policeman let go of Carroll's man.

"Get him out."

Other men from the tavern quickly pried the lid off. A bloody Dunn spilled out of the barrel and lay groaning among the roses on the dirt road, bloody pinpricks all over his face, back and shoulders. Two men helped him up to his feet.

"Dunn? I'll write up charges. Who ordered this?"

"No one, Constable Fitzhenry. I was cleaning the barrel and fell in. She started to roll is all."

"Along with the roses?"

"They were for my sweetheart."

Some of the men gave a muted laugh. Fitzhenry looked at Dunn in frustration.

"Why are you protecting them, Dunn? Tell me the truth. I'll arrest a few."

"'Twas my own fault, Constable."

Fitzhenry turned to Carroll.

"I'd take you in for assault, Carroll, if I thought I could make it stick. Next time, I promise you, I will charge you with something. All of you. It can't go on like this."

"But we're all being as good as lambs, Constable."

Fitzhenry gave Carroll a last look, then remounted.

"Keefe? Make sure Dunn gets cleaned up and send him home safe."

"Yes, Constable."

"No more of this. I warn you."

Then Fitzhenry rode away. Carroll and his men went back into the bar for drinks, as did the other patrons. Michael Keefe took Dunn into the kitchen to clean him up. Jim stayed outside a moment with Vinnie, unwilling to fall in with Carroll's crowd so easily.

"I thought I had left this kind of shite back in Tipperary, Vinnie."

"I don't know, Jim. It might be a new land but I don't think people change much."

"We're going to have to be careful."

James Keefe came back outside.

"Come on, Jim, Vinnie. Carroll's buying a round!"

Jim and Vincent followed Keefe inside.

Over the following days and weeks, Jim, Vinnie and Johannah cut a great number of sod bricks from a small open meadow on the land and then, using lumber to reinforce them, piled them to form the walls of a temporary hut. Johannah became quite skillful at the work. Her nails were broken and dirty, her apron stained with mud and she worked with little Will secured in a sheet on her back, but she was adept at piling the dirty sod. At the end of a day, she would collapse on the bed, aching and exhausted. She had never been so challenged, never worked so hard, but with the sod walls and a roof of poles, bark and oilcloths, they were building a house and a world. Johannah had never been so happy.

Jim and Vinnie opened up a hundred-foot-square clearing back from the road and planted some barley and corn. A smoky fire was constantly consuming the green trunks and branches. When the rains came, they quickly turned the raw dark earth of the new clearing into mud but it was a warm summer rain and they continued to work, their hands and clothing coated in dirt and their faces spattered. They washed and took water from a little stream that ran south through the property, and they dammed it with sod and branches to create a modest pool where they could bathe. Once, the summer rain turned torrential for almost a full day and it was impossible to work, so they all took shelter under the unfinished pieces of oilcloth and bark that was their roof. The brush fire was impossible to keep going and the little dam gave way in the swollen stream. On that day, they were wet and muddy and somewhat miserable as they looked out at the rain, but they were building the future.

"The rain comes, the rain goes," Vinnie said philosophically.

"One step at a time," Johannah offered.

"And the rain'll help that barley and corn," Jim said.

"Absolutely," Vinnie agreed. "On a summer day like today, my mother would make full use of this rain." Vinnie smiled at a memory. "She'd divide up a cake of soap and give us all pieces and send us out to wash our hair. If it kept up, we could soap up the clothes too and so we'd clean ourselves and the clothes. Once we pulled her outside with us all soapy and danced in the rain. She was laughing…"

Johannah had intuited from his stories that his mother had later re-married and moved in with a new man who did not want children, so Vinnie and his siblings had been thrown out and left homeless.

"You must miss her."

Vinnie looked out into the rain. "Yeah," he said finally. At that moment, there was a sudden increase in the downpour and the shelter of the makeshift roof proved marginal.

"Well?" Johannah held up a large white bar. "I've got the soap!"

Vinnie's face broke into a huge smile.

"Let's go," said Jim, holding baby Will, and all four of them ran out to wash and dance in the warm summer rain.

Jim and Vinnie finished the roof of their little house and before long, the humble hut was transformed into a small but dry and cozy cabin that they hoped would house them for their first couple of years of life in Canada. Johannah transplanted wild black-eyed Susans and Queen Anne's lace into beds outside the door with meadowlarks and red-winged blackbirds singing on sunny branches nearby. Jim was pleased to see Johannah add her homey touches to what he called "the estate," an inverted horseshoe over the door and makeshift curtains on the glass window Jim had bought in town. Inside the cabin, they had a table and chairs and a trunk, a small double bed Jim managed to build and a crib for Will. Jim had constructed an attached lean-to shed out of sod where Vinnie had established his own small bed and living quarters among the shovels and seed.

"It's not quite the Shelbourne," Vinnie said, referring to a luxury hotel he had once seen in Dublin, "but probably next best."

"Don't be expecting room service," Johannah warned him.

Together, they planted a few more late crops—potatoes, lettuce and three types of beans—in the truck patch, and Johannah grew to love working the earth with baby Will on her back. Jim and Vinnie built another sod shed for the pony and a pig, and a rough coop for a handful of chickens they bought from the Whalen farm just across the line. From

Jim, Johannah learned the messy business of killing and plucking a chicken and became very good with the hatchet.

"You sure you're not related to Dr. Guillotin?"

"That just may be so, so I'd watch myself if I was you."

Jim and Vinnie continued pushing back the forest one tree at a time.

Jim occasionally took the cart to town for supplies, but Johannah did not join him. Surprisingly she had not even gone to Mass yet but declared she would make up for it and God would forgive them. The weather had turned warm and sunny, and the summer flowers were in bloom, when Johannah finally declared her intention.

"We will all dress in our finest clothes and now go to St. Patrick's. This will be the all-important first impression that our family will make on the community. It will be the formal coming out for the Donnellys. We will all be on our best behaviour."

Society

As WIFE AND mother and mistress of the new Donnelly "estate," when Johannah remembered the high society coming-out party her aunt had arranged in London for her sixteenth birthday, with a jealous bevy of the daughters of earls and millionaires, all she could do was laugh at her current circumstances. She was the wife of a dirt-poor farmer four miles outside a little middle of nowhere town in Canada. If only she had Raffy and Lucy to laugh with now.

As they dressed in preparation for their first Mass, Jim shaved himself in a cracked hand mirror with Vinnie crowding in to comb his hair. Vinnie and Jim put on the good clean cotton shirts they had bought in town. Johannah had a new cotton dress that Jim said made her look very pretty. She checked the boys' presentation with a critical eye, straightening their collars and brushing off lint.

"You can never undo a first impression," Johannah told them again. "There…" She finished with them, then turned and looked at herself in the hand mirror, adjusting her hair, which she had put up in a tight bun, pinching her tanned cheeks to give them more colour, revealing what she defended as a healthy streak of vanity. Jim met her eyes as he helped her into the pony cart and she could see the pride in his eyes.

They could see St. Patrick's rapier-like spire two miles out of town. The new church had replaced a modest frame building that had burned down six years before. It was built much larger than the existing needs of the small Lucan community. The deacons and bishops reasoned that with the famine and troubles back in Ireland flooding the region with good, grateful Catholics, if you built a big church, the faithful would fill the pews and the offering plates.

Across the road, on the east side of the Roman Line, Keefe's two-storey wood frame hotel and tavern stood as if in defiance of pure Christian life and, from what Jim told Johannah and what she saw of it herself, many nights Keefe's boasted an even larger congregation than the church. But St. Patrick's ruled Sunday morning and as they made their way there for the ten o'clock service, people in their best clothes were approaching in carts and wagons and on foot from the road into the town and from the other concession lines that intersected there. Jim and Johannah, little Will and Vinnie arrived in their pony cart, tethered it in the shade to the whitewashed cemetery fence and entered the church, their eyes adjusting from the bright sunlight to the cool, still darkness of the sanctuary.

The inside of the church was even more impressive, even breath-taking to them, with golden icons and high ceilings that made the St. Patrick's back in Borrisokane seem cramped and quaint. Johannah was even tempted to refer to their new church as a "cathedral" but in truth it was not. One might even get away with calling it a basilica, for there was a certain roundness to the bay of the altar, but no, it was a church, and Johannah was happy to settle for that. And it was theirs.

The people of St. Patrick's welcomed the Donnelly family warmly that morning. They shook hands with many who greeted them before the service commenced, beginning with the congenial Keefes and their family members. They received nods and handshakes from the Feehleys, Kennedys, Carrolls and O'Connors, the men among them familiar faces Jim had met in Keefe's tavern. The priest, Father O'Brien, was an ancient, frail and pious man whose lined and sallow face suddenly melted into smiles as he greeted them.

"We were all wondering when you'd come to take the blessed sacrament with us."

"We're sorry, Father. We were just getting our things in order. Won't miss another Sunday," Johannah told him.

"Good, then. Welcome and we rejoice." Jim and Johannah exchanged a smile as the service began, the Latin words sounding like old lost friends, reawakening Johannah's spirituality, making her at home. She looked over at her husband and knew he was having the same thoughts. They had found the community they had hoped for.

After Mass they all piled aboard their little pony cart for an easy Sunday drive west into town, sightseeing the closed shops on Main Street and the stately Protestant homes in the tree-lined west end of Lucan. Jim gestured ahead toward a fine big white house with green trim and a large veranda and coach house behind.

"That's his place there, I think. Your Dr. Davis. That's how Porte described it. He said he might be back by now."

"It's beautiful. Let's go in, Jim. I'd love to see him again."

"I know he was good to you, Johannah, but I do worry…"

"I think I owe him my life, Jim. Please, let's say hello and thank him."

Just as Jim was about to turn in the driveway, three men came riding down the street toward them on horseback. Jim looked straight ahead and kept going past the Davis driveway.

"Aren't we going in?"

Jim did not answer. The three men rode past them, giving them a stern nod.

"Who is that?" Johannah asked him.

"John Carroll."

"I'd like to see Dr. Davis."

"Another time."

Johannah could see how wary, even intimidated, Jim felt.

"He's our friend. They may as well know. We have to show our colours, Jim."

"Not today," Jim told her and they turned north to make the loop back toward the Roman Line.

Jim finally felt there was great headway being made on their lot the morning Keefe brought his oxen to help him and Vinnie clear the stumps and logs. They truly were magnificent beasts, accomplishing more in two hours than two men would manage in two weeks. Their cloven hooves on stocky legs tromped and pawed and found firm footing below the slippery mud. A heavy chain was looped around one massive stump, wider than a man's arm is long, and the beasts strained to pull it from the ground. Keefe encouraged the animals, snapping a little whip over their heads, just to get their attention as never once did Jim see the lash fall on their dusty hides. Keefe had a deep affection for the lumbering behemoths.

"Hiyah! Hiyah! Haaaaaa!"

As it lifted, Jim and Vinnie chopped at the roots underneath to free the broad stump from its grip on the fertile ground. Both were aware there was a danger the big stump could fall back on them when they were underneath; there were stories of it happening more than once. Slowly the bulk of it was coming away, turning over and pulling free. Keefe eased off for a minute to rest himself and the big animals.

"I don't suppose we could just plant around the stumps?" Vinnie suggested.

"That'd be far too sensible," Jim concluded.

"You know what the dumb Irishman said when he was given free land?" Keefe asked them, wiping his sweaty neck with a sodden checkered handkerchief.

"What?"

"All this land…and the trees too!"

The three men laughed together. Jim took the moment in the hot sun to gaze around at his slowly growing muddy patch of cleared field.

"Another week and we'll have close to five acres to plant for next year."

"Aye. But I'll need you both after we're done for a week, putting up my barn."

"Done. Vinnie, why don't you stay the winter? Help with the planting in the spring."

"Well, I still have the mountains to see, but maybe they're best seen in summer."

"Good then."

Jim offered Johannah a wave as she arrived in the cart with lunch in a basket. She had driven across the cleared field and carried the young sleeping Will on her back.

"Just a few minutes, Jo. One last stump."

"Haaaa! Come on! Hiyah!"

Keefe snapped the whip over the oxen's heads. They strained their massive bodies against the chain again. The big stump came up a little more and Jim and Vinnie went under again to chop at the thick roots. Vinnie took a few more swings to cut them through or pull them free, but the roots were slow to submit.

Johannah sat watching them work. She had set up a generous lunch of sandwiches for the three of them on a split log, with bread made in her new clay and stone baking oven Jim had built, lettuce from the garden and a boiled chicken she had killed that morning.

"This damn stump's holding on for dear life! Maybe if we… tickle it," Vinnie made a goofy face and wiggled his fingers as if to do so and they laughed at Vinnie and the idea of a ticklish tree stump.

"Hiyah! Come on!"

The stump turned up further still and they continued to chop away at the last of the roots underneath, now in earnest. The oxen heaved. The big root moved up even more and almost surrendered its grip. They stepped back to safety from under the stump, but then in a split second, the chain snapped like a gunshot. Jim shouted a warning and ducked down as the stump settled and the long, freed chain sliced horizontally through the air back toward them. It missed Jim, but Vinnie was not so quick. The chain struck him across the head, knocking him off his feet, and he fell to the ground onto his back.

"Vinnie!" Johannah stood up.

Johannah and Jim both raced to him. The boy lay unconscious, his body inert, his head bloody and deeply dented and damaged by the iron chain.

"Vinnie?"

Jim wrapped Vinnie's head in his shirt, lifted him into the pony cart and he and Johannah, still carrying Will on her back, rushed him down the long Roman Line into town at a fast trot. The four miles into town seemed interminable with Vinnie moaning and writhing and Jim shouted at the pony in frustration. On the main street of Lucan, they arrived outside Dr. Davis's house.

"Doctor!" Jim shouted out to the house.

He picked Vinnie up—he felt as light as a child in his arms—and climbed the stairs to the veranda.

"Dr. Davis!"

Davis opened the door and there was a moment of surprise and pleasure.

"Johannah…Jim!"

"There's been an accident…"

Davis took one look at Vinnie's injuries, held the door open and gestured Jim inside.

"Through here. Easy now. Be gentle with him."

Jim entered the coolness of Dr. Davis's house and into his office and examining room. Johannah followed them in with Will now in her arms.

Jim laid Vinnie's trembling body on the table and stood back beside Johannah. Vinnie's eyes flickered open as Davis inspected the wounds. The damage to his head was substantial, his skull fractured, and he was losing blood, limbs shaking involuntarily. Davis applied a gauze bandage to stop the blood flow.

"Talk to him. Keep him responding."

"Vinnie? Can you hear me? Wake up, Vinnie!"

Suddenly Vinnie's eyes became clear for a moment.

"Lost my boot. Where's my boot, Jim? Dog musta got it."

"Vinnie? You'll be all right. Can you hear me?"

His eyes remained clear.

"Yes. S'alright. I can feel the rain now."

Vinnie's shaking slowly calmed. He sighed. His body relaxed. His eyes became fixed. Jim looked at Dr. Davis, who felt for a pulse. His expression confirmed their fears. Vinnie was dead.

Jim put his arms around a trembling Johannah, who now began to cry, and Jim with her. They stared down at Vinnie's face, normally so animated and expressive, now so chilling in its stillness, and they could not speak to comfort each other.

Later Dr. Davis's housekeeper brought them tea in the cool, darkened dining room and they spoke about Vinnie as they waited for the undertaker.

"He was like a little brother or even a son," Jim said.

"So many dreams," Johannah remembered.

In the midst of this grief, Davis expressed his pleasure to see them again. He asked about their travels and they described the homestead they had built so close and apologized for not having come to see him. He did a quick examination of young baby Will, finding him to be in very good health. Jim was going to ask the doctor about the level of conflict between Catholics and Protestants in the town, struggling to find a polite way into the issue, but was interrupted by the arrival of the mortician.

They buried Vincent Matthew O'Toole in St. Patrick's cemetery two days later. Jim, along with two Keefes, two Kennedys and Dr. Davis, was a pallbearer at the funeral. His jaw set, his eyes brimming, Jim lifted and carried the rough coffin to take the boy to the open grave and his final resting place. Johannah walked directly behind holding baby Will, and behind her followed two dozen members of the congregation, and they all gathered around the grave. Before Father O'Brien began, John Carroll came up to Jim to ask about Dr. Davis. Johannah and Davis overheard the question.

"What is that Protestant doing here on consecrated ground?"

"We invited him," Jim told Carroll. "He did all he could for Vinnie."

"He is not welcome here."

Dr. Davis made a move as if to leave but Jim gently took the doctor's arm to stop him.

"He's as welcome as you, Carroll. It is right that he should be here."

"He is our friend, Mr. Carroll," Johannah added.

"Your friend?" Carroll turned to Johannah, amused, his little eyes excited.

Johannah's anger at this man rose to match her grief. "It's hardly the time for this, Mr. Carroll. We're at this moment putting a fine young lad in the ground."

"So clear off," Jim told him, loud enough for many of the people gathered to hear, and Johannah touched his arm to calm him and keep his hands from turning into fists. Carroll studied both Jim and Johannah in silence for a moment with that unsettling look of amusement, then turned and walked away before the priest began.

Vinnie's casket was lowered into the grave and Jim and Johannah, Dr. Davis and others of the parish listened to the old priest's voice, which though sincere, shook with age, saying the words that would send Vinnie's young soul to heaven. Johannah couldn't control her tears and Jim would not look up at her for the same reason.

"...we therefore commit his body to the ground; earth to earth, ashes to ashes, dust to dust...in sure and certain hope of the resurrection to eternal life."

Johannah thought of all that they had been through, all the words spoken at so many funerals. And now Vinnie had been so suddenly and brutally taken away from them by cruel happenstance. Death could come from a thousand places, at a moment's notice, without reason or sense, with cruel, inexplicable intent. But human life came from only one source: a woman's body. This was Johannah's power, she only fully realized then, a power over life, and she made the resolution, in the face of death, to wield that power to its full extent. To wage war against death by creating life and creating life abundantly.

Seven Young Devils

JIM CRIMPED OVER the final nail in the final shoe of his three-year-old mare, let the hoof of the congenial beast go back down onto the ground and straightened his sore back. It had been six, almost seven years since they had found the land and claimed it. Years of prosperity and babies. Jim watched with affection as his four-year-old son, Robert, fifth born among the Donnelly boys, gathered eggs in the hen house. He was crouched unmoving in the straw, staring intently at a hen on her nest. The bird stared back at him. Jim and Johannah knew Robert, fair haired with eyes as blue as the sea, was not the brightest child—in fact, Johannah admitted he was "slow"—but he was well liked and defended by his mother and brothers. No classmate would have dared say a negative word about him and expect to go unbeaten. Robert's pleasure was to bring in the eggs, unbroken, to his mother. And at this, he was skilled. The hen finally gave her squawk and Jim watched as his son pushed the bird gently off the new egg. Robert laughed with success and picked up the final warm, wet egg, placing it gently in the basket with several more. He left the chicken coop with his basket and walked with great care and no mishap up to the farmhouse to receive his kiss from Johannah.

Jim took a moment to look around at his lively kingdom. Their farm had expanded substantially in the years they'd lived here, the old sod hut replaced by a large log house well back from the road, much of it built in one day by friends and neighbours, and a small barn with animals—six hungry pigs, two horses and a cow, in addition to the twelve chickens in the hen house—with full fifteen acres cleared. Johannah had produced seven young rough-and-tumble Donnelly boys who, except for the two very youngest, all tended the animals and did chores. The boys made for a future of good hands on the farm and Jim knew Johannah loved them all more than life itself. But he also knew Johannah hungered for a daughter. He felt her need and was willing to keep trying his best.

Dr. William Davis had overseen Johannah's pregnancies and delivered four of the boys, two local midwives handling the others. The disagreement with John Carroll over the Donnellys' friendship with Dr. Davis had not amounted to much. They had good friends now in the community, the Keefes and the Whalens and some of the Kennedys, the Portes and O'Connors and Feehleys. Jim had been quietly asked to join certain political groups of far different stripes—the Conservative Tories or the Liberal Grits, the Catholic League or the Protestant Orange Order, the Tipperary Brotherhood or the Irish Benevolent Society—and had with Johannah's approval politely, but firmly, refused each one, and had so far been left alone. He and Johannah had witnessed several brutal fights outside the bars in Lucan while passing by but Jim had not raised a fist in anger in more than seven years and Johannah was proud of him.

Though Jim loved all his boys he knew his first-born, Will, remained his favourite. Now seven years old, a strong, hard-working red-headed lad with a teasing sense of humour, Will had become a good, natural leader for the others. They had saved money to have a special boot made for him in London for his club foot and now the limp was much less noticeable.

Will and his next-youngest brother, James, were up in the open door of the loft winching up bundles of hay from the wagon to store in the top of the barn. It would dry well under the good roof for winter feed. James enjoyed a joke and his father could hear his laughter at something Will had said. Pat, who never stopped talking, and the silent, brooding Tom were fighting over a long-handled shovel Jim had been using to dig post holes for a new pigpen.

"Give it to me. I had it first. Leave it alone. Don't! Daaaaa! He bit me!"

It was true; Tom had sunk his teeth into Pat's hand, breaking the skin.

"Tom! No biting. And give Pat the shovel."

Pat pulled the shovel away from him. Tom tried to kick him, screeched and threw dirt at him as Pat walked away. Tom would need a little guidance, Jim realized.

Over in the shadow of the porch Jim observed John, the wise one, "the bookworm," already wearing his own specs, his nose buried in a school book, off in his own world. Jim mused on the mystery of how, though each child had come from the same seed, they all developed their own distinct characters.

Johannah stood high in her boots in the centre of the small corral Jim had built beside the barn, holding the lead on the two-year-old mare she was training. Jim watched her as she snapped a long whip at the horse's heels. The mare cantered in a circle with five-year-old Michael in the saddle. The boy had curly dark hair and an angelic face and he rode well, posting easily, and Jim could see Johannah found pleasure in the boy's fearlessness and natural skills, even at this young age. Johannah kept the lead very loose to allow Michael control.

Here was the best thing in Jim's life, this woman, and no question. It all began and ended with her. What she was doing with a man like him, he never quite understood, but he thanked God and didn't question it too deeply. Sure it was one of God's mysteries. She was smiling now and when she did, it seemed to him like the heavens opening up.

"That's it. Good, Michael. Very good. Jim! Have a look at Michael."

All the boys stopped their activities for a moment and they watched Michael, who rode with a serious formality, reins held thus, posting smoothly with the horse, angle of the body just so, horse and boy moving as one.

"Nice job, Mikey!" Will led his brothers in applause for Michael's skills and the fourth-born of the Donnelly boys was clearly proud of himself.

"We'll have you riding in the Royal Winter Fair," his father called out to him, thinking how much like his mother the boy rode. Johannah brought the mare to a stop, lifted Michael off and gave him a hug, then lowered him to the ground and followed him out of the corral toward his father.

"And the beast's limp is gone. Your liniment with the linseed worked well, hah?" Jim complimented her.

"Yes, it did. Swelling's gone. We should make up a batch and bottle it, sell it in town or at the fair. That's the ticket," she said enthusiastically. "Let's bottle some for the fair."

Johannah's voice trailed off as she looked over to the road. Jim followed her gaze to see that two men and a boy had arrived on horseback. They stayed out at the road for a moment. The Donnellys' black dog, Butch, began to bark a challenge at them and Jim called him back. Jim recognized Constable Fitzhenry, but didn't know the other man, who was pointing in a sweeping gesture and talking excitedly to Fitzhenry. The three rode in to the roundabout in front of the house and dismounted.

Their hearts beating a little faster, Jim and Johannah walked over together to see what the strangers wanted. The boys all watched in silence. Fitzhenry addressed them and spoke the words that had haunted their worst dreams for almost seven years.

"Hello, Jim. Mrs. Donnelly. This man is Pat Farrell. He claims he owns this land."

They both stared at Farrell. Johannah turned to Jim and saw his face was as pale as a winter moon. He responded, his voice quiet, intense.

"That's a lie. We've been here seven years. We've done the clearing. This land is mine now. It's the law."

Farrell held up documents in his hand, his eyes a little wild. "This land is mine."

Johannah went forward to take the pages. At first, Farrell resisted.

"Let her see," the constable directed him, and Farrell reluctantly passed the documents to Johannah. She began to look them over.

"There's my registration and there's your claim file. You've been here exactly six years, ten months. The squatter law don't apply 'til seven years. So now you gotta clear out...squatter."

Jim stared at Farrell, clearly too furious to speak. He was a hair away from violence. Fitzhenry seemed to sense this and stood purposefully between them.

"Well, we can't settle this today. You'll have to go to court, Jim."

"Fine by me," said Farrell. "The law's on my side. I'm claiming my land, Donnelly. And you're getting out."

Johannah was thinking, Fitzhenry or not, if a gun or an axe were close by Jim's hand, that fool Farrell would be in peril. The rhyme even made her smile for a moment, mirth in the midst of calamity. Then the darker thought came, strong and irresistible: *I told you, I told you. If we had a mortgage, at least we'd have a deed.* But she buried this thought for now. That fool Farrell was rambling on, oblivious to the peril at hand.

"You're nothing but a squatter. And from what I hear, a Blackleg."

From whom would he have heard the label "Blackleg"? Johannah wondered who his local agents were. And now she was sure Fitzhenry's presence was the only thing keeping Jim from Farrell's throat.

The constable stepped in. "Come on, now. Let's go, Farrell. Jim, you'll get your date notice of the assizes in London. They'll sort it out."

Farrell was talking to his son. "You see, Billy boy? I told you the land was beautiful. We'll build a bigger barn and clear another twenty acres."

Farrell's young son looked at Jim's face and said quietly to his father, "Let's go, Da."

Farrell, his sensible son and Fitzhenry mounted up, turned and rode away, back down the Roman Line toward town. Jim and Johannah stood there watching them depart, letting it all sink in. Jim's face was now beet red.

"He will never take my land."

Johannah bit her tongue 'til it bled.

First Justice

IN THE COURT of assizes in London, Province of Canada, the magistrate named McLeod hammered his worn gavel to re-establish order in the traditionally unruly courtroom. Big Constable Fitzhenry was there both to give evidence and provide security along with other officers. All Johannah could do was watch as Jim and Pat Farrell angrily faced each other. The courts being a great source of entertainment, friends of both men had come to see what would happen. The Donnellys had the Keefe brothers and the O'Connors and two Kennedys. Johannah was surprised to see John Carroll in the courtroom. And why was he seated with Farrell's supporters? But then, maybe she was not so surprised. It made sense to her now.

Taking the stand, Farrell stated his case as crudely as he had at the farm. Jim was so full of emotion, he couldn't speak in response and Johannah had to come forward as his proxy.

"My Lord, Mr. Farrell waited years until we had cleared much of the good land. He had his spies watching as we increased the worth of the property several times over. Now, days before the property becomes legally ours, he makes his claim."

As the unruly audience responded loudly for both parties, weary Judge McLeod hit the gavel again.

"Silence or I will empty the courtroom. Mr. Farrell? When did you become aware of Mr. Donnelly squatting on the land?"

"I had no idea Mr. Donnelly was squatting until my friend John Carroll"—Carroll nodded to the judge—"wrote to me explaining the situation only weeks ago and up I comes to sort it out immediately."

Johannah had to interrupt. "Mr. Carroll knew we were there six years ago!"

Fitzhenry again stayed between Jim and Farrell. Farrell pointed a finger at Jim. "The law's on my side and I knows the law!"

"Quiet!" McLeod shut him down, his patience gone. "My judgment is this: of the hundred acres, fifty will go to Jim Donnelly and fifty to Pat Farrell, including equal portions of the cleared land as determined by a court surveyor and equal frontage on the Roman Line. Donnelly keeps the existing house and buildings. Deeds will be issued to both. Now accept this fair ruling and find peace between yourselves."

Johannah was so deeply relieved her eyes teared up. They had secured fifty acres and the buildings. No one could question their ownership. But Jim was furious and Fitzhenry kept his place between the two men and their supporters. Jim leaned around Fitzhenry toward Farrell.

"You son of a bitch!"

"You stinking squatter."

Fitzhenry raised his arm to hold back Farrell, who wanted to go for Jim.

The judge was done. "Clear the courtroom!"

Muttering about the crazed bunch of Irishmen inhabiting his courtroom, Judge McLeod left the dais and slammed the office door behind him. Fitzhenry and the clerks encouraged the people to vacate the room

Johannah put her arms around Jim. "We won, Jimmy! We have the house and barn and fifty acres and no one can ever take it away from us. We'll have a deed!"

Jim glared at the departing Farrell.

"He stole my land."

Jim drove the wagon back up the Roman Line in brooding silence and Johannah remained quiet at his side. The buckboard was only a few weeks old, with springs and new steel wheel bearings that made for a comfortable ride and a new tawny gelding they had bought to pull it. They rode past the pleasant green fields of their neighbours on a warm summer's day, but Jim could not enjoy the trip for the dark cloud that enveloped him. He knew that logically Johannah was right. All told, with fifty acres free and clear, they had done pretty well as squatters in seven years, but he was not thinking logically. All he could see was the fifty acres he had lost, the acreage he had cleared, the field where Vinnie's blood had been spilled. It wasn't right. It took him back to the emotions of Magee's injustices on the Cavendish estate, to when his father had killed the ponies and then himself. To when they threw his people off the land so cows could graze. Cows could eat while Irish children starved.

Amid his anger and recriminations Jim realized that, just like him, Johannah had been waiting and worrying unspoken those seven years, and thinking they were almost safe when that man showed up. Jim had failed her and himself—it was the Donnelly curse—and no words, logical or placating, could make it better.

So, in the spring of '58, the Donnellys hoped Farrell would build his house off over the hill and behind the trees as a sane man would do, but no. Pat Farrell made the decision to build his house on his fifty acres as close as possible to their property line, so painfully close to the Donnellys' own house it seemed you could almost touch his building by leaning out their downstairs window. Perhaps there was logic in this, for if one house was set on fire, it was likely the other would burn too, providing mutual protection against arson.

Farrell hired a team of men to first quickly build a fence on the lot line and then to put up the framing in the new fashion of house building. Then Farrell worked slow and alone with his young boy, Billy, boarding it in, pounding away at all hours, every day. It was like water torture, each a hammer blow to Jim's head, announcing the theft of his fifty acres. Jim, and sometimes some of the boys, would stand out there at the lot line and glare at Farrell, who didn't seem to mind the attention at all. Johannah had no doubt the trouble would escalate sooner or later, like watching a nasty rainstorm coming at them and not much anyone could do about it.

Farrell had just installed a brand-new window in the house facing the Donnellys, and it was like a red flag to a bull. When the inevitable smash occurred, both Johannah and Farrell ran outside of their houses to see Jim and a couple of his boys standing close to the property line. Jim looked up at the sky, smiled at Farrell and held out a flat palm. "Hail," was what he said.

"You bastard, Donnelly. You'll pay for it."

That night Johannah spoke sternly to Jim in private. "This is childish and I'm surprised at you."

"It's not my fault."

"What kind of example are you setting for the boys?"

"They are learning to stand up for their rights."

"The right to harass your neighbour? Jim, we have to make peace. Do you hear me?"

"I'll think about it."

The next week Farrell was digging out stumps for his truck patch. Keefe had offered his oxen, but Farrell had decided on dynamite, "the lazy man's choice" as Jim declared. The noisy blasts started at six a.m. and permeated their day at regular intervals. After two days of this, putting everyone on edge, Johannah heard a gunshot just outside the house. Jim was standing with his rifle and there was a bullet hole in a tree over Farrell's head. Will, James and Tom were with him, all quite amused. Jim pointed to the tree and explained to Farrell, "Crows."

"I'm going to get the law on you, Donnelly."

"No law against hunting crows."

That evening they were eating dinner at the big table out in the summer kitchen where it was cooler. Jim was talking to his sons as he tucked into his chicken dinner.

"I'll never forget the look on his face. He thought for sure I was about to finish him off."

The brothers looked from their father to their mother, aware of the latter's disapproval, smiling at each other like guilty schoolboys.

"Can't he take a joke?" Will asked.

"You were just playing with him," Michael offered.

"No law against scaring off crows," James repeated, giggling.

"Eat your dinner," Johannah told them all.

Will made the sound of a rifle firing and they all laughed.

Johannah's anger got the best of her. "All right! I've had enough of this, Jim! You made me a promise there would be no more of this over here. No more feuding. The fight with Farrell has got to stop! Now!"

Jim looked slightly embarrassed for a moment but then he answered with a broader conviction: "It'll stop when Farrell gives me my land back."

Johannah threw down her knife and fork, breaking her dinner plate, the gravy flowing onto the oilcloth. They were all listening now.

"You've got your land, Jim. It's plenty and you'll not get any more. You leave this thing with Farrell alone, now! Or you're the biggest fool God ever breathed life into."

Just then there was a dynamite explosion much bigger and closer than the others. The plates and glasses on the table rattled. Jim stood up, threw down his napkin and went out into the backyard. They all followed. Outside they found a stump very close to the property line had been blasted into pieces and the roof of the Donnelly chicken coop just on their side of the lot line had been blown off. A dozen chickens were flying and running in panic. Farrell was standing on his property, a smile on his face.

"Stumps," he said. "Sorry about that."

Jim made as if he would go after him. "You'll pay for that, Farrell." But Johannah grabbed his arm.

"Just stop this! Both of you." She gave equal attention to Farrell. "You're behaving like children. An embarrassment to your own! You have to stop."

Johannah turned away and went back in the house, slamming the door behind her. Chastised for a moment, Jim and Farrell then glared at each other as the Donnelly boys began to scramble around the yard, rounding up the liberated chickens.

After the dynamiting of the chicken coop and Johannah's condemnation, there were a few days of peace. But then, Farrell's drinking water from his well turned bad. He and the boy went fishing with a bailing hook in the depths of the well and caught a rotted cow's head some days old. Farrell came to the Donnelly door with the ripe evidence, his poor son beside him throwing up on their flower bed. It was Johannah who opened the door and Farrell called out past her.

"Donnelly! Donnelly, you son of a bitch. I'm going to kill you."

Jim was lying low in the summer kitchen after this, his latest harassment of Farrell. Johannah answered for him.

"You can't be uttering threats like that on our doorstep, Mr. Farrell, unless you want to be prosecuted."

Farrell left soon after and a couple of hours later, a weary Constable Fitzhenry stood on the property line with Jim and Farrell, each on his side. Farrell's son was beside his father looking worried. Will and Johannah stood with Jim. Farrell pulled from a sack the rotted cow's head, still on the hook and rope for display, as if this fully explained the entire circumstance. The rest of them took a step back to breathe.

"It's from the cow he butchered last week. See the spot on her ear. That's his cow. I want him charged with poisoning and vandalism and attempted murder!"

"He was the one who threatened to kill me," Jim told Fitzhenry. "We all heard him. I want him charged."

Johannah recognized Fitzhenry's substantial patience was wearing very thin.

"I'll have to charge you with something, Jim."

"He can't prove anything. You charge *him* with making death threats, and also stealing my land while you're at it!"

Just then they all became aware of a lone figure approaching them on a donkey along the muddy Roman Line. The rider wore a wide-brimmed straw hat and the clerical collar of a priest. He was about sixty, not a young man, and he wore a pleasant, benign expression as he made his way toward them. The priest brought the donkey to a stop and they all said their respectful greetings to him. Farrell took off his hat.

The priest smiled and replied, "Good morning to you all. Are you having a difficulty here?"

Jim started. "This thief..."

Farrell cut him off, "This maniac has been driving me..."

"QUIET!" Fitzhenry reasserted his position of authority, embarrassed in front of the cleric. "I'm sorry, Father. It's a land dispute."

"A land dispute. I see. My name is Father John Connolly, originally of Tipperary. I was for many years at Notre-Dame in Montreal. I am now the new priest at St. Patrick's."

"Oh, Father! Welcome!" Johannah exclaimed, stepping forward. "Father O'Brien must be relieved you've come. He's been under the weather in recent months. Thanks be to God." She turned to glare at Jim and Farrell. "It'll be a blessing to have a little fresh divine intervention here."

Father Connolly seemed perplexed by Johannah's outspoken interruption and turned back to the men.

"Well, I'm not sure what your dispute involves but I've come to invite you all to my first Mass tomorrow. I have a special message that may inspire you. I do hope you'll be there. I'll look for you all."

"Yes, certainly, Father," Farrell responded.

"Yes, Father. Of course," Jim told him.

"Good. Good day, then."

"Good day, Father!"

Johannah took a couple of steps as if to follow him, and with Fitzhenry standing firmly between Jim and Farrell, they all watched as Father Connolly continued his slow journey on up the Roman Line without a backward look.

"Well, maybe the Father's special message can work a miracle between you two. In the meantime I'm ordering you both not to speak or be within a hundred feet or even look at each other until after Mass tomorrow or so help me, I'll arrest you both. Do you agree?"

Fitzhenry looked each man in the eye and reluctantly, each man nodded. Fitzhenry turned to Johannah.

"Can you see to that, Johannah?"

"If I have to lock him in the broom closet."

Homily

AT ST. PATRICK's Church the next morning, the old pump organ, the only thing saved from the original frame structure when it burned down, was heard playing "Nearer, My God, to Thee" as the last stragglers hurried into the packed sanctuary to attend Father Connolly's first mass. The Donnelly family found themselves sitting across the aisle from Pat Farrell and his son, Billy. Farrell and Jim exchanged hostile sidelong glances. When the organ stopped, Father Connolly began with a gentle greeting and then had the congregation sing two old hymns back to back, which he led in an enthusiastic tenor. He moved quickly then to his homily, for which there was much anticipation. He began quietly with a sense of candour and sincerity that had all of them leaning forward to listen.

"Good Catholics of Lucan...I have been sent here among you with a mission from the archdiocese. A mission of peace. Consider the word, 'peace.' It is a word synonymous with the teachings of our Lord. With how we are meant to be. With how we are meant by the Divine to carry out our relationships with one another. But here in Biddulph Township, we are not as we are meant to be. Biddulph Township is not a place of peace." Father Connolly's voice then rose with conviction. "Biddulph Township has become notorious for its violence and crime. Arson, assault, theft, drunkenness and brawling in the taverns. I am afraid that the hand of God will fall on Biddulph, if you do not repent. The archdiocese wants peace brought to this parish and in this, I will be God's instrument."

Jim smiled and in a low voice said to Johannah, "That'll keep him busy."

She shushed him.

Father Connolly set his critical gaze on Jim for a moment, distracted by his mumble, then he continued in a calm voice.

"So it is time for change, and you must change your ways and you will change your ways. I know you will."

Father Connolly's volume rose again with emotion and all were startled by his sudden passion: "In the name of almighty God, don't you realize, each time you lift a hand against another Catholic...each time you cheat or insult or steal from another Catholic, you hammer the nails deeper into our Lord's hands and feet? You thrust that cruel spear deeper into his side. Each time you transgress against a brother or sister of the Holy Mother Church, you might as well tear the bloody, beating heart out of the breast of the Christ and throw it in the dirt!"

The breathless congregation, foremost Johannah and Jim, all sat wide-eyed, listening to this florid imagery. The pews creaked as people shifted uncomfortably and cleared their throats in the silence before Connolly's eyes narrowed and his voice dropped to begin speaking again.

"These acts of violence will not be tolerated in my parish. And anyone who perpetrates these acts will be my enemy and the enemy of Jesus Christ. Over the next few days, I hope to visit each one of you and I expect to hear and see a desire for peace, a devotion to the Holy Spirit and obedience to the Holy Mother Church."

The congregation stared at him, each man, woman and child feeling the intended fear of God.

After the service, outside the church, Johannah watched from a distance as Pat Farrell hurried to speak to the new priest. John Carroll was with him, their manner obsequious, talking with bowed heads and folded hands. She almost laughed out loud at their inauthentic behaviour but it seemed to please the priest.

Johannah looked to find Jim chatting in a boisterous manner to the Keefes and Whalens, all of them joking and laughing. It was a bright sunny day and as she watched him, she went back to her confirmation day so many years ago outside St. Patrick's in Borrisokane, and Jim with his silly faces and walking the cemetery wall, her saving him from the bull. And then the kiss she gave him, which bound their hearts, yet also sent her away. She realized again that as coarse and childish as he was with this Farrell business, and as irreverent on this Sunday morning, with his sad laughing eyes, she loved the man deeply. Couldn't help herself.

Her pleasant reverie was interrupted as she saw Father Connolly listening gravely to Farrell as he gestured toward her husband, obviously supplying a long list of sins. Johannah was very aware that even though she and Jim had been awarded their half of the land, since the court ruling many in the community—those who wanted to—saw them as "squatters," and beneath them. The priest was key to her family's standing in the community. They would have to work hard to win Father Connolly to their side.

Later that very afternoon, Father Connolly arrived at their farm in a heavy coat, scarf and wide-brimmed hat and climbed off his lowly mount. Their dog, the black mongrel named Butch, ran out and began to bark and growl at him, as was his natural tendency.

"Go away!"

The barking and growling continued until Butch grabbed his pant leg under the cassock and pulled. The material tore.

"He's here!" Will called out. He had been on lookout for the priest. Johannah then peered out the small kitchen window to witness the altercation.

"Jesus, Mary and Joseph..." Johannah said under her breath.

She stormed out of the house just in time to see Connolly take a vicious swing at the dog with his walking stick.

Connolly started to yell: "Help me! Help me!"

"Butch! Leave him!" Johannah turned and called back into the house. "Jim! The Father's here!"

Jim and a few of the boys came out to see what the barking and yelling was about.

A whistle from Jim and the dog sat down obediently. Johannah hurried out to the priest.

"Oh Father, I'm so sorry." She looked at Jim, urging him to say something.

"Yes, Father. We're so sorry."

"What a welcome!" the priest said in exasperation. "I'm sure St. Francis himself would have trouble with that cur."

"He's very friendly once he knows you."

"My inclination to know him better is not strong."

Johannah took the arm of the flustered man.

"We're all so sorry. Come inside. I'll make you a nice cup of tea and mend your trousers."

They served Father Connolly tea in their front room. The seven boys all sat crowded against each other, heads bowed as the priest said the blessing, stealing looks at him, a strange visitor to their home. Jim, Johannah and Will sat nearest to him in the cramped room, polite and smiling.

"In the name of the Father, Son and Holy Ghost, bless us, oh Lord, and these Thy gifts which of Thy bounty we are about to receive through Christ our Lord, Amen. In the name of the Father, Son and Holy Ghost."

Will led the others to cross themselves properly and say the "Amen" in unison, which pleased their mother. Johannah poured tea for Father Connolly and offered corn biscuits and gooseberry jam. He had taken the pants off in the small bedroom and now sat wrapped in a towel as she carefully mended the torn leg of his pants with black thread. After the initial business with the dog, Johannah was thinking it was going well.

"Father, we're so pleased you've come to take over St. Patrick's. As much affection as we had for Father O'Brien, the parish was becoming too much for him at his age."

"Yes, he deserves his rest."

"Your donkey seems a healthy animal," Jim continued in a conversational way. "How does she ride?"

"She is a vexation. I don't know how Father O'Brien put up with her. I plan to take extra offerings to buy a horse."

"We have a couple of animals that could be suitable," Johannah suggested, glancing at a surprised and shocked Jim, but then didn't want to press the point so as to look opportunistic.

"The gift of a horse would be very well received," Father Connolly said eagerly. She knew this suggestion of a gift would not go down well with Jim and they fell into silence for a moment. She searched for something to say to please the priest and in the giddiness of having his undivided attention a powerful idea just came to her out of the blue.

"You know, we have sometimes thought our first-born, Will, could make a fine man of the cloth." She gestured toward Will, who failed to hide his absolute shock at her offering. "He reads and speaks well, has an agile mind. Perhaps you could mentor him for the priesthood..."

Will and his father exchanged alarmed glances. Johannah purposefully did not look at Will, who was now staring at her and she suspected would sooner have cut off his left arm than submit to training to become a Catholic priest. And yet, for some reason she continued down that path.

"He does have a nurturing manner and…"

Father Connolly interrupted her. "I'm sure the idea has some merit but I have come with a more important concern we must address first, Mrs. Donnelly."

Will breathed out in relief that his mother's wild offer was not pursued. Jim and Johannah waited to hear what the priest had to say.

"I've been told that you have certain friends. Protestant friends. A Dr. Davis for one."

"Yes. Dr. Davis is a good man."

Father Connolly's voice developed a lecturing tone.

"A good man, you say? I fear many Catholics have fallen away from their duties, from their obligations concerning the Holy Church. Just because we have come to a new land doesn't mean we can renege on what is required of us. It is so very important you recognize that all Catholics must be united in our struggle against them."

Johannah was puzzled for a moment. "Against 'them'? Against… Protestants?"

He stared at her, surprised that it was not crystal clear. "Yes. Of course. Among their many thousands of transgressions against us, I remind you of the martyrdom of the blessed Father Sheehy ninety-two years ago this year in Tipperary. I don't have to remind you he was executed at the hands of Protestant politicians and clergy. We cannot just go on as if nothing happened!"

Johannah finished the stitching of the trousers, knotted and bit off the thread. Jim was sorting his way through this.

"Dr. Davis has delivered most of our children. He saved my wife's life."

The priest turned to him, his eyes burning.

"You let him deliver your children? They killed the blessed Sheehy. They hanged him and then before he died cut his body into four parts with axes. They sawed off his head and placed it on a stake on the turret at Clonmel where it was ordered to remain for twenty years. We can never allow ourselves to forget."

The wide-eyed boys were fascinated by the gory imagery. Jim was listening and nodding slightly. Although the priest's attention was on Jim, Johannah felt the need to reply. "Yes, but…the Protestants here had nothing to do with that, Father."

Her conciliatory response only fuelled the priest's emotions. He glared at her, then turned back to Jim.

"Protestants are an abomination to the Holy Church. Do you not remember your history? How they invaded us and murdered us and defiled our women and took our property. We were forbidden to read and write, to say the Mass, to own a gun or a horse, or to vote! We were made slaves in our own land!"

"Yes! Yes, slaves in our own land! It's true," Jim agreed.

"Yes, Father, terrible things were done," Johannah said. "But that was all back in Ireland. Surely Jesus himself would want there to be peace between us now…here."

Connolly turned his full attention toward her, his shock complete. "Are you saying that you can better interpret the mind of our Lord…than me?"

"No, no, Father! I only meant…"

Connolly grabbed the mended pants from Johannah and addressed Jim, a raised finger spearing the air condescendingly to make his point.

"Donnelly, you must first denounce your Protestant friends. And then you must get this wife of yours under control. And finally…I want to see peace between you and Farrell. You are Catholics, comrades in arms. Save it for the Prots. They rejoice when we are divided. Any more fighting, you and your family will not be welcome in my church!"

Johannah could see Jim's face turn against the man. The priest rose and they all rose. As he stepped into the bedroom to put on his pants and button them up, Jim and Johannah's eyes met in alarm. What manner of priest was this? He returned to face them and offer the final admonishment.

"You know, at my last parish in Quebec, when I arrived on my home visits, the members of my flock would get down on their knees and kiss my ring."

"But you're only a priest, Father," Jim told him. "We should save that for at least a bishop, don't you think?"

Father Connolly stared at him. He turned and marched out of the house without another word. Jim and Johannah looked at each other again and she took a deep breath, her first, it seemed, in minutes. No question, that had all gone quite badly.

"Don't worry about him, Jo," Jim said with a smile. "He'll learn to love us yet."

On a morning soon after Father Connolly's visit, Johannah noticed out the kitchen window that Farrell and his son, William, were hoeing potatoes in a small patch close to the property line. Nearby, Jim was engaged in taking the harness from his plow horse. They glanced at each other across the fence in passing and then continued with their labours, and it occurred to her as she watched them that, say what you will about Father Connolly, his warning had had a tempering effect on Jim and Pat Farrell both.

First Blood

WILL DONNELLY HAD sharpened their three double-headed axes at the pedal wheel stone in preparation for a land clearing picnic that Saturday at the farm of a man named Maloney, who lived just off the Roman Line a couple of miles south of them. It was the early summer of 1863. The clearing day was a popular convention among the neighbours, a social time with families very welcome and the wives outdoing themselves with pot-luck dishes, and Will was excited to see friends from school and one or two girls he liked. He had been to two clearings the summer before. Despite the rigour of the labour, few neighbouring men refused Maloney's invita-tion and with each event, goodwill was logged until it was the next family's turn to have a few acres cleared, or a barn or house erected, at little expense.

Will knew it was a pleasure for his mother to get out of the house on a fine day. She had told him how she enjoyed watching and hearing the rhythm of the broad saws on the hardwood trees, a strong man on each end, as the long teeth cut deep into a mature trunk the width of a wagon wheel. And there was a sense of security in believing they were all taming the land together, bending it to their purpose. When the saw blade on one side of the trunk met up with the axe cut on the other, a giant oak would crack and shiver and begin to sway, and the warning call sounded—"She's coming down!"—the crash of the impact muffled by the thick undergrowth. The smaller trees were felled by an axe alone. As the forest was beaten back, with trees falling all over, the warning calls could overlap and the men needed to pay careful attention and be nimble. Men and boys trimmed the branches of the fallen timber and stacked the thick logs in twelve-foot lengths to later be sawed into lumber.

Will laboured hard beside his father—they spit on their hands in unison—and Jim set the example for Will of the joy and virtue in honest labour. Despite his club foot, Will was strong and agile. He and other boys dragged the green cuttings into a pile to be burned. There were a dozen men and their families with them who had come to help clear on Maloney's farm. The team of Keefe's oxen strained to extract the stumps with stubborn roots that had burrowed deep into the ground like the fingers of huge hands and were not surrendering easily. Johannah had told Will the story of Vinnie O'Toole's death and he knew she would be thinking of him this day.

The women set up an efficient kitchen on top of some wide stumps cut smooth and level, close to the action, where they prepared a good lunch for the workers with the offerings they had brought: chicken stew, roast pork, boiled river perch, slices of venison and moose, bread and lard, and potatoes and greens. They joked and laughed, appreciating the rare social time together. Will's mother was popular among the women and could turn a joke as well as any. She played down her finishing school accent and Will noticed she even mangled the Queen's English now and again just a little because it "were" fun to do. A crippled man with a threadbare top hat sat on a log nearby and played a pleasant fiddle for them and it was altogether an enjoyable day.

Pat Farrell had also come to Maloney's, along with his son, Billy, with whom Will went to school. They spoke rarely but neither were they enemies. Farrell would now even give Johannah and her sons a stern nod of greeting. Will was relieved that apart from a wary look or two, for the past years Farrell and his father had ignored each other. He noticed that Father Connolly, who had suggested Jim Donnelly stay home from Maloney's clearing bee, kept an eye on them as well. Big John Carroll, who had sided with Farrell at the land hearing, had brought horses and worked there among them with his son Jim, his team hauling away the lesser logs that Keefe's oxen left behind. Jim Donnelly ignored him as well.

Will had dragged some heavy branches to the burn site. He gave his mother a wave and a wink. He left the work for a moment to talk to his pals Martin Hogan and Pat Whalen. They had their eye on John Carroll's son Jim, walking toward them carrying a bundle of spindly branches under one arm. Jim was a heavy-set, clumsy boy. Will turned to the others.

"Watch this."

Will casually tossed a large candy cane out onto the path some distance in front of Jim Carroll as he approached. It was attached to Will's wrist by a black string. Will walked around an adjacent tree and sat down on a stump nearby, facing away. Coming down the path, Jim Carroll spotted the candy cane in front of him and went to reach down for it with one free hand. As they all watched, Will casually tugged the string and the candy jumped three feet farther down the path. Perplexed, young Jim continued after the candy cane. Just before he reached it, Will pulled the string again and it jumped another two yards. Frustrated but determined, Jim Carroll dropped his wood and ran toward the candy. Will turned and stuck out his good leg for Jim to trip over and he fell on his face. Will, Martin and Pat shared the laugh. With a long, hard pull on the string, Will brought the candy cane back around the tree to catch it in his hand. Young Jim Carroll stood up to face the tricksters.

"I don't want any candy cane from Club Foot Billy. You've got a devil's hoof!" Jim Carroll made the sign of the cross with his dirty fingers. "Get away from me, devil!"

Suddenly Will was fiercely on his feet, his fists ready. He took two steps toward Jim Carroll, coiled to strike him.

Carroll yelled and ran. Will turned to the other boys, laughing, and put the candy cane in his mouth.

There was a figure clearing brush near Will dressed in old trousers, boots and a rough shirt. At the sound of the derisive laughter, her green eyes turned toward him.

"You going to be the slacker there all day, Will Donnelly, with that candy in your mouth, or you going to do something useful?"

The slender girl in a plaid shirt and wool breeches was dark-haired Nora Kennedy, a couple of years younger than Will, whose father owned the stately farm just west of St. Patrick's Church. Her mother was a prissy stick and disapproved of her daughter's masculine clothes. Will had always liked the girl's spirit.

"Myself, I like the idea of slacking, Nora."

"Well, you know what they say," she countered. "If you're going to do nothing, don't do it here."

Will made a monkey face at her, picked up the axe and went back to trimming a felled hemlock. Nora studied him for a moment, then returned to dragging brush.

Other young girls, in the sort of frilly dresses Mrs. Kennedy would have chosen for Nora, brought buckets of cool water around to the men working. One of these girls was Maggie Thompson, a golden-haired beauty with a dazzling smile. Their place was a decent farm on the third concession, just off the Roman Line. The father was a rough man who had done well with corn and beef cattle and his wife made up for his lack of pedigree by "putting on airs," as Johannah described it.

Maggie approached Will and passed the ladle of water to him with particular care. "Hi, Will. Your throat must be dry in this sun."

"Thank you, Maggie. I could use a drop. That's a pretty dress."

"My mother bought it in Toronto. I'm surprised you noticed."

"Have you heard this one? 'A mocking eye, a pair of lips. That's often why a fellow trips!'"

Maggie laughed lightly, charmed. Nearby, Nora overheard the lame conversation and rolled her eyes as she wiped a sleeve across her dusty, sweat-clad forehead and continued dragging the next pile of brush to the fire. Maggie's mother saw the exchange between Will and her daughter and found it far too familiar.

"Maggie! Come over here."

"But I still have water."

"Don't talk back! I said, come here."

Maggie revealed to Will a look of irritation at her mother's orders, picked up her bucket and did as she was told. Will watched as she was subjected to a small lecture. He knew what it was about. Even after all these years, the Donnellys were still considered squatters by some, people who pretty young girls do not talk to. His mother was clearly right about Mrs. Thompson.

Jim was just beginning to fall a young ironwood tree when warning yells sounded as a medium-sized oak on the other side of the clearing cracked and began to topple. John Hogan's voice boomed too late: "Keefe! Look out!"

The tree crashed down into the underbrush and there was a cry of surprise and pain.

"It got Keefe!"

Jim and Will and several other men rushed to the crown of the fallen tree. Underneath, his leg cruelly pinned under a substantial limb, was Jim's friend James Keefe moaning in agony.

"Oh…oh…oh!"

"We'll get you out, James!"

The men quickly began chopping the branches around him.

"Easy! Stop chopping!" Jim ordered them. "Use the bucks, for godsakes!"

The men brought the gentler saws, anxious to free Keefe but careful not to cause more suffering in their haste. Minutes later, four of them carried Keefe out of the bush and laid him in Hogan's wagon, where Ethyl Keefe had prepared blankets. The leg was crushed—they could see the pain was extreme and he was losing blood. Jim put an oak twig between his teeth and fashioned a tourniquet from his handkerchief. Hogan had already hitched up his horses.

"I'll get him to Dr. O'Hara."

"I didn't see him there," Farrell said suddenly. It was Farrell who had felled the tree. "I'm sorry, Keefe," Farrell called out to the prone man in the wagon, but in his agony, Keefe was past hearing.

Hogan climbed aboard, took hold of the reins and set off with Keefe gasping and moaning in the wagon, his distraught wife sitting beside him, holding his hand. They all watched as the wagon disappeared down the Roman Line. Then they all stared at Pat Farrell.

With his land being cleared so quickly, Maloney was sympathetic about Keefe, but also clearly hoped it wouldn't slow the day.

"Terrible thing. But he'll get good care. Pray they save the leg. We must be careful, boys. Have an eye. We're all working hard, getting the job done. And thanks be to you for it."

Will saw his father give Farrell a hostile glance as the men went back to work.

The day had been a productive one and as the shadows began to lengthen, the men could all feel proud of their work, their hands and backs aching as they should and the blue sky open over more than four acres almost ready for planting. The only blot on the day was Farrell almost killing Keefe. It was an incompetent accident but not seen as malicious or intentional, except by Jim Donnelly. Thankfully, a rider brought word from O'Hara, the Catholic doctor beside the post office, that Keefe would keep his leg.

Johannah and the other women began to pack up the leftover victuals from the rough plank tables with the help of their younger boys and girls.

"James! Michael!" Johannah called. "Take these over to the wagon. We'll head back soon."

There were goodbyes as other families headed home in carts and wagons with sleepy children while the men went back to work for a couple more hours. Johannah left Will to stay with Jim and made off home with the wagon and the other boys. Will and Jim would help clean up that fifth acre for Maloney before nightfall.

The workers lingered a little after the meal, some of them sitting on the stumps of the trees they'd felled, enjoying a pipe or a discussion about new crops or the best breed of horse for riding versus cart versus plow. Jim Donnelly liked the tough little breed of horse called the Canadian—Bob Whalen had two—that had become popular and could do all three tasks. Young Will put on the crippled man's top hat and tried out his fiddle with interest. After a few screeches of bow against strings, and a little of the man's patient instruction, Will was delighted to stroke a couple of clean, pretty notes.

"By God, we might have a fiddle player in the family!" Jim was delighted.

Maloney came around to clap the men on the back and thank them again, so pleased was he with the outcome of the day. Father Connolly had just gone off deep into the woods for private matters and it was the moment Maloney had been waiting for.

"Sure I'm blessed with good neighbours. Look what we've done today!"

With most of the women and children and Father Connolly gone, Maloney took from under his coat a couple of forty-ounce bottles of Seagram's rye whiskey and passed them around to thank his neighbours for their work.

"There you are, lads. You've never deserved the 'cathar' more."

The crippled man took the fiddle back from Will and began to play a reel. They passed the bottles quickly among them, long, fast, deep swallows, eyes watching for Father Connolly's return. Farrell was one of the first to take his portion from one bottle. Jim took a pull from the other.

And so the mood of the labourers was refreshed and Maloney expressed his pleasure again: "Yes, it's a good day." And all agreed, and there was talk of previous clearing parties on other holdings and the prosperity of the current farms that would now soon come to Maloney. They discussed new machinery being developed for clearing and farming and the pros and cons of using dynamite versus oxen on the stumps.

One man by the name of Martin McLaughlin owned the largest farm in the Lucan area and had ordered a new combine thresher from the Toronto firm Massey Ferguson. He was proud of it and extolled the machine's abilities. He would need one-quarter the manpower this coming harvest. McLaughlin was a small man with a thick head of hair, prematurely white, though he was only twenty-eight. He had a large wife who was very active at St. Patrick's and had several young children. He seldom spoke in public, was considered shy, but he was wealthy so the other men listened attentively when he listed the benefits of his new combine.

The conversation then went to previous accidents and Jim was not coy about raising what happened to Keefe. He confronted his neighbour.

"Now what about that tree, Farrell? You want to explain yourself? You never much liked Keefe. Did you mean to do it? Or was it pure stupidity?"

It seemed there was a fight pending and Maloney interrupted.

"Oh come on now, Jim, you don't want to stir up trouble. It was an honest accident…"

"I stand by what I asked."

Jim could see Farrell was feeling the whiskey now and they were both ready for confrontation.

"Everyone knows I meant Keefe no harm, Donnelly. What are you saying?"

"Everyone knows you and Keefe have had words, but I'll give you the benefit of the doubt, in falling a tree like that on Keefe's head. You didn't mean to, fine. Then I guess it was pure stupidity."

"Donnelly…you're the biggest horse's arse ever drew breath."

"At least I don't steal a man's land!"

"Oh yes, you do! You're a fucking thief!"

"Da!" Will called out. "Don't fight!"

But without further delay, Jim and Farrell went at each other with a maniacal intensity that had been bubbling beneath the surface for three years, held in check by the priest's warnings and sobriety until now. Together they made the sound of fists on faces and the usual accompaniment of blood flying. No man dared to come between them in this contest, at least until they tired. Farrell was the bigger man, but Jim was quicker. Under the influence of the whiskey, most of the onlookers were cheering them both on. They were a fair match and punished each other terribly. The quiet McLaughlin did not cheer but he watched with fascination.

The combatants stumbled into Maloney's potato patch, throwing punches, then falling and wrestling on the ground, crushing the plants.

"You're ruining my spuds. Get out of there!" Maloney called out to them, but they were deaf to any calls for peace.

Jim Donnelly and Pat Farrell were up on their feet again, swinging their fists at each other's faces. It scared Will Donnelly to see the fury of his father's attack and his blood being spilled, but there was fury on both sides. Farrell's son, Billy, was also upset, standing beside Will as their fathers went at it.

"They're going to kill each other," Billy Farrell said to Will Donnelly.

"No. No, they'll be all right. They'll tire themselves out in another minute or two."

It was John Carroll who threw Farrell the hickory axe handle. Farrell picked it up and threatened Jim with it and then Jim was truly seeing red. Hogan tossed Jim a tree branch as thick as a forearm. Farrell and Jim Donnelly circled each other, brandishing their clubs. They both swung and smashed each other, each landing punishing blows to his rival's body, bruising and cracking ribs. The other men continued to watch and cheer them on, savouring the brutal fight that every one of them had predicted.

It was then Father Connolly returned from the woods. He was deeply alarmed as he came upon the fight—Farrell and Donnelly bloodied, their clothing torn, their faces distorted in pain and hatred.

"Stop this! In the name of God. Two Catholics fighting. You'll kill each other!"

The priest's words distracted Jim and with a lucky blow, Farrell's club found his head and knocked him decisively to the ground. Farrell raised the club again and was about to finish Jim off, when Father Connolly came between them.

"Stop this now. Stop! That's enough!"

Truly, few would disagree Farrell was about to kill Jim then and there, so Jim owed his life to the priest. Father Connolly and the other men, including Carroll, pulled Farrell away. Bloody and battered, Jim struggled slowly to his feet alone. Will tried to help him but his father shouted, "Get away!"

Jim stood there groggy and unsteady, the club still in his hand. He called out through bloody, swollen lips, "Farrell...you piece of shite."

Farrell heard this and suddenly pulled away from the grasp of the men and turned back. He ran at Jim, club raised, roaring. Alert now to his attack, Jim feinted neatly to the side. As the other man missed him and stumbled past, he instinctively landed a glancing blow with his club to the side of Farrell's head to send him on his way. Farrell went down on his hands and knees in the ruins of the potato patch.

In that moment it was as if an irresistible force took Jim over, something carnal and primitive, an animal instinct to ensure there would be no more threat to himself or his family, to finish off the fight for good. And in that moment he saw the face of George Magee as the cottages burned, he heard the cries of Lucy O'Toole, the keening of the mother of the dead Ryan twins, and finally the determined swing and crack of the sledge as his father brought it down on the heads of the ponies. And in that moment it was Magee he was fighting, finally avenging his father, it was everything all together, the rage and the shame, the legacy of every cruel injustice inflicted on him and his family forever.

Without hesitation he lifted the rough club with two hands and swung it down on the back of Farrell's head with all his might. Farrell's body flattened down among the plants, blood flowing from his ears and nose, face turned to one side. He lay still with his open eyes staring beneath his caved-in skull, his lips moving. Bob Whalen stepped between Jim Donnelly and Pat Farrell to prevent further violence but the animal savagery that had invaded his friend was just as quickly finished. And so was Pat Farrell.

Jim Donnelly looked at the bloody club in his hand, amazed at what he had done.

John Carroll and Father Connolly went to Farrell. The priest knelt beside him, placing a gentle hand on his bloody head.

"Pat? Pat, can you hear me, my son?" Farrell's eyes continued to stare, his lips moving slightly, then his raspy breathing slowed and became shallow. Father Connolly began a whispered prayer.

"Behold, O Lord, this Thy servant and in Thy loving mercy, good Lord, deliver him. From darkness and doubt, good Lord deliver him…"

"Da? Da!"

Farrell's son, Billy, who had been standing frozen, ran forward toward his father, but he was stopped by Pat Whalen and Martin Hogan. A moment later, Pat Farrell stopped breathing. John Carroll felt Farrell's neck for a pulse and shook his head. The shocked men, including Father Connolly, stared at each other, then turned to Jim Donnelly. It was Father Connolly who spoke the word.

"Murder."

The bloody tree branch dropped from Jim's hand. The word was whispered again by McLaughlin and then spoken in bold accusation by John Carroll. Jim studied the disturbed faces of the men, then abruptly turned and walked quickly away, up the Roman Line toward home, with Will following close behind.

Johannah could see Jim and Will from the kitchen window walking home up the Line, still far off. Jim didn't have his coat and he was limping and even from that distance Johannah could see there were dark stains on his face and clothing. The other boys were off on various endeavours, except for John, reading on the porch. She came out and stood beside him and her heart began to pound. As her husband came closer, she saw more clearly the blood, the torn shirt and the bruises already darkening his face. She went in to get clothes and soap and warm water from the stove kettle. As she returned outside, he was coming up on the porch, swaying a little, having difficulty with his eyes, saying nothing. Will looked at her but he too was silent. Young John Donnelly put away his book to watch and listen. Johannah sat Jim down and washed his wounds. Most were superficial, the blood congealed. A couple should have stitches. And there was terrible bruising on his cracked ribs and arms. She fashioned a bandage around his head.

Johannah went about her repair work in silence. When he was ready, Jim would tell her what happened, and he soon did. It was as bad as she could have imagined.

"I killed Farrell. They'll be coming for me."

With these words, Johannah felt as if her mare had kicked her in the stomach. She felt as bad as on the day Farrell came to claim the land.

"Truly? You killed him?"

"Yes, I did."

"You're a stupid man, Jim Donnelly."

"I can't argue with you, Jo. 'Twas a stupid thing."

"Do you realize what you've done to us?"

"Yes. I know," he said quietly. "I've never been more sorry."

"It's the end of us, Jim. Our dreams, our family together…"

"I know it's bad. But I need your forgiveness and I need your help. I love you."

"You're such a fool." Johannah gathered herself together. She knew she had to be smart and ready to help her husband. She had no choice. She needed a plan.

Fugitive

WITHIN TWO HOURS of Farrell's death, Chief Constable Fitzhenry and three other well-armed police from the borough rode up to the Donnelly farm. Fitzhenry dismounted. The other three remained on their impatient horses.

Johannah came out onto the porch with her hands on her hips and waited for Fitzhenry to speak his piece.

"Mrs. Donnelly. We've come for Jim. He's killed Pat Farrell."

"I know. The idiot told me."

"Is he here?"

"No. I threw him out. You'll not see him here again."

Two hundred yards away, Jim was watching this encounter from the safety of a thick palisade of cedar trees.

"Are you sure, Johannah?"

"He told me about the killing. There's no forgiveness for murder. I told him I didn't want to see him again. The fool took his things and he's gone."

Fitzhenry sighed quietly, not believing her.

"Do you know where he's gone, then?"

Fitzhenry scanned the cover across the pasture at the tree line as he asked the question and for a moment, Jim ducked back in the bushes, thinking he had been spotted.

"I don't know, Fitzhenry, and I don't care," she said loudly, trying to get the constable's attention back.

"Will you tell us if he comes round again?"

"Sure, but there won't be much left of him if I see him here again."

"Then you won't mind if we have a look around?"

"Search 'til your little heart is content, Fitzhenry."

That night a dozen constables searched the barn, woods and fields for Jim but he knew the land well and could easily avoid them. He told

Johannah later he spent much of the first evening watching them from the high branch of a big hemlock behind the barn.

The next morning Johannah made her way to town. She was shunned by almost all she encountered. At the post office she saw for the first time the reward poster. It was a sketch of Jim, a good one, with the offer of four hundred dollars for information leading to his arrest. Mr. Porte told her he was sorry for her troubles. While Mr. Porte was helping another customer, Johannah pulled the poster from the wall and took it away with her.

Johannah had a good chat with the boys that night.

"You should all know...the killing of Pat Farrell was a terrible thing. Even though Mr. Farrell brought it on himself, there is no way it could be right. But your father is ours and we have to do whatever is necessary to help and protect him. He has to be in hiding but he will be around the farm from time to time. You can never tell anyone. We can take him food or leave it for him. We can get him letters and gifts, things to make him comfortable. The important thing is that he loves us all and we love him, too."

As Jim began his life as a fugitive, he and Johannah discussed their systems of signals and supply, which would be used under the watching eyes of Fitzhenry, who established a two-man sentry at the farm. Johannah instructed her boys to treat the constables with respect to put them at ease, and she herself made the constables dinner, believing that if Jim was spotted, a constable might think twice before shooting a man whose wife had filled his belly.

If Johannah put two candles in the window at night, it would mean that the family had distracted the constables and Jim could come up to the barn or the out sheds or even the summer kitchen. Johannah and the boys would also find ways to leave small packages where he would find them.

On the fifth night it poured rain and Johannah filled a big knapsack with dry socks, a shirt, a warm stew dinner and a bottle. She folded it all in an oilcloth and blanket and gave it to Will. Outside the farmhouse she brought tea to the two constables to gather them together and distract them as Will slid out a side window with the sack on his back. He could move quickly through the woods—his limp and hop did not prevent a speedy lope toward his father's hideout. His mother instructed him to take a circuitous route and stop and listen from time to time to make sure he was not being followed. To be followed could lead to his father's capture, which could mean his father's life.

Jim Donnelly sat beside a tiny fire with an oilskin over his head in a rocky enclosure beside a huge fallen tree. The fire had very little smoke. He was cold and wet and alone. Through the fine, cold rainfall, he heard the snap of a twig nearby in the darkness and cocked both hammers of the shotgun in his hands.

"It's me, Da!"

Will stepped forward so his father could make him out. They did not speak but both listened, their senses now pricked for any presence of Jim's enemies, who could have followed the boy here. When he was satisfied, Jim uncocked the shotgun and took the knapsack from Will. He kept the shotgun across his knees. He took out his sheath knife and began to quickly eat his first food of the day: bread and meat stew, still warm from his wife's kitchen, apples and cider in a mason jar.

"Ma sends her love and the boys are all right. Tom broke his finger and didn't tell anybody. The constables were mean at first but now they're more friendly."

Looking to Will, Jim gestured to the food. "You'll eat with me?"

Will nodded. Jim cut Will some bread and they ate together in silence by the light of the small fire. Jim felt the need to tell his son something meaningful about why he was here and how this had happened, but how could he explain his actions when he did not understand them himself? Will reached into his sack, unfolded the wanted poster and handed it to his father to examine.

"Handsome devil. But only four hundred dollars?" Jim laughed and Will's face relaxed and he could laugh himself.

"You're worth three times that much, Da."

"Thank you, my son. I like to think so."

Buoyed by this joke, they stared into the little fire and again ate in silence for a while.

"Da?" The fire crackled and hissed. "What are you going to do?"

"Not sure yet. Still sorting things out."

They both just stared into the fire, Will waiting patiently for his father to say something.

"Your mother was right," Jim said suddenly. "About fighting with Farrell. I was a fool."

Will kept his silence, but Jim knew he was taking it in.

"She's a smart girl, Will, your mother. Smarter than any of us. Listen when she tells you something."

"I will, Da. I do."

"Good." They ate and looked into the fire some more.

"I will admit it was all by my own hand this happened. No one's fault. Only my own. But you should know, Will, about the curse. The Donnelly curse is back in full force. It is our burden and though we might make bad decisions and do wrong things, it plays its part as well. We can't forget that."

"I won't forget, Da."

Surrender

OVER THE COMING months, there were days passersby would see a woman working in the Donnelly fields, weeding or harvesting potatoes, and these neighbours would believe and report it was Johannah. Her dresses were tight on Jim but she let them out and he managed to get into them, complete with a frilly bonnet, and work the fields throughout the summer. No Donnelly boy ever smirked at their father's masquerade, nor did one ever talk to anyone outside the family about Jim's visits to the house and the barn.

Fitzhenry began to hear of the muscular figure in a dress seen from time to time in the Donnelly fields, but each time he went to investigate, Johannah claimed it had been herself. Twice, in addition to the sentries spending irregular shifts at the house, Fitzhenry set out constables to wait in the bushes on the edge of the north field and once they even surrounded him, but with a fast horse waiting close by, Jim dropped implements and was mounted and gone before they could close the trap. And Johannah's strategy of feeding the constables had worked, for on the two occasions shots were fired after him by the constables, they flew well over his head.

It was the next spring, almost a year after Farrell's demise, that Father Connolly came to visit Johannah. He had a new horse that pleased him, paid for by the parish, and which boosted his pride and confidence, if that were necessary or possible. Johannah served him tea, nervous at the questions he might ask, for she was eight months pregnant.

"You told the constable you hadn't seen your husband in a year."

The priest pointedly looked down at her ripe stomach, the new child clearly only a month or two away from delivery.

"More or less."

"I assume the child is Jim's and it is the lesser sin of lying you're guilty of, Johannah."

"There was a visit or two," Johannah admitted to the priest.

Father Connolly watched, curious, out the window as young Billy Farrell batted rounders in the yard with the Donnelly boys.

"And how has it been with the Farrell boy? Is he all right being here?"

"I think so. He's a lovely lad. It just felt like the right thing to do to take him in. He's quite at home."

After his father's death, young Billy Farrell lived in the house he and his father had built. Every afternoon, Johannah would prepare a full plate of food for Will to deliver to him. Johannah would see the boy looking through the fence at them like a lost cat and so one day she instructed Will to invite him to come and live with them if he wanted. On the eleventh day, the lad was waiting with a bag of clothes and belongings. He was welcomed into the house by all the Donnelly boys and given his own bed in the north bedroom with Michael, John and Tom.

Father Connolly had considered the boy's situation with mixed feelings, living in the house of his father's killer. But after enquiries, no family of Pat Farrell had come forward to take him and the priest had to admit Billy seemed content with the Donnellys.

Johannah waited quietly and Father Connolly finally persevered with the message he had come to deliver.

"Johannah, you know in your heart Jim has to give himself up to God's justice."

"It was self-defence."

"The truth will come out in court. But it won't be resolved while he's a fugitive. He can't continue like this."

"I know," Johannah told him, and she did.

The winter had proved hardest for Jim. The Donnelly barn was bitterly cold but to sleep in his own bed was dangerous as Fitzhenry conducted frequent night inspections at their house. Jim would occasionally stay over at the homes of supportive neighbours, the Whalens and the Feehleys, but never more than a single night. One night, through inside information or plain luck, Fitzhenry made a midnight raid at James Keefe's house when Jim was a guest. The fugitive had to hide face down in bed under the covers, hidden among three sleeping Keefe children, as the police searched the rooms around them and came up empty-handed.

"I think in your heart you're a good Catholic, Johannah. Let that be your guide in this. You're the only one that can convince him. Tell him to give himself up. Tell him to have faith, come back to the Church and God will be just."

She was listening.

Johannah came to Jim in the barn late that night with a candle and stood waiting at their appointed time. Jim left his hiding place when he was convinced she was not followed. Fitzhenry's men had gone home for the night. They embraced, then sat on a bench in the tack room with a small lantern for light, holding hands. It struck Jim in that thin light how Johannah had aged in the last year and how it was because of him. He had done this to her. She seemed rough and drawn from lack of sleep, a weariness that broke his heart, though it was plain to see her inner strength and beauty remained undiminished.

"Father Connolly is supportive," she said, getting down to business. "He promised that you'll get a fair trial. He's on our side. People think you'll maybe only spend a couple of years in jail or even be found not guilty. Some even say that Pat Farrell was a troublemaker and land stealer. You ran a fine race, Jim," she looked at him with pride and affection. "But you can't go on like this. I can't go on like this."

Jim knew this was true. He could not take another winter outside the house.

"I was such a fool, Johannah."

"Yes, you were. But we'll make it right."

He embraced her and they kissed and at her bidding, they moved to the soft hay and with great care around her prominent belly, they made love to seal their decision.

It was late spring when Bob Whalen walked into the Lucan police station accompanied by Jim Donnelly, in the women's clothing that he had worn to get there without being arrested. Chief Constable Fitzhenry saw him and laughed out loud.

"Donnelly! You crazed bastard. The lady of the fields. You're under arrest!"

"I know this, Fitzhenry. That's why I'm here. Just get on with it. And pay the man his money."

"What money?"

"The reward for Whalen here. Four hundred dollars. He captured me."

Whalen and Jim had worked out the deal. Bob would keep two

hundred dollars for his efforts and Jim would pocket the other two hundred to pay for a defence lawyer. They didn't like the way Fitzhenry laughed out loud again.

"Now wait a minute, Fitzhenry," Bob said. "That's the deal. Four hundred dollars reward."

Fitzhenry looked at Whalen, a short, ruddy-faced man.

"Or what? You're going to take him home again?" Any humour left Fitzhenry's eyes. "There will be no reward, Bob. He gave himself up, sure as a pussy's a cat. Now fuck off before I arrest you too, for contempt of court!"

Fitzhenry took Jim Donnelly down the hall to the cells and that was that.

Johannah could not be present for the arrest of her husband, as it turned out. His last child, and a demanding one, decided to make an early debut. Dr. Davis had been called away to London so Michael Keefe's wife, Anne, who was an old hand at the birthing of babies, came by, and Johannah had all she needed in her main bedroom. Will kept the six other boys occupied elsewhere and Johannah hoped she didn't scare them all with her groans as she delivered their new sibling.

"It's a girl, Johannah! A goddamn girl!" Anne announced with the appropriate enthusiasm. "You did it."

"Thank Christ!" Johannah shouted, with a convert's passion.

Such pure joy filled Johannah to see this child, blessedly without a penis, who was already crying with hearty spirit as Anne wrapped her in a thick towel and gave her to Johannah to nurse. As she tenderly held her daughter, the tiny infant suddenly calmed and took easily to the breast. After a few moments, she opened her shining blue eyes and stared intently up at Johannah.

"Hello, little one," her mother whispered. "You've come into this world outnumbered by boys, but together we'll be fine."

Anne had gone out to the barn to find Will and the boys and invite them in to see this wonder—a girl in their midst. They lined up under the direction of Anne and Will to have a look at the babe, now fed and sleeping in Johannah's arms.

"Keep your dirty paws off her," were Anne's initial instructions. "Just look."

Will was first in line. "There's not much to her," he said.

"There will be soon enough. Next!"

The brothers each filed past to get a quick look at her tiny face like a small congregation receiving Mass.

"She's got no hair."

"She'll have it soon enough."

"She looks like a piglet."

"All right, that's enough. Next. "

"What's her name, Ma?" John Donnelly asked.

Johannah had almost succumbed to sleep herself.

"Jenny is what your father and I want to call her. Her name is Jenny."

The boys tried out the name and liked it. As their mother joined the newcomer in sleep, Will gathered his brothers to go and left the Donnelly women to their rest.

The Trial

AT THE SUMMER assizes in the expanding market town of London, Jim sat in the prisoner's box, on trial for murder. Johannah sat the family as close as she could to him. It was a high-ceilinged room of heavy oak beams, in a primitive Baroque style, with the judge's dais elevated above the courtroom—a physical confirmation of his supremacy. The room was full of curious onlookers and cozy with the body heat. She sat there in the front row with their seven sons and new infant daughter, Jenny. Young Billy Farrell, son of the deceased, was also there, now one of the family.

Johannah smiled a little nervously at Father Connolly. They were in God's hands, he had assured them. Trust in God. Farrell's friends, John Carroll and Martin McLaughlin, the short, silver, well-to-do farmer who had been at the scene of the fight, were in court. Johannah did not know McLaughlin, nor what to expect of him. James Keefe and Bob Whalen were there with smiles and nods of encouragement.

The Crown first put Carroll on the stand.

"Pat Farrell was only defending himself. Donnelly was fixing for that fight from the start."

Johannah had expected this. After Carroll, Martin McLaughlin took his turn, his colours quickly becoming apparent.

"There had been some drinking and Farrell was a little drunk. Donnelly pretended to be, but I think he was pretty sober. I think he was planning the fight."

Jim's expression showed this was a lie.

Bob Whalen came to the stand for the defence. Judge Bennett was looking through his papers as Whalen offered his story.

"They'd both been drinking and both had it in for each other for years. Farrell wanted to go at it as much as Jim Donnelly. At the end, Jim was just defending himself. Farrell clubbed him and he was on the ground…"

The judge interrupted.

"Wait. Stop. You're Robert Whalen. You accompanied the defendant in and wanted the reward."

"That is so. But I didn't get nothing. Fitzhenry said…"

"You're not an indifferent witness, sir."

Whalen, to his credit, pointed to Connolly and McLaughlin.

"You think these other jokers are, Your Honour?"

"You are disqualified. The jury will ignore Mr. Whalen's comments."

Bob Whalen was a key witness for the defence and they had just lost him. Maloney was reportedly sick in bed. John Hogan would have testified but he had driven Keefe with his crushed leg to the doctor and had not been a witness to the fight. So the final witness they would depend on was Father Connolly. The priest began in a magnanimous tone.

"Of course, we all knew about the land dispute between Farrell and Donnelly. I had talked to both men, together and separately, and urged them to make peace, and it did hold for almost three years and then…it ended so tragically."

"Did either man express a desire for peace?"

"Farrell told me he wanted it to end and could live with having lost half his land if it meant peace."

"And Jim Donnelly? What did he say about it?"

"There was no talking to Jim Donnelly. He wanted what he called 'his land' back and would hear of nothing else. I was so concerned that on the day of Maloney's gathering, I had urged Donnelly to stay away. As we now all know, he should have taken my advice."

Jim and Johannah sat frozen as they heard Father Connolly turn away from them and support the dead man. Johannah could not believe her ears.

"When Donnelly arrived, did you try to keep him away from Farrell?"

"We did everything we could. But Donnelly would not listen. Jim Donnelly was determined to fight that day," Father Connolly asserted emphatically. "Neither man nor God could stop him."

Finished, he left the witness chair. As he returned to his seat, he looked with pity first at Jim and then at Johannah.

The jury took less than an hour to reach a verdict. The judge had explained they could find Jim not guilty, or guilty of first-degree or second-degree murder or manslaughter. When they returned to the courtroom, the voice of the judge rang out with his question for the foreman. "Have you reached a verdict?"

The foreman of the jury stood. He was a short man who Johannah had heard managed a hotel in Exeter. He had a long, bushy black moustache, through which he spoke.

"We have, Your Honour."

"How do you find the defendant?"

"M'lord, we find the defendant guilty of murder in the first degree."

John Carroll and Martin McLaughlin both appeared satisfied, but to twist the knife, so did Father Connolly. In most cases where a drunken fight had ended in death and the verdict was guilty, a prison term would result, but Judge Bennett put on the black cap to pass sentence.

When he spoke, his words shocked the courtroom: "James Donnelly, you are sentenced to be taken to the jail from whence you came, thence on the seventeenth day of October next to the place of execution, there to be hanged by the neck until you are dead."

Johannah listened in disbelief and rose to her feet.

"NO! NO!"

Will stood up and put a protective arm around his mother. Jim and Johannah locked eyes, helplessly. He then stared at the floor and slowly shook his head. A moment later, the guards took Jim by his shackled arms and led him away.

On Sunday morning, the sanctuary of St. Patrick's was almost full and all the talk as the people filed in was of Jim Donnelly's sentencing. It took the deacons several minutes to quiet the congregation to the point where the service could begin. Nevertheless, it was fully underway when Johannah, looking haggard, entered with her eight children and Billy Farrell. Father Connolly was standing with his back to the congregation saying the mass. Half the congregation turned to watch Johannah as Connolly spoke.

"The grace and peace of God our Father and the Lord Jesus Christ be with you."

The congregation replied distractedly, "Blessed be God, the Father of our Lord Jesus Christ."

Now every eye turned to watch Johannah Donnelly as she walked up to the altar and knelt with her children just behind the priest, looking at his back as he continued.

"Lord God almighty, creator of all life, of body and soul, we ask you to bless this water as we use it in faith to forgive our sins."

Sunlight streamed through the stained glass window portraying Saint Sebastian, which Father Connolly had commissioned the year before, the arrows protruding from the young saint's breast. Johannah's expression was a little wild as she stared up at Connolly.

"Heal us from all illness and save us from the power of evil…"

"Father," she called out.

The priest stopped speaking. The church was silent and still. Slowly, in shock, Father Connolly turned around.

"Please talk to them," Johannah implored.

"How dare you interrupt the Holy Mass."

"Don't let him die."

She had determined she would not cry in front of Father Connolly. "For the children. Plead mercy for him."

Connolly's face reflected the self-righteousness he felt in his heart.

"I cannot help you. I witnessed the murder. The judgment on your husband is a fair one. May God have mercy on his soul."

Johannah was crushed by the priest's continuing lack of compassion. She stood up but remained where she was. The sanctuary was as silent as the surface of the moon when she turned to face the congregation. She held up a piece of paper.

"They want to kill my husband. Who will sign this petition to stop them?"

Father Connolly was speechless for a moment, clearly aghast that this woman would take such liberties in his church. Johannah went to James Keefe with her petition and a sharp pencil.

"James. Our friend. Will you sign?"

James took the petition and pencil, quickly read it and was about to sign when Father Connolly finally found his voice, in which there was an angry quaver.

"I forbid it."

James hesitated, did a quick survey of the faces around him, then of the furious priest. He gave the petition back, saying, "I'm sorry, Johannah." He turned away, his eyes desperately studying the floor. Johannah hesitated, staring at him, then took the petition to the other men in the pews.

"Bob? Robert?"

"In God's name, I forbid it," Father Connolly repeated more forcefully.

The Whalens and Hogans reluctantly, in guilt, turned away from her too. Everyone felt the glare of Father Connolly upon them and would not make eye contact with her. Johannah turned to the priest and approached him, her frustration churning into a fury of wild emotions.

"You said to us that Jim should give himself up. He will find God's justice, you said. I convinced him you were right. I convinced him to give himself up because of what you said to me."

"I will pray for him."

Johannah hesitated a moment as his words sunk in. A shadow came over her face. She moved a step closer, her words as bitter as thorns.

"Save your lying prayers, priest."

He stared at her, speechless.

"You put a noose around his neck!" Johannah continued. "His death will be on your head!"

The congregation held their collective breath. Johannah turned, gathering her children.

"Come Will, Robert, James, Michael, Billy, everyone, let's go…"

Before leaving the church for good, she stopped at the door and slowly looked around, studying the congregation of Saint Patrick's, the congregation that had betrayed them. She would never trust a priest again, nor a congregation, nor perhaps even God himself. She shepherded her children from the sanctuary and out onto the steps, slamming the heavy doors behind them.

Thirteen Steps

JOHANNAH LEFT THE church and instructed Will to look after his siblings in the school playground. Taking with her only baby Jenny, she went to see Dr. Davis, having nowhere else to turn.

"Come in, come in, Johannah. I just heard about Jim's conviction."

He welcomed her with an arm around her shoulder, guiding her inside into the bright foyer of the generous house. She had saved her tears until then and they came in quiet sobs that made her body tremble.

"We'll talk this through, Johannah."

He guided her out onto his big veranda and poured tea for her, which sat untouched. He listened, as always sympathetic, anxious to help.

"You know Jim is a good man."

"I do."

"He didn't mean to kill Farrell. It was an unlucky stroke given in drink. I can't lose him like this. Is there anything you can do?"

Dr. Davis considered what he had to offer.

"Well, I was at a dinner in London last year and met the attorney general, who was speaking: Jack Macdonald. Interesting man with some vision. He might see me. I'll go speak with him in London about Jim's case. See if there's something he can do."

Johannah stood up, wiping her eyes, and embraced him. "You've been so good to us, Dr. Davis."

"I was the one who convinced you to come to Lucan, Johannah. I have a responsibility. You have created a good life here for your family. Let's see if we can salvage it."

"Please speak to him as soon as you can. You're our last hope."

But there was one other hope for them that Johannah did not want to reveal. She went home and cooked dinner for her children, her spirits apparently recovered from the confrontation with the priest. She read

Robinson Crusoe to the boys and put them all to bed. Jenny was being an angel and slept soundly in her crib.

When the children were asleep, she quietly moved the table and woven rug back to clear a space in the dining room, and on the wooden floor used a charcoal stick to draw a circle within which she could kneel. She stopped to listen and make sure the house was still before she continued. Within that circle she drew straight lines, as Raffy had secretly taught her to do so many years ago, until they made up the five points of the penta-gram. She placed Raffy's smooth river stone in the centre, then wrote Jim's name on a beeswax candle, which she lit and placed at the northernmost point of the configuration. In a saucer she combined the incense, savour-ies and musk she had gathered in the woods and dried. With a sharp knife she made a cut at the base of her thumb, as she had once done with Lucy, and added seven drops of her blood to the saucer, then added a splash of raw whiskey and lit the mixture, letting it burn a few moments. She blew the flame out and it began to smoulder, and a thin, acrid blue line of smoke rose up to the ceiling. She took Jim's shirt and brimmed hat and moved them three times through the plume of incense smoke, speaking the words quietly so the boys would not wake up.

> I hold my hands out to thee, god Dubsag Unig-Ki, patron of
> Kullabi, to be with my love.
> Ensure life and health are his,
> Let a kindly guardian march on his right,
> Let a kindly spirit march on his left.
> Nin-Anna, the mighty scribe of the underworld, add your
> pure voice to mine,
> Speak for my love an incantation of protection,
> Unto his body may evil spirits and evil men not draw nigh,
> May they wreak no violence against him. Let him live.
> And may our house be protected from their evil forever!

The children were all asleep, save one. Will watched and listened to his mother unseen from the shadowed hallway, surveying doors and windows, wondering how the dark forces she summoned to help might manifest themselves. He was apprehensive but not in disagreement with her choice. Whatever was necessary to save Da. As his mother began another verse, two of his brothers were stirring in the big bedroom and he turned away and went in to quiet them and allow his mother to continue her incantations in peace.

On the morning of Jim's execution, he was served good ham and eggs and found it a curious courtesy for a man who would not have time to digest them in this world. Then he was taken from his cell, shackled hand and foot, and accompanied by the guards and a young priest on his last walk down the hall to the gallows inside the courtyard of the London jail.

Jim had been incarcerated in a windowless five-by-eight-foot cell at the London jail for the last few months. He was allowed twenty minutes in a side yard to walk, breathe fresh air and see a patch of sky once every other day. Because of some recent violent incidents caused by heightened emotions, the families of condemned prisoners were not allowed visitation rights. Certain letters were allowed and Jim had advised Johannah on the workings of the farm that summer. Barley prices were rising and pork prices encouraged the purchase of another sow. Johannah and Will were managing well without him. And apparently they would have to continue.

It was a long walk to the gallows courtyard. The priest spoke words of comfort: "The Lord is my light and my salvation; whom then shall I fear? Yea, though I walk through the valley of the shadow of death, I will fear no evil…"

Jim raised his shackled hands and made a gesture with one for him to stop.

"Yes, thank you, Father. I can take it from here. The Church has not been of much help to me recently. If I want a chat with God, I'll do it myself."

The young priest was offended. "As you will." But he followed at a distance as Jim walked on. It was the time now, Jim mused, to sort himself out, all right. He was deeply sorry he had killed Farrell and put an end to the fine life he and his family had known. He wondered how God might look upon it. He supposed he was about to find out. No one to blame but himself. He wondered now if there was a God, a heaven, a hell. Could it be that it was all a ruse from ancient times so that men like Father Connolly could control the rest of them? It was a thought that had come to him more often of late. Even so, he supposed it was better to live life as if there was a God and be disappointed than to live as if there was no God and be surprised. Jim realized again, disappointed or surprised, he was about to find out.

Johannah sat on the long bench in the empty hallway outside the office of Attorney General John A. Macdonald, staring at the floor, listening to the muffled voices inside, her ears perked to the tone of the conversation. She would glance up at the clock on the wall opposite and then cast her eyes down again to listen. She leaned over and made a circle with her finger on the floor and crossed it five times to make an invisible pentagram. Suddenly there were rapid footsteps and a young clerk opened the door and came out into the hall, scrambling into his coat. He had a single piece of paper in one hand. He looked at her for a second, his eyes wide, then turned and ran down the hallway. Dr. Davis stepped out into the hall and saw her anxious face and his usually grave visage broke into a smile and he nodded. Johannah embraced him, tears rising, then raised her skirts and ran down the hall after the young clerk.

Located in the old courtyard and built of rough wood, the scaffold was a sturdy structure with enough of a drop to break all but the most obstinate necks. Jim was escorted to the wooden staircase and climbed very slowly, one step of the thirteen at a time, the chains from his shackled feet dragging against the lip of the rough boards as he climbed. At the top of the platform, the hangman studied him seriously to assess his demeanour, or perhaps just the girth of his neck. Jim gave him a smile.

"All in a day's work, hah?"

The man's expression did not change. Jim looked down at the officials on the ground. There was the jail warden and another man in a suit, three uniformed policemen and the priest, who had decided to stay below, which was for the best. And there at the back was Fitzhenry in a suit. Good old Fitzhenry had come to see him off. Jim smiled and raised a shackled hand in greeting. Fitzhenry raised his hand back to him but he did not smile. In fact the big chief constable looked very stern and his eyes were moist.

Imagine that, Jim thought to himself. *Fitz is going to miss me.*

The hangman guided Jim to where he had to stand, over the trap door, and he and another policeman removed the shackles from his hands and feet. They were replaced by leather straps around his ankles and ties to his hands behind his back.

"You have anything to say, now's the time," the hangman told him.

"I send my love to my wife and children. I am sorry for taking the life of Pat Farrell and I ask forgiveness here and afterwards, if there is an afterwards."

There was nothing more to say. Jim would miss this life and his children and most of all the sweet woman who had loved him despite everything. There was nothing to do now but accept the event before him with the dignity of an Irish nobleman.

"Let's get on with it."

The hangman approached him with the black hood in his hand.

"I don't want that. I'd rather do without."

"It's not for you, Donnelly. It's so the others don't see what your face does."

He put the hood roughly over Jim's head so he was now all in darkness. He could hear the young priest reciting the twenty-third psalm. Jim supposed that too was more for the others than himself. He closed his eyes, despite the hood, and went back in his thoughts to the sunny glade beside the Ballyfinboy River where he and Johannah had caught the salmon and years later made love for the first time. He waited there in that happy memory for the trap to spring.

But what he heard was the creak of another door opening and a voice calling out. "Wait! Is it done?" There was a shuffling of feet below and muffled inquiries and agitated speaking but Jim couldn't get the gist. *Can a man not die in peace?* he wondered.

A voice called his name and through the material of the hood he finally said, "Yes. I am here."

The hangman took the hood off his head and he looked down to see a small, officious man with a message in his hand. The man seemed irritable, as if Jim's case was creating disorder in his orderly day.

"You are Jim Donnelly, correct?" he asked again.

"Who else would I be?"

The small man continued with his chore. "This is from the attorney general's office. John A. MacDonald has granted you an order of clemency."

"What does that mean?"

"It means you're not to be hanged, sir. Your sentence is commuted to fifteen years in Kingston Penitentiary."

Jim let the information sink in that he would not die today. There was a brief moment of joy. He would see her again. But almost immediately he began weighing the long, hard prison time. All that time without her. Fifteen years. The noose almost seemed a kindlier destiny. But not quite.

"All right, then. I'll take it."

"No one is giving you a choice, Donnelly. You will, in fact, not die today."

In Jim's tiny prison cell in the London jail, Johannah sat on the cot and held his hand. She had been allowed, again through the generosity of Attorney General MacDonald, a rare and brief spousal visit before Jim was transferred to Kingston Penitentiary to serve his term. She brought baby Jenny to show him and she wore a cotton dress, her hair held up with combs the way he liked it, subdued as she looked around at the clammy limestone walls, clinging to the hand she would not hold again for many years. Far too many years to think about.

Jim tried to make her smile. "Well…it'll be free room and board."

Baby Jenny was gurgling and cooing, trying to talk. Johannah turned and looked into Jim's eyes, all business now.

"I'll petition for a lighter sentence. And we'll keep the farm going. Don't worry. We'll be fine, I promise. I swear we'll get through this and find a good life again. You and I are like wolves, Jimmy. We mate for life."

"Yes. We are wolves." Jim smiled at her sadly. "Do you remember the time on board the ship when you climbed on the railing and stared down at the sea? I found you and I grabbed your hand."

"Yes."

"Well, I won't be there to grab your hand. You'll have to be strong."

"I was a silly girl then. Don't you know me, Jim? I will get through this. It's you I'm worried about. It's you that must be strong. Don't change."

"You tell the boys I'll be fine. They have to look after you and stay out of trouble."

"Don't forget you have a daughter now."

He looked at the child, held out his hands and took her, bouncing her on his knee. She stared up at him, wide-eyed.

"Hello, you little one. If I stay the full term, you'll be a young lady when I see you next." At this Johannah was struggling to hold back tears. "You'll remind her over the years she has a father?"

"Every day."

The guards came to escort Johannah away.

"It's time, ma'am."

Jim and Johannah looked at each other and stood up. They held each other with the baby between them and kissed. Johannah studied his face intently. She grabbed a fistful of his coarse prison shirt and squeezed it as tight as she could, as if she could hold him here with her for good. The guards unlocked the cell.

"Goodbye, my love," he said.

"Goodbye, Jim."

Jim reached up and touched the tip of her nose.

"See you in no time."

Jim arrived at Kingston Penitentiary by open wagon with six other prisoners, all shackled together. They had been transported by train in a cattle car from London to Toronto, then from Toronto to the garrison town of Kingston six hours east, then the last two miles by wagon to arrive at the huge dark stone fortress prison on the shores of Lake Ontario, where men unfit for normal society were sent to be excluded from it.

After a scrub down and fresh clothes, Jim appeared before Warden Piggott in his office, in shackles on hands and feet, accompanied by four guards as if he might make a break for it at any moment. The warden's office windows overlooked the prison yard. His large desk had three plush armchairs of oxblood leather arranged in a half-circle in front of it. Jim wondered who sat in those chairs. Never a prisoner, he was sure.

Jim faced the warden with dignity as he came out from behind his desk. Jim met his eyes, unblinking. The warden was a tall man and he stood over him and looked down.

"Welcome to Kingston, Donnelly."

"Thank you, Warden Piggott."

"You'll grow to like it here."

"I don't think so, Warden."

The warden looked at the floor for a moment, disappointed with this response, licked his lips and gave a thin smile.

"You might be surprised. Just don't make any trouble and we'll get along fine. Do what you're told. Follow the rules. Listen to me now," he continued as if to a child. "It's very important to carefully follow the rules that we teach you. That's all we ask. Like…the swearing rule or the silence rule or raising your eyes. Do you understand?"

"What the hell is the raising your eyes rule?" Jim asked, looking directly at the warden.

"Oh no." The warden shook his head in disappointment. "There, you went and broke all three of them."

He nodded to the guards. A wooden club smashed Jim across the head and he went down. With their clubs and boots, the four guards continued beating and kicking him on the floor. And the warden watched until Jim lost all track of place and time.

PART TWO

Prologue

SPRING ASSIZES—Old Court House, London, Ontario. June 2, 1880.

"All right now, Johnny, do you feel ready to continue?"

"Yes, sir, I do. I'm sorry about before."

"That's fine. It must be hard for you."

"Yes, Mr. Irving, it is. But I think I'm ready."

"All right, then, you are still under oath. We were talking about the Donnelly family. Let's go back to that."

"Yes, sir."

"Tell us again from your point of view how the Donnellys were regarded in the neighbourhood."

"Well, some folks called them 'the terrors of Biddulph County' but to their friends, the Donnelly boys were good people and loyal and that's what I seen. They had a reputation, as they say, as drinkers and fighters and ladies' men. And 'course behind their backs, people talked about the cold fact their father was a murderer serving hard time in Kingston and so they was all tarred with that brush. Of course, I heared that any words in the schoolyard and the boys would deal with those reckless yackers with bloody noses, twisted arms and oaths it would never be talked about again."

"Johnny, do you know what the term 'Blackleg' or 'Blackfoot' means?"

"Yes, sir. Them's Catholics with Protestant friends."

"Did you ever hear the Donnellys called that?"

"Yes, sir. They was called 'Blacklegs' behind their backs. But Johannah and Will told me they didn't want to live with all the old feuds from Ireland. This were a new country, they said. The Donnellys had as many Protestant friends as Catholic and they was proud of it, and frankly made prosperous by it 'cause it were the Protestants who had the money. And as Johannah said, it were Catholics caused the problems with the land, pushed the fight with Farrell and almost got Mr. Jim hanged. It were Protestants that saved him."

"Would you agree there are lots of Catholics fraternizing with Protestants in Biddulph County?"

"Oh, sure. Most Catholics do a bit of quiet Protestant business on the side. But the Donnellys did it proud and open, especially Johannah. With their crops of corn and barley, and their horse and cattle breeding and trading, the woodlot with the little sawmill and their stagecoach business, I'd say at least half was Protestant customers. At the time before Mr. Jim came back, they was doing real good businesswise."

"Let's get back to your own experience. What else can you tell us about the Donnellys? How would you describe them when you started working there?"

"Well, the Donnelly boys was the life of any good party. They danced and played music, got into horseplay and flirting with the girls. They was big, strong good-looking fellas, most of them. They was loyal to their friends and fast to fists with their enemies. They wore the best clothes and boots, especially Michael and John and Will, and they all had a little money to jangle in their pockets and was willing to spend."

"Why do you suppose that would create enemies?"

"Well, some of the boys was getting into trouble with the ladies, you see. Courting a Blackleg Donnelly was probably the worst thing a young Catholic girl could do, but lots did. I suppose it added a little excitement to the girls' dreary lives on the farm. Drawn like moths, as they say. Many was the bar brawls I heard about over a sister or daughter's honour. There was even stories of farmers paying the Donnelly boys cash money to leave their girls alone. Imagine that!"

"But did you hear about any criminal activities they were involved in?"

"Objection. Any such information would be hearsay."

"Please rephrase, Mr. Irving."

"Very well. Johnny, in the time you worked on the Donnelly farm did you ever witness them doing anything against the law?"

"No, sir, not really."

"Just say yes or no."

"No, sir. I do remember there was high talk in town about all the things they did, what with them barns burning down and them horses being killed, men beaten up and robbed. And their mother, Johannah, ordering these actions against whoever she pleased, so the gossip went, but I never seen any of it. The truth was, some people just blamed the Donnellys for everything bad that happened around Lucan.

"Like I say, we just considered them the neighbours down the road and they never did nothing to us, in fact only favours, and frankly I can't see a Donnelly killing a horse or letting one burn in a barn. They really loved them horses."

"So you found the Donnellys to be good, law-abiding citizens?"

"Pretty much."

"Just yes or no, please."

"Yes." Johnny thought for a moment and started up again before Irving could stop him. "Mind you, they weren't angels neither. Like at Maggie Thompson's wedding. But I'd say whatever the Donnellys did, it usually didn't seriously hurt anyone and whether you were friend or foe, you'd find they was always most entertaining."

The Terrors

SINCE LATE WINTER and into the warm early spring of 1879, Will Donnelly had been deeply heartsick, sullen and morose that Maggie Thompson would do this to him. His own golden-haired Maggie who had pledged her love to him, and he to her through three summers. He'd laboured over pretty words of poetry to trap her heart, sang and played fiddle songs to her and behaved the complete gentleman, never touching her but only with her full welcome and encouragement.

Will was confident with his appearance; he had grown into a handsome man with his mother's intense green eyes and a long face and narrow nose. He chose to wear his red hair to his shoulders and had an imperial goatee on his chin. Many in town whispered how much like the devil he looked, even down to his one "cloven hoof" and his fiddle playing, and this he didn't much mind.

Will was aware for years that the Thompsons had no love for his family and though he had pressed her, Maggie would not let him approach her father for her hand. She talked of running away with him, but that didn't sit right with him. Three blissful summers they loved in sweet passion and secrecy, which was her choice—the hard winters were restrictive to their trysts as people stayed indoors and socialized less—and then came that bitter letter in which she told him all had been found out, she had confessed to her family their carnal relationship and Will had heard the mortifying news that his letters had been read by her dullard father and her brothers, Matthew and Zebadiah. He imagined them holding his letters in their clumsy paws, laughing over his most intimate disclosures. She had promised them never to see Will again and intended to stick by that evil bargain.

"I'm sorry, I'm sorry, I'm sorry," Will read in her last letter, as if plunging a knife over and over into his already battered heart.

So then Will began to wonder if her letter was penned through intimidation, and then he began to feel sure of it. As if in confirmation, another letter arrived one day in early June, a short, scrawled missive asking him simply to come and take her away!

Will decided to make the visit on horseback to the Thompson homestead with four of his brothers: Michael, James, Tom and Robert. He wanted to do it properly, respectfully, but if things went badly he would need some backup. Thompson opened the door to him and eyed him with hostility. Will had brought gifts of tobacco and whiskey, which he gave to Thompson. The old man took the gifts but did not invite him in, so standing outside Thompson's door, Will declared himself, as he thought he should have done from the beginning.

"Thompson, it would be my wish to take your daughter, Maggie, as my wife."

Old Thompson and his two sons laughed at Will's proposal.

"I would sooner see her dead than married to a Donnelly," Thompson replied with a snort.

"Then we are prepared to take her by force," Will told his friend, Hogan. The Donnelly brothers pushed the Thompsons back and entered the house. It was a large structure, but dank inside without fashion or comfort—small windows, crude male-dominated furnishings, a moose head on the wall, clothes drying on any structure and dirty dishes piled in the sink. Will was heartsick to think his Maggie lived in this house. They searched the bedrooms and then the summer kitchen where a skinned deer was hanging. Will returned to Thompson, who told him, "You could have saved yourself the trouble."

"Where is she?"

"Jean's taken Maggie someplace secret and safe, far away from you."

Will gave Old Thompson points for his bollocks as the brothers had by then grabbed hold of his arms and Will was very close to damaging him severely with his fists, and his brothers would sure have left the two Thompson sons senseless on the floor. But Will didn't feel right beating up a man in his own house, much less the father of the woman whom he still clung to the hope of marrying.

"And she's going to stay there in that secret place until she is married by her own consent."

"To whom?" Will asked, astonished.

"Pat Carroll."

The name was like a club to the head.

"What? That pitiful excuse for a man?"

"But he won the girl, didn't he? And you didn't."

God help us, Will thought, *what a waste.* Old Thompson had said it with such triumph, a broad smile displaying his broken teeth. There was nothing more to be done there without violence. In deep despair Will left the Thompson house, his brothers following behind.

"She can't stay hid forever, Will."

"If she's chosen Carroll, maybe she wasn't the one for you anyway."

"It's not the end of this, Will."

And so for the weeks leading up to the wedding—that loathsome event—Will wandered lost in his labyrinth of dark thoughts.

When Johannah Donnelly heard of these goings-on by way of Michael, she was not displeased, though she kept the feeling for the most part to herself. She had never thought much of Maggie as a suitable woman for her eldest son and believed he was making a childish fool out of himself. The girl was weak and spoiled, and the one time Johannah offered these thoughts up to Will early in the affair—"Wouldn't you rather someone with more substance?"—Will stormed off to the barn and the air was frosty between them for days. But Johannah knew there was no percentage in arguing with the power of love. Hadn't she herself succumbed to its persuasions long ago? It seemed to be a common condition of youth, like the measles or chicken pox, they all had to go through. She would bite her tongue, say a little prayer and hope her eldest would soon return to his senses.

The day of Maggie Thompson's wedding to Pat Carroll dawned a sunny spring Saturday and Will cursed the Judas sun for blessing the injustice. It was to occur at the spiritual fortress of St. Patrick's. Despite their family's estrangement from Father Connolly fifteen years before, his mother liked to go there to sit near the back and receive Sunday Mass. The priest would not deny her, but nor would he look her in the eye. The boys, some of them, joined her on occasion, if only for the socializing, for they still counted a good number of friends in the congregation.

The Thompsons were a popular family in the community despite the men's lack of graces and they were good friends of the expansive Kennedy clan. Some of the Thompsons were friends of the Donnellys and some were not. The Carrolls, family of the groom, also had many social connections, though the Carroll family name had some years back been tarnished with suspicion of thievery and arson, but all in all, Will calculated the turnout would be substantial and he would need all his brothers at the church. He wanted to give Maggie one more chance.

Will led his brothers, all seven of them mounted, all in their suits and high black boots, approaching from the north end of the cemetery, walking their animals respectfully in a line between the headstones. They didn't hurry and they didn't speak. They arrived together near the church steps and dismounted. There were horses, wagons and carriages lined up outside, and quite a few more across the street at Keefe's tavern. The church doors were closed. A pump organ was playing the wedding processional.

Inside the church, Father Connolly was presiding in his church finery at the altar as usual, and the congregation was on their feet. Will and his brothers removed their hats. The big church was filled for the wedding, bouquets of lilacs and wild roses lined the walls and covered the altar, and those present wore brighter clothing than they would have on a Sunday morning for Mass.

Will could just make out the bride through the heads of the people, as well as that miserable father of hers up at the altar beside the poor excuse for a groom, their backs to their guests. At the sound of the church doors closing, a few heads turned around to see the Donnellys newly arrived in full force. Everyone knew Will's feelings for Maggie and how her family had behaved toward him. More heads turned now in open-mouthed anticipation of what he might do. Will leaned to one side, trying to catch a glimpse of Maggie's face. Not yet noticing the Donnelly presence, the nearsighted Father Connolly commenced the ceremony in blissful ignorance.

"We are gathered together here in the sight of God and in the face of this congregation, to join together this man and this woman in holy matrimony…"

Old Thompson stepped aside and Will saw her, the radiant Maggie, looking at Pat Carroll with what Will knew was a thin, sad smile of fatal acceptance. But he was here to tell her she didn't have to do this.

"…which is an honourable estate, instituted by God in the time of man's innocence. Please be seated."

When the congregation sat down, Will and his brothers were the only ones standing other than the wedding party and more people began to notice their presence. Then Maggie glanced up, turned and stared at Will in shock. She then threw back her veil and glared at him with unmitigated exasperation. The entire congregation turned then, to find the Donnelly boys were in the church. All of them. There were gasps and whispers and apparently much amusement over Will's state of affairs.

Will was distracted for a moment by Nora Kennedy, only a few feet from him, her green eyes flashing in amusement.

"I'll be damned. Will Donnelly, you hopeless romantic."

Will looked at Nora for a moment, registering her enjoyment of the circumstances, but then returned to his mission to stop this farce. He marched up the aisle toward the altar, toward the bride and groom, and called out to Connolly, "I'd like to move along to the part, Father, where we can object. Because I object!"

Jean Thompson and Father Connolly spoke almost in unison: "How dare you!"

Maggie looked at him sadly. "Oh, Will…"

Will walked right up to the altar—the groom and his brother and best man, Jim Carroll, were frozen in surprise—and quickly, before anyone could prevent him, Will bent down, put an arm around Maggie's thighs, lifted her over his shoulder and carried her back up the aisle. The groom, his brother and Maggie's father all made an attempt to go after Will, but Tom, James and the other brothers moved in and stood in their way.

Overcoming his astonishment, Connolly once again found his voice: "Stop this! What are you doing?"

"Let's give them a moment," Michael Donnelly warned the groom and wedding party, as Will carried Maggie out through the heavy church doors.

This was too much for Pat Carroll. "You thieving Blackfeet!" he yelled. And he made the mistake of swinging his fist with incompetence, just missing Michael's pretty face. Tom stepped in with a hammer punch to Carroll's head and the fight was on, with Will's brothers against most of the male congregation.

Tom Donnelly took hold of Pat Carroll's bloody face and applied his thumbs to gouge out the groom's eyes until Michael intervened.

"Tom! Don't! Let him go!"

Father Connolly scrambled through and over people to safety behind the altar, aghast at the dozen men throwing punches in the sanctuary of his church.

"Stop this! I command you to stop!" But the men involved were past hearing. Fearful and angry mothers guided crying children to the doors, women found shelter between the pews, others joined Father Connolly behind the altar. Johnny O'Connor and his parents had crawled under a pew. His mother kept pulling Johnny down out of harm's way as he tried to see each blow of the donnybrook.

With Maggie over his shoulder, encouraged that she wasn't exactly struggling, Will quickly made his way down the steps and deep into the pastoral quiet of the green cemetery. Even there, the fight inside the church could be heard: grunts, yells, curses and breaking glass, and the admonishments of the women telling their men to stop. Will's instructions to his brothers were simply to hold them off and not do permanent damage to the people or the church, as Will took Maggie as far away into the cemetery as he could in the brief time they had.

"Will. Put me down."

They were a distance now from the church on a level table of clipped grass near several old granite headstones. He did as he was told, placing her down gently so she was sitting on the green canopy. Will sat back himself to look at her in the splendid lace gown, her blonde hair circled in tight braids beneath a small lace bonnet. A little powder and rouge on the cheeks and the full lips he had kissed so often. It was all as he had imagined, but for the fact he was not the groom.

Three men had at last hurried out from the church to save Maggie but she held up a hand as they approached.

"It's all right," she said, and they stopped. "I'm all right."

The men glared at Will, but then reluctantly retreated a few yards to give them privacy. Maggie leaned toward him and looked into his eyes with what he saw as an encouraging affection.

"Oh, Will. I told you it was over."

"But the letter you sent. To come and take you."

"It was an impulsive moment. I'm sorry."

"I went to find you."

"I know. They took me to my cousin's farm. I tried to escape."

"But they can't hide you now."

"But now, things are different."

Will fought the desire to stroke her face or take her hand.

"There were many things you told me, Maggie. Things you wrote. You said you loved me. Or have you forgotten?"

"No. I have not forgotten, but…things are more complicated."

"I love you. I want you to be my wife. Can anything be more simple?"

Maggie sighed and shook her head and they sat in silence for a moment. Will began to recite a verse they both knew:

> So the spirit bows before thee,
> To listen and adore thee;
> With a full but soft emotion,
> Like the swell of Summer's ocean.

Maggie studied him sadly, but there was emotion in her eyes. Was it love? he wondered with hope rekindled. Will's right hand was spread in the clipped grass. She placed her hand on top of it and recited a later verse.

> But the sword outwears its sheath,
> And the soul wears out the breast,
> And the heart must pause to breathe,
> And love itself have rest.

"No!" he wanted to tell her, but he was silenced by the conviction in her eyes. He wanted so much to touch her body but did not dare. She was giving him her answer and it was not what he wanted to hear. Will pulled his hand from under hers and turned away. He ran his fingers through his long hair and bit his lip.

"Maggie. You can't be in love with that…farmer. Marry me, Maggie."

"No, Will. It would never work out between our families. I don't want to live with conflict. My father would have a heart attack. My mother would disown me. I am not ready to live like that."

"Who cares about them! We can go away somewhere. I've got money. Michigan or Manitoba. Then it won't matter."

"I can't leave my family. Nor could you yours. It won't work."

The fight could be heard as it continued in the church. A chair smashed through a fine stained glass window and they both winced. Will looked at Maggie, feeling as helpless as an adolescent boy.

"I want you."

"We don't often get what we want, Will. That's how it is. I'll marry Pat Carroll and I will be…content. Can you please understand that?"

She leaned forward, put her hand on his face and kissed him on the cheek.

"I won't change my mind now," she continued. "We had some sweet times together. I will always remember those. We'll always have that. You are a beautiful man, Will, but it is not meant to be. Now please let me go back to my wedding and get on with my life."

Her hand remained on his cheek. He looked at her, his emotions raw and exposed as never before. The touch of her hand on his face was the final lifeline to what could be. She suddenly realized this and removed it, finally cutting him adrift.

Will watched Maggie go back to the church. With malignant glares at Will, the men standing by joined her. Will waited for her to turn back, just once, but she did not.

By now the crashing violence in the church had subsided and a few of his brothers were making their way out of the church. Michael was assessing the damage to his beautiful, broken nose. Pat was massaging his bloody right hand. Tom stood there with his vacant stare. Will would just be happy if Tom hadn't killed anybody. They all looked over to him for guidance. *Nothing else to be done here,* he thought. With a gesture of his hand, Will directed his brothers to their horses and home.

Johannah

As THEY ENTERED Fitzhenry's Hotel, owned by the chief constable's brother, Johannah and Jenny Donnelly could hear the slow fiddle music in the main dining room emanating from the open doors: the Thompson and Carroll wedding party. The hotel event was open and public so the Donnelly women had put on their finest dresses, bought in nearby London, and despite the rude behaviour of the males of their family earlier in the day, had decided to come to enjoy the gathering. The town was too small not to. Even after the battle in the church, Johannah knew it was important for the family to make an appearance to let everyone know the Donnellys held no grudge. The boys were parking the wagon and settling the horses. She had made sure that her boys would bring baskets with impressive gifts of food and drink, chocolates and whiskey and even wrapped gifts for the bride and groom, by way of an apology, though she would never have used that term.

After the wedding at the church, Chief Constable Fitzhenry had been called to investigate the Donnellys' transgressions, but everyone had seen Pat Carroll throw the first punch. Johannah instructed John Donnelly to immediately pay for the damages to the sanctuary with Father Connolly. So, finally, no charges were laid. But now it was time to enjoy the party and Johannah felt no small sense of celebration. Although Will had made a fool of himself, at least he would not be marrying Maggie Thompson.

Johannah and Jenny entered the main dining room, or the "ballroom" as the management coined it, arm in arm. The tables had been set to the side or removed for dancing and socializing. It was an impressively large plastered and painted room that would comfortably hold a hundred people, with a wooden and iron candelabra hanging aglow from the ceiling and three real landscape paintings from England on the wall. There were tall windows set in thick walls that provided enough room for several guests to sit on the sills. A short, heavy-set fiddler played dreary, formal music on his instrument. He was leading a small, uninspired band in a leaden waltz. The newlyweds, Pat and Maggie, were at a table opening gifts, surrounded by well-wishers, with Maggie's mother, Jean, beside them. A few guests were dancing. *What a lacklustre little affair*, Johannah thought. She enjoyed the way the members of the wedding party stared up at them with expressions of dread when her seven sons arrived just behind her. The Donnellys again, dressed in fine, fashionable suits, waistcoats and jackets, high polished boots, well-groomed with rings and pocket watches, beards combed and moustaches waxed, ready to enjoy the party, any one of them a catch for a smart Lucan girl.

Will, of course, had not wanted to come, but Johannah was determined to present a united front. It took some persuasion that honour demanded that he not hide, and Will's curiosity eventually trumped his apprehensions and heartache and he came.

The boys placed the substantial gift baskets on the table. They greeted their friends and enemies alike in the noisy good spirit of the day. The families of both bride and groom glared silently. They might well have felt the need, but no one possessed the ability to throw the Donnellys out. The young girls watched the new arrivals from a distance with great interest. Michael, with his long dark curls and flashing eyes, headed toward a gaggle of receptive young ladies.

"Hello, Judy, Winnie, Bea, you radiant creatures! I am overwhelmed with beauty here! Who was to know...Old Fitzhenry's has been transformed into the Garden of Eden full of Eves!"

The farmers' daughters were delighted with his patter. Johannah watched Michael from a distance and noted the hungry, competitive young eyes of this coterie. One in particular, the pretty young Fanny Carroll, was watching Michael closely and appeared to be biding her time. Johannah sensed that the girl saw danger there to be courted.

Young Jenny Donnelly lit up in a crowd, remembering everyone's names and joining in the gay chatter. "My daughter," Johannah said when introducing her. It still thrilled her to say it. Jenny had proved such a blessing—the last child Jim had given her was the best. She was a beauty, a female version of the curly-haired Michael, with warm brown eyes and an engaging laugh, her hair piled at the back of her head, her long neck revealed. Johannah both loved her beauty and feared it for the men who would come to steal her away.

And Johannah herself? She caught her own image in the mirror behind the bar for a moment and saw again how she had aged in the years since Jim was taken. Her dark hair was streaked with grey but there still remained a hardened beauty, and she knew she had a confidence that both intimidated and attracted the men in the room. Not that even one in fifteen years had sought her favour, not when her husband was Jim Donnelly.

Johannah knew very well some of the decisions made in the course of her life were not perfect. Falling in love with Jim Donnelly was only the beginning. She had lost her husband and then lost her church. Because of the kindness of Dr. Davis, she had made the decision to do open business with the Protestants and though this had brought prosperity to the family, she was very aware it had set some of the community against them. So be it. She would not be governed in Canada by the troubles in Tipperary.

Johannah's eyes were ever keenly on her boys and her thoughts on how proud she was of them, handsome spirited young men whom she had brought up well alone, dancing and carrying on as young men should. She hoped Jim would be pleased with them. After April 16 she would find out. That was his release date. In four weeks she would have her man back. It was all the boys talked about. Would he be happy with them all? Would he still love her? Would she still love him? But she was not ready to think about all that just yet.

One thing she was sure Jim would like was the fact that they now owned Pat Farrell's land. They owned the full hundred acres. Young Billy Farrell had lived with them as one of the family for many years and Johannah was pleased they could offer him that. He was a good lad, kind and smart and affectionate. At the age of nineteen, he wanted to seek his fortune and leave the conflicted memories of his father's death behind him. Though it was hard on Donnelly finances for a few years, Johannah had given Billy full market value and then some for his fifty acres. The boy had travelled west and built a lumber mill in the fledgling town of Yellowknife, married a Dene woman and started a family. He sent letters, calling the Donnellys "my family" more than once, and a photograph of himself and his wife that warmed Johannah's heart.

Johannah turned her full attention back to the wedding reception.

"Jean Thompson looks like she's about to turn to stone," Jenny remarked. Jean made no attempt to hide the chilling glare she offered Johannah. No surprise. Johannah, in return, responded with a generous smile and nod.

"She's already halfway there," Johannah replied lightly.

Mother and daughter laughed together and they looked around to warmer companions, waving across the dance floor to Dorothy Keefe and Loretta Hogan.

Johannah noticed James Jr. was already feeling no pain as he took a swig from his flask and grinned at the girls with his father's face and his grandfather's weakness for drink. He refused to talk to Johannah anymore about his drinking. She had Will trying to work on him about it. James now had his eye on a girl, a McLaughlin daughter who looked back at him boldly. He winked and it brought a smile from the little tart. James was always drawn to the bold ones.

Short, fiery-tempered Patrick was talking loudly to the Ryder brothers, James and Thomas.

"A 'property tax' now, they're saying! Paying tax on something you already own! We should take the government out and shoot the whole lot for even suggesting it!"

"And hang them while we're at it."

"Absolutely. For even suggesting it."

Her son Robert, slow and sweet, was dancing with a homely little girl, one of the Feehley sisters. Two young men watched them from the side. One, John Kennedy, called out to Robert as they danced by.

"Hey, Bobby. What day of the week is it?"

Robert slowed his dancing as he thought about this for a moment and Kennedy and his friend laughed at their joke. Robert realized they were only teasing him and grinned back at them in a good-natured way.

"All right. Have your fun, boys," and he danced away.

Jenny had moved some distance from her mother and placed herself alone with a pleasant, expectant smile on the edge of the dance floor, gazing around in anticipation at a few young men who seemed available. She caught the glance of two or three of them and batted her eyes in subtle invitation. All of them gave her the positive once-over, for she was a very pretty girl, but then one by one they would glance fearfully at her brothers, shuffle their feet and turn away. Jenny finally walked up to one of the younger, harmless Toohey brothers, who she had gone to school with.

"Good evening, Dennis. Would you care to shake a leg?"

The Toohey lad looked at her and, as others had done before, gave an involuntary glance toward her brothers.

"I'm sorry, Jenn. The damn ox stepped on my foot today. Sorry."

She glared at the shirker as he moved away from her, only just remembering to limp on the third step.

Johannah came up to Will and John, who were talking to the Whalen brothers.

"Rental houses. On our four lots just off Main Street," Will was telling the Whalens with enthusiasm. "We plan to expand the lumber mill. Board our own trees. Build the homes with Donnelly lumber. And a new grocery store where our renters can shop."

"But we're in need of some c-c-c-capital, gentlemen," John explained. "For a reasonable investment, you can be in on the g-g-g-ground floor with the housing."

"And did you tell them about the stagecoach line?" Will asked. "We'll be expanding our routes. We'll have a second coach to take our renters to London every morning to work. So we house them, sell them provisions and take them into town every day."

"You got this all figured out," Michael Whalen said, impressed. "Except Flanagans have the London route."

Johannah joined the conversation. "For now," she replied with a smile. "The Flanagan coaches are hacks and their fares overpriced." She waved her hand as if seeing a sign before her. "Donnelly Brothers Coachline… prompt, courteous service. The Donnelly name will stand for quality transportation."

"Full services, year r-r-r-round," John finished. "Da'll be popping a few buttons when he g-g-g-gets home."

"Yeah, your da gets out soon, eh?" asked Patrick Whalen.

"Four weeks!"

"You all must be excited."

"Yeah. It's been a long wait for us. Longer for him I'm guessing. But he'll be home soon. We plan to have the London run established by then."

"All right, but the Flanagans aren't going to like it."

"We don't want any trouble. It's just healthy competition in a growing market," Johannah said innocently.

"How much investment would youse be looking for?" Michael Whalen asked.

"Well, that all d-d-d-depends…"

As Johannah spotted Tom, she let Will and John take over the Whalen conversation and watched him. Her sixth-born was standing alone, his heavy-lidded eyes surveying the people in the room. Tom was her worry. But for him, all her boys could display compassion and affection. It was as if he was unconnected to the outside and bore some dark rage deep within. When he was seven years old, Johannah had witnessed him capturing a squirrel in his hands, which almost immediately bit him and in a second he had broken its neck. No tears, just the swift twisting action and he tossed the flaccid body away without a backward glance. She had hoped Tom's detachment would become less with time but that and his tendency to sudden violence had not. Will and the other brothers kept a careful eye on him.

If Tom had any affection it was for his simple brother, Johannah thought, as she saw him watch Robert and the Feehley girl go dancing by. As they did so, John Kennedy stuck out his foot and while the Feehley girl stumbled free, Robert tripped and fell heavily to his hands and knees on the dance floor. John Kennedy and his friend laughed out loud. Robert's face reflected his embarrassment as he got slowly to his feet. A second later Tom Donnelly had John Kennedy by the throat with one big hand, choking him against the wall.

"Why did you do that to my brother?" Tom inquired in a quiet voice.

When Kennedy's friend came to his defence, Tom easily fended him off with a backhand that knocked him down, stunned him and gave him a bloody nose. Tom pushed John, whose face was turning red, down onto his knees, his big hand like a hose clamp around his jugular.

"Why'd you do that?"

Will went quickly to Tom, standing over John Kennedy, and put his arm around his brother's massive shoulders. "Tom. That's enough. Let him go."

The crowd stood back, the dancers slowing to a stop, and watched as Tom applied more pressure. Robert Donnelly joined Will.

"Hey, Tommy? Let him go. He was just having his little joke."

"Tell my brother you're very sorry," Tom whispered.

John Kennedy spoke, choking through clenched teeth.

"...sorry."

"What did you say?"

Kennedy's voice was a strained, desperate whisper, "Sorry, Robert!"

But instead, Tom squeezed harder. John's nails raked at Tom's hands, his face bright red from lack of oxygen.

"He's killing him!" Kennedy's friend shouted, spraying blood on the onlookers from his bloody nose and trying to get through. Johannah came up beside Tom. The band's music came to a sliding stop, as all eyes turned to John Kennedy, who was kneeling on the floor with Tom standing over him, his hand clutched around Kennedy's throat.

"Tommy. Let him go."

Tom looked at his mother. "He was not nice to Bobby."

"I know. But let him go now."

Tom finally opened his hand to release Kennedy. Kennedy fell back on the floor. He convulsed, gasping for air and holding his throat, coughing. After an awkward pause, Anthony Fitzhenry gestured to the band. The music started up again with a new song, as wilted and uninspired as the last, but it eased the tension.

"Don't do that again, Tom," Johannah instructed him, looking into his eyes to make the point. Tom's expression became contrite and he nodded to his mother.

Leaving them, Will ordered a double whiskey at the bar and found he had to pay for it, those cheap Thompson bastards. His little brother Tom worried him. His other brothers would not always be there to stop him. Will took a long drink of the rye whiskey and listened to the band for a moment, a fiddle, piano, banjo and a trap drum. They were sawing along with some brutal standard that left the floor empty of all but the most intrepid dancers. He watched the newlyweds at their little table opening the last of their gifts. One was his. As he watched, Maggie held up the delicate lace shawl he had bought for her and she seemed delighted as she tried it on. She looked around and their eyes met and her appreciative smile took on the most subtle element of regret, or so it seemed to Will, and sadness came over him again. When she looked away, Will finished his whiskey. Then he heard a fresh voice in his ear.

"She's a practical girl."

He turned to find the green eyes of Nora Kennedy close beside him. She had forsaken her pants and shirt for a light summer dress that stopped him for a moment.

"I mean Maggie. Marrying Pat Carroll. She's far too practical for a romantic like you, Will. Did she even invite you here?"

"You must be joking."

"I say, consider yourself lucky, man. It was a close call."

The bartender had refreshed his glass without request. Will turned back to it, his elbows on the bar.

"I am forlorn, Nora. The dream is gone."

Nora glanced at Maggie, who was opening another gift with an eagerness that did not become her.

"Nightmare, I say. You'll get through this in the fullness of time, Will. Right now you need to get yourself out of this mood."

He turned to her.

"How do you propose I do that?"

"You can start by saving us from this tedious music. I know you can."

The band had finished their selection. Nora left the bar and Will watched as she went to speak to the fiddle player. She was persuasive, gave him a heavy coin to seal the deal and he gave up his fiddle to her. She returned and put it in Will's hands with a challenging smile. He inspected the workable instrument, quickly checked each string for tuning, making a few adjustments. He looked up at Nora's expectant expression, then went over to the band, which was making ready for the next set.

"Gentlemen?"

Will began to play a light and lively reel, in strong contrast to the previous dirge. The wedding guests immediately felt the mood change in the room. The other band members joined in and people made their way to the small dance floor. Within a few bars, there was a crowd. Will looked up from his fiddling to find Nora smiling at him. He was a good player and not shy either about showing off, adding a few trills and fancy notes for her.

At the back door of the hotel, James Jr. was speaking to Abbie McLaughlin. He patted his jacket where he had a bottle of rum. Abbie was the daughter of Martin McLaughlin, who still owned the largest farm of any Catholic in the region and was no friend of the Donnellys. The short man was standing with the Kennedys, his full head of silver hair proudly brushed back from his clean-shaven face, frowning a little at the new free nature of the music, and who was playing it. James whispered in Abbie's ear and she giggled, then glanced over toward her father, finding him pre-occupied. She put an arm around James's and left with him out the back door toward the barn and stables to "inspect the cows."

John Donnelly, small and agile, standing at the far end of the dance floor, was more comfortable in his suit, waistcoat and tie than the rest of his brothers. He had even worked at the bank in Exeter for six months wearing such an outfit every day until they discovered his father was a convicted murderer and he was let go. He summoned up his courage and approached Winnifred Ryder at a table near the back. They had known each other at a distance almost all their lives. She was a delicate girl and not unpretty when she raised her face.

"Wi…Wi…Winnifred? Would you care to d-d-d-dance?"

She looked up at him in alarm, then looked down again and shook her head.

"Then… could I maybe s-s-s-sit here?"

This time she hesitated, then nodded and he sat down beside her.

Johannah had seen John approach Winnifred and was pleased to see them talking together, John was so shy. But then she also noticed Michael and Fanny Carroll whispering in each other's ear. She didn't trust that girl with her Michael, and watched with concern as they went off together out of the ballroom, past the bar and toward the stairs to the second floor rooms. It was increasingly necessary to keep an eye on him.

The music of the band covered the sound of her footsteps as she followed them and indeed she found the couple upstairs in the darkened hallway of the quiet north wing. They were up against a closed door kissing each other without shame. Johannah stopped and remained at a distance in the shadows. At this moment the band stopped playing and Johannah heard Michael whisper, "Ah girl, don't deny me heaven."

Fanny laughed and bit his lip until he gave a yelp. "Heaven is for good boys."

"Oh, I'll be good. I'll be oh, so good. I'll have one foot in the goddamn priesthood."

"Not that good."

They laughed and Michael allowed his hand to casually slide down and cup her left buttock through the light cotton dress. With his other hand he rotated the skeleton key he had inserted in the hotel room door and turned the knob. They fell through into the small room and onto the noisy bed, the door closing behind them as the distant band began another tune. Johannah didn't exactly knock as she entered and confronted them.

"All right, you two. Fanny! What would your mother think?"

The girl was too scared to speak. She gathered herself as she jumped off the bed, ran past Johannah in the doorway and disappeared down the hall.

"Ah Ma, she was lovely and willing," Michael said as he buttoned up his shirt. "Why would you do that?"

"Saving you from yourself. Surely you can do better than a Carroll," Johannah told him.

"Any port in a storm, Ma."

"All I need is a Donnelly baby in an unmarried Carroll belly to make my life more complicated. How did you get the room?"

"Four bits an hour from Fitzhenry."

"That's about what she's worth. But Fitzhenry should be ashamed. I should tell his brother. Now do yourself up and come back to the party. I like to have my boys near me."

Michael stood up and gave her his dazzling smile.

"You'll always be my one true love, Ma."

At the end of a song, Will put down his fiddle, grabbed a glass of wine from a passing tray and addressed all those present.

"Ladies and gentlemen, I have a toast!" He had the attention of every guest once they charged their glasses. He was pleased to see Michael and his mother enter. He exchanged one last look with Maggie and put a smile on his face.

"To the happy couple. May they be blessed with many children and may we all live to be present at their golden wedding anniversary."

The guests endorsed Will's tasteful and generous toast and emptied their glasses and Johannah was proud of him. Maggie offered him a simple, public thank you. Then Will gave the fiddle back to its owner and left the party. As he passed his mother to leave, she recognized a certain distress in his hardened features.

"Will?"

He held up a warning hand as he strode past her. She was about to go after him when John called her over to a conversation he was having with Joe and James Flanagan, owners of the biggest stagecoach company in the township. The Flanagan family also owned the Central Hotel. She watched Will leave Fitzhenry's, then turned to join them.

"You should hear this, Ma. Mr. Flanagan is interested in our s-s-s-stagecoach business."

"Is that so?"

"Well, yes, Mrs. Donnelly," said James Flanagan. "We heard you were thinking of getting a second coach and a couple more teams and trying to service more routes. We really don't think that's a very good idea for anybody. We could save you a lot of trouble by giving you a fair price on your one diligence and your two teams."

"Afraid of a little healthy competition?"

"No use fighting it. There just isn't room for two coach companies in this county. And you're late half the time or breaking down. You Donnellys just don't have the experience to run a decent stagecoach line. And it's no job for a woman. So have some sense. We were thinking one thousand dollars all in. That's good money. Twice what those flea-bitten nags of yours are worth and that rattletrap you call a coach."

Johannah had been listening to the elder Flanagan brother, her tight smile growing slowly along with her temper as the man talked himself out of any hope of a deal.

"It's a funny coincidence you should be making this offer, James." She glanced at John for emphasis. "We were about to come to you to buy out the Flanagan Line."

Joe and James Flanagan stared at her for a moment, then smiled as if getting the joke.

"But we have four coaches, eight teams of four, more routes, better routes."

Johannah smiled. "Yes, your London route must make a little fortune."

"Boy, that's for sure!" Joe revealed enthusiastically. "The London route's half of our..."

"Joe!" His brother James interrupted him loudly. "Never mind. We have lots of good routes, and we're going to keep them. But my point again is there's not really room for two stagecoach lines in Biddulph."

"Maybe not."

"Good. So we'll give you… $1,500 but not a penny more for the coach, the team and leave the business."

"We'll give you $4,000 for all the Flanagan teams and coaches."

James Flanagan was starting to look mean. "Where you going get that kind of money?"

"We'll rob a bank."

"Don't be so foolish, woman. Take the offer."

She stared him down.

"Donnelly Brothers Coachline is not for sale."

Late that night, Will sat alone at Keefe's tavern finishing a bottle of Gooderham and Worts special rye and feeling sorry for himself. Except when it came to Maggie, both of these activities were rare in his experience, but when is a better time than after losing one's own true love? Even more so as he approached the bottom of the bottle. Keefe was sympathetic but he wanted to close up. It was about then that Will had the idea of bidding Maggie one final farewell. *Wait,* Will thought. *I'll give her a shivaree! It's only customary.*

So it was about two a.m. when Will started pulling apart forty feet of fence rails from Pat Carroll's paddock, piling them below the honeymooners' bedroom window. With a liberal dose of kerosene, he lit the pile on fire. Then he proceeded to ride around the bonfire, taking shots with his pistol at the stone chimney of the house from different angles. Later, he would vaguely recall singing "The Bear Went over the Mountain" at the top of his lungs. It took him little time to arouse the attention of the newlyweds inside, who opened their bedroom window.

"Donnelly! I'll get the law!"

"And all that he could see, and all that he could see, was…the other side of the mountain…"

The bonfire roared through the pile of dry rails.

"Will! Don't do this! Please go home!" Maggie called to him.

"The other side of the mountain…the other side of the mountain…"

"You'll be up on charges! I'm warning you!" Carroll shouted from the open window.

"Was all that he could see…"

Will fired another shot at the chimney and had the satisfaction of seeing Carroll duck. This was just before he fell off his horse. Will had not fallen off a horse since he was seven and now here he was sitting in the dirt in front of the woman he loved. Yes he did, there was no denying it. The bonfire was burning down now. The good feeling from the rye suddenly left him and he was just dizzy and sick. He had lost everything else and now he'd lost all that was left of his dignity. He looked up and into the light of the burning fence posts and the flames, now in decline, did serve to trigger an epiphany: Maggie was now gone from him. It was enough. They both needed to get on with their separate lives. Just then he heard a hammer cock and saw that Pat Carroll stood over him in his nightshirt with a double-barrelled shotgun aimed at his head.

"I've been plenty patient! You've got three seconds to get off my land, Donnelly. ONE!"

Carroll cocked the second hammer.

"No, Pat!" Maggie called out from the doorway.

It occurred to Will what a stupid way this would be to go, but he had difficulty expressing himself. Or standing up for that matter.

"TWO!"

"Please, Will!"

"THREE!"

"Lower the gun, Paddy. I'll take my boy home."

Johannah's horse came out of the darkness and stood in the firelight, Johannah looking down on them. She was unarmed but her presence caused Carroll to quickly lower his shotgun from the bead on Will's head.

As Johannah looked on, Will stumbled unsteadily to his feet. He found and picked up his hat. He faced the newlyweds, bowed deeply and mustered enough clarity for a final farewell.

"I'm sorry…I wish you a good night…and a good life."

Finding the trailing end of the reins, not trusting himself to mount successfully, holding onto the saddle horn to stay upright, Will led his horse away, walking unsteadily in the direction of the Roman Line, followed by his mother.

The Business

SHORTLY AFTER THE Thompson wedding, Johannah, Will and John acted on the decision to extend the routes of their Donnelly Brothers Coachline. The short-haul passenger and freight routes between Lucan and Clandeboye, Granton or Essex made them small change, but the plum of the stagecoach trade, the one the Flanagans claimed, serviced and controlled, was the Lucan to London run. They could operate two coaches, or "diligences" as they called them, all day back and forth for twenty-five cents a head each way to the stores and offices and factories of London. Once this service was regular and controlled, the houses they would build in Lucan could be rented at a higher rate. So this was the route the Donnellys were about to challenge.

Unknown to the Flanagans, the Donnellys had ordered a substantial, brand-new covered diligence quietly built for them in Goderich and painted with the name Donnelly Bros. Coachline, and an additional first-string team of four fine Arabians Michael had located and brought by train from Toronto. It cost them most of their savings. The rig could take nine passengers after driver and crew, and was finished inside with padded seats and glass windows. It was one grand stagecoach and the Donnellys were pleased with themselves.

"Imagine what Da will say!"

Michael would drive, of course. Will had done some driving for the Flanagans and could manage a rig with the best of them but Michael had the gift with horses—he could drive as well as he rode—and their motto would be "Comfort and Speed" to win the day and dominate the route. They had just as much right to it as the Flanagans.

Michael and Will had taken the rig out a couple of nights under darkness up the Roman Line to Saintsbury and across to Whalen's Corners and back, where they wouldn't be seen, urging the horses several times into a full gallop. They came back to report to Johannah the first night and by the candlelight on the kitchen table, with smiles breaking through their dusty faces, they told her the rig was very fine, well balanced and sturdy, and the four Arabians were a gift from God.

Michael, Will, John and Jenny had worked into the night on the decorations. The new Donnelly coach was festooned with the British colours of red, white and blue, streamers flying, pompoms on the harnesses and feathered headgear for the four horses. The majority of passengers bound for the banks and offices of London that Friday would be Protestant, Johannah had reasoned, with an uncompromised love of their queen. The British colours made for good business.

So on the day of the inaugural London run, the Donnellys were ready. Will rode with Michael, and Johannah kissed them goodbye.

"Make me proud of you. Remember, you're representing the Donnelly name."

They brought the new coach, all proud and sassy, down the Roman Line and onto Main Street. There were not too many folks around that morning but those that were stopped and stared. They passed through Lucan and made a left onto the Proof Line Road. Michael grinned at Will, the wind in his curls, happy in his work.

The strategy was to let the Flanagans pick up their passengers at the Central Hotel on Main Street and challenge them before they got to their second stop. The second passenger stop was a mile south of town with people coming in on the concession roads from the southern villages of Elginfield and Denfield to catch the coach to London. All they had to do was beat them there. Now just leaving town was the Flanagan coach up ahead in the distance, a worn-down, lumbering brig compared to their shiny new streamlined cutter.

Joe Flanagan was in the driver's seat with his brother James beside him. They turned around to see the Donnellys approaching.

"What the hell is that?"

Joe urged their animals to greater effort. Michael slapped the reins himself for a little more velocity and moved over into the left lane, ready to overtake the Flanagans, and the race was on.

At the crossroads coach stop for the London destination, five passengers stood waiting for the coach: two businessmen in suits, two women with empty shopping sacks and a farmer in jeans. It was quiet, calm, the businessmen checking pocket watches, others peering up the road, when suddenly they saw the two coaches appear over a slight rise, coming toward them in the distance, on the long straightaway leading to the stop. The coaches were almost abreast, a huge vortex of dust spiralling up behind them, hooves pounding, drivers hollering, running flat out, neck and neck at broken-bone speed.

The two teams of horses were at a proper gallop, though Will knew young Michael was not yet giving the Arabians full steam. Will was holding onto anything he could as they bucked and reeled over the old corduroy road. Ahead of them, the other users of the road had no rights, pedestrians, a donkey cart and a terrified penny-farthing bicyclist, who at first tried to outrun them and later headed wisely into the ditch, because nothing was going to stop this coach race.

As the coaches ran side by side down the Proof Line toward London, Michael and Will were having the time of their lives. Will called out across to the Flanagans, "Hey, Flanagan! You dragging an anchor?"

Joe Flanagan was throttling his horses with a long bullwhip. "This is our route, Donnelly!"

"Not for long!" Will laughed at him.

"You can go to hell!"

"You first!"

The stages were so close, Joe tried out his whip on Will and Michael. On the third application Will managed to grab the bullwhip in his gloved hand and there was a tug of war between the two coaches. Will pulled the whip from Joe and threw it away into the dust cloud behind them.

Inside the Flanagan coach, they could now hear the passengers shouting.

"Slow down! I want out! Let us out!"

As the two competing coaches approached the crossways, the passengers who stood waiting at the next stop were all watching the spectacle intently. They looked askance at each other, hands shading eyes, stepping out of the shadow of the crossroads chestnut tree to try and figure out the meaning of the imminent arrival of two coaches. Neck and neck now, the Flanagan passengers protested in the vain hope their driver might heed them.

"Stop! I want out! Help!"

Neither driver was about to give up. Veering wildly, Flanagan reined his coach hard into the side of the Donnellys' with a crash of wood and steel.

"Hey! He's wrecking the new rig!" Will told Michael, but his little brother had no intention of holding back.

After the first rough impact and withdrawal, Joe Flanagan turned his horses hard to the left and smashed into the Donnelly coach again, but the new rig had the weight and wider wheelbase to withstand it. This time the Flanagan coach bounced off and lost control, lurched sideways, and as the passengers screamed, it rolled over onto its side. Dragged by the excited horses, the coach slid along the right ditch for forty yards before coming to a stop in a cloud of dust and a wail of passenger fear and indignation.

Still upright, the Donnelly diligence continued down the Proof Line toward the passenger stop.

"Nice driving, Mike!" Will exclaimed as he grinned, gently elbowed his little brother and straightened his own clothes to greet their first passengers.

Mike pulled their empty coach to a squealing, horse-rearing, wheel-seizing, dust-enveloped stop in front of the amazed passengers waiting under the chestnut tree. Michael hopped down and dusted himself off. The new rig had sustained a few scratches but most of the coloured streamers and pom poms remained intact.

"Good morning to you all!" Michael greeted them and opened the door with a grand gesture. "It's the new Donnelly Brothers Coachline at your service for London. All aboard."

The passengers looked at each other nervously. No one moved to enter the coach. Michael smiled at all of them with his perfect teeth, giving them a moment to consider. From the driver's seat Will was looking back down the line to observe the fate of the rival coach's drivers and passengers. Joe and James Flanagan were standing on the road beside their overturned rig, dusty and hatless, but both in one piece. Will heard Joe call out to them on the gentle breeze.

"You sons of bitches!"

Will watched as their battered passengers, with no help from the Flanagans, slowly crawled up out of the coach door, one, two… a businessman and farm hand helped a middle-aged lady out of the door. An older man half-emerged behind her and shook a fist at the Donnellys. Will had considered going to assist but changed his mind.

"They're fine," Will concluded quietly. "Come on. Let's get these folks loaded."

Michael ran a hand through his hair and blew the dust from his nose with his red bandana and addressed their would-be clients again.

"So, ladies and gentlemen…the new Donnelly coach for London is now boarding! In you get!"

Again the men and women failed to move. They were looking down the road at the small gaggle of shaken Flanagan passengers, standing like a shipwrecked crew beside the overturned diligence.

"Look what you've done to the Flanagan coach," the younger shopper told them.

"Oh, them," Michael responded dismissively. "They've got a terrible safety record. Taking your life in your hands with the Flanagans. It'll be the Donnellys from now on. All aboard!"

Michael betrayed some impatience when no one moved. He looked at his older brother and whispered, "What do we do now?"

Will turned to address the audience. "All right, ladies and gentlemen, for today only, we're dropping the round-trip fare from fifty cents to twenty-five!"

The farmer bolted into the Donnelly coach and the other passengers followed. Michael and Will loaded their bags, took their money and helped them aboard. Michael gave the two women a wink and told one older shopper, "Shame on your husband for letting such a beauty travel alone."

One passenger, a middle-aged businessman, hesitated before boarding, looking at Michael and Will. "I don't know about this. I…I think I might wait and…"

"No time to dawdle."

Michael took his arm firmly and encouraged him into the Donnelly coach. When all were aboard, Michael and Will climbed into the seat above and off they set for London.

Joe and James Flanagan stared at the new Donnelly coach setting off down the road with their stolen passengers, making promises to themselves.

The Homecoming

JOHANNAH SAT HERSELF down on the creaky bench in front of the ancient mottled mirror to take a good long hard look. It was April 16, 1879, the day she had been waiting for. He had been released the day before and was coming home. A sigh escaped her. She arranged and rearranged her shoulder-length dark hair, a braid up, a braid down, two braids, no braids—she brushed it out again—*a bun or piled up, with combs or without?* She put on her spectacles for a better look—*the bangs are all right, but should I have ringlets? They are in fashion this year. But what will Jim care about fashion?* He would probably want her hair exactly as it was fifteen years ago, but she was no longer that woman. She took the spectacles off. Her daughter, Jenny, was sweeping the floor behind her. A few dust motes had risen, catching the sunlight through the window that faced the Roman Line going south into town. She gazed at the empty road for a moment, then went back to the untrustworthy mirror.

"Up or down?"

"Oh, down I think looks pretty, Ma."

"Down shows the grey more."

"Then up!"

"Then you see the wrinkles."

"Stop worrying. He's going to be so happy to get home. To see you after all this time. It's so romantic!"

"Romantic? I guess," she replied with a light laugh.

For fifteen years Johannah had fought to keep the farm running, the eight children fed and clothed, crops growing in the field and the household maintained. She had kept them all alive, hadn't lost one. She could see now how it was all written in the lines on her face, every bad harvest, every schoolyard fight, every neighbour's complaint, every childhood illness or broken arm, every lame horse, every tax collector's visit, the evidence there for all to see.

There had been no visits to the prison. A convicted murderer in Kingston Prison was not allowed visitors. She had written letters, at first almost every day, and at first he wrote back with short, terse communiqués he knew would be read by the prison authorities. After the first three years, these tapered off.

Johannah had dreamed of this day and yet her doubts and fears were swirling through her mind like a flock of angry crows. After all this waiting, still she yearned for just another day or two to be ready. *How much will he have changed and will whoever he has become still love me, and will I still love him?* Her thoughts flew round and round again until she felt dizzy.

They had all worked so hard on building and improving the place and deep within each of them, it was for him. *Surely he will be impressed.* The bedroom now had plaster and paint on the walls, a dressing table, a nice high-back chair and a new four-poster bed that Johannah had indulged in. Like the bed of her childhood in Ballymore, the posts almost scraping the ceiling.

Jenny finished sweeping and came over to look into the mirror with her mother. In its frame was the yellowed sketch of Jim from his wanted poster—he had never had a photograph made. Jenny laid her chin on her mother's shoulder as they studied the sketch. The face was handsome, clean shaven, wreathed in curly hair like Michael's and had a sad smile.

"Just bad luck for you he's so ugly," Jenny joked playfully.

"He was the most handsome man in the county."

"But that croaky voice and the stutter…"

Johannah laughed. "His voice could charm milk from a chicken."

"It's strange for me not knowing what he looks like, having never really met him. Only the one picture. But I feel like I know him and I think I will. My own da! Tell me about the first time you met again."

"We were kids together…"

"No, Ma, I mean afterwards. After you came back from England. The poaching in the grass."

"Oh, yes. You liked that. I caught him poaching on the estate. He was all charm and swagger. I caught him and…then he caught me."

Jenny groaned and slumped in an armchair.

"Why doesn't anything like that ever happen to me? Go on."

"Then he took me off to North America…said I'll give you a new world and a new life…and that he did." She hoped Jenny didn't catch the slight sarcasm in her final words.

"It's so romantic!" Jenny exclaimed, but she noticed her mother's face began to cloud with doubt. "Don't you be nervous now. It'll be fine."

"He'll expect to find the girl he left. He'll find me."

"Ma, he will fall on his knees and thank God when he sees the beautiful creature that awaits him."

Jenny suddenly came over from the armchair and hugged Johannah from behind and they laughed for a moment.

"Go and sweep the kitchen."

"I did."

"Well go and sweep it again!"

Jenny left with the broom. She was replaced a moment later by her eldest brother. Will came in and sat his tall slender body on the bed behind his mother, silent for a moment, his hands clasped between his knees, his large head lowered, staring at the floor. *He really could have been a priest*, Johannah mused.

"We're just heading out with the coach now to get 'im."

He raised his head and studied her reflection in the mirror as Jenny had.

"You ready for this, Ma?"

She smiled at the earnest concern in his face but didn't reply.

"It's just I've heard stories about prison. What it does to a man. He'll be changed."

"I know. So are we all. But we'll make it work, Will. We'll get through. We always do."

"Yes, we always do. You're the inspiration for that, Ma." He studied her for a moment. "All these years you always did what you had to do for us."

Will smiled, stood up, kissed the top of her head, patted her shoulder and left her alone. Johannah returned to the ruthless mirror again. The smooth little river stone from Ballymore with the flecks of red and green was on her dresser. She touched it for good luck. Jim was coming home.

Michael, with Will beside him, took the Donnelly stagecoach at double speed down Main Street heading east as they left the Central Hotel where the paddy wagon had brought Jim Donnelly for his release. The Donnelly coach, with Jim inside, sported ribbons and bows again and the four Arabians had been brushed from their full manes and silky coats to the long feathers of their forelegs. James and Patrick escorted the coach proudly on horseback, as outriders on either side.

The boys had only seen their father for a moment as he cursed his guards goodbye and carried a small sack of belongings from the prison wagon to their coach. He stopped in front of Will for a moment—his hard eyes, buried in a full beard, studying his son. Will barely recognized him.

"Will?"

"Yes, Da. It's me."

Will wanted to embrace him but something held him back. He extended a hand and they shook, he with enthusiasm and affection.

"It's good to see you, Da."

"Is your mother well?"

"Yes! We all are. They're waiting for you. See our brand-new stagecoach? You can ride like a king. The Donnellys are a going concern and we—"

"Take me home," his father cut him off as he climbed into the coach, where he remained silent and hidden behind the curtains inside. *It must be hard for him,* Will thought, *to have missed so much, but the family will lift his spirits.*

Beaming in the driver's seat, Michael called out to his brothers, "Come on, boys! Let the parish know, Mr. James Donnelly Sr. is back!"

"Our da is free!"

"Whooooooo, whooooooo! The Donnellys are together again!"

James and Patrick pulled out the pistols they had brought for the occasion and began firing them into the air. Passersby paused on the boardwalks of Lucan to watch the noisy entourage pass. Most knew what they were seeing. At the Central Hotel the response had been muted, but as they went by Fitzhenry's tavern there were a few cheers and waves. Chief Constable Fitzhenry—still very active, though an older man now—decided to let the illegal discharge of firearms within town limits go by. Will was sure Fitzhenry had bigger concerns about his father's return, with friends of Pat Farrell still around.

On the edge of town going east on Main Street they passed the O'Connors' little house on the south side and the grand 260-acre farm with the pillared house of Martin McLaughlin, who had testified with such bias against Jim fifteen years before. James and Patrick hollered and fired a few more rounds at the bottom of his lane. Will could see Mc-Laughlin watching from his front porch.

Father Connolly watched too, standing in the doorway of St. Patrick's at the crossroads. As they passed, Will tipped his hat. Connolly stood as still as a scarecrow. Then the diligence took the corner at St. Patrick's from Main north onto the Roman Line far too fast and might have been lost in the hands of a lesser driver—they almost lost Will. Michael steadied the coach in time to give a returning wave to a few men outside Keefe's tavern across from St. Patrick's, a couple of them shouting their support, then the Donnelly team galloped north up the centre of the Roman Line with a long trail of dust rising up into the still air behind them. Patrick and James reloaded as they rode.

The Donnelly coach passed the homesteads of the Flanagans, the Kennedys, the Tooheys, the Feehleys and the Carrolls. As they approached the Donnelly homestead on the west side of the Roman Line, Pat and Margaret Whalen were out hoeing in their garden a short distance from the road. When they heard the whooping and pistol shots that announced Jim Donnelly's return, they rose from their labours, stretching their backs, and watched as the stagecoach and the Donnelly boys rode by. Will waved to them and they waved back, but Will noticed their apprehensive expressions, betraying mixed feelings. Were they worried about troubles in Lucan with Jim Donnelly back? Fifteen years was a long time to maintain the unrelieved thirst of vengeful minds. Will was confident the Donnellys would put those apprehensions to rest.

The coach came wheeling into the yard and Will found himself seeing the place through his father's eyes. The house had been extended twice since he left, framed in and painted. They now had a few young beef cattle in the corral and milk cows in the distant green pasture beyond the new outbuildings. His father should be very pleased with what they'd done. Will was proud to show him.

Michael brought the rig to a dramatic stop in front of the porch, the outriders firing a couple of pistol shots, and Patrick hollered, "He's back!"

Robert, Tom and John stood on the porch in ebullient anticipation. Jenny came out of the house, took the hands of John and Robert and together they walked out to the stagecoach to greet their father. Patrick fired his last two shells and Jenny scolded him.

"Patrick! Put that away now."

Patrick stuck his pistol into his belt. Michael hopped to the ground and with ceremony, placed a wooden milk crate below the door for their father to step down on. All of them came together in a half-circle a few feet from the coach door to give him room and stood still and silent, excited, waiting.

After a moment, Will went forward, turned the handle and opened the door. From out of the darkness, their father emerged. He squinted into the afternoon sun, then stepped down on the crate and surveyed his farm. They were all struck silent to see that prison life had not been kind to their father. He was fully bearded and had an old knife gash from his temple to his mouth that had been broadly stitched. His hair was mostly grey and his face was now lined and significantly aged. There were elements of defiance, cunning and fear in his expression.

Will stepped up to him and Jim turned his attention from the farm to his family. "Welcome home, Da."

All joined in as the brothers and Jenny came forward.

"Welcome home, Da! Welcome! Sure is good to see you. Welcome home!"

Forming a line, each one spoke their name and shook his hand with enthusiasm. Jim Donnelly stared fiercely at each son and then finally at his daughter. "You're my girl?"

"I am! I'm Jenny," she confirmed. "I don't think we've met. Hello, Da." She stepped forward, did a shallow curtsy and waited as he stared at her without moving. Finally she took his big broken hand in both of hers and squeezed it as he tried to smile.

Her father looked away from her out to the old abandoned and derelict Farrell farmhouse, his face betraying some satisfaction there. There were cattle grazing on the old Farrell property.

"Whose beasts are those?"

"Ours, Da. We bought the Farrell place. We own all hundred acres now." Will surveyed the house. "We left the house up. But we took down the fence."

His father nodded slowly as he considered this.

James Jr. was eager to read a speech he had written out and Will nodded for him to go ahead.

"On this solemn yet joyful occasion, we want to welcome our father home and say that though, through the many years we have missed him, we have as a family..."

"Where's your mother?"

James stopped and Will answered for him, "In the house, Da. She's coming. Don't worry."

Ignored and hurt by the interruption, James folded and put away his speech, turned away from his father and took out his flask. It was then that Johannah stepped out onto the porch.

Will announced her. "Da? Here she is."

Johannah had reclaimed her beauty with her hair up and a new dress. She came down from the porch, across the yard and walked boldly up to Jim. They stood apart.

"Hello, Jim." Her eyes then began to tear up. The children watched her as she tried to evaluate this hard, bearded man before her and find her Jim Donnelly in there after all these years.

"Well...I've raised you seven handsome devils and one beautiful angel."

"That's me!" Jenny interjected.

Johannah concluded her statement. "Welcome home to us, Jim."

Johannah then stepped up and put her arms around him and embraced him with all her strength. Jim stood, not quite knowing what to do with his arms. He finally patted her back with one hand and she withdrew from him, knowing enough not to be hurt, knowing it would take time for him to find comfort at home, and in her. They studied one another's face for a half minute and Johannah laughed and Jim offered a ghost of a smile. Yes, it would take time, Johannah knew.

Will waited as long as he could. "See what we've done to the house, Da? Framed and plastered. And the new barns for the horses and stagecoaches. The war in the States was good for us the year after you left. We sold a lot of horses, cattle and pigs to the Yanks. We donated a little corner square of our land for a schoolhouse that's been there seven years. Now we're going to expand our lumber mill and build rental housing in town. We're doing well, Da. You don't have to worry. We're well off now."

Jim looked around at the buildings. "Well, you're squires of the county now. Got the world by the arse and a downhill haul. Didn't need me at all."

"No! This is all because of you, Jim," Johannah assured him. "Each time we'd ask, what would Jim do...what would Da do? So you see, you were at the centre of this."

"Always w-w-w-with us, Da," John added quietly.

Their husband and father looked at them, his face unused to expressing a positive emotion.

"So you didn't forget about me?"

"Not for a moment!" Michael assured him.

He looked out over the fields. "You've cleared that back section. You can almost see to the property line."

"You can!" Will exclaimed. "There's plenty acres for barley and wheat..."

"Good. At least you've not been sitting on your arses." Jim gave a short cough of a laugh and on this cue they all laughed with him.

"You taught us about hard work, Da."

"You were a good father."

"Well, I've been thinking about this moment for some time. You're all fine-looking lads."

"What about me?" Jenny asked, confronting him, and Jim Donnelly laughed.

"And a fair girl...and a fine farm..." Jim was blinking as the tears entered his eyes.

"Welcome home, Da!" Jenny told him and hugged him again and everyone took up the refrain. "Welcome home."

Jim wiped a sleeve across his eyes and nose and looked toward the house.

"All right, then. What's for grub?"

"Come inside."

Jim turned and limped his way across the yard toward the farmhouse, followed by Michael, Robert, Patrick and Tom.

"We'll show you the house, Da!" Michael offered.

"It's really nice," Robert spoke with enthusiasm.

"It's got plaster walls and new furniture and...everything," Patrick gushed as they followed him.

Johannah turned to Will and Jenny and John.

"There. He's good. He just needs a little time with us. He'll be fine," she told them with all the conviction she could muster and hurried to follow her husband inside.

Settling In

THAT NIGHT THEY were in the yard having a lively bonfire to celebrate Jim's return with family and a few friends: the Keefes—old James and his two sons, Sam and Luke—and the Whalens. Will played his fiddle and John played pipes. A painted banner proclaimed, "Welcome home Jim." Johannah danced and laughed with Michael.

As for Jim Donnelly, he sat drinking whiskey near the fire and talking over the pipe and fiddle music to James Keefe. From time to time Jim would suddenly, warily, look at the people around him, behind him. Then he would turn his attention back to James as he caught Jim up on local news. Will listened to their chat, a little jealous as his father hadn't said more than two dozen words to him since he arrived.

"I was sorry at Dr. Davis's passing," Keefe told him. "I stood outside the wall at Trinity for the service. He was a good man for a Protestant. But I wasn't sad to see John Carroll in the ground. His son Jim's grown up to be as much an idiot."

"The son has now become the enemy then?"

"The enemy? Well, I don't know…"

"In Kingston, life's pretty simple: there are friends and there are enemies."

James Keefe adjusted his leg, which still caused some pain in the evenings, sixteen years after the accident, and gave a considered response to his friend.

"But you're not in prison now, Jim. Things are better in Biddulph. It's not the law of the jungle the way it was."

"I guess we'll see."

Johnny O'Connor had been helping out after farm chores the night that Old Jim Donnelly came home. He was to serve guests and wore a clean shirt that Johannah had given him over his thin frame and had brushed his straw-blonde hair. He brought a plate of apples and cheese up to Will, who took some, then offered it to Jim and James Keefe. Johnny was a little nervous about meeting Jim Donnelly. The man had gone to prison before he was born and the plate trembled. Old Jim studied him for a moment.

"And just who are you, boy?"

"I'm Johnny O'Connor, sir. I lives near to town, sir. I do chores for your missus."

"O'Connor. I remember. The shack next to the McLaughlins' place? A pretty mother and your da's the drunk?"

"That's me. I were born a couple years after you went away. I'm glad you're free, sir."

"You may be in the minority in this town but thank you, lad. It's a pleasure to meet you."

Jim stuck out his hand and Johnny shook it, spilling a few of his apples in the effort.

"You remind me of someone," Jim told him. "A boy I knew a long time ago. His name was Vinnie."

"Must have been a handsome fella."

Jim looked at Johnny a moment and then laughed out loud at his little joke.

Jenny Donnelly had been watching her father from a distance. She remembered all the stories her mother had told of him and his rough countenance was beginning to soften in her eyes. She worked her way toward her father, passing Johnny, who she knew had a crush on her. She smiled at him and said, "Hi sweetheart."

Johnny's face went red and he quickly picked up his apples and moved along.

Jenny extended her hand to her father almost like a challenge. It was time to dance. He looked up at her, intimidated by this pretty young woman who happened to be his daughter.

"Dance with me, Da. Ma says you're pretty good at it."

He shook his head, but she wasn't about to give up.

"Come on! You got to."

"Dance where?"

"Just over there on the driveway near Will and John. It's hard and smooth."

His features softened as she spoke and when she gently took his hands and pulled him reluctantly to his feet, he did surrender and walked with her to the packed ground near the players. He tried a little jig with her. He seemed pleased and even initiated a few fancy steps.

"Kinda rusty. Not much call for dance practice in the pen."

His sons began clapping with encouragement and others joined in. Jenny was laughing. But then their father tripped and almost fell. In embarrassment he tried to escape back to his seat. Jenny playfully grabbed his arm again. He pulled it away quickly, too roughly, and sat down not looking at her. Though she covered it with a laugh, Jenny was hurt by his rejection. After he had sat down, she kissed him on the back of his head and went to get some apples herself.

Michael stood up and gestured to the musicians. The music stopped and Will and John came over beside Johannah to witness a special presentation.

"Excuse me, everyone. I have a little story you're all familiar with. Goes like this...

> A handsome young devil named James,
> got involved in some fisticuff games.
> While he was only defending,
> a man's soul went ascending,
> So hanging became the courts' aims."

Jim rubbed his beard and turned away, uncomfortable with the attention. He looked around at the others while Michael continued with his eyes on his father.

> So handsome was this fellow, Donnelly,
> they decided they couldn't hang he.
> They sent him away,
> fifteen years and a day,
> then gave him back to his good family.

Jim sat up and listened to the poem, warming to its good intentions.

> So now reunited are we.

Strong and proud is the name Donnelly.
All the girls we will kiss,
not one party we'll miss,
now Da's back from penitentiary!

For the first time their father seemed pleased. He applauded and everyone joined in. Johannah put a hand on his shoulder and smiled at him.

Robert pointed at Tom. "Tom doesn't kiss any girls. None'll have him!"

Everyone laughed, even Jim and Johannah. Tom grabbed Robert in what at first seemed a playful hold. Then Tom bent Robert's arm behind his back. Robert yelled in pain and Michael warned him, "Easy, Tom. He was only joking."

"Let him go, Tom," Will's voice was serious.

Robert said with a cry, "I was just kidding!"

The maniacal look returned to Tom's eye as he bent the arm higher. Again Robert yelled in pain. Will took hold of Tom's arm and Michael grabbed him around the shoulders but Tom would not let go of Robert. The Whalens and Keefes watched, their eyes wide at Tom's cruelty to his brother.

"Let him go!" Will shouted in his ear.

Johannah positioned herself in Tom's sightline and looked into his eyes. "Stop it, Tom."

At Johannah's word, Tom released Robert and stood back. With tears in his eyes, Robert inspected and rubbed his wounded arm and whimpered.

"He almost broke it. I thought you were my friend."

"I'm...sorry," Tom told Robert.

"He didn't mean to, Robbie," Johannah told him. "Tom, you just go too far. We'll put some ice on it. Johnny, bring some ice please. Come into the summer kitchen, Robbie."

As Johnny hurried to the ice house, Johannah led Robert into the summer kitchen to pump some cold water on his arm. Will studied Tom for a moment, then walked away to have a smoke.

In the summer kitchen the cool pump water was easing the pain in Robert's arm, but he was still upset.

"I was just kidding. Why did he do that?"

"He didn't mean to hurt you. He doesn't understand sometimes."

Johnny brought two blocks of ice and Johannah applied them to the elbow and shoulder. "Do you want to hold the stone?"

Robert nodded his head and Johannah gave him the good luck stone from Ireland to hold in his good hand. Robert showed it to Johnny.

"You see? Ma brought it all the way from Ireland. The green is for the green of Ireland where we come from and the bits of gold are for heaven and the bits of red are for the blood. Donnelly blood we all share."

Johnny listened closely even though he had heard it before. He smiled when Robert was done. "That's real smart, Robert." Robert turned the stone over and over in his hand.

Tom went to sit on the ground beside his father's chair. He put his head against his knee. Left alone, Jim put a hand on Tom's head and began speaking very quietly to him.

"You know, you're right, Tommy. This world only sees power and strength. That gets you respect. But not against a brother. You will use that power against our enemies. You understand?"

Tom looked up at him and nodded. "Yes, Da."

"Good boy. I can tell you're the strong one."

Tom nodded again.

When all their friends and neighbours had left, the candles blown out and the house quiet, Johannah led Jim into their bedroom and presented the new four-poster bed she had bought in anticipation of his return. Jim felt the lace curtains on the window with his clumsy, broken fingers. He stumbled over a velvet footstool. He admired the bed.

"Fit for a queen, Jo. Sad you were sleeping in it alone."

"Jenny sleeps with me on a cold night."

There was nothing in her life Johannah had ever wanted more than for things to be good between them now. She sat down and patted the mattress beside her.

"Sit."

"Yes, sir," Jim replied, but the joke was strained. Jim sat down beside her, rubbing his wrists, and she noticed the dark calluses from the shackles they had made him wear. He would not look her in the eye. Johannah reached out and began to massage his shoulders. He started at the unfamiliar touch and looked up at her with apprehension. She loosened his shirt and continued.

"Your shoulders are like rocks."

"It's a long time to go without a friendly touch."

As the shirt fell from one shoulder she found cruel, old lash marks that had cut the skin on his shoulders and she could see in the mirror that they ran down his back. They extended in layers, some old, some newer and some, red lipped, very recent. She touched the knife scar on his face, angry calloused skin still gaping between the careless stitches. She took and held his right hand, with the broken fingers in hers.

"They hurt you."

Jim looked down at his feet. "I hope you will be patient with me. I won't be easy for you. But I'm trying."

"We've got all the time in the world, Jim."

She gave him a warm smile then and he continued the first tentative steps on that long journey.

"You've kept your looks."

"I guess your eyesight's going," she teased and they laughed together for the first time.

"Maybe. Sure in reality you couldn't look as good as you do to me now."

"That's a lot of beard you got going on there, mister. You expect me to kiss that?"

"You might get to like it."

"If I liked kissing porcupines."

"Oh. Never mind then."

Jim looked away and then suddenly turned back to give her an unexpected kiss.

"So you still steal kisses, do you? Careful or you'll wind up back in jail for theft."

Johannah kissed him back and they studied each other again.

"I still love you."

Overcoming his reticence, Jim examined her face, extended a finger and touched the tip of her nose.

"Imagine that."

And there through the beard and the hard years of separation emerged a little of her Jim, and Johannah wanted to tell him everything.

"You should be proud of your boys. Will and John have smart heads for business. Michael knows horses inside out. He's the best trader in the county. Pat has a good job in Exeter building wagons, Robert's starting to read a little and I'm working with Tom to control his temper. And James Jr. is so excited to have you home, it's all he talked about for months. And Jenny…is an angel as you can see." She hesitated. "Jim…the past is done, right? John Carroll is dead. You're not going after anybody?"

"D'you think I'd ever risk this life with you again?"

They faced each other and she looked into his eyes.

"I believe you." She kissed him then and began to unbutton his shirt with playful affection. Jim ran his rough hands down her body, his breathing quickening. Johannah's too.

"Can you stand an old man in your bed?"

"Not an old man. Just Jim. Just you."

"I don't know what to do."

She gently pushed his fumbling hands aside and loosened his long underwear, caressing him, her fingers finding the wounds on his body. She tried to calm him, whispering that it was all right. He was back with her now and all was well.

Johannah was not expecting tenderness but the desperate brutality of the sexual act with him shocked her. It reflected all the pent-up anger and frustration and violent punishment he had endured, and she took it from him, took this rage away, and would continue to do so until it was all out of him and he was healed.

Jim Donnelly sat at the kitchen table in the sleeping house with a glass of water from the kitchen pump, looking at his broken hands. The boy Johnny was sound asleep on his cot in the room off the kitchen. Sleep was something Jim had almost given up in the last few years, or it had given up on him. Kingston Penitentiary had been the hardest thing he had ever done. What remained of the spirited romantic he once had been was buried deep beneath so many layers of scar tissue he doubted it would ever again see the light of day. And maybe that was for the best in the long run. No room for that in this world. They had broken him, not just once but many times, both his body and his mind. And when after years of resistance he finally surrendered and he had been allowed some healing time, the damage was done. He had become a new man, one who could survive in the dungeons of Kingston and even make a liveable life there at the brutal expense of others. He had had people hurt. He had learned how to happily add to the misery of others to ease his own. He had acted and reacted for so long in a state of basic survival, to kill or be killed, to undo or be undone, to avenge each slight or insult with furious action, that in this sudden vacuum of freedom, he was so untethered it made him dizzy.

Since he returned home, Jim had struggled greatly to stay calm in the presence of Johannah and his loving family. They had moved forward without him and done well. They didn't need him anymore. It was a bitter realization. But then it was in the presence of his family he found that the thing that he believed had died, had not. Not completely. He now knew it was there deep beneath the scar tissue, he felt it like a sweet distant memory: the ability to love. It was still in him like a forgotten language or an atrophied muscle. It would be such a long journey to fully access it again, but it was not yet dead.

There was, however, an old drive within him that he had come to embrace even more in his dark cell, more powerful and sweet than even love and more readily accessible, for sure. And that was his desire for revenge. It had kept him alive, alert. He was deeply disappointed that John Carroll was dead. But there were others who had betrayed him and put him away. And there would be new enemies. There always were. And Jim welcomed them and the opportunities they would give. He would take his time and have his satisfaction.

Jim finished his water and was going to lie down again when he heard a gate bang out at the barn. Then a horse whinnied. He knew everyone was in the house. He stood up and called out.

"Somebody's in the barn!"

Jim grabbed his boots by the door and put them on. Johnny O'Connor had woken up, was now sitting on his cot and groggily doing the same.

Will was the first down the hallway. He picked up the club by the door, looked out the window and yelled to the others, "Intruders!" He and Jim and Johnny ran out into the yard together.

Two horsemen coming from the barn, their faces covered, rode past them. Will went at one with the club but he was too far away and they were too fast. They headed off down the road toward town at a full gallop. Will, Johnny and Jim were joined a moment later in the yard by Michael and Tom, and then Johannah. She turned to the others.

"Anyone see who it was?"

"I think that last was a Flanagan mare," Will told her.

"They were Flanagans all right," Michael confirmed.

"What were they doing?"

They all hurried for the barn, and now a sleepy Jenny followed. The stable gates were wide open and the paddock empty.

"The Arabians are loose," Will told his mother and father. "But they just scattered them. I can see two or three out there in the field."

Michael and Tom ran into the pasture to round them up. Will lit two lamps and they went into the barn to where they kept the elegant new stagecoach. Will walked around it, raising his lamp in the inspection, his expression of relief growing.

"Doesn't look like they touched it."

"Thank God," Johannah said. "Just mischief, then."

"What were they up to?" Will wondered aloud.

Michael and Tom came back into the barn with two of the horses on leads and put them in their stalls.

"The other two are out there," Michael reassured them. "Didn't go far."

Will walked around the coach more slowly and the second time he stopped and noticed a little pile of sawdust on the floor beside a wheel.

"What's this?"

They all watched him as he went down on one knee, took and felt the sawdust in his fingers.

"There's more," Michael said as he pointed out other little piles of wood dust under the coach by each of the wheels. Will stood up and raised a protective hand toward the others.

"Stand back."

He put his hands against the side of the big coach and gave it a lateral push. The whole thing shifted sideways away from him as all four wheels collapsed under its weight, down on the axles. The wooden spokes of all the wheels had been sawed through.

"Whoa!" Michael yelled.

"Those bastards!"

"This won't stop us," Will said. "We'll get the wheels replaced. We can use that old coach tomorrow on the London route. We have to put something on the road."

Johannah stepped up to Will and spoke quietly.

"Maybe we should hold off on the London route tomorrow."

"This was just a prank, Ma. We can't give up now. It's normal competition. Free enterprise. We've got to stay in the game."

"Let's give it a couple of days to cool off. I mean it, Will. We'll do the
Friday morning run to London when there's more passengers."

"What do you think, Da?" He turned to Jim.

"Whatever your mother thinks. She's in charge."

"All right. Friday then."

Will and Johnny went out to help Michael catch the other two Arabians and Johannah came out to watch them in the moonlight. Michael
was talking to one, coaxing the mare to come to him. The horses loved
Michael. He gave the mare to Johnny to take inside while he went after
the last one. As Johnny came inside the barn he heard Jim talking quietly,
intently, to Tom, but he abruptly stopped when he saw him. Johnny wondered what they were discussing, but it was none of his business.

The Flanagans

FRIDAY MORNING, I were up and helping Michael and Will get the old coach ready to head into town to beat the Flanagan diligence on the London line again. I'm only eleven but I'm a good hand and worked hard for the Donnellys, especially with Mr. Jim home and all. Jim, Johannah and Jenny come out to see them on their way. The boys was excited now at the prospect of a race, although I seen Johannah was quiet. I seen her put her hand in her apron pocket, as she often did, and touch the smooth river stone from Ireland for luck.

Jenny said hello to me and it almost made me faint. She were so beautiful and even though she was almost a woman and I was just a kid, I felt weak and strange when she came near me with them blue eyes of hers.

"Hey Johnny, you know why you shouldn't tell a pig a secret?" she asked me and I shook my head. I had no idea. "Because they love to squeal."

She laughed at her own joke and I didn't mind if she was teasing me a bit. She could tease me all the day long if she wanted to. I wished I were ten years older.

So Mike was in the driver's seat alongside Will and ready to go.

"Our coach might be slower, but the team's better than anything the Flanagans have," Will said.

"Pass 'em on the Thamesford straightaway if you can, to pick up at the next stop," Johannah told him. "People will be watching what we do. So make it an honest race and we'll win the route."

Just then, Tom rode in from town alone, pulling up and dismounting. His gelding, the dark coat wet with sweat, drank pretty heavy at the trough.

"Hey, Tommy. Have the Flanagans surrendered yet?" Will asked.

Tom took a moment to catch his breath. "They're ready for you."

"Good. A good old showdown."

"Everything all right?" Old Jim asked Tom, and Tom nodded to him, and I admit I wondered a bit what he meant.

"All right. It's going to be a hot one. Let's go!" Michael gave rein to the horses and the rig took off. The horses was eager and strong.

"Make us proud," Johannah shouted after them, her hand blocking her eyes from the sun, still low in the morning sky.

So I seen 'em off that morning and woulda given anything to ride along with 'em, or in truth stay at the farm and get teased by Jenny, but I had to get to school or my da woulda given me a beating, and he weren't coy on that score. In the long run, it mighta been worth it to have been there on that coach and seen what happened.

That morning Johannah was canning rhubarb in the kitchen, already perspiring although it was only May, and watching through the open window as Jenny worked her quarter horse in the corral, riding the little white mare with determination through a complex barrel course. She wore pants and a plaid shirt. The horse was agile and responsive and reminded Johannah of her Cuchulain back in Tipperary. Jenny turned and rode her through the barrels again just as a wagon pulled up outside. It was driven by a good-looking young man who regarded Jenny with interest for several moments. Johannah was elbow deep in the rhubarb so she just watched him back. There was writing on the side of his wagon, "CURRIE & SON—GODERICH," and she remembered they were coming to repair the wheels of the new coach.

The young man waited patiently until Jenny noticed him, then called out, "Hello!"

Jenny rode over to him, revealing her perfect control of the horse, and pushed her long unruly hair back over her shoulder. "Hello, yourself. Can I help you?"

"The name's James Currie. Is this"—he glanced at a piece of paper—"the Doon-ley place?"

"It's Donn—elly. Just one 'o.'"

"Oh, sorry. All right. Well, I'm here with new wheels for your stagecoach."

"I'm Jenny." She glanced at the lettering. "You all the way from Goderich, then?"

"Yes, that I am, ma'am," he said, nodding.

255

"And you've never heard of the Donnellys?"

"Can't say I have."

Jenny flashed him a smile as she dismounted.

"Good! Let me show you to the barn."

On a side street in Lucan, Michael and Will pulled the old Donnelly stagecoach up to the boardwalk curb a couple blocks away from Main Street. It was just as good as the Flanagan coach, which was not due to leave town for twenty minutes. The passengers would not be at the stops yet for the eight a.m. stage. The idea was to get to the passengers after they arrived at the crossroads stops, but before the Flanagans, and scoop them all up.

Michael spotted four pretty girls outside the general store on the sidewalk. They were all watching him. They had stuffed their homely bonnets into their pockets and pinched their cheeks to make them pink. He waved to them. "HELLO, LADIES!"

Two smiled and returned the wave. As Michael climbed down from the coach, he said, "I'll be right back, Will. We have some time."

"Don't be long."

Michael wandered over to flirt with the girls. One girl watched him with particular attention: Fanny Carroll, from whom his mother had saved him. She had let her long black hair down, cinched up her dress and opened three buttons. She did not look away when Michael stepped up close to her, close enough to touch.

"Hello, Fanny. I take it your brother's not around anywhere seeing as you're waving to me."

"He don't tell me what to do. I can wave to whoever I please."

"I like a strong-minded girl." He brushed a strand of black hair out of her eyes and stroked her cheek.

Will had climbed down from the Donnelly coach and gone around to the front of the Central Hotel, where the Flanagan coach was rigged up and waiting to begin its London route. Matthew Murphy, a second-string Flanagan man, was on the driver's bench.

Will watched as Joe Flanagan came out of the hotel with a mailbag in tow. He helped a couple of passengers aboard and called out to others on the porch.

"All aboard for London, folks!"

Joe climbed up top. Murphy gave him the reins and slid over on the bench. Joe's brother James was there to see him off.

"Take care, Joey. Gonna be a hot one. Water the horses well in London."

Joe smiled at him. "Just keep my supper warm, brother."

Will made his limping run back up the side street to the Donnelly coach. Michael was still outside the store, flirting with Fanny Carroll and the others.

"Come on, Mike! They're heading out."

Michael left the girls and joined him, climbing up onto the driver's bench, then threw them all a kiss and with a slap of the reins, the brothers were on their way.

Johannah was extricating herself from the rhubarb when Jenny practically ran through the kitchen and down the hall into her bedroom, where she struggled out of her boots, pants and shirt. She returned one minute later wearing slippers and a print dress with lace. She grabbed a jug and filled it with cold water at the sink pump. Her mother looked at her askance but Jenny avoided her eyes and said nothing as she hurried out the door with the jug and two cups. Johannah decided she'd better follow.

Johannah wasn't usually one to eavesdrop on private conversations, but this was her girl and she stopped outside the open door of the barn to listen. She could see the Currie boy, impressive in his undershirt and already sweating as he had jacked up the coach and was working on replacing the sabotaged wheels, taking off the old hubs, greasing down the axles. He got up to receive the cup of water from Jenny.

"That's a pretty dress," Currie offered as he took a long drink.

"Cooler than pants," Jennie told him.

"Suppose. I wouldn't know."

Jenny laughed.

"And this is good water. Thank you."

"Thought you might like some. It's getting hotter than stink."

"It is that."

"So…what's Goderich like? You got a department store?"

"Oh yes. And a bowling alley, and a jail and a new theatre. They're putting on a play by William Shakespeare in the fall. It's growing into a big town."

"A theatre. I've never been to the theatre."

"I've only been to one show so far, about the American War of Independence. All these people standing in front of you saying things. Really quick, you forget they're just pretending and you get all caught up in the story."

"It would be so strange to be an actor, wouldn't it?"

"I'll say."

"Saying things that aren't real."

"I don't know. Sounds like half the people in Goderich."

Jenny laughed again at this.

"So what happened here with the wheels? That was a pretty nasty thing for someone to do."

"Oh, the Flanagans. We'll have to knock their heads."

"A fighter, are you? You like that? Knocking heads?"

Jenny smiled. "Got to."

Johannah stepped into the doorway as if from a long walk and spoke as sternly as she could.

"Jenny. Let the man finish his work. I need you in the house."

Currie flashed them both a charming smile. "I'm Jim Currie, ma'am. You must be Mrs. Donnelly."

"Nice to meet you. You build a fine coach."

"We try."

Johannah turned and gestured for Jenny to come.

"Nice to meet you both. I'll be done before end of day."

"Good."

Currie appeared unsure of how to take Johannah's comment, which pleased her. "Thanks for the drink, Miss Donnelly."

Jenny actually blushed. Then she made her way out of the barn toward the house and past her mother, flashing her a petulant glare.

Rumbling down the London line, Will and Michael were gaining on the Flanagan coach ahead. Joe began driving his fresh team hard. Murphy had turned around and was staring back at the Donnellys as they edged up behind them.

Flanagan begin to whip the horses with his long persuader. The Donnellys had pulled out to the other side of the road and were still gaining. The Arabians were giving the edge to the Donnellys. Their lead horses were almost up to the Flanagan coach. Joe Flanagan glanced over his shoulder toward them, then rose up from his bench into a balanced racing crouch and looped the reins tightly around his wrists. He whipped his horses, staying just ahead, moving his coach back and forth in front of the Donnellys, almost like a tease, to stop them from getting ahead.

"Flanagan knows his horses," Michael called out to Will. "But not as good as me!"

Michael had to hold back and wait for the right moment, for Joe Flanagan had blood in his eye and would drive the Donnellys' lighter coach into the ditch if he could. Joe was whipping the horses again for more speed, letting the tails meet flesh, which Michael would never do. By now the passengers were starting to call out their concerns.

"Too fast! Slow down!"

But Joe Flanagan kept his lead, looking over and back at them, cursing. Michael was laughing, urging his team forward, looking for that opportunity to pass.

The Donnelly coach was right up behind the Flanagans'. Michael swung wildly into the left lane again to pass, barely keeping the stagecoach under control. Flanagan veered his rig over in a similar move to block him, but the lead Donnelly horses were already past Flanagan's rear wheel and starting to gain. Flanagan used his coach to try to push Michael's horses into the ditch.

"You're all right, beauties. Stay the course, darlings," Michael murmured to the Arabians. The Arabians were worth every penny of their substantial price tag, plunging onward along the edge of the ditch, trusting their driver.

"Fuck you, Donnelly! It's our route!" Joe called back at them.

"Flanagan, you shite! My grandmother can drive faster than you."

"You can go to hell!"

"You first!"

Michael suddenly pulled back, slowing slightly, and veered across to the other side of the road behind him, making a surge up the open lane to pass him on the right. He was gaining, coming almost abreast on the other side before Joe Flanagan could react. He hauled right on the reins, trying to block him.

At that moment the coupling in the Flanagan rig let go, separating the coach from the horses. Without the weight of the coach, the horses surged forward as the carriage fell back. Joe Flanagan, the reins wrapped tightly around his wrists, flew forward off the seat of the slowing stagecoach, dragged by his galloping horses. He hit the road behind them on his chest.

"Jesus Christ..." Michael called out. "Let go, Flanagan!"

But the reins were as tight as shackles on the driver's wrists and the excited horses dragged Joe Flanagan behind them on the gravel road, not slowing down for what seemed an eternity. The driverless stagecoach, with the passengers screaming, careened off the road and through the ditch, with Murphy flying high through the air, then it bounced off one tree and hit another dead on. It remained miraculously upright but smashed and broken like a child's toy.

Michael brought his coach to a dust-engulfed stop only thirty yards in front of the crashed Flanagan rig, jumped down onto the road and ran back. Will was right behind him. They looked into the coach full of moaning, sobbing passengers but could see that they were all alive, hopefully with nothing worse than cuts and bruises. Michael opened the door.

"Everyone all right?"

Will found Murphy sitting up in the ditch, looking dazed but mostly unhurt after his flight through the air into a grove of soft bullrushes. Will looked up the road sixty yards ahead to where the Flanagan horses had finally stopped and behind them the figure of Joe was lying face down in the dirt, his hands still caught in the reins, the nervous prancing of the standing horses lifting his hands up and down as if Joe himself was articulating. Will stared at the flat, distant figure on the road, anxious to see movement, urging him to stand up and shake a fist, curse them, anything, but the body lay very still.

The battered passengers started crawling out of the wreckage.

"Help the passengers," Will told Michael as he began his loping run toward Joe.

The Flanagan horses were skittish. Will knelt down on one knee beside Joe, lying still in the dust at the end of the reins. He put his fingers on Joe's neck and he bowed his head when there was no life left there. He began to unwrap from Joe's wrists the cruel reins that had been his undoing.

Murphy came limping over.

"Is he...?"

"He's gone, Murphy. What happened?"

"Don't know. All of a sudden the coupling just let go."

As the horses calmed, they inspected the heavy harness ring where a thick bolt had held the rig together. There was no sign of the bolt.

"I checked that bolt myself first thing this morning when we hitched up. Nothing wrong with it."

"Let's get Joe and the passengers back to town."

Michael brought the stage to a stop in front of the Central Hotel and Will helped the injured passengers stumble out. A couple had expressed their unhappiness that they had to travel beside the dead man. Will had covered the ravaged face with his handkerchief, but that was all he could do. Will gestured for Michael to follow and then lifted Joe's body from inside the coach up in his arms and carried him to the boardwalk to face James and Pat, Joe's other brother, who was the bartender at the Central. They both stared in shock at their brother's broken body.

"Give him to us."

Will put Joe into the arms of his brothers.

"I'm sorry, Flanagan. I…"

James Flanagan and his brother, Pat, turned away from Will and Michael and carried Joe's body into the hotel.

At the end of the day, done with the rhubarb and laundry and having decided on a fat chicken for dinner, which Jenny had killed and was plucking, Johannah looked out the kitchen door to the yard to check on their visitor. Jim Currie had packed up his tools and put the broken wheels into his wagon and was slowly driving past the house out the lane. Jenny wiped the blood from her hands, took off her apron, pushed back her hair and slid by her mother and out the kitchen door into the yard and waved to the Goderich boy with enthusiasm.

"Good-bye!"

Currie stopped the rig a moment, smiled and returned the wave, hesitated as he took in Johannah's frown, then kept going. *Good teeth*, Johannah was thinking.

"Good-bye, Mr. Currie!"

"Jenny. Stop it," Johannah told her quietly.

"Stop what?"

"Don't you be getting any ideas."

"Why not?"

"You know why. His name is Currie. He's a Protestant."

Jenny dropped her hand to her side, surprised by the obvious.

"But we have Protestant friends! You do business with them all the time."

"Yes, it is true, but no daughter of mine will be romancing a Protestant. That is where I draw the line."

"He was nice."

At the gate, Currie gave a final wave and handsome smile as he turned north on the Roman Line, back to the big town of Goderich.

"Good teeth," Jenny remarked wistfully as she watched him. She glanced at her mother and didn't return his gesture.

On the night of Joe Flanagan's burial at St. Patrick's, which the Donnellys attended in full, there had been whispered talk at Stanley's store of a midnight meeting at the Cedar Swamp School. The grieving Flanagans and Maggie Thompson's husband, Pat Carroll, and his brother, Jim, arrived there, along with a dozen others—Ryders, Kennedys, McLaughlins—their faces now lit by low candlelight. They had secured their horses around the back in the trees behind so passersby on the Roman Line would not notice the gathering.

James Flanagan barely controlled his emotions.

"I put that bolt and nut and the pin in myself. A nut doesn't just fall off. It was murder. It was them did it."

Pat Carroll was with him. "They have to be stopped. It can't go on like this."

"They get bolder every day," Martin McLaughlin agreed. He checked the gold pocket watch in his waistcoat. "We should act tonight."

"But we should act within the law." It was the elder Grouchy Ryder, father of the three Ryder boys, who spoke.

"When has the law ever served us?" McLaughlin asked. "It only serves the Prots against us."

"It did put Jim Donnelly away for fifteen years," the senior Ryder reminded them.

"Not long enough," said Carroll.

"Not deep enough," said Flanagan.

"What does Father Connolly say?"

"He's away in Woodbridge."

"All right. Do we act tonight?" McLaughlin challenged. "Let's put it to a vote."

The vote was two to nine, with two abstentions. The results were sealed with whiskey, and the oath of secrecy was taken by all. They would ride tonight. Jim Carroll blew out the candles.

Jim and Johannah woke up to the sound of horses in the yard.

"Who's that?"

The glow of firelight could be seen through the windows. Will, Michael and Patrick were in the hallway.

"The barn!" Will shouted as his brothers in nightshirts and long johns ran outside. Jim and Will were the first out the door and Will called to his brothers behind him.

"Buckets! Get the buckets going!"

Five of the six masked riders had escaped past them when Jim ran out in front of the last. The man wore a woman's dress and bonnet. Jim tried to grab the horse's halter. The man swung a club that glanced sickeningly off Jim's head and he fell to the ground. The rider made his escape.

Will ran and knelt beside his father. Jim sat up, hurt but conscious.

"Son of a bitch!"

Jim got up on his feet a little unsteadily and went to help his sons. The boys were passing buckets from the large water trough to throw on the fire, but the barn was already a hopeless inferno against the black sky. Will, James and Tom charged into the flaming mouth of the barn to pull out and save the new stagecoach. Michael opened the stalls closer to the front and drove out three of the Arabians before the smoke and heat forced him back. There were two or three horses screaming, trapped deep in the barn. Will had to grab Michael around the chest to hold him back.

"It's too late!"

"No!"

Will held on, arms locked around him. The screams of the terrified horses continued as flames engulfed the building. Michael put his hands over his ears until finally the noise died out. They had lost one Arabian and two of the old horses and the old coach.

For several moments Johannah stood very still, staring at the burning barn, the crackling sparks like stars ascending into the universe above her.

The bitter feelings had remained at a distance but now came back and were so familiar: anger, frustration, helplessness.

Johannah looked into the flames and said out loud to the night, "It's starting again, isn't it."

Feud

EARLY IN THE afternoon after the Donnellys' barn was torched, I were sitting outside the Central Hotel, waiting for my da. News of the fire spread up and down the Roman Line and across town in no time. In truth, lots more was expected to happen.

Well, it were Will, Michael, Pat and Tom and the two Keefe brothers who came down Main Street just as James Flanagan and several of their boys was coming out of the Central Hotel. I heared Will holler out as they approached.

"Flanagan! That was you last night."

"You sabotaged our rig. You murdered my brother!" Flanagan responded as they come up to each other.

Michael were furious. "We never touched your goddamned rig."

Will backed him up. "It's true, Flanagan. We never touched it. We wanted a fair race."

"You're a liar!"

And so with that, Flanagan socked Michael in the face and the fight were on, as simple as that, and me with a ringside seat! It were a pitched battle in the street. Will Donnelly was tall and had them long arms to keep his face out of range for most, and his right hook was pretty deadly. He put down one of Flanagan's boys and chased t'other away. Michael was shorter but powerful and a couple of three-punch combos to the other fella's belly would wind the other guy and take him out. I remember Pat Donnelly was wrestling with James's younger brother, the bartender Pat, swearing to beat the band. The Keefe boys was solid fighters, but James Flanagan knocked one down early on and continued using fists with t'other.

Tom Donnelly were the most vicious, knocking men down, then kicking them on the ground in the ribs and head as he liked to do. Michael and Will were best with their fists or clubs but Tom and sometimes James Jr. said you punched or clubbed a man simply to get him down on the ground where the real work began, with boots to the ribs and head and privates. I myself didn't find it so honourable but it were effective if damage was the result you wanted. At least, for the most part, no one brought a gun or a knife to these things. Those weapons was considered dishonourable and also the goal was to hurt and punish your enemy, not to kill him dead.

Constable Fitzhenry had been keeping an eye on things that morning and he were on the scene of the fight there pretty quick and went wading in to stop it. He could have let them just have their go and made things easier for himself. He was still a big fellow but he were an older man and not as light-footed as he should have been. First he grabbed hold of Will to take him out of the fight, but Tom found a small club and with this he hit the constable from behind on the back of the head. Fitzhenry went down hard and lay senseless in the street. Will yelled at Tom for doing it.

The melee was over in just a few minutes, much too quick for me far as I were concerned watching from the boardwalk, and the Donnellys were victorious, leaving the Flanagans and their friends senseless, moaning in the street, a couple wounded or in retreat. Tom kicked an unconscious James Flanagan in the head, as he liked to do. I hated that sound. He were a nasty bugger.

"Tom! Stop it. Let's go," I heard Will call out.

Will, Tom and Michael was on their feet, bloodied but winners. Pat helped Samuel Keefe to his feet. Will checked the senseless Fitzhenry then looked up at me.

"Johnny! Go get the doctor for Fitzhenry." And I were up and running on my way.

That night, in the crowded kitchen, the whole family listened closely by candlelight as Michael finished the story of the Main Street battle. John and especially Robert were frustrated they had missed it. Jim, Will, Mike and James took whiskey, and Pat, John and Robert had beer as they toasted to the Donnelly victory. Jenny loved the story of her brothers' exploits. Only Johannah nursed a dark worry about this conflict. They saw it as a game, but she knew it would only get worse.

"When we left the Central, there was not one man standing."

Jim's eyes gleamed. "Not one man!"

Leaning in the doorway, Jenny laughed at her father's relish of the whole thing.

Can none of them understand how this will continue? Johannah wondered. She could see the familiar nightmare approaching. Jim should know better than to egg them on. They all should know better.

Clearly, Jim was delighted and the boys were proud of themselves. Big Tom was using a stone to sharpen two wide-bladed butcher knives at the cutting board while he listened to the others talk.

"They threw the first punch."

"But we threw the last!" Will concluded with satisfaction.

Jim laughed at this. "You threw the last. That's rich!"

Johannah looked at the faces of her men, for whom she felt love and pride and such deep fear.

"But…it will never be the last, will it?" she said.

Jim and the brothers turned to look at her.

"That's up to them, isn't it?" Jim responded.

"No!" she shouted, and the men fell silent. "We have to stop this. You have to stop it, Jim. You know it will only get worse. You promised me a peaceful life here. We had that until you killed Farrell. And it's coming around again like that unless you go and make peace with the Flanagans. Tell them we're sorry. Tell them we'll drop the London route. Tell them we want peace."

"Drop the London route?" Will asked her, incredulous.

"Yes. I was wrong. Tell them it's theirs. Out of respect for Joe."

The men remained silent for a time, musing on Johannah's words, checking each other's demeanour, until Jim spoke.

"It's important for you to understand, Johannah. If I learned anything…" His voice grew with bitter intensity. "You don't get peace by being nice to people, saying you're sorry." The anger in his words scared her. He turned to her. "Don't you remember when you convinced me to give myself up? Tell them I'm sorry? First they almost hanged me! Then they locked me away for a lifetime where I learned the most important lesson. You have to fight them." Jim slammed his fist on the table and the glasses jumped. "It's just how the world is. You fight them every time they come at you. Fight them with everything you've got. That's when you get respect." He looked directly at Tom, who had stopped sharpening his knives to listen. Jim's voice dropped to just above a whisper. "And that's when you get peace." Tom stared at him and nodded.

All the boys were listening. Johannah was shaken by the fury in her husband's words, which seemed a long way from peace.

Breaking the tension in the room, Will held up his glass of beer. "Here's to peace!"

"But let's not rush into it," Patrick suggested, and they all laughed and drank to the toast. All except Johannah.

The next night, after evening Mass, horses arrived out in the churchyard of St. Patrick's and eight men entered the church and went to the door of Father Connolly's little study. James Flanagan, bruised, with a black eye, was followed by Jim Carroll, Martin McLaughlin, a couple of Kennedys and the Ryders, father and two sons. They didn't look as if they had come to pray. Father Connolly rose up from his desk, his bones creaking, and opened his door to the men.

"Yes? It's late. What do you want?"

"Your counsel, Father." McLaughlin answered. "We have nowhere else to turn."

Father Connolly was clearly flattered. "Come in." James Flanagan explained. "Someone got into our back pasture. They killed two of our best horses! They cut them..." Flanagan could not go on.

McLaughlin continued for him. "They were opened up with a big knife or axe, their guts spilling out. While they stood in the field! I saw the results. Horrible. They died slowly, in agony."

Father Connolly was very aware of the suspicions that the Donnellys had sabotaged the Flanagan coach and killed Joe. He had full reports on the big fight on Main Street, but this was the first he had heard of the horses.

Flanagan appeared shaken. "That any man could do that to a horse..."

"Do you have proof it was the Donnellys?"

"Who else could it be?" Jim Carroll asked.

Martin McLaughlin continued. "Our goal is simple, Father. All we want is to stop the Donnellys and have peace in the parish."

"Yes. Yes, Father. Peace. Exactly," Grouchy Ryder agreed.

"And you want to do this in a lawful manner, of course?" Father Connolly asked them, sliding into his pulpit voice.

"Yes. Within the law." McLaughlin said. "What do you advise?"

"I think what we must do is find a constable to replace Fitzhenry. He is too soft on them. He's in the hospital in London now. They're not even sure he'll recover."

Jim Carroll responded. "I can do it, Father. I want to do it."

"You?"

"I have army training. I have studied the law. I know the citizens of Lucan. And I know how the Donnellys work."

"Yes. I suppose that would be a good start. We will all sign a petition that Jim Carroll be appointed 'special constable' for Lucan."

"I'm for that," said McLaughlin.

The other men were in agreement.

"We could go out there tonight," James Flanagan offered.

"No. No, you said you wanted to work within the law. Jim Carroll must be sworn in and have legal warrants for his actions. To achieve justice, we must be patient and legal."

"Yes, patient and legal," Ryder repeated.

Connolly laid down a piece of paper and began to write a simple document. When he was done he read it out loud for any who couldn't read.

"We, the good citizens of the town of Lucan, do petition the courts of London, Ontario, to appoint Jim Francis Carroll as the new special constable for this community..."

Mrs. Thompson's Cow

THREE DAYS AFTER the street fight in Lucan, James, Michael, Patrick and Tom were at work framing in the new barn over the charred remnants of the old, the sound of their hammers echoing in the still air. Out of respect for Joe Flanagan, the Donnelly stagecoach business had been suspended for the time being. On the porch of the farmhouse, Will was sitting on the railing tuning his fiddle, talking to John and his da, who sat in porch chairs. On a small table between them, John sorted carefully through a pile of invoices. Jim smoked a new clay pipe.

"...the studding is one-quarter of our income, Da. We can expand the breeding. But you see, John and I think we should diversify."

"Where'd you get that five-dollar word?"

"We should have a variety of b-b-b-businesses," John told him.

"I know what it means; I'm not stupid."

"Cut our own trees, mill them and use the lumber to put up rental houses on that land in town. Steady income, year-round. And a store. We'll build and run a big grocery store. Lucan only has two."

John was nodding. He showed his father the want ads in the London paper. Johannah came out to listen to the conversation.

"Look, Da. See? All these people want to rent houses in north London. Lucan is only a few miles more."

"This is smart, Jim," Johannah agreed. "We build a few houses in Lucan, rent them to people, sell them goods from our store..."

"And d-d-d-drive them into London on our stagecoach every m-m-morning," John finished.

Will was the first to see the big open wagon coming north on the Roman Line. There were two horsemen following it. "What's this now?"

The entourage pulled into the yard and made a circle in front of the house. In the wagon were three uniformed constables; one was Jim Carroll, driving with his new silver badge shining in the sun. The Donnellys' neighbour old Jean Thompson, the mother of Maggie, was also in the wagon with them, in her bonnet and skirts. The riders were Martin McLaughlin and James Flanagan.

Johannah walked a few steps out into the yard, holding a shading hand over her eyes. The three constables got out of the wagon. They carried billy clubs. Carroll had documents in his hand.

"Well, if it isn't the young Carroll. What a shiny new badge and uniform you have there," Johannah told him with a smile.

"I'm the new special constable for Lucan. I have assault warrants for Tom, Michael and Will."

Carroll held out the warrants but Johannah didn't look at them.

"Oh, you do? For defending themselves?"

"They have to come with us. It's all legal. Also a warrant against Will for the killing of the two Flanagan horses."

"You have any evidence?"

"And also, Mrs. Thompson's cow has been stolen. We're searching your place. If we find her, you and your husband will come in too."

Mrs. Thompson climbed out of the wagon. Jim Carroll gestured to the horsemen and they dismounted. The three constables stood abreast in the yard, their billy clubs ready.

Will and Johannah faced them. James, Patrick, Michael and Tom had climbed down from the barn and walked over to the visitors with their various tools in hand. Jim Donnelly had gone in the house and come back outside, casually holding a double-barrelled shotgun in the crook of his arm. The two conscripted constables glanced at each other, looking a little worried, and waited for Carroll's next move.

Johannah turned to her neighbour, Jean Thompson. "Are you accusing me, Jean?"

"Yes, you. Or your boys. She's a good cow."

"Where would we keep her?" Patrick asked. "They've burned down our blessed barn!" At this point, Jenny and Robert came out to see what was going on. Jenny crossed her arms and leaned against the doorway.

"Maybe she's having tea with us in the parlour," Johannah added with a sigh. "Jean, you have to stop drinking that blackcurrant wine. It's making you crazy. Go home. The cow'll show up."

Jenny and others laughed at this but Jean continued defiantly. "I think you got her."

"We have a search warrant," Carroll said and waved another paper.

Jim came forward, his gun still hanging loose.

"Then do what you have to do and to hell with you."

"These men have been deputized." Carroll turned to Flanagan and McLaughlin. "Search the house."

Flanagan and McLaughlin walked into the house. Almost immediately there was the sound of breaking dishes and a lamp hitting the floor.

"You'll pay for that, Carroll," Johannah told him. She was studying one of the other constables.

"Isn't that young Sticky? Sticky Murphy. We used to feed you when your mother couldn't. You remember?"

Murphy looked embarrassed in front of the others. "Yes, ma'am."

"We gave your da a mule so he could make a living. And a few dollars, too. How is he?"

"He's good, ma'am. Still has the mule and a few acres."

"Good. And now you're here doing this to us?" Murphy couldn't look her in the eye. "Arresting me for stealing a cow?"

Carroll told her, "You talk to me, not him."

But the damage was done. Murphy quickly turned to Carroll. "I…I want no part of this, Carroll. You didn't tell me it'd be like this. This is stupid."

Sticky Murphy turned and began to walk back to town.

Jim Carroll called out to him. "Murphy! MURPHY! Where you going?"

At this point, Jim and Will approached Carroll and the second constable. Behind them came Tom, Michael, James and Patrick. Each had something—a shovel, an axe, a pitchfork—in their hands. They confronted the two men, their smiles a worry.

"And who's this other fella you've got here, Carroll?" Will asked him. "O'Leary, isn't it? From Thamesford. Are you here looking for your mother?"

O'Leary responded, "You shut up about my mother!"

"You mean the one you left back in that poorhouse, back in the old country in Roscrea?"

O'Leary raised his billy club to Will. "Shut up!"

The brothers moved closer to O'Leary, weapons ready. Will smiled. "Oh you shouldn't have raised your club, O'Leary. We'll have to beat you now." O'Leary looked terrified. He glanced at Carroll. "Unless…you're gone in the count of three. One…two…"

O'Leary backed away from them. Then he turned and ran toward town, following Murphy.

Tom, Michael and James went into the house and they came out again hauling McLaughlin and Flanagan by the arms and held them there. McLaughlin had a bloody nose.

"You better take these deputies with you before they do themselves damage," Will said.

Patrick joined Robert, Will and John to surround Jim Carroll, now alone and sweating. "You're a poor judge of men, Carroll," Will continued, "to add to your other shortcomings."

Johannah offered her comments from the porch. "You're nothing but a blackguard and a rogue, Carroll."

Carroll turned toward Johannah, his eyes a little desperate. "There! I'm arresting you for using insulting language to me!"

Carroll suddenly took out a pistol and pointed it at Johannah, then at Will and the others. They all tensed but no one backed away. Will spread his hands and shook his head looking skyward as if beseeching God.

"What are you doing, man?"

"I'll shoot. I will!"

Jim calmly raised his shotgun and took a bead on Carroll.

Will continued. "Yes. You can shoot one or even possibly two of us. But then the others—my da"—he gestured to the shotgun—"will kill you in a blink. You know, best all round, I'd just put that thing away."

At that moment a local farmer, John Donovan, came along leading the cow in question.

"Jean? This your cow?"

"Uh, yes. That's my cow!" She went to the cow and patted the brown head. "It must have got away from the Donnellys."

"No, she's been in my woodlot all night."

Donovan put the cow's rope lead in Jean Thompson's hand. Will tried to control his laughter. All the Donnellys were trying not to laugh, until they did.

"You are the biggest fool I've ever seen," Will told Carroll.

Carroll hesitated, the pistol still levelled. He was clearly thinking about how he could come out of this situation with dignity.

"I'll have at least one of you. Will Donnelly. You're under arrest. Get into this wagon."

"I'm not going anywhere, Carroll." Will picked up his fiddle, checked the tuning and began to play "Bony over the Alps" in merry jig time. He sang along with the music:

> Thank you, Mr. Carroll, for your kind visit.
> The law is surely on your side, or is it?
> Here is my ass and I invite you to kiss it.
> Thank you, Mr. Carroll, for your kind visit!

When the laughter died it was Johannah who warned him again: "You come around here threatening us with guns and trumped-up charges? Get back on your wagon, Carroll, if you know what's good for you. It's your only choice."

Will began to count. "One...two..."

At this point, Carroll lost heart. He looked at the roughed-up McLaughlin and Flanagan, still being held by Tom, James and Michael.

"Get on your horses." The Donnelly boys helped them do so.

Carroll backed away from the Donnellys, made it to the wagon and climbed up into the seat. Then he put his pistol away, picked up the reins and, along with McLaughlin and Flanagan, all now in total disgrace, set off back to town with Will's fiddle music and Donnelly laughter playing in their ears. Alone now, Jean Thompson looked at Johannah for a moment.

"Care for a cup of tea, Jean?"

Without a word, Thompson turned around and walked home with her cow.

The Donnellys didn't show up for church that Sunday when Father Connolly had an important message for the people, but I were there with my ma and da.

"O God, whose blessed Son was manifested that he might destroy the works of the devil, and make us heirs to eternal life, grant us, we beseech Thee, that we may purify ourselves, even as He is pure."

Father Connolly stops then and looked out at all us poor sinners.

"It is a grave sin to disrespect the Church and her priests and it is a sin to disrespect the laws of the land. Yet there are those among us who do. And I say unto them, may balls of fire fall upon your house!"

Father Connolly's face gets all red and he gets louder as he looks out over everybody.

"I have taken it upon myself to form an association called the St. Patrick's Peace Society. There is an oath book at the back for all good Roman Catholics to sign. And any who decline to join this society I will consider backsliders and sympathizers of those who cause the violent depredations in this parish. And if you or yours take sick, or need last rites, do not send for me. You are either with us or against us."

In the vestibule at the back of the church, like Father Connolly told us, the Peace Society book was lying open on a small table. After the service the men lines up, including my da, to sign it. I got a look at it and it said: "We, the undersigned, do solemnly pledge to aid in every way our priest in the putting down of crime in our parish."

I were never accused of being the brightest light but even I knowed this were directed at the Donnellys.

Queen Victoria Day

EVEN THOUGH THE annual event was only four years old, the Lucan Victoria Day Fair on the 24th of May weekend were a thing of great pride to our community and my second favourite holiday after Christmas, what with spring here and a long lazy summer stretching out. Well, not so lazy for me that year 'cause Da were on the sauce again and Ma needed all the chore money I could bring in, but you know what I mean. When he wasn't drunk and beating us, my da were a nice enough man, given to regret after and as kind as can be while sober.

The fair in Lucan were a chance after the long winter for most of the good citizens to air out all the feuds and jealousies and petty grievances that had festered in their little minds through a long, dark winter. Then in spring come the purifying sunshine of heaven. The fair showed the best side of the town. And them Donnellys loved a public gathering, which could often bring trouble, and you know for some of them, that was probably the draw.

The fair were centred on Main Street and spilled out down to the public lands and the racetrack south of the town. From the Central Hotel, red, white and blue bunting had been stretched out along the fronts of them buildings, and banners was paraded from a dozen societies, from the Oddfellows to the Loyal Order of Calithumpians on horseback with plumes and ribbons and all. Booths of food and wares was set up and hawkers lured the gawking crowds to their offerings, and always music was going on, whether a lone polka clarinet or a full brass band. Clowns, jugglers, fire-eaters and acrobats strolled through the streets of our town like they did this every day and the good folk of Lucan town, me included, spent the weekend in a state of "mesmerization." Like that word? It's Miss Johannah's. There was mind-readers and ventriloquists and bell-ringers and cartoonists who could draw a picture of you real funny.

The Donnelly family would never miss the Victoria Day Fair. In fairs before, Johannah entered pies in the pastry contest and twice she won a prize in the quilting competitions. Jenny's calf got a red ribbon two years before.

I seen the Donnellys arrive in their buckboard and three on horseback. I ties up the horses for them and gives them water. Will tells the family to stay within shouting distance. You never knows what could happen. Johannah smiled and greeted me, and Will and Robert did too. There was a number of booths demonstrating new inventions. I had been through them all and told different Donnellys about things that might interest them. A man was cranking a generator to make this glass bulb glow like a candle. Johannah touched the bulb when it came on, went bright and then faded away. She smiled, all delighted, at me and at Old Jim.

"Imagine that."

John was trying out a slick new "typewriter" with one finger. He liked the clear letters that went onto the paper. Will listened to a "phonograph" with the sound of a woman singing coming out. He looked into the horn, around the moving pipe thing and underneath. I suppose he were expecting a tiny woman to be there. Ha, ha.

Patrick sat in a booth and listened into the ear phone at the end of a wire. Then he spoke into the mouthpiece of a telephone.

"...hello...hello...Robert! Can you hear me? Robert? Can you hear me?"

At another booth close by, Robert waved to Patrick, all excited. He spoke into the ear phone and then listened, all disappointed, at the mouthpiece.

"No. I can't hear a thing."

The Temperance League had tables and displays. I seen James smiling at the frowning temperance people and he held up his flask and drank to their health.

On my say so, Johannah invested a nickel and looked in the viewer of an animation machine I showed her. She invited Jim to take a look, their faces pushed together. I had spent that whole nickel to see the show already. The machine showed a jumpy picture of a cute little girl spraying a fat man with a water hose. He tries to grab her but slips and falls. It was real funny. Jim and Johannah both laughed and that made me happy.

"How do they do that? That's amazing!" Johannah asked, but it were beyond me.

I let Jim and Johannah Donnelly go ahead. I'd tag along well behind. I were pleased they liked the moving picture machine. But as they walked on, looking at the displays, I seen that they was being watched. Jim Carroll followed them at a distance through the crowd. He had with him four men in normal suits but they all had the stiff look like the law. Three was good-sized, sturdy men—not one I recognized—but the fourth was something else. They called him Joe and I learnt later his last name was Berryman. He were nothing short of a giant. He coulda been one of the attractions at the freak show there beside the fat woman and the rubber man. He had a shaved head like a barrel and were at least a head taller than anyone else in the crowd, had a chest like a bull with massive arms, yet he moved with this quickness, not like a fat man, and his eyes was watchful and smart as Carroll pointed out the members of the Donnelly family to this Joe fellow and his other new pals.

The Donnelly stagecoach comes down Main Street all dressed in bows and ribbons with Michael at the reins in his Sunday suit and four or five young women inside. Jim and Johannah and Will cheered and waved to Michael. I tells Will about Jim Carroll and the four men with him and Will thanks me and tells me not to worry.

By this time I'd gone back to my favourite thing of all: the elephant ride. Oh my gosh, what a strange and bizarre creature she were. I talked to her owner, a dark-skinned man with a turban on his head, who said he come all the way from Timbuktu in Africa, but he spoke pretty good English. The elephant's name was Daisy and you could take her for a ride around a little corral. He said all the money goes to an orphanage in Toronto. I touched her hide and grabs her tail and I couldn't believe anything so unusual existed in our whole world, let alone Lucan. I didn't have the ten cents to ride, but after I'd been there awhile and asking questions the owner finally let me ride once for free! I were in heaven. So high up! Like riding a Clydesdale only even bigger. Anyway, I remember thinking, them people from Timbuktu, Africa, are real nice.

It was after my elephant ride I seen Jenny Donnelly walking in the crowd, so pretty. She had two girlfriends with her and were joking and chatting away about the displays. They were almost hit by a man on a penny farthing bicycle advertising a miracle tonic from Dr. Crystal. I think he had had a bit too much. But when Jenny seed Daisy the elephant, she couldn't keep her eyes off the beast. I knewed she'd like her. She said a nice hello to me and then went on to talk to the owner with the turban. All at once Jenny started to laugh. She put up her hands to the man's turban and raised it up and everyone could see Daisy's owner were a white man with some dye on his face. Jenny introduced him to her girlfriends as Jim Currie, a wagon builder from Goderich. He weren't from Timbuktu at all, but he had me going! Anyway it were all in fun until he explained he were raising money for the orphanage through the Protestant Orange Order.

You could see Jenny's friends was shocked they was even talking to a Protestant, which is kind of silly. Mr. Currie wanted Jenny to ride the elephant, but she decided not to, even though I could see she wanted to. She continued on with her friends and I could see Mr. Currie was disappointed too.

There were a thing that happened, big in my mind, on the Saturday noon of the fair that I'm embarrassed to tell. My father had been drinking and he found me with some of my friends and he had something against me. I don't honestly remember, maybe something about chores undone, or him not liking how I was behaving, but anyways he comes at me and grabs me and first he yells, which was shameful in front of my friends, and then he slaps and then punches me, closed fist. He'd done this before but not with others watching. He hits my eye and hits my nose and there's blood and then one hard in the head 'til I seed stars and couldn't stand. A small crowd stopped and I thought with all the fire-eaters and jugglers, why are they looking at me and my da. This ain't no show. I'm so embarrassed. Now I were eleven and strong, almost strong enough to fight him back but not quite, and he were my da, so I couldn't do that yet.

He's winding up and about to hit me again when I hears a voice say, "Enough, Seamus." And I felt Da pulled back from me by strong arms and when I looked up, there was Old Jim Donnelly who had ahold of him. Da took a poke at him and Mr. Jim slapped him across the face to sober him a little. *Oh my God, what now?* I think. Mr. Jim held him firm.

"You have to stop hitting the boy, Seamus. He's a good lad and if you ever beat him again, I'll come after you and you'll answer to me."

And Da listened! He listened and then he nodded and then he walks away. My face was hot and I were blushing at Mr. Jim's kind words. No one ever said that about me being good before. And in truth my da never hit me again after that day, so you can see I owed a lot to Mr. Jim. And any shame I felt among my friends was more than made up for that day by the fact that Old Jim Donnelly, the murderer and ex-convict, stood up for me.

Toward the end of Saturday afternoon come an event that were always a crowd pleaser at the fair, the six o'clock freestyle horse race. Everyone with a four-legged beast of any sort had tried out earlier in the week but by the time of the big race there would only be the best horses and riders in the field. There was fourteen and I loved to watch them prepare, fixing their saddles, tightening up the bridles and taking sidelong glances at the competition. And one was a female! Nora Kennedy had made the cut and prepared to ride a tawny gelding. This were a rough race for a woman but some liked to say she was more a man, which ain't fair 'cause I thought she was real pretty. I were standing closest to Michael Donnelly, who was riding his favourite, a black Arabian by the name of Tipperary Tiger, and nearby him were none other than Jim Carroll on a big bay named Lightning. You could feel the tension between 'em 'cause they never once looked at each other.

Now I heared men say that women are hard to understand but it were at this point that Fanny Carroll came to flirt with Michael, so bold right in front of her older brother.

"Hi, Michael. Going to win for me?" says she.

"I race for the family. If Tip wins, we can double our studding fees."

Fanny had on her playful look. "How much are your studding fees?"

"You better watch out for your brother, Fanny. You're talking to a Donnelly."

"He can't tell me what to do."

"Don't expect any man can. You're a beautiful force unto yourself."

This seemed to please her. There were no doubt, as he got ready for the race, Jim Carroll was aware his little sister was talking to Michael.

Fanny took off her scarf. "Wear my colours. 'Less you're scared to."

"You troublemaker."

She ties the light yellow scarf around the right shoulder strap of Michael's ranger shirt. Now Jim Carroll were looking directly at her. As she sent Michael on his way, I saw her turn and give her brother a look of "so there." And he looked right back at her, his eyes staring as some say like two piss holes in the snow. And I remembers saying to myself, "Johnny, this horse race are going to be some interesting."

There were few things Will Donnelly would have loved more than to join the Victoria Day horse race as he had done in past years, even winning it the second year, but his little brother Michael was the artist with the horses and it was a tougher field these days. Will was surprised to see Nora Kennedy in the mix but why not? He knew she was a fine rider. She had a plaid shirt and studded chaps that fit her hips well and a big Stetson hat she'd be bound to lose at any decent speed. Will was satisfied to watch with his father and mother and two of his brothers. He was also being vigilant against the forces that opposed his family, waiting to see what they might do. The presence of Carroll's men concerned him more than he revealed. At least with Jim Carroll in the race their leader was occupied, but you never know, and so he studied the faces—both strange and familiar—of the men in the crowd that pressed around them.

Today, as they stood at the track rail near where the horses were gathering, his mother seemed her old self: happily chatting with her friends, showing off her family, waiting to cheer on Michael in his horse race. Will was pleased to see the excited anticipation in her face. His father was arm in arm with her, just savouring her presence, his freedom and the fresh air.

Will's brother John, in a fine checked suit and bowler hat, was beside him as they waited for the race to begin. John had found a place for himself near the timid Winnifred Ryder, sister of Tom and James, daughter of Grouchy, watching the horses with interest. It was rare that Winnifred's eyes were not lowered in public, but today as she studied the horses in competition, they were luminous and appraising.

John lost himself for a moment in their hazel splendour. "Beautiful animals, aren't they, Winnie? That bay and the b-b-b-b-black gelding."

"Oh…yes." She nodded her head and lowered her eyes again.

"I wonder if they see b-b-b-beauty in each other, as people do. Do horses recognize aesthetics? I think so. I hope so."

Will was amused to overhear a little flirtatious chat coming out of John.

"They must," she said quietly.

"Yes, and then of course it's all about smell," John continued. "Each with their own aroma. Maybe humans should p-p-p-put more importance in smell. I think yours is l-l-l-lilac, am I right?"

Winnifred giggled. Will was surprised at his brother's banter but had to turn away as the horses had been called up to the line and the race was about to begin.

The Victoria Day race was a little different from the normal weekend horse races in that there was a cross-country element to it. Three times around the track and then a quarter-mile out across the public lands to a heavy pole, there for the purpose, and then back, three final circuits of the track and across the finish line.

The horses were lined up abreast at the starting line, with two tiers behind the starters. They had plenty of time to come from behind. There was that moment of stillness before the pistol cracked, then it did so and the race was on.

The first three circuits were chaotic, with several riders desperately vying for the lead. The Donnellys and Winnifred were all cheering loudly for Michael and urging speed. But they knew what he was doing: staying back from the fray, biding his time, letting the others wear themselves out on the track.

Once the riders were off the track and galloping across the public pasture toward the pole, the race opened up and Michael broke up through the pack and put Tiger to work. He passed his leading competitors one by one until only Jim Carroll and a few others were ahead. It was easy to make Michael out with that yellow scarf on his shoulder. Four horses bunched into a vicious knot rounding the pole. A rider fell and one horse went down, but Jim Carroll broke away and galloped into the home stretch, closely pursued by Michael. Behind him came Nora Kennedy— riding well, and remarkably still with her Stetson hat on her head. It was really just the three of them out in front in the final circuits of the track.

It now came down to the fastest horse and Michael, slowly gaining, came up behind Carroll by the end of the second circuit of the track. He kept edging forward until they were neck and neck a hundred yards from the finish line directly in front of them. The big bay, Lightning, and the Arabian, Tipperary Tiger, were well matched.

John, Robert and Johannah were yelling, "COME ON, MICHAEL!"

Winnifred finally joined in. "Come on, Michael! FOR GODSAKES, RUN!"

They all glanced at Winnifred—those were the first words any of them had heard her say above a whisper.

Nora was riding no more than a length behind the two leaders, now on a perfect dead heat in the home stretch, with either man the victor. Carroll could no longer ignore Fanny's yellow scarf on Michael's shoulder. He veered his bay toward Michael and reached out to grab the scarf. Michael somehow anticipated this fatal move and leaned forward, out of range. Carroll missed the scarf and the bay lurched back, stumbled and dropped a half-length behind. In that moment, Nora Kennedy made her move past Carroll into second place and Michael galloped across the finish line, the winner. The Donnellys were cheering wildly as the crowded gaggle of also-ran horses crossed the finish line. Winnifred surprised John by giving him an enthusiastic hug.

At the officials' booth, one of three judges made the announcement to the crowd: "And the winner is…MICHAEL DONNELLY on TIP-PERARY TIGER!"

A few minutes later, Michael led his mount into the crowded winner's circle beside the judge's booth. The judge congratulated Michael on a hard-fought race and handed him the silver cup. Michael smiled and raised the cup to receive the crowd's adulation. Fanny Carroll embraced him and gave him a heated kiss and then held onto his arm possessively. Jim Carroll had left the track but the Flanagans were there in the crowd, looking daggers at Mike. Johannah was clapping and cheering for her son like a kid. Her enthusiasm was contagious and Jim joined in. Michael saw her, extricated himself from Fanny and came straight through the crowd with his cup to kiss Johannah.

"I'm so proud of you!" she told him.

Nora Kennedy was being congratulated on her second-place finish by her family and friends and reached over to shake hands with Michael. She turned and looked at Will and tipped him that Stetson as if she knew he would be watching her.

Rising Stakes

THERE WAS A good band playing at the Victoria Day dinner in the packed-to-spilling-over main dining hall of Fitzhenry's Hotel. Jim Donnelly was revelling in the festivities, a happy drunk this night, talking loudly with the Whalens and Keefes, proud of his family and feeling no pain. Will was very pleased for his father, and for his mother, who was truly enjoying herself, confident that public honours were replacing Father Connolly's stigma on the Donnelly name.

Will noticed Jim Currie near the dance floor. Will walked over and complimented Currie on the quality and workmanship of the diligence and the speedy replacement of the sabotaged wheels, and Currie thanked him.

Jenny was standing nearby with her back to Currie. The coachmaker smiled at Will and spoke to her.

"Miss Donnelly. I hope you're well tonight."

Jenny turned toward him, showing surprise and interest, but then seemed to give him the cold shoulder. "Fine."

"If I couldn't interest you in an elephant ride today, could I interest you in a dance? Hopefully not a similar experience."

"I'm rather busy."

"You're busy?"

Her girlfriends had their eyes on them and were talking among themselves. She took him aside.

"You never told me you were a Protestant."

"Oh. I'm sorry." Currie touched his index finger between his eyebrows. "I was sure you'd noticed the mark of Satan."

Jenny smiled a little despite herself. The band had just begun to play a very danceable tune and couples were coming onto the dance floor.

"I can't help being a Protestant. I was born this way. But I dance as well as a Catholic."

Jenny was amused but hesitant.

"And...I promise I don't burn to touch. Not at first."

Currie held out his hand as Will watched. Will himself couldn't have cared less but he knew a romantic liaison with a Protestant might not sit well with his mother or father, despite their Protestant friends. Business was business but romance between people from two different churches was something else. Tossing a defiant look at her girlfriends, and then Will, who raised his eyebrows in wide innocence, Jenny took Currie's hand and they went out on the dance floor.

"What does she think she's doing?" Will was surprised to hear his brother Patrick say as he came up beside him. Will was happy to see the spirit of music at work, even if he then noticed Winnifred Ryder shake her head to an invitation from John.

"Well, Donnelly," Will heard a voice say in his ear and turned to find Nora Kennedy, but it was a Nora Kennedy he had never seen before. Gone were the chaps and Stetson and boots, replaced by a light cotton flower print dress that showed off the curves of her slender figure. Her long black hair piled in braids above her delicately powdered neck, rouge lightly applied to her cheeks and lips, and a darkening on the lids of her green eyes all belied the horsewoman who had that day come in second by half a length, and for that matter the girl he had known since childhood, or thought he had. This night the former tomboy was transformed and he was impressed.

Nora put her hands on her hips. "Are you going to ask me to dance or will I have to do the job?"

Will was still in shock at her transformation. He held out his hand and she took it as he led her onto the dance floor. Will and Nora fit together nicely. *Why have we not done this before?* Will asked himself.

Jenny and Jim Currie were moving to the music beside them.

"I've never danced with a 'dirty Protestant' before," Jenny told Jim, looking up into his eyes.

"How is it so far?"

"Not totally disagreeable."

"You sweet talker."

Jenny's face was lit up. Will noticed his mother had spotted them and her face revealed some alarm. He hoped she'd give it a rest and let them alone. People already called the Donnellys Blacklegs for having Protestant friends and doing business with them. So why not allow a little romance with one? He wanted to see his sister happy.

In the barn behind the hotel and tavern there were several men in police uniforms, checking their pistols and placing their night sticks in their belts. Jim Carroll and eight other armed constables were making ready to arrest the Donnellys. These were professionals, including the enormous mountain of a man they called Joe. Carroll was convinced this team would be able to arrest them all and do so in public. He would be redeemed in the town! Carroll gave them final instructions.

"The big one with the cropped hair is Tom. Go for him first. And then Will, the tall redhead with long hair and a beard."

Will danced Nora round and round the dance floor, wondering again why he hadn't done this before. It was a pleasant surprise whenever he changed the placement of his hands on her thin waist, brushing her muscular behind, his own chest discovering the cushions of her breasts. He was quite taken with her confident air in this new context, and she danced beautifully.

"So, are you over Maggie Thompson, then?" she asked him.

"Who?"

"That's the proper answer. I've been thinking some on what a man like you needs."

"Really? What'd you come up with?"

"Me."

Her refreshing directness amused him. "I might give it some consideration."

Will looked around the room as they danced and noticed that Nora's drunken brother, John, with whom Will had grown up as friends, was watching him dance with his sister. His expression said he didn't like it. Will felt the heat of Kennedy's glare and revelled in the spice it gave to their dance together. Will looked around to see if others were enjoying the night as much as he was. He could see his brother John off in a corner talking with Winnifred, who was actually giggling. John held out his hand. She found the courage, grabbed hold and they too went out on the dance floor. Will took stock of his other brothers. Michael, the man of the day with his win, danced very close with Fanny Carroll—how ironic—and Will could see neither had been forced into the situation. There were other girls there watching Michael, especially a very pretty redhead Will did not know. *Enjoy it all, my brother*, he thought. *Glory is fleeting. But for now, enjoy.*

Nora was light in his arms and he felt like he could dance with her all night. The swirling rhythm of the music and the beer he had consumed had him slightly light-headed, in a pleasant way. Nora suddenly began to explain something as if she had been debating it within herself for a while and was now presenting it.

"We've known each other all our lives, Will. We understand each other. And think what beautiful kids we'll have."

Nora was amused at the shock and confusion on his face. "What?"

"All in the fullness of time. There's a fine little house with a few acres at Whalen's Corners, just a few miles from your folks. Good stables. Reasonable price."

Will laughed out loud, without a grain of derision. "You have it all figured out."

She beamed and nodded. "I do."

The dance ended. Patrick's sour face was still glaring at Jim Currie, whose hand was holding Jenny's. He and Johannah approached them together, Patrick's look remaining hostile. Johannah spoke to her daughter.

"Jenny? What did I tell you."

"I'm not marrying the man," Jenny's eyes flashed. "I'm just dancing with him."

In the moments before the band started again, Will glanced at the antagonistic John Kennedy and, never shy at making public addresses, he took Nora's hand and called out to the people around them.

"LADIES AND GENTLEMEN. I HAVE AN ANNOUNCE-MENT TO MAKE," he declared. And the room went quiet. He had made a decision. You could say it had taken twenty years, or five minutes, but it was made.

"In this romantic environment, where perhaps hearts trump heads, the beautiful Nora Kennedy has just proposed to me. And...more importantly...I accept!"

There were looks of shock and surprise, several angry faces among the Kennedy clan, many stumbled expressions of congratulations and then, when the surprise eased, overwhelming applause. Will put his arm around Nora and gave her the kiss he should have given her years ago.

"I propose a toast to my fiancée. Please charge your glasses."

Will saw John Kennedy pick up an empty bottle by the neck and he seemed intent on coming toward Will with it, just before a voice boomed across the dance floor.

"BY THE AUTHORITY VESTED IN ME…" Jim Carroll called out. Obviously he had practised his theatrical tone. Eight constables rushed into the hotel and confronted the Donnellys with arrest warrants in one hand and their billy clubs in the other.

"…I am arresting you, Will Donnelly and Tom Donnelly and Michael Donnelly, for assault and battery against the Flanagans, perpetrated in front of the Central Hotel!"

Will stared at Carroll. "What are you talking about?"

"Put the cuffs on them, men."

The huge Joe Berryman confronted Tom and grabbed an arm to cuff. Tom could not pull free. Tom glanced to Will for guidance. As their mother and father looked on in alarm, two constables each grabbed Will and Michael.

"Carroll, you son of a bitch," Will called out. "This can wait until tomorrow!"

Johannah stepped out to confront her sons.

"Will, listen to me. You have to go along with it. We can answer the charges in court."

"We can't just give in to this stupidity, Ma. They're making us criminals."

"Go along with them for me this time. We can afford a good lawyer. Please."

Will studied her for a moment and was about to comply and surrender to the constables, but just then Berryman tried to cuff Tom's other hand and Tom pulled back. Berryman lurched after him and Tom punched him hard in the face with almost no effect.

Michael and Will both pulled away from their captors. They would not be going quietly. Two officers took out pistols and aimed them dangerously at Will and Michael. Robert and Patrick grabbed the officers from behind. One pistol discharged into the floor and people started screaming and running from the hall. The band members abandoned their instruments and escaped out the back door. Jenny and Johannah ran into the foyer, from which they could safely watch. The Donnelly brothers and the Keefes stood back to back in the centre as the constables and the Kennedys and Flanagans came at them.

Tom, the cuff dangling from his left wrist, faced Berryman and fought with a vicious obsession, breaking a chair over the man's huge head, hitting him again and again with his fists, a chair leg, a bottle, anything he could find, but Berryman kept coming after him.

Jim Carroll choked Michael on a table. Robert hit Carroll over the back of the head with a chair leg, momentarily stunning him and freeing Michael. John was exchanging blows and wrestling with a Kennedy, and knocked over the abandoned drum kit, with cymbals crashing.

Jim Currie was alarmed to find himself in the thick of it with them. Patrick was fighting with one of the constables. Another had cocked his pistol and raised it, about to fire it point-blank at Patrick, but Currie knocked it out of his hand. The constable turned on Currie, raising his nightstick, and the Protestant had to apply a right hook in self-defence. Currie knocked his man to the ground as Jenny watched him, thrilled. Another officer grabbed Currie and he was forced into a wrestling match.

As the donnybrook continued, the constables were beginning to lose. Robert, James and Patrick confronted two bloody and battered policemen near the door. The officers turned and ran outside and kept running. The brothers followed them into the street. Will fought Carroll for his pistol. He won it and pointed it at Carroll.

"Stay back!" Will warned, but Carroll could see the police were losing ground and he couldn't abide another failure.

With a wild look in his eye, Carroll ran straight at Will. Will aimed low and fired twice. The second shot hit Carroll in the leg and he collapsed to the floor in pain.

"You've shot me!"

"You'll live," Will told him.

Will looked at the pistol in disdain and threw it away. Tom had finally got Joe Berryman unconscious on the ground and was kicking his head.

"Tom. That's enough," Will told him. Tom kicked him one last time, then reluctantly stopped. Tom picked up two pistols from among the debris on the floor, stuck them in his belt and left.

Will looked around at the scene of wreckage. A large portrait of a frowning Queen Victoria draped in bunting was left looking down on the sorry aftermath. Broken chairs and bottles were scattered across the floor. The place was deserted except for three remaining constables; one of them lay moaning against the wall and Big Joe Berryman had been left a bloody, unconscious mess. Jim Carroll sat on the ground binding up his shot leg. The bartender came out from behind the shelter of the bar. He looked at Will and poured two four-fingered whiskeys for each of them and they downed them in silence.

Just then Johannah came in and stared around at the carnage.

"Will? Are you all right?"

Two constables came in with a stretcher to take Carroll for medical aid. "Yes, I'm fine, Ma. I saw Robert, James and Patrick head out front. And Tom. I think they're all good. Not sure where Michael has gone, though. Where's Da?"

"He's across the street at the Queen's."

"I want you and Da to find Jenny and John—I think John'll be clear of any charges—and take the wagon and go home right now, all right?"

"What are you going to do?"

The constables had Carroll on the stretcher and were carrying him out in obvious distress. "Reinforcements are coming, Donnelly. They'll deal with you."

"I think we better turn ourselves in," Will said. "Tom, Robert, Pat if he's willing…Michael if I can find him. James, probably. You were right, Ma. It's time to clear this all up in the courts. It's getting ridiculous. Will you go home?"

Johannah nodded and kissed him on the cheek with affection. "I'll bring the bail money." Then she turned and left Fitzhenry's.

Jenny Donnelly was on a side street kissing Jim Currie farewell. His horse was saddled and he was about to ride out of Lucan. It was still a couple hours from dawn.

"I'm so proud of you. You were fighting side by side with my brothers."

But Currie was troubled. "Look, Jenny…"

"What's wrong?" she asked with sudden alarm.

"Your family…"

"What about them?"

"They're just a little…crazy."

"Well, maybe they're a little wild. The Donnellys are never boring."

"But...I was asking around. I could never live like this, with feuds and violence."

"That's just how life is."

"No. No, I don't think so. Not in other towns. Not in other families."

"We're just defending ourselves. We have no choice."

"No, I think your family chooses it. It's not normal, Jen. I could never get married or raise kids in the middle of this. I couldn't, I...I'm sorry."

"What do you mean?"

"I mean...I'm sorry, Jenny." He studied her sadly for a moment. "Goodbye."

"But, we..."

He mounted his horse and she watched him ride off, angry with herself for the tears that wanted to come.

Just as dawn broke, a company of soldiers, the Fourth Rifle Brigade of the Sixth Battalion from London, came marching into Lucan to capture the Donnellys.

After arriving at the now-empty Fitzhenry's, the soldiers heard a distant fiddle playing and followed the sound into the Queen's Hotel across the street, where they found Will Donnelly waiting for them, playing a lonely serenade at the bar with a drink in front of him. They surrounded him at gunpoint. He stopped playing, put down his fiddle, looked at them calmly and finished his drink.

In the barn behind the hotel, six soldiers confronted Michael Donnelly and Fanny Carroll sleeping in the hay, their clothes half off. The soldiers aimed their rifles at Michael. As Fanny grabbed her dress to cover up, Michael began to laugh at it all.

The company commander heard pistol shots out in the street and led eight soldiers down a Lucan side street to where Tom was engaged in target practice against a wall with the two pistols he had taken from the constables. They spread out into a half-circle behind him, pointing their weapons at his back.

The corporal shouted, "Drop the guns!"

Tom turned for a moment to look at the commander with his strange half-smile, then casually aimed and took another shot at the wall.

"I said drop them or we shoot!"

There was a crazed moment when it was apparent Tom thought about taking them all on. The nervous young soldiers looked down the sights of their rifles, spoiling to have a reason to fire them. Tom did think about his options for a moment, both ways, then he opened his hands and the pistols fell into the dirt.

Will and his brothers were to appear before the London spring assizes to answer the earlier charges of assault against the Flanagans and more charges from the Victoria Day battle. The authorities seemed to forget about Jim Currie and the Keefe brothers' involvement and no charges were ever pressed against them. Carroll's entire focus was on the Donnelly boys. He had arranged that they were denied bail, so they spent a month together apart from family and friends in the filthy London jailhouse. Will coached his brothers on their testimony, to speak clearly and confidently and never let the accusations make them angry. Be unconcerned, even smile, to indicate to the jury the charges are ridiculous. Johannah visited them often with food and clean clothes.

The charges against the Donnellys were heard in Courtroom C, the largest of the three modern courts, as there was a substantial audience to be accommodated from Lucan, both for and against the brothers. All the Donnellys were there save Jenny, who had decided to stay home to feed the beasts and keep the home fires burning. Carroll had been busy and the Donnelly boys were charged with a long string of offenses against "Our Lady the Queen, her crown and dignity." The prosecutor read them out against each defendant, starting with Will.

"...assaulting a constable, disturbing the peace, resisting arrest..."

They all sat on a bench, chained hand and foot, before the overflowing courtroom: Michael, Tom, Robert, James, Patrick and Will. Will was stoic, Michael was bored, James desperately needed a drink and Patrick's knee constantly bounced up and down as he glared at the prosecution. Johannah, Jim and John were in the second row.

"...assault with a firearm, common assault, illegal possession of a firearm, assault with intent to kill, uttering threats, attempted murder..."

The curious press had come to report. One journalist had spoken to Johannah and she believed he was sympathetic to them. His name was Frank Simon and he was from the *Toronto Mail* newspaper. He had a somewhat honest face compared to the other muckrakers and was respectful. Father

Connolly was also there, in his suit and clerical collar, to make sure his justice was done, and in front of him, sitting with the prosecutor, was Jim Carroll. Judge George Morgan turned to the Donnellys.

"How do you plead?"

Will spoke for them all.

"Not guilty, Your Honour. We acted in self-defence. We were having a lovely dinner toasting the Queen when these private men you call 'special constables' decided to make trouble for personal reasons."

There were groans and whispered declarations for and against them in the courtroom. There were quiet calls of "shame" and Will was unsure if they were for what he had claimed or what Carroll had done. As the case continued, Jim Carroll made a detailed statement of the events at Fitzhenry's tavern that night. He implicated all of them in the litany of crimes, even Robert, who he testified had assaulted him, a police officer in the course of his duty, by hitting him on the head with a table leg. Jim Donnelly called out in the middle of his testimony, "You'll sup sorrow yet, Carroll."

Judge Morgan told Jim if he spoke out again, he'd be barred from the courtroom. Carroll called the first witness for the prosecution: Paul Toohey.

"I saw da whole ting. Them Donnellys is evil. The constaples comes up to them, eh, and day say…day say. The constaples say…"

The judge intervened. "Sir! You've been drinking."

"No."

"Yes, you have. I can smell your breath even from here."

"Jus' a nip…"

John Donnelly, sitting in the courtroom, looked at Will and subtly patted his coat, under which was an all but finished bottle.

"Get out of my courtroom before I have you in contempt!" Carroll stood up in alarm as he watched as Toohey was escorted out of the courtroom. He glared at John and Will. The prosecutor gestured for him to sit down. "Next witness!"

Carroll's next witness was Thomas Ryder. John had had a serious word with him.

"But it was Will Donnelly you saw fire the shot that wounded Constable Carroll. Correct?"

Will fixed the witness with a look that left no doubt to his intentions should Thomas Ryder prove an enemy to the Donnellys. There was deep apprehension in Ryder's voice.

"Well..." said Ryder. "It could have been. And then again, I can't be sure. There was just so much going on..."

Ryder would not meet Carroll's eyes as he left the witness box. After that, the prosecutor was looking around for witnesses in the courtroom.

"Constable Dearing?" There was no response. "Constable Braythwaite?" Still no response. They hadn't shown up. Carroll began to appear panicked.

"Don't you have a Constable Berryman on your witness list?" the judge asked.

"He's still in hospital, Your Honour," Carroll told the judge. "After he was assaulted by Tom Donnelly!"

The Donnelly defence lawyer, a man named Quinn, objected that this assertion had not been proven and Judge Morgan had the statement stricken from the record.

"Have you any other witnesses, Constable Carroll?"

Carroll glared at Will, then turned to the judge and shook his head.

"Rather poorly prepared, Special Constable Carroll. Let the record show there are no more witnesses for the prosecution."

The witnesses for the defence included Sam Keefe and Pat Whalen, who asserted that the Donnelly actions were all in self-defence, and a senior police constable who had not been involved in the altercation gave his opinion that the attempted arrests by Carroll were not technically legal under the circumstances.

The one mistake defence lawyer Quinn made was having Robert testify. Will should have warned him. While on the stand, Robert pointed at Constable Jim Carroll and testified, "That constable is lying! He said he saw me hit him on the head but he couldn't have seen me hit him on the head because I was behind him when I did it!"

The brothers all groaned and shook their heads at Robert's public admission. There was some muted laughter in the courtroom. Robert looked over at his brothers, wondering why they were all so disappointed with his astute defence.

"What? What's wrong? I was!"

Judge Morgan declared a ten-minute recess to review his notes, and when he returned, he promptly addressed the court with his ruling.

"I'm afraid this has been a very poor showing by the prosecution. So many witnesses missing, including the other constables. And very little useful evidence. It is little more than Special Constable Carroll's word against the Donnelly family's. I do find Robert Donnelly guilty of assault on a constable by his own admission and I sentence him to nine months in prison."

"No, but he was lying!" Robert said again, very upset, pointing at Carroll. Johannah, too, was stricken by Robert's sentence but she was anxious to hear the rest of the ruling.

"As for the other charges, bearing in mind the lack of solid evidence and some indication of a personal grudge held by Constable Carroll, I can only find the defendants on all counts not guilty."

In shock, Father Connolly suddenly stood up in the court, his face red, and addressed the judge directly.

"What do you think you are doing? You can't just let them go! They're a scourge."

Judge Morgan turned toward the priest, revealing his offence at this interruption.

"I don't offer editorial advice on your homilies, Father. You will be quiet in my courtroom."

"If you magistrates do not do justice by them, then I will have them punished!"

It was clear from the judge's expression Father Connolly had crossed a line.

"Another word out of you, Father, and I'll have you charged and arrested for threatening! Now sit down."

Connolly took a moment, searching unsuccessfully for words, then he finally sat.

"Save for Robert Donnelly, all the defendants are free to go." Judge Morgan told the court. "And as a personal observation, I do suspect the free use of liquor is at the bottom of Lucan's problems. If you were to take liquor away, I'd wager the Donnellys would be as innocent as lambs. This trial is concluded."

Will saw the journalist Frank Simon copy down the quote, "as innocent as lambs." Will turned to his mother and nodded toward his brothers as the guards unlocked their chains.

"The Lucan Lambs," Will said out loud and they all laughed.

Outside the courthouse, the Donnellys' high spirits were tempered by the loss of their favourite brother for nine months. They waited outside the side doors of the courthouse until the constables escorted him, still in shackles and with a lost expression, to the wagon that would take him away to the jail.

"We'll come and visit," Johannah told him. "It won't be long, baby. Be brave."

"You're a Donnelly, Robby. Be strong," Patrick instructed.

They all waved as the wagon left to take him to the London jail and as he was driven away, he seemed to take heart and he waved to them and almost smiled.

Frank Simon came up beside Jim and Johannah with a notebook. "Do you have a statement, Mrs. Donnelly?"

"The courts in their wisdom have realized my boys, beyond merely defending themselves, are innocent. Including my son Robert, who was convicted today, but we will work on getting him out early."

"What are you going to do now?"

"Go back to Lucan and celebrate."

Among the bystanders was James Ryder, who saw Johannah talking to the journalist and shouted out to them from a safe distance away.

"TO HELL WITH THE DONNELLYS!"

His brother Thomas added, "AND THEIR OLD WITCH!"

Johannah's cheeks turned red. Will and his brothers were all ready to go and shut their faces but Johannah called out, warning them.

"Will! Leave it alone, now. Let's get to the wagon and go home. We have won."

Through substantial self-control, Will and the others made their way to the wagon, ignoring the Ryders' taunts.

Jim Donnelly held his son James back and spoke quietly with a smile. "Jamie, did you hear what they called your mother?"

"Yes, Da."

"In good time, they must be punished."

"Yes, Da. I understand."

The Elopement

IT WAS DAWN when the large wagon full of Donnellys headed north after a very late stop at Keefe's tavern and moved slowly up the Roman Line. John was at the reins. Jim and James were asleep. Will was an outrider on horseback. Tom, Patrick and Michael were passing a bottle and singing yet again, though quieter out of respect for those asleep. They had been celebrating all night, from Fitzhenry's to the Central to Keefe's, and were now heading home.

> We're poor little lambs who've lost our way,
> Baa! Baa! Baa!
> We're little black sheep who've gone astray,
> Baa—aa—aa!

Johannah was sitting on pillows in the wagon, quietly enjoying the boys' celebration and the sweet victory of the trial. The Donnellys were redeemed. Will held in his hand the evening newspaper someone had ridden in with from London. The headline read: "LUCAN LAMBS LET LOOSE."

> "Gentlemen-rankers out on a spree,
> Damned from here to eternity,
> God ha' mercy on such as we,
> Baa! Yah! Baa!"

Patrick made the comment, "I have to say it again. I already miss Robert. It isn't fair."

"We'll petition to get him out early," Johannah told them.

"Goddamn Carroll." Patrick's eyes blazed.

"C-c-c-c-could have been much worse," John cautioned.

Their wagon rolled past the farm of their disapproving neighbour Jean Thompson, who was out in the chicken pen collecting eggs. She looked up at the Donnelly boys and they turned and sang to her:

> We're poor little lambs who've lost our way,
> Baa! Baa! Baa!
> We're little black sheep who've gone astray,
> Baa—aa—aa…

Her hands on her hips, Jean Thompson glared at them and they waved cheerfully back at the old crow.

They arrived home and realized they'd have to carry their father and James and maybe Michael to bed. They would start with their unconscious father. While they were getting themselves organized, Johannah got out of the wagon.

"I want to tell Jenny what happened. She'll be worried."

"She won't be up yet," Will warned her.

"Then I'll get her up." Johannah went on inside.

As they were dealing with the snoring bodies, their mother came bursting out of the house with a note in her hand. "Lord give me patience!"

"Ma? What's going on?" Will asked her.

"Jenny's gone. She's taken her things. She's gone off with that Currie boy."

"That son of a bitch Protestant!" said Patrick.

"Shhh! If your da finds out, he'll kill him. The stove's still warm. They can't be gone that long. I'm going after them. Any still able are welcome to join me after you put Da to bed."

The brothers hurriedly carried their father inside while Johannah went to saddle a fresh horse. They were on the road to Goderich fifteen minutes later, riding hard: Patrick, Tom, Michael and Will, led by a mother intent on retrieving her daughter.

Two hours later, they spotted them up ahead in Currie's buckboard, with Jenny's arm around Jim. Jenny heard them coming and turned to see her family approach. She cursed under her breath. With lovemaking and then packing, and then feeding the damn horses, she and Jim had left leaving too late. Jenny picked up the whip and began driving the horses to go faster. Then Currie took the whip away from her.

"We can't outrun them. We'll have to have this out."

He pulled on the reins and the buckboard stopped. The Donnellys dismounted and surrounded them. Patrick silently approached the wagon and grabbed and dragged Currie out of the driver's seat. Jenny jumped out.

"Wait! Don't hurt him!"

Will took her arms gently but firmly and held her back. Tom and Michael restrained Currie for Patrick to hit. He punched him a good one in the face.

"Don't hurt him!" Jenny repeated.

Johannah turned on Jenny as her brothers continued with Currie. "So it's come to this. Running off with a Protestant in the middle of the night."

Patrick punched Currie again, hard enough that Tom and Michael almost went down with him.

"I love him. I want to marry him."

"Don't be silly. You can't marry him. Neither church will have you. Friends will turn away. It will be a blight on the family name."

"A blight on the family name?" Jenny shouted this, half laughing, half furious as she continued. Fist raised, Patrick paused his assault on Currie to listen.

"A blight! We're the Donnellys for godsakes, Ma! We have the most blighted name in Biddulph County!"

Johannah was taken aback, struggling to find words.

"You're coming home," she said finally. "That man…is not of our Church."

Jenny's eyes flashed and she took a step toward her mother. "Our Church? What has the Catholic Church ever done for you?" Jenny said, pointing a finger at her. "That priest treats you—treats us all"—making a gesture toward her brothers—"like dirt! The Church would have let Da hang! They wouldn't even christen me, would they, after that? You said I was christened but I wasn't, was I? I checked the record."

Johannah was silent. It was true.

"The whole parish talks behind our backs," Jenny continued in full flight. "The Roman Catholic Church is a nasty arrogant business that goes against everything natural and human and if I have to turn my back on it to find the man I love, then I will! And to hell with them."

Patrick set up and punched the bloody-faced Currie one more half-hearted time and Jenny suddenly turned on him.

"I said stop it, Patrick! Stop hitting him!"

The anger and passion in her voice made Patrick back away from Currie and wait. The brothers were all looking at the ground. Only Currie was staring at Jenny through his sweat and blood, unsteady on his feet, still held up by Tom and Michael. He was impressed, even a little awed, by Jenny's declarations to her family.

Jenny turned away from Patrick back to her mother, her conviction thickening the air between them, her voice quieter but no less forceful.

"Now listen to me. I'm going to Goderich to marry Jim and have lots of children and live a peaceful life. A peaceful life. Without fighting all the time."

Patrick glanced at his raw fist, then Currie's bleeding face, and took another step away from him. Will was silent, taken aback, for he'd never heard Jenny be so strong with her mother.

"I don't care about Protestants or Catholics or Whiteboys or Blacklegs. I don't want to look over my shoulder every moment. I don't want to hate anybody. I don't want to worry about my brothers being killed or us being burned up in our beds! I don't want to be…I don't want to end up like…like you."

Jenny fell silent. Her last words had hurt Johannah deeply and she knew it, and she had meant for them to.

After a moment of digesting Jenny's words, Johannah nodded slightly a few times, then turned to Tom and Michael. "All right. Let him go."

Tom and Michael did so. Unsupported, Currie swayed a little but managed to stay on his feet. Michael and Patrick straightened out the punch-drunk Currie's clothes and gave him his hat back, Patrick rubbed the blood off Currie's face with his handkerchief and gently slapped his cheek and rubbed his shoulders to make sure he was all right.

Johannah came up close to Jenny, their faces only inches apart. "I have given you life and a way to live it. I don't expect you to be like me. Do you think I wanted to live like this?" Then Johannah let the sting of Jenny's words direct her own, words that she would regret almost immediately. "But if you go, don't come back."

Johannah took her mother's locket from around her neck, grabbed Jenny's hand and put it in her palm.

"Here. Your grandmother's. This is all I owe you."

Jenny studied the locket in her hand, then her mother, in defiant silence. Johannah turned and climbed back up on her horse. She looked at her boys.

"Let's go. Now."

As Michael, Patrick and Tom retrieved the reins to their horses and mounted, their mother rode away. Will went to Jenny and gave her a hug and a kiss on the cheek.

"We'll come visit."

He turned to Currie and shook his hand.

"Sorry, Currie. Sorry. Really. Good luck to you."

Currie nodded and put a comforting arm around Will's now-tearful sister. Will mounted his horse beside his brothers and waved a sad farewell to Jenny. Then they rode after their mother, now a determined, receding form on the horizon.

Blessings of the Church

JOHANNAH FOUND HIM out behind the rectory in a small glade where he kept five wooden hives of honeybees. The priest had on heavy gloves and a canvas hood with netting, so he didn't hear her as he collected the honey from one of the hives. She had never seen this done and studied him for a moment or two and mused on the nature of the tiny creatures, who could give both sweet nourishment and pain. And also on the nature of a man who could be so caring to tiny creatures and so cruel to her family.

She cleared her throat. "Father?"

The priest turned to see her, moved away from the bees and took off his hood. She realized her presence shocked him. No surprise, really.

"Mrs. Donnelly?"

"Yes, Father."

"What do you want?"

"I wanted to see you. I hoped to talk to you. About the difficulties between us. Between you and the family."

"Difficulties!"

The quiet buzzing of the bees was almost comforting.

"I want to make amends. I want to come back to my Church. I want my sons to come and offer you apologies for any troubles they have created. Will is thinking of marriage and I would love him to be married in the church."

"You and yours have insulted the holy Church with your violence. You have shown your wicked pride at every turn."

"I know there must be penance and I'm willing. My boys will be willing. Silence, prayer...substantial tithes. What would satisfy you?"

"It is not me you must satisfy. It is Almighty God!"

"God, then."

"I think it may be too late."

"Maybe for you, but surely not for God."

"You see, there is already arrogance in your tone."

"I am sorry. There must be a way to forgiveness. Please, Father."

"No. Your son will never be married in my church. Perhaps if I had seen substantial change, Johannah. But now you have let your daughter go off with a Protestant. A Protestant!"

"She has her own will. Will's fiancée is Catholic."

"Still you prevaricate and try to bargain with me. It is too late. I suggest your son Will should go to London city hall for his needs. Now leave me in peace."

Johannah watched as the priest put his hood back on and turned away from her to his tiny wards. She regarded him for a moment longer. She recalled the image of the judge in Jim's murder trial putting on the black cap just before he sentenced him to death. Then she turned her back on Father Connolly and walked away from St. Patrick's for the last time.

Nora and Will took the advice the priest had given Johannah and got married in London at the city hall in September. At first Johannah saw it as her failure, but Nora and Will liked the modern idea. No one from Nora's family was going to come anyway, as the Kennedy opposition to having a Donnelly in-law had not diminished. Will had himself gone to Nora's father, mother and brothers but they could not be turned. They opposed the marriage and that was the end of it. So Will and Nora had a party of eighteen family and friends for the ceremony, his family and the regular crew of Keefes and Whalens, and a fine dinner afterwards at Stroud's Dining Emporium near the London train station. The raw estrangement of Johannah and Jenny had not healed, so despite Will and Nora's special invitation, Jenny and her husband did not come down from Goderich.

After the wedding, Will and Nora were blessedly on their own as they rode in their buggy back to their new house at Whalen's Corners. Nora had started to show with their first child.

"Oh look, there's a nice house. I wonder who lives there?" Nora said with a laugh. It was the little two-storey place she had told him about the night they decided to marry, with a picket fence around the neat front yard and small but decent stables behind that could be added to, and it was located just a few miles from the Donnelly homestead. They had bought it the week before. Nora was elegantly dressed from the wedding in an off-white lace gown with a short train and was still holding the bouquet of roses Johannah had given her. Will could not hide the pride he felt in his new wife. He was in a good, fitted pinstriped suit with a waistcoat and they had looked a fine pair.

"I think we should just move in. No one will mind, will they?" Will helped her down and they walked with arms around each other toward the front door.

"You know, this is all still a bit of a shock to me, Mrs. Donnelly. A new house, a new loving wife…"

"Oh …" she said in mock surprise. "Do I have to love you?"

"Sure there was something about that in the vows."

"I guess I could manage. In the fullness of time."

At the doorway, they stopped and shared a long, slow kiss. Nora took off Will's jacket and waistcoat, then undid his tie and shirt. He began to fumble with the hooks at the back of her wedding gown. They laughed, still kissing. Nora managed to get his shirt off, then drew him half-naked into the dark house to "reaffirm the blessing," as Nora explained, "that God bestowed on men when he created women."

Miss Johannah, she had asked me to come up to the Donnelly homestead most every day through the summer to check to see that things was in good shape and chores done. I liked that she trusted me and sometimes liked someone to gab with. Old Jim would sit on the porch of the Donnelly farmhouse with some whiskey in his hand and stare a hole in the side of the new barn like it were about to jump. With all them things he'd seen and done in his life I wished his demons would take it easy on him.

There were one day in mid-September, Mr. Jim was out on the porch and I had just finished feeding all the cattle beasts in the corral who was destined for market. We all heard the sound of the Donnelly stage coming up the Roman Line and looked up to see Michael at the reins, calling to the horses as he did. He pulled up outside the farmhouse porch near Mr. Jim.

"We got a surprise for you, Da!"

Mr. Jim stood up slowly and came down the steps toward the stagecoach. At the sound of the horses, Johannah comes out of the house to see the doings, along with Will and Nora, who was visiting. A pretty woman of maybe thirty years steps down, her clothes was plain but clean, smiling sadly like she were a little embarrassed.

Michael did the introductions. "This is Bridget, Da. Your sister's daughter. All the way from Tipperary."

Mr. Jim studied her face. "Little Bridget? Theresa's daughter? Are you really?"

"We found her at Porte's asking about Donnellys," Michael told us, proud of himself.

"Hello, Uncle Jimmy."

"God help us, you sound like Theresa."

Bridget approached Mr. Jim and gave him a warm hug. They was both delighted to see one another.

"I still have the two letters you sent to Ma. I knew if I could just get to the town of Lucan, Ontario, that I'd find you somehow."

"And so you did. But how's Theresa...?

Tears come then to Bridget's bright eyes. "She's with the angels, Uncle. Got the fever late last winter. There was no time to write. I got no one left. Been a hard life, Uncle. With the last of our money I took the ship and came to Canada. You were kind to me when I was little."

Johannah had been looking at all this and there were no doubt it sat well with her, having another female on the place after Jenny was gone. The big hug she gave Bridget came natural to her.

"You're a brave girl travelling so far. Come inside for some tea and get to know your family."

"This is your new home now," Mr. Jim told her, taking her arm and escorting her into the house as Michael brought in her two worn canvas bags. "And you'll want for nothing."

I smiled at how the old boy could be charming and generous when he put his mind to it. I knew he'd been missing Jenny and his niece being around would go a ways to easing that pain.

"Thank you," she said and gave him a little kiss on his furry cheek. So this was how cousin Bridget came to live with the Donnellys. She fit in well and, though she were some older, she were as pleasant and peppery as Jenny and there's no doubt she and Johannah, feeling a little like a mother and daughter, helped take away some of the pain of each losing people so close to them.

Sarah Keefe's Wedding

IT WAS A frosty, star-studded winter night when Will's whole family headed to Sarah Keefe's wedding reception on the third day of February. The ceremony had been private for family only at St. Patrick's, or so Will had been told, but they were invited to the party afterwards. Johannah, Bridget and Nora, her pregnancy now quite apparent, Will noted proudly, rode in the buckboard on pillows with blankets over their legs to keep warm, driven by John. The snow had been beaten down on the Roman Line so a wagon was still more practical than a sled. Will escorted the wagon on horseback, along with his father and brothers.

They missed Robert, who remained in prison, though he still didn't quite understand why, given his brilliant defence. And they missed Jenny, though she had sent word she was happily married to Jim Currie in Goderich. Along the way, their talk was of the outstanding charges of "using insulting language" levelled against Jim and Johannah by Jim Carroll during the episode with Mrs. Thompson's "stolen" cow. They laughed at the charges, which would certainly be dismissed, but they were due in court the following day to answer them. It was all right. Johannah needed to do a little shopping in town.

"You should c-c-c-c-counter-charge Carroll for being so ugly in a p-p-p-public place!" John suggested.

The Donnellys did have a weakness for fashion. Will's brothers and even their father were all in suits and waistcoats, all sporting a fashionable variety of facial hair groomed by the Lucan barber. The ladies were all in long lace-trimmed dresses and jewellery. Will noticed Johannah had on her old necklace of pearls from Ireland. The few missing did not detract. At Will's urging she told them the story again of how she had once sold a third of them for food to eat on the ship, but she was proud of the ones she had left and they showed very well.

"All I can say is it's a miracle Sarah Keefe found herself a man. She's the homeliest mutt…"

"Shhhhhh, stop that right now, Patrick," Johannah told him. "You'll be eating their food and drink and we shall celebrate among them with true hearts."

"Yes, we will," Will agreed.

Michael picked up on Pat's direction. "Even if he's as round as she is."

"Yes, even so," Will confirmed.

The brothers laughed.

"I think we should find Patrick a wife," Michael suggested. "Might calm him down."

"Oh, no. Not me. I can burn my own dinner, thank you."

"Anyway, the marriage of two young people is a sign of hope for peace and prosperity," said Johannah grandly. "Bridget, you'll see the good side of life in Canada here tonight."

"I'm blessed by it all," her niece replied.

As they approached the farmhouse, they could make out numerous wagons and horses outside and hear the music from within. Guests were smoking and drinking out in the cold winter air. Will and his family were all in good spirits as they parked the wagon and dismounted a distance from the farmhouse. The men helped the ladies out of the rig and the Donnellys headed for the house. Will noticed his father walking slowly behind him together with James and speaking quietly about something. James was nodding that he understood. Will was pleased they had grown closer. James had been drinking more than ever. He needed his father's attention. Then Will saw his father hand James a mickey of whiskey, before turning and calling out to Bridget, who had gone ahead with Johannah.

"You must save a dance for me, Bridget. For old times."

"Sure and I will, Uncle Jim."

A rosy-faced James Keefe gave a toast to the fifty or sixty people who had gathered in the great pine-log room, a fire roaring in the hearth, with his arms around the short, round bride and groom, almost spilling his drink. "Ladies and gentlemen, in the spirit of this new marriage, let us raise a glass to peace…and reconciliation between neighbours."

There was an awkward hesitation. Will and his family were surrounded by Kennedys and Flanagans and Purtells, staring them down. Keefe raised his glass emphatically. So did Will. And so did the blacksmith Martin Hogan, an old ally, neighbour Pat Whalen and several others. Will noted the Donnellys had faithful friends.

"To peace!"

With only a brief pause, everyone drank the toast. The small band at the other end of the great room began to play again. Girls balanced serving trays of beer for the men and cordials for the women. Father Connolly and several members of the Peace Society, including Martin McLaughlin and Jim Carroll, were standing in the hallway just outside the room. Cold looks passed between them and Will.

Jim took Bridget out onto the floor for his dance. Will was impressed; his father swung her around like a man twenty years younger. It inspired Will to go and find Nora and have her join him on the dance floor. She was more than halfway along with their child but he liked the feel of her growing belly as he held her close.

"Will?" She spoke quietly. "Why do you have a pistol in your pocket?"

"You sure it's a pistol?"

"It's a pistol. I'm serious. Why do you have that?"

"Nothing. Honestly." He smiled into her green eyes. "Just a precaution."

Will looked around the dance floor to keep track of his brothers. He saw John and Winnifred Ryder go outside together. One of the Ryders had an eye on them.

Near Will, Michael was being charming and chatting with two other pretty girls, ignoring Fanny Carroll. It was clear Fanny was unhappy and becoming more so. She confronted him.

"Michael. I'm thirsty," she said.

"One of the girls'll bring you something."

"I'm thirsty now. A gentleman would get me a lemonade."

"That's certainly true. I'll keep my eyes open for a gentleman," he said and went back to flirting with the two beauties. They were joined by a third girl, an attractive young redhead with a seductive smile.

"Hello," Michael said to her. "Excuse me, did it hurt?" The redhead gave him a quizzical look. Michael continued. "I mean, when you fell from heaven?"

The other girls laughed. The redhead appeared amused.

"Did the sun come out? Or was that just your smile?"

Fanny's eyes turned to smouldering coals. Will watched as she turned and headed for the backyard.

Nora wanted a little respite from the cigar smoke, so Will found her wrap and they stepped out onto the long kitchen porch, where they could see their breath under the stars with other couples. John was there speaking intently to Winnifred, both studying the universe on this frosty winter night.

"...scientists say the light from them has been t-t-t-travelling for a hundred years to get to the earth. Some of the ones you see burned out a hundred years ago but the light continues on to us! That's how long it t-t-t-takes to get here."

"Goodness! How do people know that?"

"It's all scientific knowledge. We've advanced so far."

"Sometimes I wish we were back in the magical time when people believed angels moved the moon and stars around. I'd like to believe angels are behind everything. May not be real but it's comforting, don't you think?"

Will was surprised by Winnifred Ryder's sudden, uncharacteristic verbosity. More words than he'd ever heard her speak. She was a homely little thing—with Ryder as a last name she couldn't help herself—but tonight John's attention was bringing out a confidence and a luminosity, even radiance, in her.

Nora and Will continued to examine the formations of the stars— they were truly intense that night—while standing among the others on the porch. Some low clouds parted and a half moon came out to show the gentle contours of the light snow lying on the sleeping fields.

Nearby John continued his quiet conversation.

"Winnifred...maybe the angels still do move the stars around. I d-d-d-don't know. But I do know...I would like you to be my wife."

Winnifred looked up at him in shock, then her eyes sparkled.

"I know your b-b-b-brothers hate us," John continued, "but I promise we'll m-m-m-make it work." His voice increased in volume to the point it made the conversation public and Will and Nora could hear.

"Winnifred Ryder, will you marry me?"

Nora and Will looked at each other in surprise and held their breath.

Winnifred smiled. "Oh..." And she nodded her head with enthusiasm, and even said a breathless "yes."

Nora and Will applauded. John and Winnifred noticed them, turning all shades of embarrassment, until Nora gave Winnifred a hug. Other couples had looked askance and Nora informed them.

"They're getting married!" She turned to her new soon-to-be sister-in-law.

"Congratulations, Winnie!"

They hugged. Three other couples offered applause. "Well done, John!" Will clapped his brother on the shoulder and embraced Winnifred. "Another Donnelly merger! Welcome."

I were there at the Keefe wedding in my best shirt and coat. They had hired me to tend all the horses, making sure they was watered and had a little feed on that cold night and t'keep 'em company a bit. Some was in the barn and others were outside but I found those ones some blankets and they was good. I got to eat the cakes and had a little cider inside but I spent most of the night around the barn and that's when I saw James Donnelly drinking whiskey with young Abbie McLaughlin in the hay loft. Those Donnellys and their girls in the hay lofts, I tell you. The horses was moving around and making sounds, so they didn't hear me. They was in the hay both having lost a good amount of their clothes, drunk and laughing and having a gay old time.

"Careful, James. You'll spill," says she.

I were about to quietly leave when they started the argument.

"I gotta go, Abbie. I got something to do."

Abbie kissed him. "Later. Not now."

"No. I promised." He was pretty sure of it and started to get up and pull his clothes together. But Abbie held onto him tightly.

"You're staying with me!"

"No, I gotta go."

James stood up then to get into his pants and Abbie was showing herself way beyond anything I shoulda seen and so I didn't look.

"Don't leave me alone here. Whatever it is, it can wait."

"No! That's the thing. It can't," James told her as he pulled away.

They was both pretty drunk and James Jr. tried to yank his arm away and in doing so, he hit Abbie pretty hard in the eye with the back of his hand and she cried out.

"You hit me!"

"I'm sorry. I didn't mean to…" He stood unsteadily as he buckled his belt. "I gotta go."

Like I say, I kept low so's they'd never see me. It would have been some embarrassing. James sobered a little and was clothed and mounted on a Keefe horse. He had a heavy knapsack he tied to the saddle. Abbie was angry and drunk and sobbing, holding her bruised eye, as James rode off into the night.

"You bastard!" she called out to him as one last thing and I snuck out the side door so she wouldn't see me.

The drunken James Jr. arrived on the obliging Keefe horse at the Ryder farm a mile away. It was simple. After the trial back in the spring, outside the courthouse young Thomas Ryder had called his mother a witch, and now they would pay. James and his father figured they'd all be at the wedding reception. The horses would be gone from the barn. James opened the barn doors and released the cattle out into the yard. He had brought a large can of coal oil and took his happy time pouring the liquid on the walls of the main barn, singing softly to himself.

"Give me oil in my lamp, keep me burning. Give me oil in my lamp, I pray…"

He stood back to consider his work.

"Give me oil in my lamp, keep me burning…"

James lit the torch and stood ready to throw it.

"Keep me burning till the break of day."

Holding the torch ready, James took a long, deep swallow from the whiskey bottle in his other hand. "Sing hosanna, sing hosanna, sing hosanna to the…" A shot rang out. James staggered, hit.

James Ryder stood beside the house with his Winchester rifle. He had stayed behind from the party. He levered another shell into the breech and fired again, missing James Donnelly this time. The burning torch fell to the ground as James, slowed by the whiskey and a heavy bullet in his side, struggled to mount his horse, made skittish by the rifle shots. Ryder shot again. James rode off as Ryder fired two more times.

Ryder ran up to where James had been standing. He picked up the flaming torch. He watched the retreating horseman, considering the situation. The cows were outside. The barn had been over-insured for five hundred dollars, they needed that money, and here was evidence that a

Donnelly had done it and Ryder was a witness. He hesitated for only a moment, then he threw the torch against the wall of the barn. The coal oil ignited with a roar running along the base of the building, climbing the walls and quickly sending the barn up in flames.

Blood Moon

Fanny Carroll came out on the Keefe porch beside Will and Nora. She called out Michael's name and then turned to Will.

"Have you seen that brother of yours?"

"Good evening, Miss Carroll," Will said. "I hope you're well and enjoying the evening. I suppose you mean Michael? The last time I saw him, he was in the dining room."

"If you see him around, tell him I want to talk to him."

Then she turned and went inside again.

"Rude little thing," Nora observed.

In the kitchen, Fanny asked a distracted Mrs. Keefe if she had seen Michael Donnelly. The mother of the bride called back that she had not and she took two more pies out to the great room. The cellar door in the kitchen was open and as Fanny was about to leave, she heard over the music in the dining room the shush of whispered voices below. Cautiously, quietly, Fanny began to descend the steep steps into the cellar, where a soft glow suggested a candle was burning. At the bottom of the steps, Fanny Carroll listened. She heard urgent gasps and whispers coming from the cold room next to the stairs. She moved closer and looked through the half-open door to see by the light of one candle Michael Donnelly's naked ass as he fornicated with the red-headed girl on top of a bin of potatoes. Fanny watched transfixed for a moment as Michael's thrusts became more resolute. Her expression became cold and hard as she watched them pleasuring themselves and finally heard him finish, producing the same moan as the times when he had finished with her. Fanny quietly withdrew, the sound of her careful steps covered by the music from upstairs.

Will felt something unusual in the air that night and was trying to explain it to Nora.

"I'm not sure, maybe the intensity of the stars or the cold winter night, but it made John propose to Winnifred and Michael's running around like a rabbit in heat."

"I feel it too. It's like…anticipation."

Michael came out onto the porch beside Will and Nora with rouge on his face, adjusting his clothes.

"You having a good night, Michael?"

"It's splendid, so far," Michael told him, fastening his belt.

"You know, little brother," Will told him quietly, "you might want to exercise some caution these days. We have enemies. Maybe keep it in your pants."

Michael shrugged and smiled at him. "I could."

Then Michael looked up and noticed Fanny Carroll was standing at the corner of the barn, as if waiting for him. She gave him a smile and Michael waved back to her. She withdrew around the corner of the barn.

"Or then again…" Michael left Will and Nora and went to join Fanny.

James Donnelly Jr. arrived back at the Keefe house and walked unsteadily into the living room. He had failed. In his hasty escape, he hadn't burned the barn. He had dropped the torch. And he had a bullet in his side. He knew it was bad. He had messed up. Just like so many things in his life. He saw his father in the living room with Keefe. He would have to tell him and face his disappointment. He took a drink of whiskey and staggered. Drops of blood hit the floor from his jacket hem, which had absorbed the blood from the bullet wound in his side. He coughed up a little, touched his lips with his fingers and saw the red. The wound was worse than he first thought. No one noticed. The whiskey washed down the blood and eased the jagged pain in his side.

James turned as a Feehley boy looked out the window and pointed to a distant glow through the trees.

"LOOK! FIRE! IT'S THE RYDER PLACE!"

James shuffled to the window and stared at the horizon in amazement. It was true. Distant flames consumed the Ryder barn a mile away. He had done it after all!

Michael Donnelly came around the corner of the barn and made out Fanny, who had withdrawn and was standing under some trees watching him with her compelling smile. He headed toward her.

"There she is, my Madonna in the moonlight!"

She was strangely silent as he approached her.

"Are you all right?" he asked and her eyes glittered.

Then Michael found himself surrounded by three men. Jim Carroll and Matthew Thompson, Maggie's brother, grabbed Michael as Fanny watched.

"Fanny?" Michael looked at her.

He then recognized James Flanagan, whose stage had overturned and whose brother Joe had been killed. Flanagan had a knife in his hand. As the others held him, James stepped behind Michael and whispered in his ear.

"This is for Joe."

Flanagan quickly applied the knife blade under Michael's chin, cut deep and right across his throat. The others let Michael go and he fell to the snowy ground, his eyes wide, both hands trying to stem the blood flowing from his jugular. The assailants all disappeared except for Fanny, who remained a moment longer staring at Michael, his heels kicking weakly against the white snow as the lifeblood drained from his body. Her brother returned and grabbed her arm and they headed for their horses.

Laughing lightly to himself over the unexpected success of his barn burning, James stumbled out on the porch near Will and Nora to watch the distant growing inferno. It was a well-made barn and in fact Will, Michael and James had been at the barn-raising to help a few years before when the Donnellys and Ryders were on friendlier terms.

Tom Ryder and his father, Grouchy, and their friends raced to their horses and wagons to get to the fire and save anything they could. Other men followed. More wedding guests came outside to better see the flames in the distance. Will was about to go to his horse, to join the other men and see if anything could be done, when his brother James came up and took his arm.

"Willy, my brother. How you doing?"

"James, you see this fire?"

"Oh yes. Lovely isn't it? "

"No, it's not. No good's going to come out of this. Probably try to blame us."

James went to take a long pull to finish the mickey in his pocket. In sudden impatience Will took hold of James's wrist.

"Look, put that away. We have to be smart tonight."

James staggered and fell against him. Will's hand went under James' jacket to steady him and found his ribs were warm and sticky. He withdrew his hand and stared at the red on his fingers.

"What's this? You're bleeding!"

"Oh, yeah. Was going to mention that. Got shot."

"Shot! Who shot you? Where?"

James looked out toward the flaming Ryder barn with satisfaction, his words slurred.

"Oh…I don't know. Didn't see him. Guess it's open season on Donnellys."

James coughed and his lips were red again. He wiped it off with the back of his hand.

"Who did this, Jimmy? Who shot you?"

"Doesn't matter."

Will stared at him as the realization became all too clear.

"You torched the Ryder barn!"

James gave a weak smile. "Yeah."

"But why? For Chrissake! Why did you do that, James?"

"Had it coming."

James stumbled as if he would fall.

Will whistled and called out, "TOM! PAT! MICHAEL! I NEED HELP!"

James's knees buckled. Will caught him as he collapsed. He put his coat down and laid James on the cold planks of the porch.

"We'll get you to a doctor. We'll get this fixed."

"No! Listen, Will," James stared intently into his eyes, now surprisingly sober. "Don't take me to a doctor. Please. It can't be fixed."

"There's a good surgeon in London."

"No. I want to be at home with the family. Just take me home, Will. Please."

"Lie still."

Will was trying to think. He gently examined the bleeding bullet hole in his brother's back. It was from a rifle and would have torn him up badly inside. James coughed blood again. His lips were crimson and Will suddenly realized James Jr. was not going to make it.

"I want to go home, Will."

"All right. We'll take you home. Rest now. We'll get you out of here."
James grabbed his shoulder and drew him close.

"Will? I'm sorry."

"It's all right, James."

Patrick and Tom arrived on the porch. Patrick went down on his knee.

"James? What's wrong, buddy, one drink too many?"

"He's been shot."

Both brothers stared at Will in shock.

"We'll need bandages and water. Make a bed for him in the wagon. We all have to get out of here, now."

Patrick ran inside. Tom lifted James up in his arms and carried him to the wagon.

Where was Michael? Will had seen him go out toward the barn to see Fanny Carroll. They were probably just up in the hay. He called out.

"MIKE? MICHAEL?"

A fear gripped him as he began to walk toward the barn. His brother's phrase rang in his head: "Open season on Donnellys." He began to run.

Inside the barn he called out to Michael, his voice betraying the beginnings of panic, but the barn was empty. Will came out again. There were tracks in the snow that went around the corner of the barn. He went around the structure to the side yard and there he stopped. The night sky was clear, the starlight strong, and he could see that a short distance away, lying on the snowy ground in the moon shadow from a big oak, was Michael. He lay on his back, his eyes open as if pondering the stars, one hand at the gaping wound at his throat, his warm blood still pooling in the snow.

"Michael! No!" Will fell to his knees, took Michael in his arms and held him.

"No, no, no...!" he said, rocking him. His brother's blood smeared the front of his good shirt and the palms of his hands. "Oh, Michael."

In Retreat

THEY MOVED AS quick as they could in the buckboard on the hard Roman Line, the Donnellys taking home their dead and dying, the body of Michael covered by a blanket and the wounded James beside him. The remaining guests at the Keefe party had watched them leave. They had taken off their hats and a few gave their condolences, but no one helped. Never had Will felt his family so threatened and isolated. Now he rode behind the wagon, wheeling his horse around periodically to see if anyone followed. They were not well armed, a couple of pistols, sitting ducks for their enemies.

His mother held James's head on her lap, stroking his temple. James was still alive but very weak. Patrick and Tom had bandaged him up to slow the bleeding. Cousin Bridget was shaking, her mouth clamped shut, her eyes like a startled deer's as she stared at Michael's covered form. Nora held a blanket around her to warm and comfort her. Johannah and Jim were both very quiet and Will knew them to be in anguish, as they all were. Patrick was too angry and emotional to speak.

Inside the Donnelly farmhouse, Tom laid out Michael's body on the big table in the summer kitchen with a gentle affection Will had never seen in him before. Patrick and Tom then carried James Jr. into the main kitchen and laid him down on the cot near the stove.

"Good…thank you…" James whispered. He was happy to be home. His mother stayed by his side as Nora stoked the fire and lit several candles.

James's bandages were blood soaked but when Nora offered to change them, he did not want her to.

"Good to be home."

Bridget remained silent, sitting on the wood pile staring at James with wide eyes, her mouth slightly open to breathe, as if she were preparing herself to run.

Will called out to his brothers. "Patrick! Tom! Get your clubs. And your rifles. Tonight we'll teach our enemies a lesson. We start with the Flanagans."

"I'll c-c-c-come too."

"All right, John. Come then."

Will could see his mother in the candlelight, her beautiful face contorted by grief. Her hands were covered in James's blood. She looked small and lost and defeated.

Suddenly James called out, his voice a rattle, fresh blood on his lips. "Da! Da!"

Their father had kept to himself, sitting brooding in a corner of the room, saying nothing, looking no one in the eye, but at James's call he went and knelt down beside him.

"I'm here, Jamie."

James took his father's hand in his bloody one and made him look into his eyes.

"Did I do all right?"

"Yes, you did well, Jamie."

"I kept it all secret."

A cold realization entered Will: his father had ordered James to burn the Ryders' barn.

"I poured it all over the walls like you said. Got the barn going real well. They shouldn't have talked to Ma like that after the trial, should they? We had to defend her honour, didn't we?"

"Yes, we did," Jim Donnelly told him. "You did well, James. I'm very proud of you."

James smiled and was calmed by his father's praise. Then he coughed more blood, grimaced from the pain and settled again. His lips moved and he began to sing just under his breath.

> Give my oil in my lamp, keep me burning.
> Give me oil in my lamp, I pray.
> Give me oil in my lamp, keep me burning.
> Keep me burning till the break of day...

His eyes and lips became still, the last breath left his body and he was gone.

Johannah embraced James and held him tight for several moments. She growled and moaned and they all remained silent. Then she let him go and breathed an enormous sigh.

Jim would not meet Will's eyes.

"Put him beside Mike in the summer kitchen," Will told Tom.

Tom reached down and picked up James's body in his arms. Will followed him into the summer kitchen where their breath made clouds in the cold air. Moonlight streamed through the window as Johannah came in and knelt beside the bodies of her sons, side by side on the big harvest table they used in the summer. She placed her hands on them both and put her face against James's still-warm chest, and began to keen. Will watched as his mother grieved, the hopeless tones of her voice chilling him even more than the sight of the bodies of his brothers. He turned and went back in to confront his father.

In the living room, Patrick, Tom and John were loading their pistols and rifles and preparing for battle. Jim sat on a rigid chair, one eye open, checking down the barrels of his shotgun for cleanliness. Will came up to his father. The older man still would not meet his eyes. Will turned to his brothers.

"We will not go after our enemies tonight."

Patrick froze and stared at him. "What? Why the hell not?"

Will gestured to his father. "Ask him."

Will then turned to Tom. "Tom?" His brother turned his cold eyes to Will. "It was you who killed those two Flanagan horses in the field." Tom remained silent. "And it was you who loosened the bolt on the Flanagan coach the day Joe was killed, wasn't it?"

Tom looked at their father for guidance. His silent appeal confirmed it was all true as surely as a confession.

"The Flanagans were right," Will said, addressing his family and making eye contact with each one that would. "We killed Joe. And that's why they killed Michael."

Will confronted his father.

"Look at me, Da!" Slowly his father's defiant eyes found Will's. "You put Tom up to it, didn't you?"

Again, silence told the truth. Will was furious with his father, and with himself for not seeing it sooner.

"You brought this all on us. You put James up to burning the Ryder barn. You put Tom up to fixing the Flanagan coach and killing the horses. You've been carrying on your goddamn feuds and now two of my brothers are dead! God damn you. I wish to Christ you'd never come home!"

His father remained silent. Will turned and went out into the summer kitchen and kissed his mother and put a heavy blanket around her.

"Ma?" She looked up at him slowly. "Nora and I are going to go home. We'll come back in the morning and make some decisions. Will you be all right?" She nodded. "You've got Patrick and Tom. There are loaded rifles at the door. I've asked Johnny O'Connor to come stay here tonight so he can do the chores in the morning. You need anything? Anything I can do?"

She looked up at him, considering his question, her face a mask of grief and defiance. "Yes. There is. You can let me die before you. I don't care what you do, but give me that."

Will put a hand on her shoulder and she reached across her chest to grip his hand tight, then she let go. The image of her kneeling beside the bodies of her sons in the moonlight, her breath forming small white clouds of sorrow, seared through him.

Will returned to the kitchen and took Nora by the hand and she stood up. Patrick was surprised.

"Where the hell are you going?"

"We're going home, Pat. You and Tom stay here and look after things. Keep an eye open. One of you come and get me if you need anything. We'll take John."

Will turned to his quiet brother. "You coming?"

John nodded and they left.

Devil's Work

JOHANNAH REMAINED OUT in the summer kitchen beside her boys for a long time, until the cold crept under the blanket Will had given her and she was trembling, even disoriented by exhaustion and the very idea that they were gone. For truly the spirits that were Michael and James had departed, these bodies mere flesh and bone, dead husks that no longer housed any real portion of her sons, who only hours before had laughed and loved, felt heat and cold, pain and pleasure. Anything here was only a memory to touch, a cruel metaphor for what had been lost. And yet she could not leave them and go inside to him. She did not know how she could return to the presence of the man who had caused their deaths.

It was late when Jim came to her. He looked at the boys and knelt beside her. Her husband had knelt with her before, but this time she did not believe it, and his presence betrayed the sanctity of their deaths.

When she spoke, her breath was visible. "Two of my sons are dead." Johannah turned on Jim, her voice rising. "It's true, isn't it? You told James to burn the Ryders' barn?"

"They insulted you," he said quietly.

"Don't you dare use me in this. I should have known. You had Tom fix the Flanagan stage and kill those horses, didn't you?"

"The Flanagans had it coming," his tone defensive, weak.

Johannah was dizzy and nauseous at the realization that Jim was behind it all. She touched the faces of her dead sons.

"Don't you understand? I gave them life, I nursed them, taught them and saw them grow into men. And now they are dead! And the only one to blame is you."

It was then she began to cry, the tears finally coming. And she felt Jim's tentative hands on her shoulders, the hands she had once loved. He rubbed her shoulders to comfort her as he had done long before and she turned to him, the tears flowing freely now.

"Do you remember your promise to me years ago? No more violence. No more fighting. Then Farrell. Now this. How fine our life could have been together. Well, you're a liar, aren't you? And you've destroyed it all… again!"

"Johannah…"

"LIAR!"

She could see that the icy plume of her word affected him. For Jim, grief was overcoming pride and deep loss was smothering the passion for revenge. He began to speak. "As long as I remember, in my life I have been guided and sustained and enslaved by an overwhelming desire for… revenge. It was revenge…even with you."

She turned in surprise and studied him as he continued quietly.

"When I was a boy we raised two little ponies your father wanted as a gift for you. My father wouldn't sell them to him. Your father was going to take them anyway, so to stop him, my father killed them— these things he loved—and then he killed himself. I could not stand the sorrow and the shame of his madness. First I thought of murdering your father, but what I wanted more was to make him feel pain as I had. So as vengeance against him, I made plans to kill you. But then I had a better idea. I would steal you from him and let him know it was me."

She stared at him. "Our life together, for you…was nothing but an act of revenge?"

"At the beginning. But then I…I fell in love with you, Jo."

His grizzled chin quivered with emotion.

"And the deeper I fell in love, the weaker became my desire for revenge. You and love almost cured me of my curse. Almost. But then Farrell came with the face of your father and it all came out again. And now this. I have inherited the madness of my own father."

She looked up at him, studying his tortured face.

"We have lost two of us. Two of our beautiful sons, Jim. You must make their sacrifice mean something. Tomorrow we will go openly to our enemies, house to house, and ask them all, each one of them, in the names of our dead sons for…a truce…for forgiveness…for peace."

Jim looked at Michael and James and slowly nodded.

"We'll go to each one of them," she repeated. "First thing you'll have Johnny rig up the wagon and we'll go. Now swear it to me."

"I swear."

"Say it!"

"I swear we will go and make peace with our enemies in the name of our sons."

"Yes," she said, closing her eyes.

Jim straightened the blanket carefully around her shoulders and stood up unsteadily, his joints creaking, gaining purchase on the table that held the bodies of his sons. He reached down and gently took her hands in his to help her to her feet.

"Come inside now, Jo. You'll catch your death."

The meeting of the St. Patrick's Peace Society took place just about the hour of James's passing, as they gathered at the burning ruins of the Ryder barn. Among them were Father Connolly, the Ryder brothers, Jim Carroll, a couple of Kennedys, James Flanagan, a fairly new but enthusiastic adherent named Purtell and several other interested parties. Martin McLaughlin had brought his still-inebriated daughter Abbie there, her face bruised now, and McLaughlin held her arm and made her repeat to them the entire story.

"Tell them."

"It was James Donnelly. He made me drink from his bottle and got me all drunk so's my head was swimming and then he took me out to the barn and I didn't know what I was doing."

"Go on, Abbie."

"He made advances on me in the hay and grabbed me in private places and I pushed him away and said no—I'm a good Catholic girl—and then he hit me. He hit me and threatened to hurt me again. Then he had his way with me anyway. It's all a nightmare."

"He had his way with you?" Father Connolly asked, watching her intently.

"Yes, he did."

"Tell them what you saw then." Martin McLaughlin stood over her, urging her on.

"I seen James Donnelly ride off toward the Ryders' with a can of coal oil."

"Do you swear to that?" Jim Carroll asked her.

"I do, sir."

After Abbie's confessions, it was Father Connolly's turn to speak to the vigilantes.

"You have heard the girl. The Donnellys, led by that crippled devil and the evil woman, defy all peaceful and law-abiding citizens. I have concluded that Johannah Donnelly must practice the black arts. How else have they escaped justice for so long? This night they have burned a barn and raped one of your daughters, only the last of so many crimes against the community. The law has failed you," Connolly told them. "The members of the St. Patrick's Peace Society have done everything reasonable to stop the outrages. Desperate times require desperate actions." He turned to Jim Carroll. "You have to do whatever you think best to put an end to it and bring them all to justice. In the name of the Father, Son and Holy Ghost...I give you my blessing."

I got to the Donnellys' late that night. It were near the end of the Keefe party, Will Donnelly finds me and tells me that James and Mike have been hurt and asks me to come and help out at the farmhouse. But I got no rides so I walked and when I got there my toes was frozen. I noticed a lantern in the barn and some goings on there and I went in to find Patrick saddling a horse. He was talking to himself kind of low and crazy, or maybe to the angels, when I got there. Was saying, "...not going to do something...? Let 'em get away...? Sit on our arses...? Well, I'M going to do something..."

He had a shotgun, and a rifle and two pistols in his belt. He were a strange one, I knew, given to tempers, but I asked him politely what was up and he told me they had killed Michael and James. I were pole-axed by this certain information. So then Patrick mounts his horse with all his armaments, told me again he was going to do something about it and rode out of the barn, heading for town. I didn't like the sound of that or of his chances, but he was gone before I could speak an opinion and anyway I were only a kid.

I went down to the house real quiet to see if I could help. I went in through the summer kitchen where the door was open and by God there they was, the two laid out on the table. And I'm not shy to say I had tears in my eyes. Then I went around to the front door where big Tom let me in. And Old Jim was staring at the floor and I could hear Johannah crying softly in the living room. I told them I was so sorry for their loss. It were such a sad place that house that night and I tried to be small and quiet.

There were a cot in the kitchen where I usually slept if I was staying over and I put my coat there. Someone had throwed a blanket over the cot and when I pulled it back, there was fresh dark stains that came away on my fingers and I knowed it was blood. Poor James, I guessed. I put some split wood in the stove and boiled water for tea to give the Irish girl Bridget, 'cause she was in bad shape, crying and trembling, any loud voices shaking her. Old Jim came into the kitchen and sat near the stove and he had a basket of sweet apples from their tree and Tom came in and we all ate a couple in silence. Old Jim told me to remember tomorrow to get the rig ready early and to feed the pigs and chickens early and not too much oats for the horses and I promised I would.

While we was sitting there, there come a knock on the door. Old Jim let the steel lock slide and in comes Jim Feehley to give his condolences. I'd never much cared for the man and Old Jim didn't want him disturbing Johannah and Feehley said that was fine. When the condolences offering was done he talked about walking up the road to Will's house to do the same.

"The night's clearer than I thought," he told Old Jim. "D'you mind if I leave my rain slicker here to pick up on my way back?"

"We're going to bed soon."

"That's all right. I don't want to disturb anyone. I'll just hang it here and if you leave the door unlocked, I can grab it when I come by on my way back and I won't wake you."

Old Jim agreed to this. Just as Feehley left, Johannah comes into the kitchen. I could not look into her sad eyes and when I tried to give my sympathies they stuck in my throat. So Old Jim said we might as well all go to bed. I could see they was all exhausted and so was I. Bridget had been terrified by the killings of Michael and James, and Johannah put a kind arm around her shoulders. "It's all right now. D'you want to sleep with me?" Johannah asked her and Bridget nodded she did. That time of year in February, the Donnellys often closed off the upstairs attic bedrooms with a door that kept the warm air downstairs.

"All right, we'll sleep in the north bedroom and Johnny, you sleep with Jim in the big bed."

So after filling the stove to stay hot we all undressed for bed down to our long underwear. Tom took the bed in the first small room off the kitchen. I settled in with Jim in the bigger bedroom on the wall side of the bed under the window. It were a fine and wide mattress and I'd never slept on it before. You know, some people said it must have felt strange sleeping next to a convicted murderer but it never crossed my mind. He was warm and didn't move much, nor snore too bad. There was worse things I could be sleeping beside. Old Jim gave me his heavy wool coat for a pillow.

"All right Johnny, you'll get up at first light and light the fire. When she's going real good, go out and harness the horses, feed 'em like I said, and slop the pigs. Give extra to the sow, she's in the family way."

"Yes, sir."

He blew out the lantern and we settled down.

Patrick had ridden all the way into Lucan, but not by way of the public roads. He had made a short cut across the fields and swamps and because of this, did not encounter the Peace Society, in fact just missed them coming north. Patrick came out on the road west of McLaughlin's farm and rode up the deserted Main Street in front of the Central Hotel, then he began to yell.

"WHERE ARE YOU, YOU COWARDS! CARROLLS! FLA-NAGANS! RYDERS! THOMPSONS! KENNEDYS! COME OUT HERE!"

Patrick fired off a couple of pistol shots. Dogs barked.

"COME OUT AND FIGHT LIKE MEN!"

He let loose with one of his shotguns so everyone heard him and knew he was there, but no one came out.

"Where is everyone?" Patrick asked the moon.

The bars were closed and most citizens had gone to bed, and those he was looking for were by this time riding north on the Roman Line.

The Peace Society

I DON'T KNOW why my eyes opened that night but I woke up feeling a little trembly from crazy dreams I had about wild men on horses. Then I thought I heard horses. I was lying in the big bed beside Old Jim with moonlight coming in the little window above my head and the fire in the kitchen stove had burned low so I could see my breath. Tom were snoring in the small room. Old Jim were still beside me in dreamland. Then between Tom's snores, I heard something outside. The wind? Patrick coming back? No, it were whispered voices and feet walking careful on crunchy snow.

I raised myself up on my knees to the window and pulled the curtain aside and there they was! Thirty men or more, just like in my dream, their eerie bodies in the torchlight, armed men in wild costumes, spread out across the yard, coming for us with guns and clubs! In the weird moving light, I saw men in blackened faces and masks. Others adjusted their funny hats and wore women's dresses or shawls over their heads.

"Mr. Jim! There is men outside," I said, but it only came out a whisper. I was frozen, looking out the frosted window, then suddenly a ghoul's painted face was right there, his nose two inches from mine own looking in at me and we locked eyes like, and he was one of the Ryder boys and I prayed to Jesus and all his angels to forgive my past sins and deliver us all from these demons.

I dropped the curtain, shook Old Jim's arm and repeated, "Mr. Jim. There is men outside!"

I shaked him hard to wake him up. Then I looked up through the open door into the kitchen and I seen Jim Carroll in his constable uniform coming in through the unlocked kitchen door. He lights a candle and holds it up to see who was where. The dog barked and growled. Jim Carroll kicked the dog aside and came to the doorway of the bedroom with

328

his candle. He had this wild look and I wondered what he was doing with them crazy people outside.

"Donnelly! I have a warrant for your arrest. And your wife too."

Old Jim was finally awake and sat up on the bed in his long johns. He threw the blanket over me and said to go back to sleep.

"Carroll? What is this nonsense?"

The fire was down and the air had cooled and I handed Old Jim his greatcoat I was using as a pillow. He put it on. I whispered, "There's more outside. A whole bunch."

I'm not sure he understood this. Carroll started whistling a tune, a humorous tune like one you'd do a jig to. He had handcuffs in one hand and then he put down the candle, turned and went into the room where Tom were sleeping on the cot and I guess he was able to cuff his hands together in front while he were asleep. Tom woke up, groggy and angry and looked down at his hands.

"What? Who's...? Carroll!"

He stared at the handcuffs on his wrists, then tried to break the chain.

Johannah stood in the kitchen doorway. I could tell she were afraid but she kept easy and turned to Bridget who was awake and stood behind her, scared and whimpering. Johannah spoke to her in a low voice: "It's all right, Brid. We have a guest. Build up the fire and put on the kettle." Johannah lighted a lantern hanging from the ceiling and two candles for the kitchen table, then put on her apron over her nightdress. Bridget was staring at Carroll from the hallway door with wide eyes, then silently did what she was told, building up the fire in the stove and lighting two more candles.

I remember I were sitting up in the bed and there was a moment that was very still and quiet and Jim Carroll smiled at Mr. Jim. Tom was standing in the kitchen doorway with his back to me and his hands in cuffs and Mr. Jim saw him like that.

"He's cuffed you, Tom."

"Yeah. He thinks he's smart."

Mr. Jim turned to Carroll.

"All right. Show me the warrant."

"There'll be plenty of time for that. Right now there are chores to be done!" Carroll's voice got this weird excitement in it.

"NOW!"

A dozen wild men in their costumes burst through the door into the kitchen with clubs and shovels, shouting and whooping. I seen Carroll swing his billy club and hit Mr. Jim across the head. Jim just stares at him, not believing what he'd done, and Carroll hit him again.

Tom seed his father being hit and roared in a terrible rage. He jumped and knocked Carroll aside and fought back against three of them as they beat him with clubs, as he tried to protect his father. It were so crowded in the kitchen, and I could tell the men was half drunk, they had difficulty getting clear swings and Tom was a terror even with his hands cuffed, knocking a couple down and hurting them. The lantern in the kitchen were hanging on a line and it got hit and were swinging back and forth giving a real strange look to the room, the light shifting back and forth as I watched it all, making me dizzy.

I remember cousin Bridget gave a terrible scream and ran upstairs to the attic. I figured it were a good idea. So I slid out of the bed, ran into the main room and followed her up the stairs. She managed to get through the door but then she slams and locks it behind her. I figure she thought I was one of them after her. I pounded a few times and called her name but I guess she were too far gone. From up on the open stairs I could see everything that were going on in the main room and the kitchen and I saw someone hit Johannah and knock her sideways but she was still on her feet with her arms up to protect her head. I saw the men face her in the kitchen with their clubs. They was scared of her, I could see, and no one wanted to strike her first.

She shouts at them, "You cowards! You're all damned to hell. I'll see you there!"

Finally Jim Carroll raised a club and brought it down on Johannah's head. Johannah fell to her knees. Mr. Jim and Tom both pulled away from their attackers and tried to protect Johannah. Them vigilantes used their clubs under the swinging light.

I tried again to open the upstairs door but I gave it up and scrambled down the stairs again, crossed the floor and went back into the bedroom. It was as if I were invisible, for no one seemed to lay eyes on me, in that if they did and properly thought to kill me as a witness, I were surely gone. There was one moment when Jim Carroll stared right at me but then his attention went back to the others and I slid under the bed again and hid behind a laundry basket. I looked out through the wide bedroom door to watch the horrors going on in the kitchen. Again the open door let me see clearly into the main room and the kitchen. There was wild shadows on the wall as the lantern swung back and forth to show the crazy made-up faces of the vigilantes, raining clubs down on their victims, who held up arms to protect themselves. And yet they was still alive! On their knees and all bloody, Jim and Tom trying to protect Johannah, fending off the blows. Jim was finally knocked down and unmoving. The dog barked and moaned, then cowered. Johannah went to Tom and I heard her shout.

"TOM! GET OUT! GO AND GET WILL!"

I heared this horrible howl come from Tom and he rose up through the clubbing, all bloody and big and knocking people back and he charged out the front door. Many of the men followed him outside. Kneeling on the floor, Johannah glares up at the few assailants left in the kitchen with her bloody face and clear green eyes.

"Give me a moment to pray."

The vigilantes stepped back. It were a weird moment in among all the weird moments. Johannah looked over at her husband, bloodied and unconscious on the floor beside her, closed her eyes and her lips moved, saying prayers for a moment. Jim Carroll looked at the others, standing mute and frozen. Then he said, "That's enough! She's had plenty of time."

Johannah opened her eyes and I heared her say, "God in heaven, I curse you all!"

Carroll swung his club again and it hit Johannah's head and she fell to the floor, silent.

A floorboard creaked in the upstairs attic. Carroll looked at John Purtell.

"Someone upstairs."

Purtell and two others ran past my bedroom door and headed up the staircase. They wasn't looking for me at all in the bedroom and I was curious about Tom outside so's I slid out from under the bed and edged up to the window again to see and there outside in the front yard was Tom surrounded by a circle of vigilantes. He had someways with his cuffed hands been able to pull a club from one of them and was swinging, knocking a couple of them down and holding them back for a moment, but then they all runs in and grabs the club and surrounds him. Still, he were on his feet. He screamed and howled, angry with the cuffs on. He turned to confront Tom Ryder, who held a pitchfork. Tom Ryder looked really scared but I seen him move forward hard and he drove the pitchfork deep into Tom's chest. Tom Donnelly screamed and fell to his knees, holding onto the fork that went out the other side of him. I seen the prongs sticking out his back. It took him three tries but Ryder finally pulled the pitchfork out. Tom fell face down in the snow. I knew that were the end of him. I slid down under the bed again and closed my eyes for a moment, then I peeked out from behind the basket.

In the kitchen, the vigilantes still stood over Johannah, on the floor all slippery with blood. Her open eyes stared up at them, her lips moving. Beside her, Old Jim gave out a moan. I couldn't believe he were still alive. I seen Martin McLaughlin bring his club down and Jim's moaning stopped.

In the attic upstairs, I heard the work of other men. They was onto cousin Bridget, who was making desperate screams. The men in the kitchen stood still and looked upward, listening. Then the screams was muffled there for a while, she was gasping and crying. I wondered what they was doing, but I guess I knowed. The men in the kitchen all lowered their eyes and just stood there with their clubs hanging down. I was sure glad she hadn't opened that door to me or I'da been up there with her.

"Finish up, up there!" Carroll shouted to the attic. Then Bridget's screams come again and I couldn't stand it. There was a thud sound above and the noise suddenly stopped in the middle of her scream.

About then four men dragged poor Tom's big body inside, slipping on the pools of blood, one man falling, and dropped Tom beside his mother on the kitchen floor. I heard Tom moan and someone said, "Hit him. Break his skull open." And that's exactly what Mr. Ryder did with a spade he'd brought.

John Purtell come down from upstairs.

"That one's done," he says to Carroll.

I could hear the two other men who had gone up was dragging Bridget's body down the stairs. Her head must have been right back as I heard it banging against the wooden steps and Jim Carroll snarled at them.

"Lift her up!"

They did so and carried her body with more respect I guess, laying it down on the floor in the living room. From under the bed I could have touched her foot with a long broom handle, I was that close. Purtell walked into the kitchen and slipped on the bloody floor. He fell on his arse, putting both his hands in the pool of blood. I remember he stared at the blood on his hands and pants. The dog started barking again and a vigilante swung a club. I didn't see the dog hit but it yelped and was quiet. Then Mr. Purtell had an axe and took a swing at the dog. For a moment everything were silent and still. From under that bed I could see the three bodies in the kitchen and Bridget in the main room with her dull eyes open and her terrible face looking at me and the men in the kitchen standing around wondering what to do.

Then the boots of two men came into my bedroom and I figured they'd remembered me and come looking and this were my end. They stood with their boots two feet from my nose and I heard the splash on the bed above me and smelled the coal oil being poured. Then they step back and set the bed on fire above me! 'Twas all I could do to stop myself from making a run for it, but the coal oil didn't seep through the bed and so I stayed quiet. Then they splashed the coal oil around the living room, on Bridget's body, and lit that too. I couldn't look. When I could hear the flames crackling above me, the vigilantes turned and hurried from the house, out the kitchen door, slipping on the bloody floor, catching each other as they stepped over the bodies. It might have been funny, some of them in their costumes and masks, slipping and falling, helping each other up, if it weren't just one long scene from hell.

Now the house were empty but for me and the dead. I was feeling the heat on my back as the flames grew on the bed above me, but I waited a bit more. The Peace Society men were still outside—I saw some through the open kitchen door—and if they seed me trying to leave the house, they would kill me, that much I knowed. I pushed the basket aside and got out from under the flaming bed. Through the kitchen door, I could see on the front yard the Peace Society members with their torches watching the flames go up the house, their faces looking in, horrified and fascinated. I were surrounded by the flames up the walls now and couldn't wait much longer, trying to choose between staying in the fire and going that way or going out to their clubs and pitchforks. But then I looks again and the torches are gone! The men have left and none too soon for me.

So's I go past the flaming body of Bridget, trying not to look at that horror, and into the kitchen and stepped over the others. I seen something against the wall, a bloody ball that I seen was the dog's head. Purtell had cut it off with the axe. But here's the thing. Flames roaring all around me, I'm headed for the open door and I sees movement! Miss Johannah was still breathing! So was Mr. Jim! But both was so terribly wounded. Mr. Jim's head was open and his smashed lips were moving with curses and Johannah's lips moved in what I figured was prayer.

"Miss Johannah!" I called and she moaned a little. "Come on, Miss Johannah! We got to get out!"

I took her broken, bloody hand and tried to pull her toward the door but she screamed in pain. I couldn't do it and the flames was burning us both now. I was coughing and choking with the smoke. The whole kitchen, walls and ceiling was burning around us.

"COME ON!" I hollered at her. Weren't much of me left. The roaring of the flames made me deaf, but I still tried to pull her to the door. There weren't much purchase on the slippery floor and I couldn't move her. Then I saw her looking up at me with her one good eye in her awful, battered face. She seemed calm to me, if you can believe it, and through her smashed lips she spoke the word.

"Go."

"No, we can do it, Miss Johannah. Come on."

"Run," she whispered, then she looks me in the eyes and her face said it was all right. My back was burning now and my hair singed, chunks of fire was falling from the ceiling and I knew I couldn't do any more. Then I noticed something on the floor beside her. It was the little river stone, the piece of Ireland she kept in her apron that had fallen out, and for some reason I grabbed it, all sticky with her blood. I stuffed it in my pocket and her one good eye was watching me and whispered it were all right. I squeezed her hand one last time, her eye closed and I let go of her. Then I stepped over Tom and Mr. Jim and the body of the dog and I scrambled outside.

I remember that feel of the cold air as I tumbled out of the flaming farmhouse face down into the blood-splattered snow, a cooling remedy to my singed body. I was barefoot and without a coat, but I were alive.

I looked up the road and could see the gang of Peace Society men spread out riding away. They did not see me.

I looked back and the house were now fully in flame and sparks had drifted over to the old Farrell place and started her going too. The Farrell house laid empty and rotting all these years and for a moment I thought it just seemed right that the two houses, representing all the troubles for so many years, should go up in flames together. But I didn't think on this at any great length. I ran to the ditch, then across the road and down fifty yards to the house where Patrick Whalen lived.

In the cruel inferno of the kitchen, with the flames descending, her body numb, Johannah's dreams had instinctively gone back to the happiest times. She was riding Cuchulain along the ridge from where you could see the Ballyfinboy River meandering on its untroubled way down to the sea, with Lucy holding tight against her back, her mouth close to her ear, her voice humming "Irish Soldier Laddie." And then they were passing through the enchanted woodlot, Lucy's voice calling forth the nymphs and faeries, Cuchulain slowing down to walk along the long, cool willow-shaded path by the fishing stream, then Lucy's voice in her ear urging speed across the hard pasture, clearing two sheep walls, practically free of gravity, and it felt as if they could ride on like this forever. And then Johannah found herself drifting up into consciousness. She pushed back the terrible pain, pushed it back and turned her head to look at Jim beside her. She found his hand beside hers, took it and squeezed his broken fingers. She was amazed when, very faintly, he returned the pressure. Then he opened the one good eye in his bloody battered head and she with her smashed mouth and vision swiftly closing in, managed to tell him, "Love you."

And with the last of his strength, his eye intently on her, he raised out his good hand, one bloody, broken finger, and tried to touch her nose.

"Imagine that…"

The roof of the house made a long, mournful groan and the flaming log joists above them consumed by the fire could hold no more and collapsed as a ball of flame falling on top of them, and that was their end.

Oh, I banged at that door what seemed a long time, shifting from one bare foot to t'other, before Mr. and Mrs. Whalen comes and I can hear the scuffling as they takes the bars and chairs off the door and opens it. My feet was pretty frozen, all right. Their faces was looking at me, terrified like I were a ghost or something. They knowed what had gone on across the road and didn't want nothing to do with it, and who could blame them?

"Can I come in?"

They looked up the Line toward the Peace Society men, the last few of them still visible on the road, heading north toward the home of Will Donnelly. The Whalens looked across at the flames of the Donnelly farmhouse, then Mrs. Whalen grabbed my arm and pulled me inside and slammed the door.

No Rest for the Wicked

WILL WAS LYING beside Nora in the upstairs bedroom of their house, his eyes wide open. She had made love to him to take his mind off the deep sadness of his brothers' killings, to both acknowledge death and celebrate life. And now she slept. The lanterns and candles were extinguished, though a strong moon illuminated the inside of the room. John was sleeping in the little bedroom below, off the kitchen, with their friend and neighbour Martin Hogan. They had talked well into the night about Michael and James, who the killers were and what to do now. Martin was a blacksmith and he was shoeing one of Will's geldings in the morning so he stayed over. Will remembered that his parents were supposed to go to London tomorrow. John was going to drive them in the buggy to answer the crazy charges against them by Carroll, but the brothers had agreed, with two sons dead, the courts would forgive them if they didn't appear. The important thing, Will knew, was to face their enemies in Lucan tomorrow and make peace.

John was as close to Michael as Will and even in his grief, he declared the best course of action for the Donnellys: live and procreate and make peace with their enemies, may they all go to hell. He would be married to Winnifred and have many children and this hopeful endeavour was the right response to what had happened.

But as Will lay there, he heard the sound of horses walking quietly on the frozen road, slowing down just beyond their picket fence. His eyes opened wide. Suddenly alert, he slid out of bed and went to the window. Outside he could see twenty armed members of the Peace Society, some in disguise and some not. He clearly made out Jim Carroll in uniform and he knew they were in trouble.

Will ran downstairs and double-locked the front door and put a chair against it. He found his rifle and a pistol in the closet and returned upstairs. With the guns in his hand, he peeked out the bedroom window again. Nora woke up and rolled out of bed beside him, very sleepy, her belly pushing out her nightgown.

"What is it?" she mumbled.

Will whispered. "Keep your head down."

"Is someone out there?" Starting to awaken now, she wanted to look out the window but he held her down.

"The Society."

"What?"

Nora was suddenly alert. Will gestured for her to keep away from the window as he peeked outside. He watched as the Peace Society vigilantes, all armed with guns or clubs, stood outside the fence passing bottles of whiskey. Some of them came onto the property and headed over to the barn and Will heard his stallion start to scream. They were beating him or worse. Two of them called out. "FIRE! FIRE! BARN'S BURNING! BETTER COME OUT, BILLY!"

There was drunken laughter.

Will was shocked to see all these men so boldly presenting themselves. *How reckless*, he thought, *unless they expect no witnesses to be left alive.* The thought chilled him. Then he realized they would already have been to his family's farmhouse, which was on the way from town.

"Nora, they've come to kill us," he whispered to his wife. Better she know the truth.

Out the window, he could see that several of the vigilantes, including John Kennedy, Nora's brother, had dismounted and were approaching their front door with a shotgun.

"COME ON OUT, BILLY!" one of them yelled.

Will determined they would just wait and not show their presence, but he forgot John was sleeping downstairs. John shuffled, groggy and unaware of the danger, toward the front door. He called to the visitors outside.

"Who is it? What d-d-d-do you want?"

"Will Donnelly," came the answer and then Will heard John fumble with the chair at the door.

"John! Don't open it!" Will called down to him. But then he heard the iron bolt slide and realized John was opening the door.

"JOHN! DON'T OPEN THE DOOR!" But it was too late.

"Yes? He's..."

From above, Will saw John Kennedy fire his shotgun at John. It signalled the others and they all started to fire into the doorway from just outside the picket fence.

The vigilantes kept up their rifle and pistol fire, shooting at the house from a dozen weapons and breaking all the front windows, upstairs and down. When Will fired back twice with the rifle, they all aimed at his broken window and fired. He could only hold himself over Nora down on the floor to protect her from bullets and flying glass as rifle and shotgun fire destroyed the window and frames and ricocheted around the room.

Then Carroll's voice rang out. "ALL RIGHT! CEASE FIRE! STOP IT!"

The gunfire slowly subsided and the night was suddenly silent and still.

On the floor of their bedroom, Nora and Will were dusted and cut by glass fragments.

"Are you all right?" Will whispered and Nora nodded. Martin Hogan had crept up the stairs behind them and whispered urgently from the landing. "Keep quiet. They'll think we're dead."

Carroll then announced to the vigilantes below, "Good work! That's done. Now we go on to Keefe's for the next visit."

"Keefe's?" It was the voice of Martin McLaughlin.

"He's a Donnelly lover," Thomas Ryder confirmed.

Will noted a lack of momentum in the conversation. Other voices chimed in that he did not recognize.

"I gotta get back to milk the cows."

"The wife'll be having some questions."

"I forgot to feed my pigs."

McLaughlin's voice came in again. "Maybe we've done enough for one night."

But then Nora's brother John Kennedy spoke and through the shattered window, Nora and Will heard him say with satisfaction, "At least brother-in-law rests easy at last."

Nora gasped.

"What was that?" Jim Carroll asked. The vigilantes below had all heard the sound Nora made in the stillness through the shattered window.

"The woman's still alive in there." It was Martin McLaughlin's voice. John Kennedy spoke next.

"We should go in and finish the job."

"She's your sister, John." McLaughlin again.

"She's no sister of mine. She's made her choice."

Will had his arms around Nora. He could feel her try to stand up into the shattered window and shout at them, but he held her tight and whispered, "We're alive, my love. Don't." And finally her struggling subsided and she lay still in his arms.

"Let's let it be, John," Grouchy Ryder said. "Least we got the cripple." Below was further discussion among the murderers.

"Do we go on to Keefe's?" Will heard Jim Carroll ask. "We should finish the job at Keefe's."

"The Donnellys are done. I think I've had enough blood tonight, boys," James Flanagan answered and several more made noises of agreement. Will carefully peeked over the windowsill. Most had taken their masks off, thrown away their hats or now tore off the women's dresses.

"All right. We've done what was needed," Carroll told them. "Now listen, all of you. The oath!" All raised their hands. "We of the Peace Society will not speak to anyone about what has happened tonight, including wives, family and friends, and if anyone questions you, you will deny everything. Say it!"

The Peace Society members with their hands raised spoke in unison: "I will deny everything. On this I swear or may the fires of Hell be my future, so help me God."

"Good!" Carroll told them. "Good work tonight, men. Return to your homes with your mouths shut like good Catholics."

The Peace Society members mounted up, turned and rode slowly back down the Roman Line, now in twos and threes.

Will raced down the stairs past Martin Hogan with Nora close behind. The front door was open and John's body had been thrown well back by gunfire and he lay on the kitchen floor in a pool of blood. On his knees, Will folded a towel and put it under his head. There was a sucking chest wound from Kennedy's shotgun blast and bullet wounds in John's neck and shoulder. Nora was beside him.

"Is he dying?" Nora asked and Will nodded to her. She hurried away with purpose.

"Will...?" John spoke.

"Oh, Johnny..."

John was spitting out blood, his breathing raspy.

"My God, Will, I'm murdered. May God have m-m-m-mercy on my soul. And I've lost my glasses. Will?"

"I'm here."

Nora came back with the stub of a holy candle and some holy water. She lit the candle with a match and folded John's weak hand around it. She wiped the blood from John's face, applied some of the holy water and prayed in a whisper.

"Behold, O Lord, this Thy servant, and in Thy loving mercy deliver him. From darkness and doubt, deliver him. By Thy cross and passion, deliver him. We sinners do beseech Thee, oh Lord, if it please Thee to forgive all his sins."

"Will? My glasses..."

Will found the glasses on the floor nearby and wiped the lenses clean of blood on his shirt. He put them on John and it seemed to calm him. His brother grabbed Will's hand tight.

"Will...Will...t-t-t-tell her..."

He stared at the candle light for a moment—eternity was in the bright flame—then his eyes went dull in death.

Oh, God help me, there I were in the back of the Whalens' wagon making its way down the Roman Line, hid under a couple of musty blankets. Pat Whalen was driving me into London. As I warmed up at the stove, I'd told my story to them and they got more and more upset. And when I tells them about Johannah getting clubbed, they tells me to stop. They did not want to hear it. Since a constable was involved, I should tell it to a judge. It weren't an easy decision for Whalen to go out on the road that night, but the last thing he and the missus wanted was for the Peace Society men to catch me in their house or they'd a torched it too. So the missus gave me an old coat and boots, and Whalen harnessed up his rig and went to drive me into town. Thing was, when we started down the road, we comes in among the Peace Society men returning back from their exploits! I had a peek out to see who it was, but then Whalen growled at me to keep my head down or we'd all be killed. The horsemen was all riding at a walk spread along over a quarter mile and we felt like young calfs moving quiet through a pack of wolves. I knowed Whalen said not to, but I couldn't help myself peeking out from under the blanket to see what's what. Whalen started going fast and we passed several of the mounted vigilantes talking as they ambled their horses down the road. Whalen looked straight ahead and didn't speak to any of them.

I heared John Purtell call out, "Whalen? Whalen, where you off to this time of the morning?"

Whalen ignored them and was driving on but it was Flanagan who spurred his animal to a trot and took hold of the harness to stop Whalen's rig.

"The man asked where you were headed, " Flanagan told Whalen.

"Going in to London to pick up seed and lumber. Getting an early start."

Flanagan guided his roan close beside the wagon and I thought he might pull the blanket off and I froze still underneath. But just then, Carroll rode up.

"Whalen, you hear about anything?"

"No, not a thing."

"But you know the Donnelly house was burned last night, didn't you? Just across the Line from you."

"Yeah, I guess I saw some flames. Not my business."

"Arsonists. That's who we're looking for now. Terrible thing."

"Yes, terrible."

"So keep your eyes peeled, Whalen, and let us know if you see anybody around."

"I will, I certainly will."

Flanagan stood aside and Whalen pulled away from them. When Whalen was clear, he drove the horse on toward London like he was a chariot driver in one of them Roman races, and me bouncing on the frozen road so's I almost lost my teeth.

By dawn that morning, me and Mr. Whalen pulled up outside the judge's house in London. Even after we left the Peace Society men, Whalen made me stay under the blanket all the way to London. It were the worst ride I ever knew.

At first the old judge were as angry as a wet tomcat, being wakened up and all.

"What is it? What can't wait?"

"Judge MacPherson, Your Grace, I'm sorry but my name's Pat Whalen, from out on the Roman Line outside Lucan, and this is Johnny O'Connor."

"Yes. What's that to me?"

The judge being gruff didn't bother him and Pat Whalen were strong to make him listen to his story.

"You're going to want to hear what this boy has to say, sir."

The Light of Day

WITH NORA'S HELP, Will took John and laid him on the kitchen table, as they had Michael and James at the farm, his face and lips white in the absence of life. The house was very cold now with winter winds passing through the shattered windows. Will saddled his two second-best horses—the stallion still recovering from the vigilante beating—and had Hogan ride Nora over to his place, where she would be safe. Then, it was about dawn when Will rode for his parents' farm.

Will first saw the smoke a mile away. As he approached, he could see the house was gone and there was a crowd of the curious assembled around the black, smoking ruins. One constable he did not know was on guard. The floor and the roof beams that had collapsed still fed a substantial fire in the centre, but the onlookers tried to get closer.

Will pulled up, jumped from his horse and ran forward until the flames were scorching his face. The constable pushed him back. Though the floor had burned and collapsed, he stared through the smouldering joists, counting in numb horror the charred black forms, clearly visible in the ruins. There were three where the kitchen had been, and another in the main room and then two others, side by side where the summer kitchen had been—Michael and James, he realized.

The crowd was pushing forward, intent on seeing what was left of the bodies. The constable, with arms outstretched as if to gather them in, issued a warning.

"EVERYBODY BACK! DON'T TOUCH ANYTHING!"

One young man went in as close as he could and found a teapot intact in the rubble, still sizzling hot, and lifted it up with his leather gloves and hurried back to the others. Two other men went in as close as they dared. One picked up an axe head, another a blackened knife.

The constable raised his billy club. "The next one does that will be charged with looting! Now stay back!"

But then another raced in deeper than the others and clutched a blackened orb with his gloved hands, turned and in triumph tried to make his getaway. He ran away from the constable but came close by Will, who grabbed him by the throat and pressed his pistol to his head. What did he have to lose by pulling the trigger? And much satisfaction to be gained. But instead, Will clubbed him once with the weapon and the man fell stunned to the ground, dropping his prize.

Will heard the collective gasp from the people around him as they pulled back. "It's Will Donnelly. Look! It's him! He's alive. Will Donnelly."

Will bent down to retrieve the blackened object the looter had dropped and found it was, as he feared, a charred human skull. It was impossible to say which one of his people it belonged to. The constable was as shaken as the others and unsure what to do. No more attempts were made by the souvenir hunters.

"Mr. Donnelly. I'm so sorry," he said to Will. He was unsure if the constable was repentant for the massacre of his family or the near theft of the skull or his own sad incompetence at guarding the crime site. Will wrapped the skull gently in his handkerchief and laid it on the top step of the front stone staircase, which had survived. Numb, he studied the faces of the onlookers, then he went as close as he could to view what was left of the other bodies. There was very little to show they had once been human.

As a survivor, Will truly felt in a dream from which he very much wished to awaken, but could not. This nightmare became only more focused as he saw Father Connolly approach on horseback from the south. The priest did not see Will, but dismounted, all his attention on what was left of the farmhouse. He walked closer to the smouldering ruins, his eyes wide as he stared at the charred bodies.

"Father Connolly," Will said, and the priest turned to see him for the first time. He stepped back from Will in fear, his hand clutching the crucifix on his neck.

"No...no..."

Will saw the guilt in his eyes and then he knew. Moving away from Will, the priest slipped in the snow made slushy by the fire and fell down, his horrified eyes now fixed on Will as he slithered away in the mud, then got to his feet in his now-filthy robes and stumbled off to catch his horse, which had wandered away.

Will gathered himself to determine the proper course of action now. He instructed the constable to keep everyone away from his family and the ruins of the house until other constables and detectives arrived. The man promised to do so. There was nothing more Will could do for now, so he found the loose reins to his horse, climbed up onto its back and headed for town.

It was to Fitzhenry he went first. Good old Vincent Fitzhenry, pleased to be retired from so demanding a position as Lucan Town chief constable, but when Will explained the circumstances, he rose to the occasion. In fact, Fitzhenry had just received detailed word of the fire at the farm and a messenger came to him with a telegram from Judge Mac-Pherson in London, whom he knew, to confirm the extraordinary events. Fitzhenry explained to Will, "A dozen constables are on their way, men who've never served near Lucan. They might have heard of the Donnellys but never been involved with you."

At this news, Will leaned against Fitzhenry's porch railing, head down, catching his breath. Had it all really happened? He felt trapped in the nightmare.

"There was a surviving eyewitness," Fitzhenry told him quietly, and Will's head snapped up, his eyes locked on Fitzhenry's.

"An eyewitness? Who is the witness?"

"The young lad, Johnny O'Connor."

Will was standing with Fitzhenry on the porch of the Queen's Hotel in Lucan when the two horse-drawn paddy wagons from London arrived, flanked by four mounted constables. Several more policemen emerged from the wagons and more were coming, they told them, plus a couple of police detectives from Toronto by train. Will had described the events and the murder at his own house to Fitzhenry and named those he recognized and Fitzhenry had written it all down. They also had the list of men that Johnny had clearly identified by name. There were six. Four were on Will's own list. Judge MacPherson had laid out the charges that would be executed in Will's name.

Four constables, Fitzhenry and Will Donnelly arrived at the door of Jim Carroll's rundown rented house just off Main Street in east end Lucan. Neighbours came out of other little frame houses, mothers and kids and old men, to watch. Will stood back behind the constables with a slouch hat down over his eyes. A sleepy Jim Carroll came to the door to face them and Will watched him startle at the uniforms. The fool had actually thought himself safe.

Fitzhenry had never liked Carroll, Will knew, and there was a clear note of satisfaction in his voice as he said, "Jim Carroll, you're under arrest for five counts of murder."

"What? On what evidence?"

"An eyewitness."

Carroll appeared to be trying to keep calm. "Who brought the charges?"

"Will Donnelly."

Will was delighted to see the look on his face.

"Will Donnelly is alive?"

Will stepped forward so Carroll could see him and he truly looked at him as if seeing a ghost.

"Remember? 'We've done what was needed, men. Let's go home.' Well, you didn't finish the job, Carroll."

His jaw slack, staring at Will, Carroll was cuffed and shackled by the constables and they marched him away to the lockup.

Their next visit took them out to John Kennedy's family farm, the house painted white and the barn new with two hands in the yard loading some fine cattle stock into wagons. It was his pretty wife who came to the door, with a young girl underfoot and a babe in her arms. "We're looking for John Kennedy."

"He's having his breakfast with the other John. I'll go get 'im."

Kennedy came to the door and for a second he was as startled as Carroll, hearing the charges against him and seeing Will alive.

Will looked Kennedy in the eye and said, "Brother-in-law does not lie easy now, Kennedy. Brother-in-law is going to see you hang."

Kennedy quickly overcame his initial panic, calmed himself and remained silent as Fitzhenry read to him his rights and the constables cuffed and shackled him.

Kennedy's "guest," on the other hand, was not so composed. John Purtell made a wild run out the back door and into the arms of two constables Fitzhenry had placed there.

Reassuring his wife it was all a mistake, Kennedy kissed her and the children goodbye, stared at Will with a moment of unconcealed hatred and went quietly. Purtell fought the cuffing and babbled, "Please. It wasn't me. I didn't do anything. It wasn't my fault."

Kennedy snarled at him.

"Purtell! For God's sake, shut up!"

They loaded Kennedy and Purtell into the wagon they had brought from town and continued on their mission.

At the ramshackle Ryder farm, the constables found, arrested and cuffed Thomas and James Ryder and Martin McLaughlin, who was with them. Like Purtell, James made a break for it out the back door where two constables waited. The weak attempt at flight would not help his case. All chose silence as the Ryder children and wives and elderly parents looked on while they were led to the wagon, all but the youngest child shocked and growing tearful. Will stared into the eyes of each of the accused. They were going to hang for what they did and he hoped they knew it. As they glared back at him, he happily helped load them into the wagon.

In the constable's office in Lucan, under the eye of Fitzhenry, the six prisoners waited in three small cells. Purtell was obsessively rubbing his hands on his shirt and pants as if to clean them. He was blubbering, at the point of panic, and it was infecting the others.

"They're going to string us up. We're all going to hang! You got us into this, Carroll. It was your idea. They won't execute us if we confess."

There was a quick movement and Purtell's body was thrown and held against the wall. Carroll had him by the throat.

"Shut up, you little shite! No one's confessing to anything!"

Outside the jail, Will was approached by Frank Simon of the *Toronto Mail* and asked politely for a statement. Will remembered Simon's reporting from the spring assizes where the journalist had coined the phrase "Lucan Lambs." Humour was not required at this point but Simon seemed a sincere man to Will, unhurried and sensitive to the emotions swirling in Will's brain.

"Only if now is a good time."

Will took a deep breath. "They have killed most of my family and tried to kill me. The truth will be known and they will pay the price."

About noon, Nora and Will found Patrick. Will was so relieved he was alive. Having found no nemesis in the town the previous night to accept his invitation to fight, Patrick had wandered the streets and someone out back of the Central Hotel had finally handed him a bottle to calm him down. Not long after that, he had passed out on the Central's porch—it was amazing he hadn't frozen to death. Pat sobered slowly to the harsh reality of the night's horrors. He kept repeating that he should have been there. Nora and Will held him and they wept as the pent-up emotions of all of them, previously frozen in their shock, began to melt. They had to get word to Robert in prison and, an even more terrible prospect, to Jenny in Goderich before the newspapers got hold of the story. And Will had to make a visit to St. Patrick's.

Nora, Patrick and Will entered the sanctuary of the church just after the four o'clock Mass and walked toward the confessional, where a line of parishioners waited for Father Connolly to hear their confessions. They all pulled back from Will as he went forward and opened the confessional door. Inside, Connolly stared at him in fear as he had done at the burned house, only this time he was trapped. Will apologized to the current confessor and placed his hands on the material of Connolly's vestments, took hold and dragged Connolly out into the sanctuary on his knees.

"You can confess to me!" Will shouted at him.

The priest began screaming, "Help! Help me, my children! Protect me!"

The lineup of parishioners had come apart. They all stood there staring at Connolly but made no move.

Will dragged the priest to his feet, shook him and demanded an answer. "Why is my family dead?"

Connolly did not want to look at him. Nor did he look toward heaven. "I don't know. I don't know. Leave me alone."

Will shook him again. "You told them to murder."

"No...no," he was almost whimpering.

"You gave them your blessing, didn't you?"

"No, it's not true. I never meant to…"

"The blood of my family is on your hands!"

Will shook him again. Connolly put his guilty hands together in supplication and tried silently to pray. Will finally pushed the priest away from him and Connolly sprawled on the floor in front of the wide-eyed parishioners, his lips still moving in prayer.

Will stood back to look at him. "And on your soul."

Father Connolly's prayers ended. He stared at Will, then suddenly broke down and wept. Will realized the tears were not for his family's dead but for the priest himself. He turned away in disgust and together with Patrick and Nora left the church.

Several more police detectives came in from Toronto on the train to join the first two and put together evidence for the Crown's case. They operated out of the Central Hotel and interviewed scores of community citizens, including many Peace Society members. To hear it from the citizens of Lucan, no one was anything but a friend of the Donnellys. Two physicians did autopsies on the incinerated dead, which they admitted offered little information.

Only John's body could tell them a story. They found and identified the calibre of two rifle bullets and the pistol shot in his chest, as well as the distinctive pellet spread of Kennedy's shotgun blast that had torn into him. The Crown detectives and the constables searched the homes of the vigilantes and found a rifle above the hearth in Martin McLaughlin's house that matched one of the bullets they found in John. And they found Kennedy's shotgun and, though it was difficult to determine a match, they could prove the weapon had been discharged in the last forty-eight hours. And they found pants with substantial human bloodstains hidden in John Purtell's shed.

Though the sadness of his family's loss was deeper than he could ever have imagined, Will was confident the men who committed the murders would pay.

Jim Donnelly had purchased two small plots of land in St. Patrick's cemetery many years before. Two coffins would be buried side by side in one plot, one holding Jim, Johannah, Tom and Bridget—for what was left of them, one was all that was required—and John had his own. The other

plot a short distance away would hold Michael and James. The grave dig-
ger had worked hard and fast to give them safe places to put their loved
ones in the frozen earth.

At the interment on February 7, four days after the night of the murders, Father Connolly was not present. Will had decided to conduct the
funerals himself, reading from the bible passages that his mother had
marked. Two hundred people came, including the religious, their friends,
the Keefes and Whalens, and of course the curious gawkers and several
reporters from the newspapers: the *London Free Press*, the *Toronto Mail*,
the *Hamilton Spectator* and the *Detroit Free Press*.

"Rest eternal grant upon them, oh Lord, and let light perpetual shine
upon them…"

Will had done his best to calm Patrick, who was this day in a state of
rage. Only for the sake of the family's honour at the funeral did he contain
himself. Winnifred Ryder, newly engaged to the dead John, whom her
brothers had helped kill, wept openly beside his coffin.

"…give rest, oh lord, to Thy servants with Thy saints, where sorrow and
pain are no more, neither sighing, but life everlasting…"

Will stopped his prayer as he saw a wagon approach and draw to a
stop. Jenny climbed out, holding flowers. Followed by her husband, she
walked slowly to the coffins and tried to stand firm and straight in front
of them but was clearly overwhelmed: she had lost most of her family.
She picked out the light wood of the sarcophagus holding what was left
of her mother and father and Tom and Bridget, their names written on
a white ribbon, then laid her hands and face on the box and wept. Her
husband, Jim Currie, placed a comforting arm around her as she keened
for them, as her mother had keened for Michael and James. Will closed
his eyes. All waited, heads bowed, until she had expressed her grief. When
she regained control and stood back, her face red and tearful, Will studied
his beautiful little sister, realizing how much she resembled her mother,
as her blue eyes went from one coffin to the other. They formed a flotilla
of her loved ones, about to set sail for a dark eternity. For her, Will began
the service again.

"Rest eternal grant upon them, oh Lord, and let light perpetual shine
upon them."

Testament

THE FIRST DAY of the trial at the London spring assizes was big doings for me. The courtroom was filled and many people was turned away. There was the men from the newspapers. One was named Frank Simon, who Will liked and had us shake hands. But Mr. Irving said I couldn't talk to him, I had to save it for the trial. It were nearly three months since the massacre.

Once I had told my tale to Judge MacPherson that early morning after, they took me to the Grand Hotel and I were under guard by two policemen. Just 'cause I had got myself out of that burning farmhouse didn't mean I was safe. There was six men wanted me dead and probably a bunch more. The thing was, Ma and Da came to visit me and moved into the hotel for two weeks and started charging food and bottles of whiskey to the tab of the prosecution until they was told to leave, and then they threatened not to let me testify so Mr. Irving had to give them money so's they'd go back home. It was so embarrassing. But the policemen guarding me were nice. And they stayed with me going to the courthouse.

They also had extra police to look after the noisy crowd that waited outside the courtroom. The Crown prosecutor was Mr. Aemilius Irving, who had a bald head and a neck like a chicken and piercing scary eyes. But he was fair with me. He told me to just ignore all the crowds and tell my story. As the jury of twelve men listened to my testimony, I told the story again.

"…and then Jim Carroll shouts out 'NOW!' and they all comes running in. It was Carroll and then Tom Ryder who first clubbed Mr. Donnelly." And on I went again.

At the front of the courtroom was Robert Donnelly, who they released from prison on what they called "compassionate grounds," sitting with

Patrick and Will and Will's wife, Nora, and their new child, born in April, a boy named John William, and finally pretty Jenny Donnelly and her husband from Goderich, all listening to me. I was so sorry for my terrible story. I knew it were hard for them to hear it. I guess I talked mostly to the jury men, who listened very closely to me. They were important men, many in from London, farmers and businessmen in suits, some bearded, some clean shaved, a few moustaches, Catholic and Protestant both (united, imagine that!), who sat mostly with their arms folded and I were very careful in the story I told, I never talked about my feelings, but just the truth of what I seen.

"A whole crowd of them jumped in and began hammering the men with clubs. At first no one would hit Miss Johannah 'til Jim Carroll done it. Then they all had a go on her. And I seen Martin McLaughlin finish off old Jim. Then they brought in big Tom's body. Blood all over. James Ryder were one of them carrying. Think Tom Ryder were too, but I'm not sure. James for sure. Didn't see the others clear.

"Bridget was still screaming upstairs. Then she suddenly stopped and I seen it were John Purtell came down with others and he said she were 'done.'"

I looked over at John Purtell when I said this and he began to cry quietly. As well he should. The defendants were lined up off to my left so I didn't look at them much but when I did, I saw they was all in shock at the doings I seen. I felt fine about that. These men done terrible things. Father Connolly was beside them and had a similar look on his face. It'd be fair if he had a similar fate.

After me comes Will and his turn in the court. Mr. Irving didn't want Will and me to talk leading up to the trial so we didn't, but I could tell Will was happy I hadn't been killed and could tell my story. He would smile in appreciation when I seen him. When Will Donnelly took the stand to tell his story, everyone were so quiet you could hear a fly burp.

"When the shooting stopped, we could hear them through the broken window. John Kennedy said to Carroll, 'Brother-in-law rests easy at last.'"

Will looked at Kennedy. "But I didn't. And I won't rest easy until you're dead. All of you."

There was some talk then in the room, and the newspaper men was making hurried notes and Judge Armour had to quiet everybody and say, "The witness will confine his comments to answering the questions."

Will apologized to the court but he got his point across to the accused.

The court had ruled that Nora weren't allowed to testify because of her being Will's wife and one defendant's sister so's she'd be biased. It seemed much strange to me she'd be stopped—she'd know better than any of them—but even when the prosecution argued for her, the judge would not allow it.

Next come the "cross-examination" of me by the defence lawyer, Mr. William Meredith, who were a kindly-looking man but he were a slippery one too.

"Now Johnny…it was very late and you'd had a busy day. Isn't it possible you just dreamed all of this."

"Those dead bodies weren't no dream."

I seen he didn't like this answer, but he was still smiling.

"All right, but Johnny…it must have been very dark in the kitchen with only a candle…"

"No sir," I told him and talked to the jury. "Miss Johannah had lit the lantern and a few candles. It were like church at Easter. And later when they lit fire to the bed, their faces was bright as noon."

"But you said many of the men had masks or blackened faces. How could you possibly recognize them?"

"The names I named had no black faces or masks or they'd taken them off."

"It must have been terrifying to see these things. All of this noise, violence and blood. You must have felt overwhelmed…confused…"

"No, sir. I seen what happened very clear. I see it over and over." I turned to the jury because I wanted them to believe me. "I think I'll see it every day'til I'm in my grave. There was some men looked familiar. Others I think I knew. But the names I named was those I saw," and I pointed them out to make it certain.

"Jim Carroll…James Ryder and his brother Tom…Martin McLaughlin…John Purtell…and John Kennedy. Of them, there ain't doubt in my mind."

At the end of the cross-examination, I could see the Donnellys was satisfied and the six defendants was looking none too cheerful. John Purtell's face were crumpled up in grief and sorrow, though whether it was for the ones he helped kill or for his own hide that was about to be hung, I did not know.

I headed home that Friday in a closed wagon with my three constables looking after me. I figured I were safe now as I'd said my piece in the court and done any damage I could to the Peace Society. No reason to kill me now. Why'd they blame me? I didn't have much choice. They should blame themselves in their evil minds for letting me live.

I really wanted to put this thing behind me, get them images out of my head and go back to normal. So when Saturday comes I sneak out my window to get away from the police officers and go over to St. Patrick's where I was an altar boy, as I always did before the trouble, to sweep up, dust the altar and polish the candelabra before the services the next day. I liked the quiet in the sanctuary on a Saturday afternoon. The dust were rising from my broom, the low sunlight comes sparkling through it, coloured by the stained glass of the window showing a smiling Saint Paddy. I even began to almost forget for a while what had happened.

My quiet was broken when a carriage pulled up outside the doors of the church and I heared the lock of Father Connolly's study open. He comes out with his eyes on the double front doors of the church and I were shocked to see he held a shotgun in his hand. I stepped behind the statue of Saint Mary and he didn't see me. But who came in next were none less than a full bishop in a long black coat and one of them funny hats like a muffin. There was two young priests with him as he walked up the aisle toward Father Connolly, who slid the shotgun outta sight behind a pew and called out to him.

"Bishop Walsh! Your Excellency! Oh, it's so good to see you..." Father Connolly went down on his knees and kissed the bishop's ring. "Terrible things have happened. It's been a nightmare for me..."

"Yes. Our concerns are not so much with your well-being, Father. Now get up. I don't have all afternoon."

It were clear the bishop didn't think much of Father Connolly by the way he talked to him. He made a beeline for the study and Father Connolly followed him. One priest stayed with the bishop while the other stayed near the front doors, watching them. He stared at the stained glass of Saint Paddy, walking back and forth on the squeaky floor. Being so caught up in this with the murders and all, I know what I wants. I wants to hear what that bishop had to say. So as the young priest walks on the creaky floor with his eyes on the window, looking at it from different angles, so did I move to a place outside the study door. One, two, three steps and stop. One, two, three steps and stop. In twelve steps I were at the door, unseen or heard by him and I slipped behind the curtain to listen at the door to what was going on in the office and it were worth my trouble. Oh, Bishop Walsh were not pleased.

"You can imagine our deep concern, Father Connolly. Many years ago, we brought you in to deal with the troubles in this parish, but not to contribute to them! Is it true you gave your blessing to this…'Peace Society'?"

The bishop was pacing.

"Well, I…"

"Never mind. I don't really want to know. All I know is that if six members of this 'Peace Society,' which you formed in the name of St. Patrick's and the Holy Church, are convicted of multiple murders…it's just unthinkable."

"I am so sorry, your Excellency. I…I…"

Father Connolly sounded like he might cry, but the bishop were unmoved, his voice cold.

"Father Connolly…for God's sake, pull yourself together."

"But what will we do? I am implicated in all of this."

Father Connolly did then sob a bit for a moment. The bishop continued impatiently.

"Listen to me. It is not too late. These situations can be dealt with. Appropriate measures are already being taken."

"Really?" Father Connolly sounded almost joyful. "I'm so grateful."

"Well, we'll see. Just stay out of it. Don't talk to anyone. Not a word."

"Upon my soul, Excellency."

The bishop stood then and headed for the door followed by his young priest.

"Yes," the old boy told Connolly as he went out. "Your soul, indeed."

When I left the church I had to get back home before the constables knowed I were gone so I couldn't get to Will at Whalen's Corners to tell him what I heared. I figured I could talk to him in the courtroom on Monday morning, but on Monday when we got there, the constables wouldn't let me near him. They said I couldn't talk to him on account that he could "influence my testimony." I don't think anything he could say to me would make my testimony any worse for the defendants, but I never got a chance to tell him what I heared at St. Patrick's.

Justice is Done

ON MONDAY MORNING, bright and early, what was left of the Donnelly family—Pat, Robert, Jenny, Nora, Jim Currie and Will—reassumed their seats at the front of the courtroom. Aemilius Irving of the prosecution had a couple more witnesses to present and then William Meredith would present the defence. Will was ready to hear what desperate gambits they might come up with to save their skins.

Again the courtroom was packed, only this time there appeared to be more enemies than friends, antagonists who bore the scars of fights and feuds and grudges with the Donnellys, and more clustered out in the hallway, damning the constables who would admit no more inside. Everyone present could hear them swear and they once rushed the constables, who were nearly overcome. *To hell with them*, Will thought. *To hell with them all.* As the proceedings were about to begin in the small, packed courtroom, the clerk of the court stood up to make an announcement.

"Silence in the courtroom! Silence! I am here to inform you that Judge Armour has unfortunately fallen ill. It is not serious and the court wishes him a quick recovery. His replacement is Judge Matthew Cameron. All rise!"

They all stood as Judge Cameron swept into the courtroom and took his seat behind the bench. He was a slender man with sad eyes and he was clean-shaven but for long curly tufts of mutton chop beard that were joined under his chin, across his throat. Will noticed that Father Connolly seemed markedly relieved and wondered what sort of mischief was afoot. Judge Cameron's voice called out ahead of his clerk, quickly getting down to business, "Court is now in session."

Patrick Whalen, who had taken Johnny O'Connor into town to see Judge MacPherson, was on the stand and very uncomfortable. Prosecutor Irving was not getting the answers he wanted.

"You have told the constables of the men you recognized at approximately one-thirty a.m. riding back into town on the Roman Line on the morning of the murders. Who were they?"

Though the day was cool, Whalen's forehead glistened and he appeared deeply uncertain. He looked around the silent courtroom, finding the stony faces of the Peace Society listening, their eyes unblinking.

"Well...it was very dark."

And Will's heart sank. Irving became exasperated.

"But you told the constables their names. Tell us those names now."

Whalen was almost in pain. Will realized the Peace Society had gotten to him. "I wasn't looking too close. It was dark. I just looked straight ahead."

"But you knew them. They called out to you. You told the constables the names before. You repeated them to me. Say them now."

Whalen looked around the courtroom again and at the defendants. He swallowed hard. He glanced up at Will and then quickly away. Will couldn't believe he would betray them like this. Whalen appeared suitably ashamed, staring at the floor.

"I was mistaken. I don't know who they were."

Will lowered his head and closed his eyes.

The last witness for the prosecution was Martin Hogan, who had been with Will and John during the attack. They had called his name in the courtroom and in the halls and outside on the street. They had taken a fifteen-minute recess to send messengers to check taverns and stores in the vicinity. The blacksmith Martin Hogan had disappeared.

At precisely fifteen minutes, Judge Cameron called the courtroom to order. "Let's get on with this!"

It was time now for William Meredith to present the defence. He chose as his first witness James Toohey, brother of Dennis and Paul and a buddy of the Ryders.

"We was at the Ryder barn that the Donnellys burned down."

"Objection! There is no proof that..."

"Sustained. Go on, witness."

"Yeah, we was at the burned barn with James and Tom Ryder, trying to find tools and stuff in the ashes. Terrible thing. They was with us all night, searching through the destruction. They never left."

Next was Michael Heenan, who had once had a dispute with the Donnellys over the price of a mare.

"No, McLaughlin's calf was pretty sick. He came home early from the Keefe wedding. We all stayed up with her most of the night. And McLaughlin was there all that time."

The next was a man Will had never laid eyes on before by the name of Thomas Kinsella.

"At midnight that night, after the Keefe wedding party, Purtell and Kennedy bought me a drink at Hennessey's Hotel in Strathroy. We played cards and they was there 'til almost dawn."

"That's a lie!" Will could no longer contain himself and the judge pounced on him.

"One more outburst, Mr. Donnelly, and you will be removed from the courtroom."

Prosecutor Irving patted Will's shoulder with sympathy but also encouragement to obey.

Constable Berryman, the man mountain, came forward and was sworn in. Berryman, his face and head still bearing witness to the beating Tom had given him, told the court, "That night, Jim Carroll was assisting me on a case in Grafton. He was with me all night."

By mid-afternoon Will and his family were numb. The testimony for the defence was all a lying connivance! And yet it was accepted. No one else was standing up to scream "liar," though the impulse hit Will several more times over the course of the day.

Prosecutor Irving cross-examined each witness aggressively but they all just repeated what they had said as if by rote and would offer nothing more, nor less.

"Was McLaughlin's calf male or female?"

"I'm not sure."

"Who else was with you at the Ryder barn?"

"I don't recall."

"What was the case in Grafton Mr. Carroll was assisting you with?"

"I don't remember."

When Irving appealed for the judge to instruct them to answer questions more fully, Judge Cameron sided with the witnesses. And when Irving became aggressive with anyone, he received a warning from the judge to "stop bullying" the witnesses.

When he could do no more, Mr. Irving sat down and Judge Cameron gave his charge to the jury.

"The truth is, when all is said and done, the only real evidence against these men is the testimony of a confused young boy and that of an angry brother and son of the victims, himself with a record of criminal violence, who no doubt wants revenge. But we are not here for revenge. We are here for justice."

Prosecutor Irving, seeing all benefit of his work slipping expeditiously away, was suddenly on his feet.

"I object, Your Grace, to the biased nature of your charge to the jury. You are not telling them what they should think about but rather what they should think."

"I will allow the record to duly note your objection, Mr. Irving, but you have interrupted me in my charge to the jury, which is not your right. I want you to sit down now so I may finish."

Irving hesitated, then recognized clearly the battle was not on a level playing field. More words from him would not help. He sat down in his chair.

"As I was saying, we are here for justice. The defendants before you are all respected men of the community," Judge Cameron continued. "Land-owners and church-goers, fathers and husbands, friends and neighbours. And other respected men of the community have testified they were no-where near the Donnelly farm that night. Can they all be lying? Gentle-men of the jury, what you must ask yourselves: Are you prepared to see these six farmers and family men, pillars of this community, taken from their wives, taken from their children, taken to the jail and hanged by the neck until dead? It could mean the effective destruction of this com-munity! And all on nothing more than the word of an addled boy and an accused criminal? I would ask you to think very hard on it. Now please go and determine your verdict."

The Donnellys were all numbed to hear the bias of the judge's charge. After the jury had retired and the court was adjourned, Frank Simon of the *Mail* said as much to Will: "I've never heard a charge so strongly opinionated. It could be grounds for a mistrial."

Will did not want to think about that. He made encouraging com-ments to his family members, although he himself had doubts. But surely the jurors would find the truth.

After an hour the jury returned. This short sequester was good, Will thought, the conclusion obvious. The courtroom filled again quickly and

Cameron wasted no time. The defendants were ordered to stand, their faces like granite but for Purtell, whose mouth was moving and eyes flittering around the courtroom.

"Mr. Foreman? What is your finding?"

The foreman of the jury stood.

"My Lords, we find the prisoners…NOT GUILTY of murder."

The courtroom exploded with contrasting emotions. Patrick stood up and hurled obscenities at the jury members. The family and the friends of the defendants were overjoyed and some rushed forward to shake their shackled hands or to thank the jurists. Will examined each face of those jury members looking for contradiction or disagreement but they were all, in the shame they must feel, determinedly without expression.

"Case dismissed" the judge proclaimed. "The defendants are discharged. The session is closed."

Judge Cameron, his job done, quickly exited the courtroom. Guards swiftly removed the shackles and the defendants stepped down from the dais onto the floor to greet family and friends, hugging them and shaking their hands. Congratulations and laughter filled the air and the press asked them questions about their relief. It was only reporter Frank Simon who came to Will and placed a hand on his shoulder in condolence. The jury members began to reveal that they were pleased with themselves, not wanting the responsibility for six men being executed, six more families devastated. Father Connolly was deeply relieved and moved among the freed prisoners, shaking hands.

Patrick, Robert, Jenny, Nora, Jim Currie and Will sat on the front bench in frozen, shocked defeat while everyone seemed to be moving around them. Johnny came and sat with them in silence for a moment, then finally spoke to Will.

"They figured out just how they wanted everything to go long before I even had that bible in my hand, didn't they?"

Will nodded slowly.

Crown Prosecutor Irving sat down with them, held Jenny's tear-moistened hand and spoke forcefully to Will.

"There is a just God in heaven who sees all and he needs no jury or courts to mete out his own retribution."

Will seemed to find some solace in this idea. "Thank you, Mr. Irving. I hope so. I can still hear her voice. I can't believe she's gone."

And Jenny began to cry again. They all remained there in silence until long after the courtroom had cleared.

The Peace Society showed up at the Queen's Hotel to celebrate with the freed men, as did Judge Matthew Cameron and Father Connolly. Society members were pouring the defendants free drinks and referring to "The Accomplishment." A marginal fiddle player was ruining a jig. John Purtell was quite drunk. He kept staring at his hands and rubbing them obsessively.

Outside, a lone figure in a duster approached the tavern. Will Donnelly paused just outside the door a moment to listen and he heard someone say, "They couldn't find them guilty. It would mean hanging half the township!"

The nervous laughter went on too long. Will stepped inside and raised his voice above the chatter just as the fiddle music stopped.

"YES GENTLEMEN...DRINK UP!" he called out from inside the doorway. The celebrants fell silent and the musicians froze. The six defendants were lined up at the bar, convenient for Will's intent.

"In fact, I insist you all have a drink on me."

It could have been the commanding tone in his voice, or curiosity about what he had to say, or the two double-barrelled shotguns, cocked and pointed toward the former defendants. In any case, Will had their attention.

"Fill your glasses."

Will gestured to the bartender with the barrels of one gun and the man scrambled to fill the vigilantes' glasses with whisky. Then brought a shot of whisky to Will, who had two more pistols in his belt.

"Now...a toast to the Donnellys. Repeat after me: "Here is a toast to the Donnellys who we murdered."

The vigilantes stood silent, unmoving. Will fired one shot into the ceiling above their heads, then aimed both guns at them again. A scattering of debris flew and a cloud of plaster descended slowly to the floor, a light dust on the surface in the liquid of each glass. No one moved or spoke. Will stared into their faces to give the warning.

"You heard me, gentlemen! A toast to the Donnellys who we murdered. Say it!"

The Peace Society men were fearful at the end of his weapons. He used the barrels as a choir director might lead his followers and each man complied. They spoke the words haltingly, but all voiced them in ragged recitation as Will stared them down.

"A toast to the Donnellys who we murdered!"

"Good. Good. Jim...Johannah...John...Tom...Bridget...James and Michael. Drink with me to the Donnellys."

He kept the left shotgun trained on them. He laid the right shotgun on the bar as he threw back the shot the bartender had poured him, banged the empty glass back on the bar and picked up the shotgun again. All the vigilantes drank on cue except for Jim Carroll. Carroll stayed very still, watching Will Donnelly. Will knew Carroll found it quite unfortunate he was still on this earth. He hadn't taken his drink. Will moved closer to him.

"Drink."

Still Carroll didn't move. Will put the two barrels of one gun up under Carroll's chin and looked him in the eye. His finger tightened on the trigger.

"Drink. Or...don't drink. Truly, I got nothing to lose anymore. One... two..."

Carroll reached down and picked up his whiskey. His hand trembled a little as he put it to his lips, for he heard the conviction in Will's voice.

"Here's to the Donnellys," he said clearly, his eyes locked on Will's, "who I murdered."

Carroll drank it dry. Will was satisfied. He lowered his guns and nodded. Then he turned and left the Queen's.

Epilogue

ST. PATRICK'S CEMETERY, Lucan, Ontario. June 26, 1930

Gives me chills to be back here at old St. Paddy's. It's been fifty years and nothing much has changed with the big yellow-brick church, the sharp spire like a sword aimed at heaven. There's even a couple rigs with horses still, though the horse sheds was pulled down years ago. Now it's mostly automobiles parked. There is a few in the overgrown lot across the Roman Line where Keefe's tavern used to stand before they burned it down. The little Ford coupe I rented in London is parked there. I came up on the train from Detroit yesterday to sign the papers to sell off the last of my father's land in Lucan and also to see this funeral that's now going on inside. It's a funeral for the last of the vigilantes, Martin McLaughlin. Didn't want to miss that. Killing two birds with the one stone, you could say.

Didn't get much for Da's land. The town's a lot smaller, quieter now with people moving into the cities. Only one tavern left out of the seven when I was a boy. Truth is, in the years after the massacre and trial, a lot of people moved away from the taint that it gave to Lucan town.

The cemetery has greened up nicely this time of year as it always did and the birds is singing. I'm sitting on a bench close to the old Donnelly graves. There's Michael and James together under a separate stone. Then Tom and Bridget, and Old Jim and then of course Johannah, buried all together in one casket and their names on one big black headstone. On that headstone too is John Donnelly in his own casket alongside. And on that headstone, it tells you after each name that they was murdered. Will insisted on that and I can tell you it wasn't a popular decision with the St. Pat's crowd. Will defied anyone to stop him and he got his way. At least the headstone tells the truth.

You can hear the funeral service going on in the church now. They sang "Holy God We Praise Thy Name" before and now somebody's speaking the eulogy but I'm not interested in what they have to say. I know what kind of man McLaughlin was. He was one of the worst: smart, wealthy and educated. Made the others feel legitimate. Closer to the church, south of the Donnelly graves, is a fresh open grave, dung-brown dirt piled beside it waiting for the old boy. I went and had a look at it to make sure it were nice and deep and I'm satisfied. Shouldn't be long now.

I'm sure they all feel fine and righteous in there but I got to admit this place makes me nervous. Is there anyone left would come after me? It's been fifty years but you never know. The day after the trial was finished they burned my house down and tried to kill me! And I was just a boy of twelve, and me and my parents had to go live with my cousins in St. Catherines, so yes, it were long ago but you never know. These people have long memories, their sons and grandsons.

After the trial, people got on with their lives. Jenny and her Jim moved to Glencoe, closer to Lucan than Goderich, and they had a good number of kids and a quiet life there. Pat, Will, Nora and Robert lived in Lucan for a year after the murders and hired lawyers. Tried to have it declared a mistrial and to get a new trial going—they wrote me a letter and I would have testified again, but they was pretty much ignored and no trial ever happened. I'm surprised the Peace Society didn't go after the three Donnellys left and finish the job, seeing how easy they got off with the first murders, but after that, Lucan come to be a fairly law-abiding town. I think Pat finally gave up and moved to Thorold and went into black-smithing. Robert stayed on the farm and rebuilt the house. Will and Nora moved on to Appin with their one baby and had another daughter I met, and they ran the St. Nicholas Hotel. Will is buried in Appin and the others is scattered in various towns.

As for the Peace Society bunch, their families still live in Lucan or along the Roman Line. In truth, a lot of them died young from unknown ailments and farm accidents, or their wives or family members did. Will went to some of those funerals, and he used to love to blame his mother's curse when he heard of tragic misfortunes among the families of the Peace Society members. He kept the whole list and sent it to me just before he died, passing the torch, sorta like. Soon after the trial, John Purtell disappeared and his family never heard from him again. Jim Carroll headed west and there was talk he killed a man in a lumber camp in the West Kootenays and lived out his life in a hospital for the criminally insane.

McLaughlin, Kennedy and the two Ryder brothers stayed on their farms, expanded their families and lived peaceful lives for a while. But "Shotgun" Kennedy's wife died very young and "Pitchfork" Tom Ryder died of a nasty cancer and his brother "Spadey" James Ryder, who I saw kill Tom, was killed himself in a knife fight three years after. The Feehley who left his coat so's the door to the Donnelly kitchen would be unlocked lost his son and infant daughter to the influenza two years after the massacre.

Father Connolly stayed on for years at St. Patrick's. I heared he left in 1894 to go back to Ireland and he died the next year. I visited Will once or twice over the years and he was happy to hear Connolly was dead. Like with all the other deaths, he blamed this one on his mother's curse, but I don't. I figure it's just life and there's no one really keeping score.

As for me, I've travelled some, out to work in Manitoba and Saskatchewan, worked in Chicago, then went down to California for awhile. I'm now in Detroit and have done all right for myself in the automobile business. I have a good wife, Rachel, and the two kids, William and Jenny, is all growed up.

Truth is, it don't give me much joy being here for this funeral. Being witness to what happened has been my life's burden. I've always had terrible nightmares since. Terrible guilt I couldn't save her, or any of them, that night. Still do. Still have trouble sleeping. Still dream about the horsemen coming, more'n a hundred hooves kicking up ice and dirt, horses' eyes wild, coats lathered, frosty breath, men with feathered hats tied on with rope, carnival masks and clown paint, and that thick metal smell of blood in the kitchen. Some nights it all comes back.

How much longer are they gonna drone on in there? I check my watch. If they knock off soon I could still make the four o'clock train back to Detroit.

I've come to believe that evil is something that is always out there flying around the world and sometimes it just settles somewhere and normal people do terrible things. That's what happened here, I believe, and I seen it. I don't have a better explanation.

All right, they're coming now with the coffin. The burial is under way. Get it? Under way. Will would have laughed at that one. The people have come out of the church and followed the coffin to the open grave and the men are rigging up the ropes and the young priest is opening his book. I'm looking now at the family at the graveside: the adult children, grandchildren and great-grandchildren all grieving for the deceased. Good-looking people, several generations sired by that murdering bastard. None of them would exist if he had hanged, but I don't find much consolation there. The young priest is reading. It's almost time for my bit.

"Thou carriest them away as with a flood and they are even as a sleep; in the morning they are like grass that growth up."

There are tears for this old boy but I must say, he lived a long and lucky life compared to most of the others, considering the evil he got up to, and if you put any stock in Johannah's curse.

"In the morning it is green and groweth up, but in the evening, it is cut down and withered. For we consume away in Thy displeasure, and we are afraid at Thy wrathful indignation."

I walks up to the gathering by the grave and people start to look up at me. Many of the older ones know who I am and I can see I am expected. I see they's uncomfortable and want me to go away. I see fear and resentment, but I also see guilt.

"Thou hast set our misdeeds before Thee and our secret sins in the light of Thy countenance…"

Then the young priest spots me and his voice trails away and he goes quiet. The mourners actually stand back to make way. I steps up to the grave and looks down at the coffin for a moment. His wife is already buried there and on the stone under his name is the birth date but not yet the date of his demise. The stone says, "Martin Edward McLaughlin." And I think it should say, "The last of the vigilantes that murdered the Donnellys." But it never will.

The mourners are silent and even cowering away from me. I clears my throat twice, leans over the open grave and spits very generous-like down on the coffin and tells old McLaughlin, "May you go straight to hell."

No one moves or speaks. I pick up a shovel, scoops a heaping blade full of dirt and throws it down on the coffin with a heavy thump. I am satisfied. I turns away from the grave and let them finish with their respects to the old boy. I'm finished with mine.

So I go back to the Donnelly graves then and tell them all, "Well, that's the last of them." I reach down into my pocket and find what I'm looking for. It is the smooth, round river stone with the bits of green and gold and red, the little piece of Ireland, of fairy dust and blood, that Johannah always kept with her and I took that night and kept with me.

It's been around for a million years and will last another million, long after we and our tribulations is all gone. I do feel it protected me well that night and brought me luck over fifty years of my life and I thank her for it. I place it carefully on the ledge of the family gravestone. I go down on one knee and lay my hand flat on the trimmed grass of the grave where she lies, which has been warmed by the summer sun.

"Rest peaceful now, Miss Johannah."

Then, after a moment, I stand and look out across the graves of the friends and foes of the Donnellys. Then I head over to my Ford and I turn my back on Lucan for the last time.